To
Queen Margaret University

F. M. McCarthy

The

Zeta

Waves

By
F. M. McCarthy

MARZIPAN BOOKS

Published in Great Britain by
Marzipan Books, P.O. Box 1186, Yateley, Hampshire, GU477BR
First published in 2007

Printed and bound in Great Britain by
Cox & Wyman Ltd, Reading, Berkshire

ISBN 978-0-9555292-0-7

www.marzipanbooks.co.uk

Chapter one

"The Chronoguiser is behind that curtain! It is big. It is wonderful! It is most amazing invention that we will ever have the chance to see!" Hundreds of people said these words and millions of minds chanted the same, in silent unison, "The Chronoguiser is behind that curtain!"

Moments before they had witnessed the flying of the National Flag. They had watched the faces of the Anthem singers, and they had all been surprised to discover that the Flag had in fact concealed a shimmering blue circular curtain, six metres high and wide.

Three hours into the Forum, the late afternoon sun shone brightly onto the Natural History Museum. While the gathering outside stared fixedly at the huge Mega Screens, the Delegates inside gazed entranced at the Forum Stage - all frightened to miss a moment of the auspicious unveiling ceremony. At home, indoors, millions of viewers - also watching the Stage - glued their eyes to their television sets.

Teasingly flashing intermittent images of an expectant audience and the massive concealing curtain, the Forum auditorium cameras zoomed in on Professor Doherty.

"We have reached Section Four of the Forum!" he called out excitedly, his televised image almost alive with the intensity of his thoughts. "The unveiling of the Chronoguiser!"

Everyone inside and outside of the Museum tensed with excitement.

"I can sense your anticipation!" bellowed the Professor, standing on the beautiful Forum Stage in front of the tantalizing curtain. "You will never have to fear the past again! We now have the ability to change anything that we find unsatisfactory about history! You will never again have to bear the burden of mistake or injury! Or dread the prospect of a bleak and angry future!"

The Stage-Band, *The Inventors* - stationed before the Professor's podium - played a drum-roll. Booming out through the Mega

Speakers over Cromwell Road and all the surrounding London Parks, that drum-roll caused all to hush.

Professor Doherty paused, stretched out his arms and smiled out at everyone, from where he stood on the Stage, from the huge Mega Screens positioned all around Knightsbridge and from millions of television screens.

"Behold! Ladies and Gentlemen. We call it the Chronological Reorganiser. I present to you, on behalf of TT Corporation - *the Chronoguiser*!"

As the auditorium cameras focused purely on the glistening blue shroud - the curtain dropped. Falling slowly onto the large Forum Stage, it brushed the shoulders of ten Security men. Pushing gently at their backs, it prompted them forward.

Millions of eyes now loomed in on the space where the curtain had been. Projected on the back wall of the Stage they saw an enchanting moving mural of the Solar System. Lined up in front of that mural stood the Security men. Between the men and the mural, they saw... *nothing*!

To everyone's immense disappointment, the curtain had concealed an empty circle! TT Vox Populi laughed. Faith Firebell gasped. People in the Parks and in the street outside the Natural History Museum screamed. Inside the nearby Knightsbridge - Queens Gate - apartment, the seated youth, Dominic, was livid!

"It's all a shameful hoax!" yelled a large group of outside spectators, angry and puzzled.

"It's been stolen!" cried one hysterical woman.

From the Parks, the deafening roar of hissing and booing seeped pervasively into the Forum auditorium. Inside that auditorium, the audience stared in disbelief at the elaborate Stage, decorated on all sides with tiny stars. They glanced at the Professor's mahogany podium on the right, the Stand of Stupidity booth on the left and the three television screens mounted on an overhead pelmet at the front of the Stage. They looked at TT's private Balcony compartment jutting out on the right wall of the auditorium. Then turning their heads like small children, they gazed wide-eyed, hurt and disappointed at Professor Doherty.

The Professor regarded them kindly. "The Chronoguiser is here. It is here," he assured them in a raised, gentle voice. "The marvellous phenomenon can make itself invisible."

Thousands of mouths gaped open, in awe and wonderment at this surprising revelation.

Professor Doherty laughed loudly and shouted happily at his captivated guests. "The Chronological Reorganiser has an automatic camouflage function! It *is* here, I assure you. Everyone, bear with me! You'll all be able to see it in a moment!"

He nodded to TT in the Balcony compartment. While the Professor walked to the far right side of the Forum Stage, climbed the podium and turned a dial, TT reprogrammed the Chronoguiser with his remote-control device.

Quickly the low wall of silver mist that covered the Stage began to thicken and to rise. All the lights within the auditorium were extinguished. Higher and higher the mist rose, until *The Inventors* and the Security team were entirely lost from view.

The Professor's head bobbed above a sea of silver vapour. "Soon..." he whispered.

Hushed with anticipation his audience strained their eyes to see within the enveloping mist, until, when the thick silver vapour was at a height of six metres, something mysteriously began to materialize.

At that instant, the entire worldwide audience gasped in amazement. Their eyes widened in awe and their mouths relaxed, gaping in pleased astonishment. Numerous people hurriedly put on their spectacles, took them off, cleaned them, then put them on again. Everyone, but everyone stared silently.

The Forum Delegates were unequivocally astounded. The people in the streets and the Royal Parks were astonished. The viewers at home were dumbfounded. Quickly everyone moved closer to their screens, at home, or in the Parks, in order to admire in detail the merits of the fantastic creation.

Professor Doherty glanced behind him. "There she is," he thought proudly. "My lifetime's endeavour - the Chronological Reorganizer. Whenever I see her, I always think the same. She is more beautiful in reality, than I ever dreamt she could be."

Behind him, radiating sparkling blue light, and mesmerizing the worldwide audience, a huge gossamer ball of azure light beams completely encompassed a glowing, floating, silver Sphere.

Unexpectedly, startling the stunned audience, TT's fine baritone voice roared out over the heads of the Delegates, "I give you, the most aesthetically stunning machine, *ever created!*"

Suddenly three thousand antenna shaped rays of bright, blue light emitted from the apex of the Sphere. Each ray ended in six, short, interconnecting prongs and each prong discharged a faint musical note. The combined effect of the eighteen thousand musical notes filled the silent auditorium with the most enchanting pervasive melody ever imagined.

The audience seated in the auditorium Gallery cheered. Streamers flew from the Balcony, tumbled onto the Delegates in the Stalls and draped across their heads and shoulders. In the Parks and the streets, the people went wild. Professor Doherty whistled as loudly as he could, and everyone clapped.

Moments later, controlled by TT, the music from the Chronoguiser suddenly dissipated, together with the intense blue light. Two silver panels slid open, one revealing a wide viewing window, the other revealing an access hatch at the base of the Sphere. From that hatch, a ramp of steps slid quickly to the Stage Floor. Once again, the applause was deafening.

When the din from the audience had subsided, *The Inventors* began to play a lulling melody and the silver cloud of mist began to fall and dissipate. Professor Doherty, still standing on the podium, with the mist hovering gently below him, wiped his brow with a handkerchief that he withdrew from his coat pocket. Gently he tapped on his microphone. He smiled.

"Ladies and Gentlemen," he shouted. "It is time to christen the Chronoguiser!" Grabbing two large bottles of champagne from inside the podium, he hastened down the podium steps and ran to the edge of the Stage. "Have you guessed the name?" he asked a sensitive lady, seated in the front row of the Stalls.

"I think the Chronoguiser is called 'The Dandelion'," she answered.

The Professor called out to his audience of Delegates, "This lovely lady thinks the Chronoguiser has been called 'The Dandelion'. Who else goes with Dandelion?"

"*I* go with Dandelion," shouted a man at the back of the auditorium.

"So do I!" called another man.

His audience, guessing at names, hurriedly made bets on which name would be chosen.

After handing the sensitive lady her promised bottle of champagne, Professor Doherty bounded towards the floating Chronoguiser. He raced up the boarding steps until he reached the ship's hull. Holding the second bottle of champagne in his outstretched arm, he tapped it against the Chronoguiser. Strangely, it made no noise.

"I give you our prototype Chronoguiser!" he shouted. Then he shattered the bottle of champagne on the glowing silver Sphere.

Tinkling as it fell, the broken glass cut holes through the silver mist. Splashing, the champagne rained out over the Stage. Consequently, the spilt alcohol reacted with the hull of the Sphere. Large embossed lettering, charmingly decorated by the dandelion flower, now appeared on the silver hull.

"The Dandy Lion!" shouted Professor Doherty.

While the auditorium audience applauded and the crowd in the Parks cheered exuberantly, the Professor descended the boarding steps. After striding across the Stage, he climbed the podium stairs. Speaking in an excited raised voice, he enthused about the astonishing vessel.

"The Chronoguiser is a multi-functional time-machine," he said proudly. "With the addition of Space travel, submersible and air-flight functions, it outstrips any craft ever made in terms of performance, design and quality. One of the groundbreaking features of this vessel is its buoyancy. It will float high into the atmosphere the moment the magnetic anchor is released. The anchor automatically resets every twelve hours, so there is no danger of losing the amazing vessel."

"How many does it seat?" called a man from the front of the auditorium.

The Professor laughed. "Five - room for all the family."

"I'll be able to take my family to the Theme Park on the moon!" called out the same man.

"Yes," said the Professor, "You'll no longer have to rely on the Spacebus. You will be able to travel in the comfort of your own vehicle to the Satellite Aquarium, the Satellite Gardens, even visit the Mining Station on Mars for a tour of their facility. TT Corporation has just launched a new Satellite Robotic attraction for your enjoyment, in orbit as I speak. Entry is free for one year to all owners of Chronoguisers and their families."

"Where can I buy a Chronoguiser?" asked a stout Delegate, sitting with her husband.

The Professor eyed her curiously.

"I'm sorry. I haven't been fitted for a palmdisk... yet," she explained. She flushed with embarrassment.

Professor Doherty inhaled and coughed. "Four hundred Chronoguisers are waiting at the TT Showroom in West London," he replied. "They will go on sale tomorrow morning."

"This glowing Sphere - you say it's a Spaceship," said a journalist from *Science and You*. "My readers will want to know how it works."

"Well, get out your recorder," said the Professor. "For all the readers of *Science and You*. This is how the Chronoguiser works!" He paused. "There is a natural untapped power source in the Universe. Can anyone tell me what that power source is?"

"Gravity," proffered a fragile, snowy-haired man.

"Yes," agreed the Professor. "The Chronoguiser can tap into that power source."

"Amazing!" responded the fragile man, genuinely impressed.

"The Chronoguiser can fix onto any gravitational field in the Universe," continued the Professor. "Harnessing the natural power source of the Cosmos it flies through Space, pollution free, and it won't cost a penny for fuel!"

"I can hear faint music coming from the Sphere," said a thin lady in the front row. "Why?"

"Once the gravity drive is activated the Chronoguiser will always play an audible tune," the Professor replied. "Consider that gravitational fields are melodious sound fields, beyond our range of hearing, and that each planet is a musical instrument. The Chronoguiser can tune into any gravitational melody on the Universal map. When the light field around the Chronoguiser hums, it is echoing a particular gravitational field."

"Like a radio, echoing the sounds of a radio station!"

"Exactly."

"OK, the power source is gravity," said the journalist from *Science and You*. "But you haven't explained how the Chronoguiser flies through time."

"Using maps," responded the Professor cheerfully.

"You're kidding - it's that simple. Maps?"

"Yes. Visualize if you may, that the Universe is a clock, and as the planets move in their respective orbits, the hands of the clock change. The position of the gravitational fields, they are the hands of the clock. They graphically represent the time. The Chronoguiser is equipped with a database of all the star maps for the last three thousand years... and the projected charts for the next ten million!"

"Wow, that's a hell of a lot of maps!" said the *New York Times* Reporter.

The audience laughed.

"Yes," agreed Professor Doherty. "These star maps form the basis of the Navigational System for the Chronoguiser."

"OK, Professor. The maps represent the time. Once you have the right map how does the machine get there?" asked a journalist from *Science for Scientists*.

Faith Firebell, seated in the middle of the auditorium audience stood up. "The Chronoguiser uses the map to tune into a particular weave of gravity fields," she said earnestly. "Harnessing the amalgamated power of those gravitational fields, it is pulled through time."

The assemblage were hushed and stared at her.

"Is that right?" she asked nervously.

"I'm overwhelmed," said the Professor. "You've been reading my published Research Papers."

Noticing several people in the Stalls grinning at her, Faith suddenly felt self-conscious and sat down.

The Professor now temporarily left the Stage and *The Inventors* played a ballad during his absence. While waiting for his return, the worldwide audience chatted excitedly. They wondered whether the Chronoguiser would fit into their carports - imagining the look of envy on their neighbour's faces. Simultaneously, the Reporters in the auditorium frantically scribbled onto their note pads and the Scientific community looked proud and satisfied.

After the ballad, the drummer clanged his drums noisily and the Delegates became silent.

Carrying a large gold envelope and an unusual electronic key, Professor Doherty, now returned, stood at Centre Stage. There he beckoned to Green, seated in the Stalls. Prompted forward, Green - the previously chosen 'Section Three' volunteer - quietly left his seat. Walking through the aisle, he solemnly stepped onto the Stage.

"Take a bow, Green," said the Professor.

Green bowed and the Forum audience clapped.

Glancing behind him at the head of the Security team, the Professor called to the Chief, "Chief, please give me your Medal of Valour."

Striding forward and unpinning his medal from his jacket, the Chief handed that emblem of bravery to the Professor.

"Remain standing here," instructed the Professor. After which he looked sternly at his audience of Delegates. "This is Section Five of the Forum and the demonstration you are about to witness is a weighty one. You are all very much involved in this matter, so I want the full attention of everyone. That includes the people outside, in the Parks and at home. After the demonstration, I will be asking questions," he warned.

"Now to the logistics of the demonstration. Firstly, I want you all to draw an imaginary line through the auditorium and divide the area into neat halves. The people on the right of the Hall are to focus their attention on the Security Chief. Pay particular attention to what he is wearing: - a blue jacket, blue trousers and black shoes. He is also wearing a holster containing his gun and his knife. I have taken the Chief's Medal of Valour and I am going to hand it to Green."

Green promptly took the medal handed to him and deposited it in his front shirt pocket.

"As soon as the Dandy Lion flies out of the domed-roof of the auditorium, I want you all to stare at the Chief. *Don't* take your eyes off him - for three minutes! Is everyone agreed?"

All the people on the right shouted, "Yes!" in unison.

"Those of you on the left of the auditorium are to focus on the *empty* Stand of Stupidity. You can watch the Chronoguiser leave, but as soon as it does, don't take your eyes off that glass booth! Agreed?"

"Yes, Professor!" shouted the people on the left.

"Green will be travelling to the past - a week before our Forum. His destination will be TT's office in West London. TT's office has an open roof, by the way. The Chronoguiser can't pass through walls! Amazing as it is, it can't do that! Green will arrive at midnight to avoid detection. He will open a Wall-Safe, with this key." The Professor held the key over his head for the audience to see. "This gold envelope in my hand contains written instructions," said the Professor, holding up the envelope in his other hand. "Green will put the envelope and medal inside TT's Safe. He will keep the key on his person and return to us." Turning to face Green, he handed him the key and the envelope. "Green, are you clear about your assignment?"

"I am," replied Green.

"Put your hands together for the first citizen to fly our time-machine - the Chronoguiser!" called the Professor.

Encrgetically the audience clapped. They watched eagerly as Green and Professor Doherty walked ceremoniously towards the boarding stairs of the Dandy Lion. Both bounded up the steps and bowing thcir heads so as not to hit the ceiling, entered the glowing Sphere. Crouching over they squeezed into their places inside the small cockpit.

Green immediately noticed the calibration instruments and the Flight Controls on the dashboard in front of him, plus the onboard computer before the front passenger's seat. Glancing behind him, he observed three additional passenger seats, flipped up and secured against the rear of the craft. Then he ran his eye over the ceiling, noting a globe the size of a basketball mounted in the centre on extendable arms.

"That's the gravity drive," pointed out the Professor. "It drops down into the apex of the craft when the flight function is activated. Aeronautical flight uses the gravity of the moon as a power source. For Space flight, gravity is tapped from the selection of stars and planets that provide the best flight path. Time travel is a precise art with the Chronoguiser accessing power from over three thousand planetary bodies." The Professor paused. "1 need to give you a quick run down on the workings of the vessel, so you must concentrate. The audience are impatient to move on with the demonstration so my instructions will be rapid."

"Go ahead, I'm listening," responded Green cnthusiastically.

"The coordinates of your journey have been preset by TT," said the Professor hurriedly. "He is custodian of the Dandy Lion's remote-control apparatus which overrides all of that Chronoguiser's Systems. Rest assured, nothing can go wrong. Incorporated into the craft is an automatic homing mechanism that can't be disengaged. After an elapsed time of thirty minutes, the ship will return to the address of the registered owner. The Dandy Lion also keeps a secure log of all its journeys so we will always know where it has been and who was onboard."

Green smiled at the Professor. "I'm not planning any grand larceny today," he joked. "But I guess it gives you peace of mind that I can't steal your time-machine."

Ignoring this remark, the Professor continued hastily, "Underneath the calibration instruments and the Navigation screen are the Flight Controls. The manual pilot pulls forward from the console when required, but you won't be using it for your journey today. The Flight

Controls, which do concern you, are those six functions switches on the left, the six departure buttons in the centre and the two boarding levers on the right. They are all colour coded. When you push down the black boarding lever, the steps will withdraw, and the hatch will close. The white lever powers up the craft causing the gravity drive to drop down and lock into position. The cabin of the craft will then fill with blue light beams, shooting out from the apex of the drive and you will hear quiet lulling music. Next, you will set the four function switches required for your journey. The red, orange and yellow switches on the left column set the air-flight, Space-flight and Time-flight options. The violet switch at the bottom of that column is the automatic pilot. The pushbuttons in the centre of the console activate the functions you have set, so push the red, orange, yellow and violet when you are ready to depart."

"What are two remaining switches and two buttons used for?" interrupted Green.

"The blue switch on the top left column is the submersible function. The indigo switch sets the camouflage - makes the Dandy Lion invisible to the naked eye. The corresponding buttons in the centre of the console activate those functions. Don't press indigo, whatever you do, Green. We don't want to spoil the show!"

Green nodded his head in agreement and the Professor continued swiftly. "Your entire flight will take exactly 200 seconds. The flight to the past will be over in a split second. The craft needs to be in Outer Space - during normal operation - before the Time-flight function can activate. Once you have entered Space, the shield over your viewing window will automatically close for your protection. Expect your journey to be slightly uncomfortable for the split second you time travel."

"*How* uncomfortable?" asked Green."

"From your position in the craft, you will feel like you are being dragged forward out of your seat, upwards and downwards. That's why, as you can see, there are fittings on each seat to secure the head and feet in position. The dragging sensation occurs because the drive links to the enormous force of gravity from three thousand planets and stars. When the Time-flight function comes into play, that amalgamated gravity attempts to pull the Chronoguiser towards a non-existent location. Essentially, gravity from three thousand celestial bodies tries to rip apart the whole Sphere, from all sides.

"Cripes," said Green. Rather impressed, he stared at the instrument panel. "Why *doesn't* the ship rip apart? What stops it?"

"That's my secret, Green, but suffice to say you are completely safe."

"You reckon," responded Green disbelievingly.

Professor Doherty chuckled.

"Anything else that I should know?" asked Green.

"The Chronoguiser will rock as it accesses the thousands of stars for power. That also will be momentary."

"Fine," said Green. "Continue."

"Once the date on your instrument panel in front of you displays last week, you have completed your flight back in time. The Chronoguiser will automatically take you back down to Earth, direct to TT's office. Do your job. Then return."

"What if something goes wrong?" asked Green.

"Nothing will go wrong with the Dandy Lion. If, however, you are caught in TT's office, Security will think you are a thief or a spy. Show them this, and they will let you proceed."

The Professor handed Green a small badge with the letters *TT5000* written in gold around the edges. The centre was made of an unusual black enamel.

"Once they see the badge, they will let me go?"

"Yes," replied the Professor. "Now, instructions for the return trip."

"Let me see if I can manage this on my own," said Green sarcastically. "I press 'Return'."

The Professor laughed. "I'll leave this in your capable hands then, shall I?"

Green pulled the Safety harness across both his shoulders, fastened the buckle in the centre of his chest and waved the Professor away.

"Don't mess this up, Green, or there will be hell to pay," warned Professor Doherty. "TT Vox Populi has a distinctively harsh side." Promptly he left the Sphere, hurried down the steps and dispersed the ten Security men.

All eyes now watched excitedly as the boarding steps withdrew into the craft and the hatch closed. An aura of blue light from the Chronoguiser diffused onto the Stage. Wafting through the auditorium, soft enchanting music emitted from that vessel. Harnessing the gravity of the moon as a power source, the Dandy

Lion rose slowly through the auditorium's domed-roof, into the world outside.

Everyone in Knightsbridge and the Royal Parks craned their necks and gazed at the sky as the Dandy Lion shot up into the heavens. Millions of viewers at home stared at their television screens. Suddenly they all felt very proud.

The Dandy Lion reached Outer Space in less than two minutes. Now the Bubble3 Space Telescope focused on the amazing Sphere. Consequently, the Mega Screens in the Parks, the three screens in the auditorium, and the British News Television Station all transmitted captivating feed of the silver Dandy Lion flying through Space, cocooned by a network of sparkling blue light. While the viewers watched, the aura around the vessel deepened to cobalt blue. Then unexpectedly, the ship disappeared.

Five seconds elapsed. The Dandy Lion reappeared. The intense blue light previously surrounding that Chronoguiser faded to a soft blue glow. As the glowing Sphere descended into the Earth's atmosphere, the people in Central London eagerly watched the sky.

Meanwhile in the Forum auditorium, something remarkable had happened. The audience were incredulous. The Chief, still standing at Centre Stage, was viewing his clothes in amazement. He no longer wore his blue jacket and blue trousers. He no longer carried his gun. Instead, he wore work boots, baggy grey trousers and a black polo shirt. Pinned on the left of his polo shirt was his Medal of Valour.

The sensitive lady was smiling. She had been brought onto the Forum Stage and was shaking hands with the occupant of the previously empty Stand of Stupidity.

"Sir Holmes, I thought you had been hurt," she said kindly to the Peace Prize Winner.

"So did I," he replied, "but as you can see, not a scratch!"

"The Dandy Lion..."

He cut her short in mid-sentence. "The what?"

All her words came out in a rush. "The Dandy Lion - the Chronoguiser. It disappeared, and then you appeared - out of thin air! At the same instant, the Security Chief transformed, before our eyes! I swear - we were watching him the whole time. He *was* dressed the same as the other Security men. Now he's dressed in different clothes. Look too, he got his Medal of Valour back. He's wearing it on his chest!"

"Slow down. Start from the beginning," Kepplar suggested. "This is a lot of new information to take in at once. A moment ago, I was in hospital with a bullet in my side, after being shot inside this very booth, not more than thirty minutes ago. Now I'm watching a sparkling silver Sphere descend through the domed-roof above my head."

"Yes. I will explain everything from the beginning," she said kindly. "But for now, I do believe Professor Doherty requires our attention." After which she glanced towards the Professor, who was clapping his hands and shouting for order.

The Dandy Lion was hovering above the Stage and the Security men had returned to their positions. While everyone watched, the Dandy Lion's hatch opened. The boarding stairs descended and Green bounded down the steps, greeted by enthusiastic cheers and whistles. The Professor stepped forward and energetically shook his hand, followed by the Chief, the sensitive lady, and a bemused Kepplar Holmes. Many of the Delegates stormed the Stage. Green was beaming.

A giant roar from the Royal Parks filtered through the walls of the auditorium. "Hip, hip, hooray! Hip, hip, hooray!"

When the congratulations were over, Professor Doherty climbed up the steps onto his podium. "Back into your seats, everyone," he shouted. "We have one last section to complete before our Forum is finished! Back into your seats, please!"

When everyone had returned to their seats, or their positions in the aisles, and all were ready to listen, the Professor spoke clearly.

"The instrument panel on the Dandy Lion confirms that the Time Travel Function *has been operational*! The readings pinpoint the exact time the ship departed, arrived, the destination, and the time and place of return. Now, does everyone want to know what was in the letter that Green took to the past?"

"I already know!" exclaimed a man in the Balcony, wearing a Union Jack shirt.

"I suspected that many of you may have guessed," responded the Professor good-naturedly. "Well, tell me then."

The man wearing the Union Jack grinned and spoke, clearly and precisely, "The letter contained instructions. The Chief was to wear casual clothes to the Forum and be unarmed."

"What about his Medal of Valour?" asked a lady wearing a red, flamenco dress.

"The instructions said: Give the Security Chief back his Medal," revealed Professor Doherty.

Comprehension dawned on many faces.

The Professor looked satisfied, then eagerly continued. "Ladies and Gentlemen, I ask you to join me in a discussion concerning a nightmare. The subject of the nightmare is our Global Peace Prize Winner, who has returned to his seat in the Stalls. Please stand, Holmes, so that the whole assembly may see you clearly."

Holmes stood up in front of his seat and slowly turned in a circle.

"Raise your hand, anyone in the Forum auditorium who had a recent nightmare featuring Sir Kepplar Holmes," asked Professor Doherty.

Everyone in the Hall raised their hands.

The Professor continued. "Lower your hand if the nightmare is still vivid in your memory."

The entire group lowered their hands.

"I'm going to ask you, at random, to tell me exactly what happened in your nightmares. Starting with you, Sir."

"Kepplar Holmes was shot," answered a man in the front Stalls.

"I had the same dream," whispered the stout Delegate to her husband.

"Faith, tell us your nightmare?" asked the Professor.

"Holmes was shot, Professor. A gun was dropped onto the Stage and fired as it landed."

"A woman wearing a red sweater ran onto the Stage and jumped on Professor Doherty!" shouted the young Reporter from the *New York Times*.

Everyone in the Stalls chuckled.

"She grabbed the gun from the Chief's holster," said the lady from *Tokyo News*. "And dropped it onto the Stage."

"I never did!" shouted a woman suddenly jumping up from her seat at the front of the auditorium. "I only *dreamt* I cannon balled Professor Doherty!"

Once again his guests laughed.

"I dreamt I grabbed the gun from the Chief," the woman continued. "It fell out of my hand onto the floor and discharged. I suspected the Chronoguiser was behind the Flag and I wanted to get to it. I never intended anyone to be harmed."

"No one is blaming you, Madam. Everything is fine," said the Professor. "Please sit down. Now tell me, Audience, where was Holmes when he was shot?"

"In the Stand of Stupidity!" shouted a gentleman wearing a terribly expensive suit.

"Ladies and Gentlemen!" shouted Professor Doherty cautiously. "You *must* be entirely honest. Raise your hands if you all had exactly the same nightmare!"

Every hand in the auditorium was raised.

The Delegates were hushed and astounded.

"We all had the exactly the same dream," said the stout Delegate who sat with her husband. "Over five hundred people all had the same dream."

The Delegates listening nodded their heads in agreement.

"I'm sorry, Madam, but you are wrong," said Professor Doherty.

She looked disappointed. "But everyone agreed... How can I be wrong?"

"Not five hundred, but millions of people had the same dream. Every one who watched or participated in the Forum today had the same nightmare. We are confirming this in writing as I speak. TT Corporation representatives are asking everyone in the streets and in the Parks. They are calling everyone at home. They are asking the same question of everyone. Did you have the same dream? The evidence will be conclusive. Yes!"

The stout Delegate was placated. Her husband smiled at her and placed his arm around her shoulders.

The Professor spoke steadily. "The point I am making is this: the trauma of the recent shooting of Holmes still exists. We can't replace the past with something else, no matter how much we want to, but we *can* make ourselves a better present, and future." He paused. Then said brightly and sincerely, "Ladies and Gentlemen, we have successfully reorganized time! We have conquered the past!"

His guests beamed. The Professor climbed down from the podium and signalled *The Inventors*. There followed a loud crash of drums from the musicians behind him.

"Ladies and Gentlemen," he shouted, "We have come to Section Six, and are nearing the end of our Forum. Please put your hands together for *The Inventors*!"

The gathering inside and outside the Natural History Museum clapped their hands in appreciation as the musicians bowed, waved, and left the Stage.

"Before we finish there is one last task to be performed," said the Professor, "that is, to announce the winner of the *best idea* competition."

The Delegates tensed with anticipation.

"The Chief of TT Corporation will present the winner with the keys to his or her new super-car, plus an executive employment contract! TT Vox Populi, please join us on Stage!" shouted Professor Doherty.

The audience clapped and cheered. The Reporter from the *New York Times* whistled loudly. TT, who had been waiting in the wings for several minutes, walked theatrically out onto the Stage. Changed from his cream suit and wearing a vertically striped red and blue jacket, baggy blue trousers and a silver top hat, he stood at Centre Stage and addressed the Delegates enthusiastically.

"Ladies and Gentlemen, thank you for your active participation during our Forum, and for sharing your ideas with us! TT Corporation wish to show their appreciation by presenting one of you with a deluxe super-car."

The audience tensed.

"The winner today, for her contribution to the TT Forum, is... Faith Firebell!" shouted TT.

Faith was shocked. While the audience gave her a hearty round of applause Faith's associates rallied around. Her cameraman hugged her. The cheeky young Reporter from the *New York Times* kissed her on the lips. The *Herald* Reporter shook her hand and the lady from *Tokyo News* patted her shoulder.

"Well done, Faith," she said, in congratulations.

Not everyone was pleased.

"Faith already has a great job. Now she's got two," remarked a prim, middle-aged woman in a cream frock - one of the previously rejected 'Section Three' volunteers. "Some people have all the luck."

Hearing this, the man sitting on the left of Kepplar responded darkly, "I wouldn't *want* to work for TT."

"Faith Firebell, please join us to receive your prize!" shouted Professor Doherty, beckoning her forward.

While Faith made her way to the Stage, the people in the aisles squeezed back to allow her passage, and congratulated her as she passed. She climbed up the steps onto the Stage and stood between TT and Professor Doherty.

"Congratulations Faith," said TT, smiling at her benignly, while handing her a scroll and a key tied with a red ribbon. "Please accept the keys of your super-car and this employment contract."

"Thank you, Mr. Vox Populi. I never imagined you would pick me. I'm overwhelmed!"

"Will you work for me, Faith?" TT asked.

"Yes, yes!" replied Faith, smiling happily.

Both TT and the Professor held hands with Faith. Then both men raised Faith's hands high in the air.

"Ladies and Gentlemen, give a round of applause for our winner today, Faith Firebell!"

The Delegates clapped. The throng outside cheered and all the British viewers smiled, pleased that a familiar face had won such an immense prize. The men lowered their hands, letting go of Faith.

Professor Doherty stepped forward. "Ladies and Gentlemen," his voice boomed out, hushing the hubbub of the auditorium. "We have come to the end of the Time Travel Forum. You have been attentive, intelligent company. Thank you very much for your attendance, and your participation. Also for those of you in the Parks, streets, and at home, thank you for voting, and thank you for watching."

His guests cheered in appreciation and the roar of applause from outside seeped through the walls of the auditorium.

The Professor's voice took on a youthful, excited tone as he shouted out enthusiastically, "You *were* afraid of yesterday! You *were* afraid of today! You *were* afraid of tomorrow! Today, thanks to TT Corporation and our brilliant band of scientists, you will never be afraid again!"

There was another avalanche of applause. Outside the auditorium, the multitude cheered and yelled. Super-car drivers honked their horns. Train drivers blew their whistles. The tumult was deafening.

Professor Doherty bowed to his audience. Over the uproar, he yelled out, "Goodbye, good luck, good ... life!"

"The Time travel Forum is over," said Dominic. Relaxing in Zeta's nearby Queens Gate apartment - in her Sitting room - he passed his hand over the coffee table switch, turning off the television.

"Were you impressed?" asked Zeta.

From where he sat on the claret sofa - beside Zeta - he quickly glanced to his left at the two sash windows overlooking the street. He admired the centrepiece of the toffee and beige room - a transparent vase full of genetically modified water lilies. Then he looked at the antique fireplace overhung by a large gilded mirror on the wall behind him. Finally, he appreciated the painted frieze of the English Lakes on the wall opposite.

"Definitely. It was quite a show," he answered. "A day to remember for everyone. Worthy of watching over and over again." He grinned.

"You mean that?"

"Sure," he answered sincerely.

"The prizes were good," said Zeta. "I'd like to go on a ride in a zeppelin."

"You can join me, if you like."

"You won a zeppelin ride?"

Dominic mimicked Professor Doherty. *"Congratulations our sixth winner today. Balloon Card number 4454. You have just won a zeppelin ride for two!"* Then he continued in his own voice, "Look at my prize card. It's still in your pocket."

Zeta retrieved his card from her skirt pocket and read the number on the back. Remembering his invitation, her face flushed.

"You still haven't opened your balloon-gifts, Zeta," Dominic said, glancing at the two parcels on the crystal coffee table before him. "Open them now," he suggested. "You may have received something interesting."

Zeta put her puppy, To-do, previously asleep on her lap, beside her on the sofa. Lifting a cerise gift from the coffee table, she tore off the wrapping.

"Shall we see what I won?" she said cheerfully. Pausing, disappointed, she found an empty box. She turned the box upside down and shook it. A small jagged piece of yellow parchment fluttered to the floor. "Looks like I got the booby prize," she said quietly. "The gift is empty."

"Try the pink gift," Dominic casually suggested.

Zeta tore off the paper on the second parcel. Finding the second gift also empty, she turned it upside down. Another piece of jagged yellow parchment fluttered to the floor.

"What's on the bits of paper that fell out?" asked Dominic. "There are two bits. Your left foot is on one of them."

Zeta moved her foot, picked up both pieces of paper, then read the first one out aloud:

"*Your gift is a Roa...*
Please co...
From TT Co..."

"It doesn't mean anything," said Zeta crossly, handing Dominic the first parchment. "The second piece says:

...ming-Ring,
...llect it
...rporation."

After studying the first piece of parchment, Dominic placed it on the coffee table. "Match it with other half," he suggested.

Zeta's hands trembled a little as she placed the two pieces of paper side by side and read the message, "*Your gift is a Roaming-Ring. Please collect it from TT Corporation.*"

"Wow, Dominic! What an immense gift!" she exclaimed, standing up to leave. "I'm going to collect my Roaming-Ring from the Showroom. Right now. Let's go!"

"And I was so comfortable, too," he said.

Before they had a chance to make a move however, they both heard the apartment door open with a crash.

"Dad's home," said Zeta, smiling at Dominic.

"His usual entrance?" queried Dominic, in reference to the commotion in the adjacent entry hall.

"Yes," replied Zeta, "When he brings guests to his Tea Parties he's rather boisterous."

Dominic watched eight people enter the Sitting room with them.

"Hello, Dad," said Zeta, addressing a regal intimidating man standing at the fore of the group.

"Everyone, this is my daughter, Zeta," her father, Professor Doherty announced. And this is her friend..."

"Dominic," responded Zeta.

Standing up and moving away from the sofa, Dominic shook the Professor's hand. "Glad to meet you, Professor Doherty," he said amiably.

"I'd like to introduce you to my guests, Zeta," said the Professor proudly, after nodding sternly at Dominic. "This is TT Vox Populi - Chief of TT Corporation!"

TT stepped forward and shook Zeta's hand.

Zeta, looking up at the round face of that charismatic man considered thanking him for her Roaming-Ring, but was too shy.

"This is Faith Firebell. She is the winner of the Delegate's best-idea competition," continued Zeta's father. "And of course you know Isabelle."

Faith and Isabelle smiled politely in greeting.

"These two feisty fellows are brothers. They were on Stage protecting the Chronoguiser. The elder is Garrett Bourne. The younger is Eddie Bourne."

Two Security men stepped forward and in turn, gently shook Zeta's hand. Then they energetically shook Dominic's hand.

Eddie turned towards the Professor and spoke excitedly, "The human brain waves, the Zeta Waves. Did you...?"

"Yes, I named the waves after my daughter. She inspires me! In actual fact, the Roaming-Ring was her idea!"

Eddie grinned at Zeta admiringly.

The Professor continued his introductions. "Zeta, this gentleman, wearing the most terribly expensive suit I have ever seen, is my Bank Manager. You may have met before."

"Yes, I have seen your daughter in my Bank," said the gentleman. Nodding greeting to Zeta, he looking back at the Professor.

The Professor gestured towards the wall frieze in his Sitting room and boasted, "Observe the delicate artistry. Don't you think the frieze perfectly captures the rugged, bewitching beauty of The Lake District?"

His Bank Manager glanced at the mural and silently nodded.

"My daughter painted that," Professor Doherty revealed proudly.

Zeta hid her face in her hands.

Returning to his task of introduction, the Professor continued, "Finally, yet importantly, this snowy-haired pariah is Professor Holmes, Zeta. I'm going to pick his brains later. He is an exceptional scientist!"

The fragile, snowy-haired man smiled kindly at Zeta.

"Holmes... Are you related to the Global Peace Prize winner?" asked Dominic.

"Yes, I am his father," replied Professor Holmes.

"Is Sir Kepplar alright?" enquired Dominic.

"Yes. He is completely unharmed, thanks to that marvellous invention, the Chronoguiser. Thank you, young man, for your concern."

Professor Doherty pretended not to be surprised. Having not realized the connection between the snowy-haired man and Kepplar Holmes, he felt awkward and resented Dominic.

Aware of the problem, Dominic remarked casually, "Zeta doesn't resemble you either, Professor."

"Lucky for her," joked TT.

"How old are you, Dominic? Do you work?" asked Professor Doherty.

"I'm fifteen, and no, I don't work," replied Dominic.

"How do you know Zeta?"

"We met at a music recital, at the Bandstand in Kensington Gardens."

"Do you go to school?"

"No."

Sensing the heightening tension, TT interjected, "Well then, Hugh? What should we do with this idle young man?"

The Professor stood with his arms crossed, and raised his eyebrows.

TT addressed Dominic. "A strong lad like you; I'll give you a job. You can work alongside these two," he offered, gesturing towards the smirking Security men.

"Where is the job?" asked Dominic.

"At the TT Research Facility. Farnborough."

"I'd have to cut my hair short," responded Dominic.

"I can take that as a *no*, then?" said TT.

"You can take that as a *yes*!" said Dominic. "When do I start?"

TT handed Dominic a card.

"You can start tomorrow. Call me, first light. Now, where is the magnificent Tea Party you promised us, Hugh?"

"I'm famished," said the Bank Manager.

"Yes, where's the grub?" asked Garrett.

"This way if you please," said Hugh Doherty, herding his guests back into the entry hall towards the Dining room. "Please join us, Dominic?" he proffered grudgingly.

"Thank you, but I'd rather not," replied Dominic.

"Zeta?"

"Perhaps later, Dad. After Dominic leaves."

While Zeta and Dominic remained in the Sitting room, the Professor joined his guests, waiting for him outside the closed Dining room doors.

"I have laid out a sumptuous feast for you all," the Professor boasted. With a flourish, he opened the double oak doors.

The apartment suddenly went quiet.

"Something's wrong, Dominic," Zeta said nervously, a few minutes later. "Dad's not being loud. He is *always* loud when he's entertaining. There is a problem. I know it."

"Let's go and see," Dominic suggested.

Walking quickly to the stately Dining room, they cautiously peered inside. Professor Doherty was sitting at the head of a magnificent round oak table. A cream Corinthian Column stood in each of the front corners of the toffee and beige room. Behind the Professor, his guests stood grouped before a large rear sash window framed with velvet claret curtains.

"Dad, where is all the food? What is that lump of stuff in the middle of the table? Where is the Tea Party?" asked Zeta.

"Are you trying to be funny, Zeta?" responded the Professor, in an icy tone.

"No," said Zeta meekly.

"Perhaps you would be so kind, as to enlighten me to the whereabouts of our refreshments?"

"I don't know what happened to the refreshments," responded Zeta.

"What happened to the disk recording of 'The Conversation'?" the Professor asked resentfully.

"There is no recording," she responded.

"Obviously!" her father raged at her. "You sabotaged my Tea Party, Zeta! You took my Tea Party and replaced it with a lump of porridge on a plate!"

"No, Dad," said Zeta distressed.

"Did *he* put you up to it?" he asked, staring crossly at Dominic.

"We didn't do anything wrong," replied Zeta.

Garrett moved towards the table. "This isn't porridge," he said, sticking his finger into the square lump of food. "It has the consistency of ice-cream." Scooping a spoonful into his mouth with his finger, he tasted it thoughtfully. "It definitely isn't porridge."

TT frowned and clasped his hands behind his back.

"Looks like porridge to me," said Eddie, moving over to the table beside his brother. "Hmm, tastes like porridge too."

Professor Holmes also moved towards the table and tested the food. "I recognize this nourishment. This is Space food, designed for astronauts. It contains everything a human body needs to sustain life - protein, vitamins, fibre, essential fats, carbohydrates."

"Will you all shut up analysing the porridge!" shouted Professor Doherty. "I don't give two hoots what the stuff is! Zeta, a joke is a joke. Just return my food to the table, and I'll forget all about this little incident."

"I'm sorry, Dad -"

"Not you too!" said the Professor in an exasperated voice, as TT also moved towards the table and tasted the food. TT however, unlike the others, did not comment and looked decidedly troubled.

"Where is my Tea Party?" Professor Doherty shouted at Zeta.

"It's been a long day, Hugh," said TT. "We can all visit my Head Office and join the big shindig my father is hosting. It's his going-away bash."

"Right then. Everyone out!" shouted Professor Doherty, hustling everyone out of the Dining room, until only TT remained.

"Have you changed your mind about our living arrangements?" asked the Professor, striding towards Zeta.

TT intercepted him and draped his arm across the Professor's shoulders. "There are some executives at the going away bash who are dying to meet you, Hugh."

The Professor shrugged and relaxed. Then the two men walked out of the Dining room, past Zeta and Dominic, and out of the apartment.

Zeta followed them, running from the apartment into the foyer. She called after her dad, only to see him slamming the heavy house door behind him.

"Dad? When will I see-?"

Zeta's voice crackled and stopped in mid-sentence. There was an audible clunk, followed by a mechanical humming and whizzing sound, ending with another loud clunk. Then there was nothing. Not a whisper. Nor a sigh. Nor the sound of the busy London afternoon.

Chapter two

Five hours earlier...

Propellers whirled amidst the clouds, chopped and ruffled the vibrant summer sunlight and spread a calming mantra over the thriving cultured town. Celebrating the onset of a new era, the Forum day began as grand festival. Thousands of zeppelins filled the skies. Bountiful decorative beacons they floated encouragingly over lofty buildings, towering terraces, landmark structures and city Gardens.

Bubbly laughter from countless merrymakers rose in the atmosphere like a heady sweet bouquet, and the heart of London - Knightsbridge and its four neighbouring Royal Parks - was abuzz with the chatter of a massive crowd.

Ambling forward, numerous members of that flowing crowd sang exuberantly, hugged random strangers and spoke vociferously, until, interrupting their revelry, the melodious sounds of a salvaged ship's bell rang out stirringly over London.

Heralded by those chimes, the Orator's voice called, "You are afraid of yesterday! You are afraid of today! You are afraid of tomorrow!"

Entranced by his promise of a utopian world, a stream of bobbing heads coursed its way through the city streets, from the nearest Royal Park, Kensington Gardens, towards the Natural History Museum.

Standing splendid and palatial on the corner of Cromwell Road and Queens Gate, that Museum beckoned emphatically in the early afternoon sunshine. Throngs of eager faced spectators crammed the huge frontage of the blue-flecked, brown brick building. In thousands they pressed against the black gates of the regal Museum and with one thought only, that of somehow gaining entry, they gazed wishfully towards the enormous, arched entrance.

Summoned by an overwhelming curiosity, the public gathering enviously watched the invited guests waiting inside the gates, on the front steps of the Museum. In turn, those Forum Delegates smiled.

Armed with their prized invitations, the Delegates avidly gazed in through the double glass doors, up at the beautifully plastered ceilings, the high arched portals and the marble Corinthian columns of the still empty, Great Entrance Hall.

Booming out from inside the Museum, the eager multitude now once again heard the deep cultured voice of their Orator calling to them. Wrapping around his audience of listeners, his dulcet tones filled the Forum auditorium wherein he stood, shot out of the massive Speaker System integrated throughout London and soared out over the crowd.

Flooding over everything in its path like a fast moving watercourse, his euphonic chant swept forward, flowed along Queens Gate into Kensington High Street, spilt onto the steps of the Prince Albert Memorial, then washed unimpeded over the pristine lawns of the surrounding Parks. Rippling further through the outlying streets, his riveting voice thundered out over the throngs of expectant people, tumbled over the heads of the excited gathering and tossed their thoughts away.

So strongly did the Orator's gripping proclamations eclipse all other extraneous and intriguing sounds, that his voice categorically quashed the tumultuous clamour of a white vintage helicopter that suddenly appeared as a daunting haze on the azure horizon. Fast approaching the Museum, flying high over the Royal Parks and hauling a mysterious blue glowing crate underneath its long fuselage, the propeller blades of that helicopter chopped noisily through the air and its long shadow, cast by the bright sun, swam unseen through the huge distracted crowd.

Roaring out steadily over the locality, the Orator's pervasive voice continued to overshadow the arrival of the helicopter, presently hovering over the rooftop of the Museum. Lowering its secret gleaming payload through the open domed-roof of the auditorium, the helicopter set the crate down onto the Forum Stage.

So overwhelming were the Orator's pronouncements that the powerful helicopter, free of its payload, landed on the rooftop without audience. Rhythmically slicing the air, the rotor blades of that stationary craft were still spinning rapidly - throwing dust and debris chaotically upward - when the door of the helicopter slid open. Two men of similar ages stood proudly in the entrance of that vessel. Jumping down onto the rooftop, they entered the Museum through the rooftop access. Abruptly the Orator's pronouncements stopped.

Currently entering the now crowded Great Entrance Hall the two men moved towards the grand rear staircase. There they climbed the marble steps to the central landing where the stairs branched off to the left, and to the right. Instantly spotted and besieged by Overseas Correspondents, local Newspaper Reporters and Journalists, they smiled affably.

The British News Reporter - Mrs. Firebell - was the first of the members of Press to reach them. While she spoke into her microphone, her cameraman proudly filmed her, standing to the left of these two well-dressed celebrities.

"I am Faith Firebell," she said excitedly, "reporting to you from the Great Hall in the Natural History Museum, London. We don't want anyone to miss participating in the events of today. So, make sure you are settled at home in front of your television or you can see one of the Mega Screens in our Royal Parks or in Cromwell Road. This is an exciting day for all of us. Precisely forty minutes from now, the TT Forum will begin!"

The viewing audience enjoyed a panoramic view of the Great Entrance Hall of the National History Museum, as the cameraman quickly transmitted live footage of the spectacle in front of Faith. His pictures showed a huge beautiful Hall crammed with people from every country in the world. Many were dressed in their National costume and the variety and colour of their attire caused the Hall to sparkle enchantingly. To the additional surprise of the viewers, they also saw that several of the Delegates wore a jewelled platinum Ring around their foreheads.

"Five hundred Delegates from neighbouring nations have flown to London to participate in the TT Forum," Faith continued, once again the focus of the cameraman. "During the Forum these Delegates will contribute towards the new Chronoguiser Legislation. This legislation will protect us all and will revolutionize our lives. Speaking to you today, I have Chancellor Judgewell, and of course, the organizer of the Forum, Mr. TT Vox Populi!"

As the cameraman zoomed in on a close-up of the bald head of Mr. TT Vox Populi, TT grinned precociously. Unexpectedly he grabbed the microphone from Faith, smiled into the camera and exclaimed in a friendly voice, "Thank you, Faith! She is such a gorgeous lady. Isn't she a gorgeous lady, Audience? Welcome to all the Delegates in the Great Hall before me! Hello to all the viewers at home. Hello to the people gathered in Cromwell Road and in the Royal Parks! Lovely day, isn't it?"

Enthralled by his charisma, the Delegates in the Great Hall turned to face TT. Immediately there followed a loud roar from outside of the Museum as the multitude in Cromwell Road shouted back, "Hello!" in return.

TT responded by stepping forward. Beaming, he danced a jig - much to the delight of his worldwide audience.

"I have a surprise for all of you wonderful people gathered together today in the Royal Parks!" TT continued, after he had finished his impressive dance. "I can hear you already. You are asking, what is the surprise, TT? You'll find out, sweethearts, in fifteen minutes from...." He held his arm out in front of him and looked at his timeband. "Now!"

"Mr. Vox Populi?" asked Faith, also stepping forward, pleased and smiling. "Can you tell us the agenda of the Forum today?"

"I can't do that, Faith!" TT exclaimed in mock horror. "If I did, I would spoil the surprise! However, I *can* tell you that TT Corporation are running three competitions during the next four hours and that the winners of those competitions will be announced during the Forum."

"Mr. Vox Populi, can you tell our viewers the details of these competitions?"

"Why certainly. The first competition is for the viewers at home. Watch to see if your citizen card number is called during the TT Forum, then immediately dial TTCASH11 to claim your prize. Each prize is one week's basic wage, in cash.

The second competition is for those people in the Royal Parks. You will all be offered a card before the TT Forum officially begins. If your card number is broadcast, dial TTSKYRIDEI1 to claim your ride for two, in one of our many zeppelins.

The third competition is only available to the Delegates at the TT Forum. TT Corporation is always searching for people with original ideas. The Delegate who comes up with the best idea will win a super-car, plus a job at TT Corporation!"

Pausing and taking Faith by surprise, TT kissed her lightly, his thick brown moustache tickling her cheek.

"This is a grand slam day for all of us!" he continued enthusiastically. "My compliments to you all! Enjoy the show!" Returning the microphone to Faith, he moved back to stand casually to the left of the Chancellor.

Four Reporters, each given the opportunity of interviewing TT and the Chancellor, now stood on the landing, grouped in a half circle around these two celebrities.

The first Reporter inline was Faith Firebell of the *British News*. A short, tanned, muscular man from the *Australian Herald* stood beside her. The third Reporter, a slim youth, wore a badge on his breast pocket that read, *New York Times*. Lastly, a beautiful woman with almond shaped eyes from *Tokyo News* was the fourth Reporter granted an exclusive interview.

While the cameraman transmitted footage all around the world, and the Delegates in the Great Hall quietly listened, Faith put forth her initial question.

"Chancellor, we all know what the Chronoguiser does. Do you support the general public using this invention?"

"The best interests of the nation will always be my top priority," replied the Chancellor.

Faith, disappointed by the diplomatic answer, brushed her long black hair back from her pretty face, and frowned.

"Will everyone get to have a Chronoguiser?" asked the Reporter from the *Herald*.

"We will have to wait and see," the Chancellor replied. "The Chronoguiser Bill will be read in the next sitting of Parliament."

"Will a special Police Force be established to control the use of the Chronoguiser?" asked the lady from *Tokyo News*.

"Yes," he confirmed. "The Chronometer Department is a new department initialised to control the day to day operation of the invention. The Chronometer Department will be responsible for policing the law."

"In the event of the Chronoguiser causing property or personal damage; will there be avenues for compensation?" asked the *New York Times* Reporter.

"The new legislation will address all your concerns including the issue of damages," replied the Chancellor. "The laws dealing with Life Insurance and Accident Policies, together with Property Insurance will be read in Parliament tomorrow."

"Chancellor, there are rumours that the Chronoguiser Legislation will not be passed. Is this true?" asked Faith.

"That decision will be reached soon. We have the best minds in the world formulating these new laws."

"Last question, but on a different topic," asked the Reporter from the *Herald.* "Will the Chronoguiser make us all rich?"

"The Chronoguiser is an invention that promises to improve our quality of life," replied the Chancellor.

"Thank you, Chancellor," said Faith, as the four Reporters now turned their questions to TT, standing by the Chancellor's side.

"Mr. Vox Populi, is it true that TT Corporation has changed leadership?" asked the *New York Times* Reporter.

TT removed his star glasses revealing his large thoughtful green eyes and his round pleasant face.

"Please call me TT," he replied. "My father - the Honourable Wiggy Vox Populi - retired from his position as Corporate Chief, this morning. You are looking at the new head of TT Corporation. Under my leadership, TT Corporation, already the most dynamic Corporation in the world, will also be the biggest and most powerful. Invest in your future. Invest in TT Corporation!"

"TT, will the issues of health and safety be a priority to TT Corporation?" asked the *Herald* Reporter.

"My Corporation is committed to providing the safest-"

"Independent sources confirm that several scientists employed by TT Corporation have died during the production of the Chronoguiser," accused the *New York Times* Reporter, cutting TT off in mid-sentence. "Is this true?"

"No one has died," replied TT firmly. "Please rest assured that TT Corporation have the highest Health and Safety Standards in the world!"

Moving closer to him, the lady from *Tokyo News,* smiled. "On a lighter note," she asked positively, "When can I buy a Chronoguiser, and how much will it cost?"

"Mass production of the Chronoguisers will begin as soon as the relevant legislation is passed," TT replied amiably. "Pending that legislation, four hundred Chronoguisers will be available for sale, tomorrow morning, in our Showroom in West London. The retail price for these Chronoguisers will be negotiated on application to purchase. However, I assure you that we, at TT Corporation, are dedicated to keeping production costs to a minimal level, passing on those savings to the consumer in a lower retail price."

"Will there be an age limit imposed on the use of the Chronoguiser?" asked Faith. "Can my nephew, Jimmy, use the invention to get to school on time?"

"We do not envisage age limits, Faith. And yes, the Chronoguiser will be a useful tool to ensure that Jimmy gets to school on time."

"Are there financial or legal barriers to the use of the Chronoguiser?" asked the youth reporting for *The New York Times*.

"There certainly are no financial barriers. If the need arises, TT Corporation will provide access to a Chronoguiser regardless of nationality, age, race or financial status. I cannot comment on legal barriers until the legislation is passed."

Faith's cameraman, who had previously been silent, called out suddenly, "TT, will our viewers see a Chronoguiser today? TT Corporation have kept the invention so secret that nobody actually knows what the Chronoguiser looks like!"

TT smiled. "This afternoon, during the TT Forum, TT Corporation's crowning achievement - the Chronoguiser - will be unveiled!"

"Ah, but can TT Corporation prove that your amazing invention actually works?" asked the cameraman.

TT smiled casually. "Yes, we can. Following the unveiling there will be a practical demonstration."

"Please, TT, on another subject?" asked the lady from *Tokyo News*. "We would like to ask you about the Roaming-Ring. If that is acceptable?"

"I would love to tell you about the Roaming-Ring!" replied TT with great enthusiasm.

"TT," she continued eagerly. "We know that TT Corporation have developed a second new product, called a Roaming-Ring. The Roaming-Ring went on sale today and already has surpassed anything ever invented, in popularity and sales. Why, as we look around us we can see that many of the Delegates in this Great Hall are already wearing these beautiful diadems."

"Yes," said TT. He smiled graciously at the Delegates gathered around the landing. "Besides being functional, the Roaming-Ring is also decorative. Made with platinum, each Ring is set with jewels in an exquisite design."

"We have been advised by your Marketing Department that the Roaming-Ring offers unlimited potential for travel. Is this true?"

"The Roaming-Ring requires a certain level of acquired skill to operate. However, with practice, any one, of any age, can operate the device. What you were told is true - within reasonable limitations of skill, the Roaming-Ring does offer unlimited potential for travel!"

"Can you tell us, and our viewers at home, precisely what the Roaming-Ring is, and what it does?" asked the youth from the *New York Times*.

"The Roaming-Ring, TT Corporation's wonderful new product, is completely safe. It is a sensory device, worn on the head, which triggers the movement of the individual psyche - the energy field of the mind. The *out of body* experience that ensues allows the wearer to travel anywhere without ever having to move a muscle. Psyche travel is the newest advancement of our cultured society. Stationary consciousness now belongs in the past!"

"Wow!" exclaimed the youth. "Will I be awake when this happens?"

"It is only possible to psyche travel when one is asleep," TT replied. "Set a timer on the Ring for the duration of any trip and activate the device with either a secret password or by brushing your hand across the front of the Ring. Once activated, the Roaming-Ring puts the wearer to sleep and automatically wakes them when the holiday time is over. Naturally, if a slumbering body is disturbed during the trip, the sleeper will awaken. The *out of body* experience *is* wonderful."

"Where can I buy a Roaming-Ring?" asked the grinning youth.

"At our Showroom. You can be fitted -"

"The price you are charging for the Roaming-Ring is exorbitant!" cut in Faith.

TT regarded her sympathetically. "No, Faith. That isn't true," he replied sincerely. "We at TT Corporation believe the price to be fair. Included in the outlay for the Roaming-Ring is compulsory Property Insurance. We also provide free Breakdown Service. Considering the value of the Roaming-Ring to the wearer, the price, equivalent to only one holiday on a Spacebus to Mars, is very reasonable."

"How many holidays can I take using the Roaming-Ring? How much will each holiday cost, and where can I travel?" asked Faith, placated.

"You can take countless holidays, Faith, to any place your mind can take you. The only cost involved is the initial outlay for the Roaming-Ring."

TT smiled and paused. Then he glanced at his timeband. "The TT Forum is due to begin," he announced proudly. "We need to wrap up our question time. Any last minute queries?"

"No more questions," said Faith, smiling.

The lady from the *Tokyo News* shook her head.

"Thanks for the interview, Mr. Vox Populi," said the Reporter from the *Herald*.

"Yeah, thanks," added the youth from the *New York Times*.

"My pleasure," replied TT happily. "We are now all required in the Forum auditorium."

All four Reporters nodded courteously to the Chancellor, who all the while had been waiting patiently by TT's side. Cameras flashed like fireflies. The Reporters and cameraman descended the stairs where, together with the Delegates, they were ushered quickly out of the Great Hall towards the Forum auditorium.

While everyone else was shepherded into the auditorium, the Chancellor and TT turned to their right, moved up from the landing and climbed two flights of the marbled staircase. Leaving the stairs behind them and reaching a private compartment that overlooked the Forum Stage, they halted. TT pushed the compartment door open. Then he grinned, as he was greeted by a loud blast of music. Followed by the Chancellor, he entered a small room furnished with four plush, red velvet chairs.

"Those Musos are lively chaps," remarked the Curator of the Museum, over the noise of the band. He had been waiting inside the compartment for their arrival and enthusiastically shook the Chancellor's hand. "I was lucky to get them. They are in huge demand."

"I can appreciate why," said the Chancellor. "Marvellous vocals. The lyrics are thoughtful. And the music is…" He paused for a moment. "Quite brilliant!"

In response, the Curator abruptly slapped the Chancellor on the back. "Glad to have you here, chaps!" he said jovially, pushing them both into their seats. "Refreshments?"

Shoving two glasses of iced tea towards the Chancellor, he dropped a large bucket of popcorn in TT's lap. After which he moved towards the balcony.

"There are two functions on the front railing of the balcony," he explained. "A microphone - if either of you want to address the audience - and an intercom direct to the Stage Manager and Security." After this brief speech, the Curator grinned at both of them with a delighted expression on his wizened face. "If you need me, chaps, simply holler!" he said. Then he promptly left the room.

Looking over the balcony the Chancellor subsequently admired the most prominent and principal feature of the Stage - the huge National Flag, suspended tautly from floor to ceiling, six metres back from the front of the Stage. Before the Flag stood a line of ten Security men. Several metres behind the Flag, a fascinating moving mural of the Solar System peeped out, radiating warm shafts of yellow light around the National Banner. Curiously, he also noted the mysterious addition of azure light beams mingling impartially amongst those golden rays.

"What do you think of the Stage, Chancellor?" asked TT.

"The man-size, glass booth and the podium at the front look promising," replied the Chancellor. "But I can only hazard a guess as to what is hidden behind the Flag. You can't let me in on the secret before the unveiling, can you?"

TT laughed.

Suddenly the lead singer of *The Inventors*, standing in front of the podium - finishing his song - strummed his guitar loudly and playfully.

"Thank you!" he called to his audience. Along with subtle intonations in his voice, the tiny disks that speckled his white suit changed colour, swinging from one end of the light spectrum to the other. "We are *The Inventors*!" he shouted, his outfit shimmering with a purple haze as he did so. "We have, and will continue to enjoy performing for you this afternoon! After a short interval, we will return. Thank you!"

Applauded by five hundred Delegates, he left the Stage, accompanied by his drummer, pianist and two additional guitarists.

"Wait for it, Chancellor," cautioned TT, pre-empting a sudden loud chime.

Seconds later, the clang of a ships bell rang out over Central London, startling the Delegates and the outside assembly. The Orator, Professor Doherty, strode out across the auditorium Stage - the bell announcing his entrance. Seen by all - in person, through their television screens or through the Mega Screens - the Orator stood tall and imposing on the Forum Stage. Raising his arms out at his sides - level with his shoulders - he tilted up his face, looked through the open domed-roof and roared, "Look up to your future!"

Immediately the three Stage screens blinked on, projecting televised footage of the sky over London. Subsequently the Delegates stared at those screens.

Outside the Museum, as directed, the assembly looked up at the wispy clouds overhead. The throngs in Cromwell Road and in Queens Gate moved to the centre of each of those streets. Tilting their faces upwards, they scanned the sky above the five-storey terraces. Whilst they did so, the multitude in the Parks peered through the trees at the pale blue atmosphere that moved gently above them.

Looking questioningly at the sky, all were now party to the colourful sight of thousands of zeppelins floating above them. Each zeppelin towed a huge, buoyant, sparkling red bauble.

Suddenly, as countless curious faces gazed up, all of those baubles exploded. Cascading down over the multitude below, a million balloons of various sizes spilled out. Each iridescent balloon was marked with the letters 'TT'. Tied to each balloon by a coloured string, a beautifully wrapped gift and a personalised card floated downwards.

A delighted murmur swept through the huge crowd, all waiting wide-eyed for their gifts to descend. Eager moments later, the balloon-gifts floated tantalizingly above the heads of a thrilled multitude. Fitted with a miniature propeller, each gift was equipped with a scanner that matched the gift with the recipient, by age and gender. Consequently, the packages flew higgledy-piggledy amongst the crowd, seeking their owners.

In St. James Park and Green Park, the assembly cheered. While in Hyde Park and Kensington Gardens, the crowd, of quieter persuasion, smiled and laughed cheerfully.

The patrons in Kensington Gardens were strolling languidly. Numerous large trees cast round leafy shadows over the generous lawns around them. The flowered walkways, thoughtfully planted with begonias, filled the Gardens with a sweet aroma.

Standing at the Queens Gate entrance to Kensington Gardens, two ladies were gazing up, watching two small balloon-gifts float gently towards them. One lady was matronly with thick, auburn hair. The other was a prim, middle-aged woman wearing a light, cream frock.

"Oh!" gasped the matronly lady. Catching one of the gifts, she held it excitedly.

"How astonishing!" said the prim, middle-aged woman, also catching her balloon-gift.

Both ladies smiled. Together with vibrant people from many different nations, they strolled into the Park towards a flowered walkway, bordered with colourful annuals. They chatted eagerly and happily. On their way, they stopped beside a teenage boy and girl. The prim, middle-aged woman opened her gift. Pleased to receive a voucher for her favourite shop, she read her heart-shaped card out aloud.

"To a dear lady, invest in your future, invest in TT!" Turning over her card, she read the back. "Keep this card for a lottery prize draw during the Show."

"She seems happy," remarked the teenage girl, noting the woman's pleased expression.

The youth nodded in agreement. Springing high into the air, he volleyed a small balloon towards his friend. She caught the balloon, held it by the cerise string and smiled.

"Pretty smile," he said cheerfully.

Again he jumped high in the air, this time volleying a balloon-gift with a fluffy pink string towards his companion. When she caught the balloon, he reached towards her, snapping the propellers off both her brightly wrapped gifts.

"Thanks Dominic," she said happily.

"Anytime," he replied. "It pays to be lanky sometimes. I'm five foot eight and still growing!"

Eyeing up a group of small balloon-gifts as they floated towards him, he jumped for and caught a balloon with a multi-coloured plaited string.

"This is the non-gender, non ageist variety," he remarked casually. Breaking off the propeller and detaching the string, he let the balloon float away. Pulling the star-shaped card from the gift, he quickly read the words inside.

"To a special person. Invest in TT. Invest in your future!" Turning the card over, he read the back aloud, "*Number 4454.*"

Thoughtful for a moment, he looked innocently at his friend. "Do you think I have a chance of winning, Zeta?"

"No," she laughed.

Roughly tearing open the packaging on his balloon-gift, Dominic discovered a hand-painted miniature by the respected artist, 'Constable'.

"No frame," he said. Winking at Zeta, he continued lightly, "I thought I'd get something weird!"

She laughed. "To match your hairstyle?"

"It's a wig, I tell you!" he exclaimed jokingly, patting his sleek, shoulder length, light-blond hair. "You'll break my heart if you don't like it."

"I like it, peach streaks and all," said Zeta, raising her eyebrows and regarding him critically.

Grinning, Dominic paraded himself happily before her. "Admire if you dare, dear girl," he boasted, "my well preserved and lovingly worn Designer ensemble! As you can see, my baggy twill trousers are flattering and chicly threadbare, and the torn and useless pockets fashionably state my altruistic nature. My T-shirt has holes in *all* the right places. And besides being a *definite* aid to tanning - being rather translucent as it is - it does show off my handsome physique rather well."

Zeta laughed warmly. "Your clothes have only one merit, Dominic, and that is that they're clean!" She stretched out her hand towards him. "Here, you'd better give me the miniature artwork and the star-card to keep for you."

"What?" he asked, handing her his painting and card. "Do you disagree that the tantalizing glimpses of my physique are not praiseworthy of my attire?"

Again she laughed. She looked at him fondly, but asked uncertainly, "Will we meet next week at our usual place?"

Dominic's eyes twinkled. "Ah, the Bandstand. Such happy memories!" he mused dreamily.

"Be serious?" Zeta asked, smiling and moving closer to him.

Dominic keenly regarded the slim, fourteen-year old girl standing by his side. He noted her rose coloured complexion, her wide face, full mouth and large, dreamy grey eyes. He coolly observed her clothes - a pink vest with a matching pink cotton kilt. Then he looked at her long brown hair, worn up and pinned by several pretty slides and combs. Finally, he gazed around him appreciatively at the green grass, the flowers, trees, and the contented, smiling people.

"What will we do now?" he asked his friend cheerfully.

Zeta grabbed his arm encouragingly. "We could go back to my place," she suggested. "Dad's at the Forum and my auntie, Marjorie, has returned to her house in Hampshire. She lives in Farnborough, near the TT Research Facility, so no one is at home. The TT Forum is on television, from 2pm until 6pm. We can watch it together. You never know - you might win something!"

"I thought you'd never ask," replied Dominic. "I was beginning to think I'd lost my savoir-faire. We've been friends for *months*!"

"Sorry, I wanted to ask you, but I wasn't allowed visitors."

"What changed?"

"My dad's in a great mood because of the Forum, so I'm allowed guests for once."

"I hope his good humour lasts," said Dominic optimistically. "Race you!"

From where they had been standing in the flowered walkway, they raced back towards the Queens Gate exit.

Glinting through the treetops, the sun beaming down over the gardens flickered rays of light hither and thither. Watching Dominic and Zeta disappearing from view, several people imagined that they saw the lad's retreating image shimmer and glow, like a ghostly silhouette in the dappled sunlight. Brushing the cobwebs of light from their eyes, they gazed around them at the festive gathering, then casually continued to enjoy their day.

Weaving their way through the crowd, the racing pair exited from the Park into Kensington High Street. Once there, they cautiously crossed into Queens Gate. Dashing along, Dominic was a long way in front.

"You all right back there?" he shouted.

Glancing at the Victorian mansion to his left, he sprang up the front steps onto the porch. Leaning against the ornate balustrade, he waited for Zeta to catch up. While he waited, he noted the flowered house-trellis that decorated the left side of the building, extending from the basement to the fifth floor apartment. On that trellis, dense clusters of scented pink clematis, woven tightly through the lattice, cascaded downward, spilling a sweet fragrance onto the porch.

Reaching him a few moments later, Zeta stared. "How fast can you run? I almost lost sight of you, you were moving so quickly."

"I'm glad you're impressed," replied Dominic casually. "Are we going inside, or what?"

Moving towards the front entrance, Zeta put her metal key into the door lock. Pushing open the heavy door with her shoulder - alongside Dominic - she entered her building.

Dominic, who had been in her foyer before, immediately recognized the familiar surroundings - the green plush carpet, the pale golden walls and the elegant, wrought iron staircase.

Accompanying Zeta to her apartment, ten metres further into the foyer, he admired - as he always did when he saw Zeta home - the paintings hanging from dado rails on both sides of the foyer. Glancing towards Zeta, he noticed a thread of purple light across her door.

"What's that?" he asked, pointing at the thread of light.

Zeta pulled a disbelieving face. "Where have you been all your life? The thread of light is the doorbell. Haven't you noticed it before?"

"Nope. I was too busy admiring the Art on previous occasions. Besides, I was expecting something a little more high-tech than a beam of light for a doorbell."

"Such as?"

"What about a Robotic Butler incorporated into the door?"

Zeta laughed. "I'm sorry," she responded sarcastically, while at the same time admiring her large, wood-panelled entrance door. "This is a listed building, Dominic. As residents, we are not permitted to demolish any of the original features."

Grinning, she held her electronic key quite close to her mouth and whispered something into the built-in microphone. The thread of purple light disappeared. The door swung open and they both entered her spacious apartment - decorated with toffee walls, oak woodwork and beige carpets.

Dominic immediately observed that the apartment was arranged over two levels with a Dining room to the left, a Study and a Sitting room to the right and a descending spiral staircase at the rear of the entrance.

"What's downstairs," he asked. Stopping outside the closed Dining room doors, he peered curiously through the glass panels.

"A kitchen, bathroom and two bedrooms," replied Zeta, closing her apartment door. "You can go into the Dining room if you like," she suggested. "By the expression on your face this is the first time you have ever seen a table laid for a Tea Party."

Opening the doors, Dominic stepped inside the stately Dining room. "There's a lot of food for ten guests, Zeta," he called, after counting the chairs arranged around the table. Moving further inside, he closely observed the round oak dining table, fashioned into three distinct revolving rings. The outer ring was dressed with smoky crockery and gold cutlery. Positioned on the next ring Dominic saw many plates of luxurious, mouth-watering food, suitable for all palates. Interested, he admired bowls of fragrant jasmine and rose interspersed with wreaths of eucalyptus, artistically arranged on the smallest ring. Finally, Dominic looked to the centrepiece of the table, where he saw - on an ornate Stand - a Compact Disc, labelled 'The Conversation'.

"I've never heard that recording before," he remarked curiously, glancing around as Zeta entered.

"Everyone who has been to one of Dad's Tea Parties within the last two years has heard it. It's a party favourite."

"What is it?" he asked. "Music, comedy, poetry?"

"None of those, Dominic. 'The Conversation' is a tête-à-tête between my dad and me. We only ever have the one stressful exchange, so he made a recording of what is said when he talks to me."

"Why did your dad go to the expense and fuss of making a disc of a private conversation?"

"Dad got tired of repeating himself, Dominic. He plays the disc every time he sees me because he is tired of arguing with me. Time is money to dad, so ultimately it is cheaper to make a disc and listen to that, than talk to me. It shaves a few minutes off his day."

"Does he talk to you at all?"

"He plays the disc. When it is finished he says one sentence."

"And that is?"

"He says, 'Have you changed your mind?'"

"What then?"

"He leaves to see his girlfriend."

"Does anyone else know your dad doesn't talk to you?"

"His girlfriend knows."

Both teenagers were silent. While Zeta watched, Dominic took the disk, slid it into the player fitted in the bottom of the stand and pressed 'START'.

The first voice he heard was a man's - irritated and condescending. The second voice he recognized as Zeta's. Rather than her familiar calm, sweet voice, he heard her speaking quickly in a nervous and high-pitched tone.

"Listen to me Zeta!" said the man's recorded voice. "I'm your father! That gives me rights."

"If you say so, Dad."

"You have put your mother on a pedestal."

"Mum made this place a home for me."

"Forget your mother, Zeta!" the man's voice shouted. "Isabelle is my partner now. We can all live together. We can all be comfortable. But I need you to give the go-ahead. Will you do that?"

"No thanks."

"There's a picture of your mother in your bedroom," the man's voice said testily, "pasted to your mirror. There isn't a picture of me."

"You're never home, Dad."

"Your mother disappeared years ago, Zeta. Isn't it time you forgot about her? She is not coming back. *I* am the one you see every day, not her! I am the one who looks after you. You could try and give me some respect."

"My mother is missing. You don't care how I feel,"

"I tried my best to find your mother - if only to prove to you that she isn't missing, that she ran away, that she doesn't care about us."

"My mother does care. She loves me."

"You love a ghost."

"You think mum's dead?"

"I didn't say that."

"Make up your mind, Dad. First, you say mum ran away, then you contradict yourself and imply she is dead."

"I don't know, Zeta, if your mother is dead or alive. I'm sorry."

Dominic listened to Zeta's recorded voice, a voice that had become resolved and determined.

"Mum's missing. I know she is still alive."

"You have to live your life with me, Zeta. You haven't got any choice in the matter," the man's voice said coldly.

"Mum must have had her reasons for going away. I need more time before I can make any decisions, Dad. I care for her. I miss her. That's how I feel."

"So, it's wait and see," said the man's icy voice.

"I can't stop caring because it inconveniences you!"

"The arrangement I am offering you is a good one."

"For who, Dad? For you."

"Be practical."

"Why? You and Isabelle have the monopoly on being practical. There is enough *practical* to go around. I don't have to add to it."

"Zeta, you're trying to live a dream."

"I don't want to hurt you, but I can't live the way you want, Dad."

"Don't waste your life waiting for someone who doesn't care about you, Zeta. Life with your mother is the past. You and I, and Isabelle, can work things out together. She is ready to move in with us, as soon as you say yes."

"I said no."

The recorded dialogue stopped. Zeta reached over the table, removed the disc from the player and put it back on the stand.

"How long has your mum been missing, Zeta?" asked Dominic.

"She disappeared not long after my ninth birthday."

"Your dad's not the bad guy, you know."

"I know," replied Zeta resignedly. "But I don't understand why dad plays that recording to all of his guests."

"This is my guess," replied Dominic. "One, he's pretty cold. Two, he thinks 'The Conversation' is interesting."

"Aren't his friends appalled?"

"Sure, but it saves them asking him about you and gives them something to ask him."

"And that is?"

"Haven't you got any music?"

A bell rang suddenly from within the apartment. It tinkled prettily several times.

"Dominic, will you wait in the Sitting room while I answer the door," Zeta asked, quickly walking away. "Please close the Dining room doors behind you."

Dominic left the Dining room. Rather than enter the Sitting room, he stepped briskly into the Study instead. Facing a large oak desk and a floor to ceiling wall library, he stealthily moved towards the desk. There he stopped before a pile of handwritten notes arranged neatly on the desktop. The notes flicked over quickly, as if blown by a sudden breeze. Then just as abruptly, they returned to their original position. Seconds after he had entered, Dominic left the Study.

Strolling casually into the Sitting room, he headed towards the two sash windows overlooking the street. Halting when he reached the centre of the room, he glanced at the sofa, the fireplace and the overhanging gilded mirror to his left. Frowning at his own reflection - his ghostly complexion and colourless eyes - a concentrated look passed over his youthful face. When he looked in the mirror again, his complexion appeared normal and his eyes were pale blue. Satisfied with the results of his mental exertions he walked across to the right side of the room to study the painted frieze.

Meanwhile, Zeta had reached the entrance door.

"Zeta love," called a woman's voice from outside. "It's Isabelle."

Looking through the spy-hole in the door, Zeta saw the image of a small plump woman with ruby-red cropped hair and a friendly smile. Curiously, she noted that the woman was wearing a cherry coat, even though the day was warm. Her arms were crossed loosely in front of her, suggesting she was holding something.

Zeta quickly stood back from the door. She took the electronic key from her skirt pocket and whispered a password, causing the door to swing open suddenly.

Stepping into the apartment, Isabelle spoke in a rush. "I'm not staying, Zeta sweet. I'm speeding off to the Museum to catch the beginning of the Forum." Unbuttoning her coat with one hand, Isabelle withdrew a small, furry bundle with the other. "For you, Zeta," she said quietly, pushing a tiny, golden puppy into Zeta's arms. "I won't take no for an answer! Now I must dash. See you when I see you!" Turning away, Isabelle quickly ran from the foyer into the street, and away.

Cradling the bundle in one of her arms, Zeta let the door swing shut. Grabbing her balloon-gifts, she walked into the Sitting room. Dumping her balloon-gifts on the coffee table before the sofa, she stepped towards Dominic.

"Look Dominic, Isabelle gave me a pup."

"*The* Isabelle on the recording?"

"The very one."

Dominic looked at the light golden pup squirming happily in Zeta's grasp, noticing its calm soft brown eyes. "It likes you," he remarked.

"And I like it. I always wanted a puppy."

Crossing the room, Zeta sat cheerily on a mound of black and white checked blankets bunched on the sofa, cradling her new puppy.

"Who sleeps on the sofa?" asked Dominic. Sweeping a bunch of blankets onto the floor, he sat down next to her.

"Dad, when he's at home."

"I take it he's not often at home?"

"Lately he's been spending every night at the TT Showroom in West London. He has become good friends with the Security men."

"What does he do at the TT Showroom?"

"He admires the products."

"I suspect its not much fun for you being alone at night."

"I'm not always alone," responded Zeta, "Auntie Marjorie sleeps over, when she's in town. We sleep downstairs."

Trying to wiggle free of Zeta's grasp, the puppy nipped nervously at the hem of her vest top. Accidentally it tore the fine fabric with its sharp little teeth.

"Oh!" exclaimed Zeta, examining her torn top. "The puppy doesn't like me after all!"

"Here, give it to me," Dominic said. Grabbing the puppy from her lap, he held it up. "Do you actually know anything about puppies?"

"No," Zeta bashfully replied.

"Do you know the breed?"

"Sure, it's this new breed."

"And that breed is...?"

"Wait. Let me think... it's a Clode! A miniature."

"*It's* a he, by the way," Dominic advised. "Have you thought of a name, or are you going to call him 'The Puppy' forever?"

"I'll call him *To-do*," said Zeta.

Dominic laughed and so did Zeta. Grabbing the checked blankets, she tossed them over the side of the claret sofa. She took To-do from Dominic and relaxed back into her seat. After watching her face intently, To-do curled up on her lap.

Glancing at her timeband, Zeta asked politely, "The Forum starts any minute now, Dominic. Turn on the television, would you please?"

In response, Dominic moved his hand over a switch on the crystal coffee table before him, causing a roll-down television screen on the wall opposite - above the frieze - to wind down to the floor and illuminate.

Suddenly a series of loud explosions resonated throughout the skies over the nearby Parks. Consequently, several brilliant flashes of coloured light flickered through the long, cream, voile curtains veiling the sash windows of their room. Striking the large gilded mirror that overhung the fireplace, red, orange and purple light beams danced on the high walls. In the intervals between the frequent explosions, Dominic and Zeta heard singing and laughter from the street outside.

Running to one of the windows, with To-do in her arms, Zeta called to her friend, "Come and see the fireworks!"

Dominic remained sitting on the claret sofa. "The Forum has started, Zeta. Come and sit down. You'll miss it."

"The sky is ablaze with beautiful colours, Dominic, shaped like Christmas decorations. It's a wonderful sight!"

"Sit down," he encouraged. "You'll be sorry."

For several minutes, Zeta watched the fireworks display, marvelling at the colourful arrangements the exploding rockets made in the sky. When the fireworks ended, she heard the distinctive sound of propellers. Several modern light aeroplanes soaring overhead ejected streams of coloured paper in their wake. The sky was now raining confetti. Swaying to imaginary music, she watched the delighted crowd outside her home, dancing underneath that paper rain.

Swirling as it fell down to earth, the confetti pattered softly on the rooftops. Tumbling into the guttering of the houses, it collected in little neat piles on the eaves. Covering the blossoms of pink clematis on the house-trellis, it spotted the green leaves of that climbing plant. Continuing to fall, the paper rain brushed against the window where Zeta stood and speckled the glass with tiny, coloured dots. Hopping and drifting, it finally settled in little heaps in the corners of the window ledge.

Minutes passed in silence. Zeta ceased to look out. She brushed the cream curtain away, turned to face Dominic and pressed To-do's soft little face against her own. The wide, gilded mirror reflected the large tears that now welled in her dreamy grey eyes and fell, making little splashes on To-do's silken fur.

Unsure of how to respond to his friend's sadness, Dominic drummed the slender fingers of his right hand onto the arm of the sofa.

"You're missing your mother," he stated exactly. Stretching out his left arm, he prompted her to join him on the claret sofa.

Embarrassed, Zeta half turned back to face the window.

"Come on, Zeta," he said encouragingly. "Watch the Forum. *The Inventors* are on Stage performing and their music is quite brilliant. They have three more songs to perform, none of which you would want to miss. The last song is one of your favourite ballads. The Stage around them looks great. Blanketed with a metre-high pearly mist, it is nicely crisscrossed with hundreds of purple light beams."

"What else?" asked Zeta.

"The Forum auditorium is jammed with people. Besides the seated Delegates, others have been granted admission. They are standing shoulder to shoulder in the aisles. Some are hanging from bronze ladders propped up against the walls. There is even a team of five acrobats standing balanced precariously on each others shoulders at the back of the Hall."

"What else?" asked Zeta, turning to face him.

"Floating at the back of the auditorium are balloons carrying baskets of refreshments. The balloons are shaped like Candy Cane, Bonbons and Soda Pop bottles."

Zeta grinned. "You're kidding?"

"I kid you not. Come and sit down."

Chapter three

Grabbing at the air with vaporous, outstretched hands, pearly clouds of mist bubbled out from behind the National Colours, then crashed in waves, submerging the rear of the Forum Stage in a deep mysterious, silvery sea. Nudging forward, the high silvery mist rolled and tumbled, blanketing the raised wooded platform over which it flowed. Suddenly dissipating, the mist then fell shallow, forward of the Stage, where it lapped a metre high against the glass booth and the mahogany podium, to finally tickle the elbows of *The Inventors*, presently performing their final ballad.

"I'm taking all bets now for the steeple chase, Ascot at 5pm," whispered a fat TT Security man who went by the name of Garrett 'Ret' Bourne.

Concealed by the silvery mist floating over the Forum Stage, Ret stood in front of the National Flag - on the far left. Part of a line of ten Security men, he was accepting money from his nine colleagues. Simultaneously he tapped information into a small disk bonded to the palm of his hand.

"What are the odds on *Roan Lady*?" asked an ugly Security man - standing close to the centre of the line, beside their Security Chief.

"One hundred to one," replied Ret.

"Who is the favourite, brother?" asked a brown-haired, tanned youth of sixteen, who stood beside him.

"We're not taking bets from you, Eddie," said Ret.

"Because I have a progress conviction?" asked Eddie.

"That's right," replied Ret, grinning menacingly.

"I'm not afraid of you, bro," said Eddie. "Despite you being horrible."

"Give your little brother a go. A progress conviction never stopped any *other* gamblers," growled the ugly Security man.

"Who is the favourite?" Eddie repeated, pushing his money into his brother's hand.

"*Piebald Penny*, if you must know," replied Ret.

"I put ten credits on *Piebald Penny,*" said Eddie. "And fifty on *Chestnut Boy.*"

"Sorry, brother, *Chestnut Boy* has been scratched," replied Ret.

"One thousand credits on *Roan Lady*, to win!" said their Security 'Chief'.

"*Chief?*" asked Ret, concerned.

"I'm sure," responded the Chief.

"I changed my mind," said Eddie. "I'm also betting my sixty credits on *Roan Lady*."

The conversation continued in muffled tones until each man had placed his bet with Ret.

When they had finished laying their bets, their Chief walked quickly along his line of Security men. After checking over their clothes - a blue bulletproof jacket with the TT emblem on both sleeves, blue trousers and black brogues - he spoke to each man in turn, starting with the youngest.

"You must make a good impression, in case anyone looks at you, Eddie."

"No one is looking," said Eddie despondently.

"Give it time," said the Chief, "you will be noticed."

"Sure," replied Eddie sulkily.

"No one is to get past us - to the Flag," said the Chief firmly.

"No one will get to the Flag," said Eddie.

When he had spoken to every man in this way, the Chief checked his own handgun. Resuming his position in the centre of the line of men, he puffed up with pride, pulled in his belly and stood to attention.

"What's a Zeta Wave?" whispered the ugly Security man, who stood to the left of the Chief. "People in the audience are talking about TT's interview with the media - things we are in the dark about. We want to know what an 'out of body' experience is, and what 'Roaming' is?"

"You're wasting your time asking him. He doesn't know," said Ret.

"Just because I carry a gun, you think I am minus a brain," said the Chief. "I happen to be quite an authority on the subject. I was the one in charge of securing the Section that was testing the Roaming-Ring."

"I know what a Zeta Wave is," interrupted Eddie excitedly. "It's a human brain wave. Each of us has small quantities of them floating around our heads all the time. The Roaming-Ring produces Zeta Waves in large quantities. Those waves trigger the release of the psyche from the body. That is what the 'out of body' experience is - the release of the psyche. I've roamed already - at the Research Lab in Farnborough. They tested a Roaming-Ring on me. It was fantastic! I psyche travelled to Monte Carlos. I could see and hear, just like in real life. I could even move things about! It was the best experience I have ever had. I'm saving up for one."

"On *your* wage? How long will that take?" asked the ugly Security man.

"Only four months. But it's worth all the work."

"Since when did you become a guinea pig?" asked the Chief, addressing Eddie gruffly. "I was the one to be doing the telling, Smart Alec. Now, zip it lad, and let me have a go." The Chief looked at the faces of his grinning men and then his own face relaxed into a good-natured smile. "The movement of the spirit to different locations is termed 'roaming'," he said in a knowing tone of voice. "A mind, or psyche if you prefer, that is travelling out of it's body is called a 'Roamer'. With the aid of the Roaming-Ring, anyone can travel anywhere in spirit - as the lad here proved by travelling to Monte Carlos."

"Inside your head is just thoughts, dreams; static," said a young snowy-haired Security man, standing to the right of the Chief.

"No, that's not true," said the Chief emphatically. "What's inside your head is a physical thing that can move. It has physical properties."

"Tell me, Chief? What's inside my head?" asked Eddie.

"A timeless, spaceless, energy field," replied the Chief solemnly.

"Our Chief is a regular treasure of information," remarked the ugly Security man, causing the other men alongside him to chuckle.

The Chief looked at his timeband - a bracelet of light, projected from a jewel pasted onto his wrist. "See those three television screens on the pelmet up at the front of the Stage," he advised. "They'll be turned on in two minutes. *The Inventors* will stop playing. The Orator will return to the Stage and the congregation will all look this way. They'll see us through the fading mist. They'll notice us laughing."

"What screens?" asked Eddie.

"The ones hanging from the roof, you daft brush!" replied the Chief.

The Security men muffled their laughter. Forcing themselves into solemn attitudes, they landed friendly punches on each other.

Suddenly, as the Chief had warned, the television screens flashed into life.

"Chief?" asked Eddie.

"Shut up, all of you gamblers," remarked the Chief, without turning his head. "This mist before the Flag is dissipating. The audience are looking at the screens. They can see us."

The audience within the Forum auditorium were indeed watching the three activated screens. One screen broadcast ancient footage of war, famine and disease. Another screen transmitted current documentaries of natural disasters and famine. The last screen broadcast fabricated future accounts of world peace and prosperity.

The Orator - as the Chief had advised his Security team - had returned to the Forum Stage and was pacing up and down, staring coolly at his audience. Of mediocre beauty, with a somewhat clinical countenance, he was undoubtedly a most intimidating man. Dressed in a purple silk shirt with a black tie and matching black pinstriped trousers, his overall appearance was regal. An attractive, grey moustache tickled his upper lip and his hair was grey, cut short at the back of the neck.

The gathering outside the building and in all four Parks watched him eagerly - the immense screens erected twenty metres in the air holding them spellbound.

As the Orator abruptly stopped at Centre Stage, the auditorium cameraman zoomed in on the startled, bearded face of a dark, portly man, seated in the right aisle, in the last row of Stalls.

"You are afraid!" the Orator shouted, staring at that man. "I am talking to the Delegate who wears a green patterned shirt. Yes, you there! You are afraid! He sits in the last row! He wears a green bell-patterned shirt and a black bow tie," continued the Orator. "Yes, look at him! Everyone, look at him. Turn in your seats. For those standing, twist your bodies and look behind you. Turn your heads! Look at him!"

Everyone in the auditorium swivelled in their seats and craned their heads to look at the man in the bell-patterned shirt. Simultaneously everyone in the Parks and in Cromwell Road looked towards the massive Mega Screens.

"Stand up!" the Orator called. "We are going to call you Green!"

"I'm not afraid!" shouted the man, angrily jumping to his feet.

"Oh yes you are!" the Orator said sternly. "You have just been released from prison, have you not? You are on parole, are you not?

You are afraid that your past will hurt you! Most certainly, you are afraid!"

The man stared at the Orator, speechless.

"Now sit down," said the Orator dismissively.

Mystified, the man sat down.

The Orator stood tall. Focusing on the entire audience, he shouted cordially, "Ladies and Gentlemen! Welcome! The Natural History Museum and TT Corporation are delighted that you could join with us on this auspicious occasion! I am Hugh Doherty, Professor of Physics and Mathematics. It is my pleasure to lead our Forum today!"

A balloon burst at the back of the auditorium, followed by a startled gasp from a lady.

Ignoring the mild annoyance the Professor continued unperturbed. "We are ready to begin our discussion on the subject of reorganizing time!"

The assembly clapped heartily and when the noise died down, the Professor proceeded.

"The TT Forum is divided into six sections. During Sections one and two, we will debate on the benefits and the dangers of reorganising the past and the future. I expect your energetic participation. The Draft Legislation pertaining to any debated issues will be included at the end of each of those two sections. Additionally, throughout these two sections, I will be announcing the winners of the citizen card and balloon card competitions. Viewers at home, stay tuned to see if you have won a week's wages. Spectators in the Parks and the streets - keep watching those Mega screens. You may have won a ride in a zeppelin!

During Section three of our Forum, I will be asking for a volunteer. That individual will have the honour of being the first member of the public to use the Chronoguiser! We will be asking the gathering and the viewers to vote on the person of their choice. Their chosen candidate needs no prior knowledge of technology, must not be an employee of TT Corporation, and must be aged twenty one or over. Immediately following the selection of a volunteer we will proceed to the fourth Section - the inaugural presentation of TT Corporation's crowning achievement, the Chronoguiser!"

"We get to actually see the Chronoguiser!" shouted a man from the back of the Hall.

The assemblage laughed, clapped and whistled.

"Thank you very much for your elaboration," said the Professor cheerfully. Then he continued in a sober tone. "During the fifth Section of our Forum, we will ask your chosen volunteer to join us on the Stage, where you will see the wonderful work of the Chronoguiser demonstrated!"

The conference clapped and stamped their feet. The watching crowd outside cheered enthusiastically, as did the crowds in the Parks.

"Finally, in Section six, we will announce the winner of the employment contract, and the super car!" the Professor concluded.

After glancing at his timeband and at his palmdisk - a Global Communications Device - Professor Doherty looked directly into the camera that filmed the Stage.

"We begin!" he said, smiling broadly. "Section One! And the first order of the day is to announce a winner! Congratulations, Citizen XZA. You are our first winner. You have just won a week's wages! Enjoy!" Grinning at his audience, he shouted, "Section One - reorganising the past!" After which, he gestured cordially to the man in the green bell patterned shirt. "The member of our group who we can all recognise by sight, the man wearing the bell-patterned shirt. We will all call him Green. Green, will you please stand? I want to talk to you!" the Professor called.

The man dubbed as Green stood up.

"You have recently been released from prison, have you not?" asked the Professor.

"Yes," replied the man stonily.

"The past tells us you are a danger to society."

"That is not true. My most recent past proves that I have reformed."

"The public didn't see you reform. You were locked away, invisible to us."

"You afford me *no* privacy. You shame me in public. But the worst of it is, you refuse to acknowledge that I have paid for my crime!" Green shouted. Angrily he sprang forward towards the Stage, to abruptly halt - seconds later. Sulkily he glared at the Professor. Then he turned and faced his fellow Delegates.

"I am sorry," he said gruffly and loudly. "I *am* afraid of my past, afraid that it will haunt me forever. Afraid that the remorse I feel will never end." He bowed his head and went quietly back to his seat.

"He *is* a danger to society," remarked a stout Delegate seated two rows in front of Green. "He can't even control his temper."

"Hush," advised her husband, who sat beside her. "We don't want any trouble."

She swivelled around in her chair and stared rudely at Green with intent to chastise.

"Ahem," said the Professor. When he stared at her accusingly, she settled quietly back in her seat. Professor Doherty then looked elegantly at his audience of eminent Doctors and Professors. He smiled and began to slowly pace the Stage. "Green has conceded," he announced. "He is afraid of his history. He is afraid of his past."

Green coughed and his face flushed.

The Professor continued in a kindly voice, "Ladies and Gentlemen, the Majority are not afraid of the past, because they are, in most circumstances, the conquerors. But when the individual suffers misfortune, makes mistakes that seem insurmountable, or loses a loved one, the past may rear its head and snarl."

Many of the Delegates nodded their heads in agreement.

"Green made a serious mistake," the Professor continued. "His mistake is a crushing burden to him. He has demonstrated to us all that the past may represent a real threat of which we are deeply afraid. For being such a good sport, *and* for being here with us today, please give Green a round of applause!"

The crowd clapped heartily.

Once again, the Professor looked at his timeband, palmdisk, and at the Stage-camera. He smiled widely. "Congratulations Balloon card number: 9900! You are the second winner of the day! You have just won a zeppelin ride for two!" he shouted. Then he continued in a sober voice. "Ladies and Gentlemen, we will continue to conquer the past. The Chronoguiser is a Chronological Reorganizer. It is a tool to enable us to reorganize time." Professor Doherty glanced again at his timeband. "Citizen GHT, our third winner of the day! You have just won a week's wages! Congratulations!" The Professor paused and said solemnly. "Consider the regrettable events of the past, and all the bitterness that follows. Consider if we could travel back through time and *prevent* those bad things from happening. We wouldn't be able to give ourselves a new past of course, but we would be able to make life better in the present."

"That would be wonderful!" said a sensitive lady in the front row, left aisle.

Overhearing, the Professor nodded. "Yes. That would be wonderful, dear lady."

The lady blushed and bowed her head.

The Professor continued. "As a second alternative, consider what we could achieve on a humanitarian level, if we could physically travel backwards in time." He glanced at his timeband, then called, "The fourth prize of today goes to Citizen PQD! You have just won a week's wages! Congratulations!"

"We could prepare for environmental disaster such as floods, fires and earthquakes!" shouted a man in the aisles.

"We could prevent accidents and crime!" shouted a muscular man wearing a Union Jack shirt.

"We could prevent aircraft and shipping disasters!" shouted the stout Delegate who sat with her hubby.

"Yes! We could conquer the past!" yelled the Professor. "Prevention of the worst in life is not the only benefit of time reorganization. The benefits to society on a purely educational level are phenomenal, and the scope for leisure is boundless!" The Professor shot a glance at his timeband and grinned at the Stage-camera, "Congratulations Citizen QBN! You have become the fifth lucky winner! You have just won a week's wages. Well done!"

"What are the arguments against travel into the past?" asked the Reporter from *The Herald*.

"I want you to tell me," said Professor Doherty. "However, I warn you. You are all intelligent people, and I expect original ideas from you. Anyone who dares quote me old ideas, or ideas from films, will be placed on the Stand of Stupidity - that glass booth to the left of our Stage!"

Many of the onlookers laughed. Many looked nervous.

The Professor glanced at his timeband for a sixth time. He held his head up high and winked at the Stage-camera. "Congratulations to our sixth winner today. Balloon Card number 4454. You have just won a zeppelin ride for two! Congratulations, Citizen HHD. You are our seventh lucky winner today! You have just won a weeks wages, compliments of TT Corporation!" The Professor then studied his guests questioningly. "For all of you who want to risk being placed in the Stand of Stupidity, raise your hands! First idea?"

Several people in the assembly immediately raised their hands.

"Yes," said the Professor, prompting a fragile, snowy-haired man to speak.

"Travelling into the past violates individual security and privacy - especially psyche travel. At present, there is nothing to stop a mind travelling anywhere, anytime. How would someone feel if an invisible energy field - a Roamer - turned up in his or her private bathroom, constantly visited his or her home, or even invaded a secret meeting?"

"I wouldn't welcome a spying energy field in my home," yelled the stout Delegate with the hubby.

"You are suggesting that the Roaming-Ring can be used to time travel?" asked the Professor, looking in awe at the fragile man.

"Obviously, in the right conditions and with the right mindset."

Those Delegates in the Forum who were wearing Roaming-Rings looked decidedly pleased and smug.

"Please join me in my home after the Forum? I would like to speak with you?" asked the Professor.

"Most certainly," replied the fragile, snowy-haired man.

"Ahem," interrupted the raised voice of TT from his Balcony compartment. "Ladies and Gentlemen," said TT smoothly. "Before we continue, I would like to put your minds at ease concerning the issue of unwanted Roamers invading private premises. TT Corporation will provide a security device to prevent the invasion of unwanted Roamers. The Security Device is purely a barrier - it will not harm Roamers in any way."

The stout Delegate with her husband smiled confidently. A few people seemed disappointed that their roaming would be restricted. Most were relieved and happy.

"Moving on," said the Professor. "Next idea?"

"There is a danger of shocking people who live in the past. They may disapprove of our behaviour, our beliefs, our culture and even our looks. Why, they may even believe we are aliens!" said a woman with long, black hair, wearing a sari.

"Excellent point, excellent!"

"Receptive individuals in the past could be influenced by our thoughts. This could result in social chaos and disharmony," said the Reporter from the *Herald*.

"Good, good. Next idea?"

A woman standing in the aisles, wearing wooden clogs and a peaked white bonnet, put her hand up nervously.

"I would presume that past cultures are not socially, morally or intellectually equipped to deal with modern technology. The introduction of future technology to the past could have dire consequences."

"A well thought idea. Thank you, Madam." The Professor scanned his assemblage and smiled. "You wish to add something useful, Green?" he asked, noticing that the man wearing the green bell-patterned shirt had raised his hand.

"If we try to reorganize time we run the risk of people changing history, prompted by greed."

"A good idea, but unfortunately for you, an old one! Come up to the Stage, Green. We are banishing you to the Stand of Stupidity!"

Green grinned good-naturedly and stepped up to the Stage. Entering the Stand of Stupidity, he stood casually surveying the onlookers from his now excellent vantage position.

The Professor scanned the company. Only the eminent scientists were willing to offer ideas now, with the exception of Faith Firebell.

"Mrs. Firebell," said Professor Doherty, "you wish to offer us your wisdom?"

"Yes, Professor. I do," she replied. "Having considered all the dangers of reorganizing the past, I believe that the biggest danger is the loss of the life of the traveller, through murder!"

"Please elaborate, Faith," prompted the Professor.

"If a person ventures into the past or future, by psyche travel or physically, they run the risk of being killed, with absolutely no repercussions to the murderer. There is no proof that the murder took place because there is no record of the victim's existence in that period."

"The converse is true," added a woman with a sallow complexion. She wore a delightful, red, flamenco dress and her hair was pinned with several feathery combs. "A traveller could commit assault or murder and easily avoid apprehension. He or she need only return to their own era."

Faith nodded her head in agreement and smiled at the lady.

"Can you suggest any way to prevent these murders, Faith?" asked the Professor.

"Restricting travel to safe zones would be an effective preventative measure," she proffered.

"How exciting!" shouted a sarcastic man on the Balcony.

"The zones could provide rides in the oldest or the newest vessels, and zoos of prehistoric or evolved animals," continued Faith. "Imagine the different types of food - a treat for any palette. The local people would be dressed in marvellous clothes. There would be *lots* of attractions."

"Great. I sure want to go to the past or the future to see a lousy *Theme Park*," shouted the same sarcastic man.

Professor Doherty considered the man with raised eyebrows. "Thank you, Faith," he said. Then he addressed the entire assemblage. "Mrs. Firebell has pointed out the most significant danger of reorganizing time, both in the past and in the future. We have now reached the final part of Section One."

The Professor, presently standing in front of the mahogany podium, took a book from a lower inner shelf, opened it and began to read out aloud, "The Draft Legislation on the subject of reorganizing past time states:

1. Our time travel technology will research the past.

2. Travel into the past must not violate individual security and privacy.

3. Travellers will be required to undergo a course of study to familiarize themselves with the beliefs and culture of the past. They are legally obliged to respect that culture and must dress commensurate with the period.

4. It is illegal to introduce future technology into the past.

5. It is against the law to harm or murder a person travelling to the past of future. Conversely, it is illegal for a traveller to harm or murder any person during their travels. The Chronometer Department will be responsible for all related investigations and will apply great diligence in the apprehension and punishment of criminals.

6. All new technology must be equipped with a sealed log of all trips, including dates, times and identification of users. All logs must be registered and handed into the Chronometer Department annually.

7. Citizens are authorised to use the new technology for educational and leisure purposes only."

Finished reading out the Draft Legislation, Professor Doherty glanced at his timeband. "Congratulations Citizen SSV! You are the winner of a week's wages! Ladies and Gentlemen, we have reached Section Two of the Forum - Reorganizing the future!"

While the Delegates clapped enthusiastically, the Professor continued, "The future is not a certainty until it happens. There are so many affecting variables that it is futile for one individual to attempt to change it. Even though this point is debatable, I believe much of the future is inevitable. This is because of the fundamental instinct of all things living to pursue their needs."

"I disagree, " said a gentleman wearing a terribly expensive suit.

"Let me explain," said Professor Doherty. "Consider a tree. If you block its light from above, it will grow taller. If you block its light from the right, it will grow to the left. Akin to trees, mankind will always strive towards the light. Hence, much of the future is inevitable."

"You're supposed to be a scientist, not a spiritualist," called a woman disparagingly. She was balancing on a ladder with a group of her friends. She waved her hand at the Professor dismissively and her friends laughed.

"Don't lose your balance, ma'am!" responded the Professor.

Many in the audience smiled and looked smugly at their feet.

"Question time!" said the Professor. "What is the most positive aspect of knowing the future?"

A robust woman held up her hand, and answered nervously, "We can plan the future. We can be sure we will survive."

"A text book answer, Madam. Thank you. We have a responsibility to protect the citizens of the future, but our main responsibility is our own survival. What is the danger of travel to the future, apart from murder? Yes, Madam."

"Our primitive minds may cause shock, chaos and destruction," said a young woman wearing a kimono in the first row. "We may even cause a future society to degenerate. Why, they might lock us in a Zoo believing we are animals."

"Good point. Thank you."

A thin bald man wearing a green kilt and a matching jacket raised his hand. "We could infect the people of the future with diseases that we are immune to. Or we could carry a disease back from the future and destroy our entire population."

"Excellent answer, Sir."

The Professor glanced at his timeband and palmdisk. "Balloon card number 177095, you have just won a ride for two in a zeppelin! Citizen ZXK, you are the final winner of our card competition. You have just won a week's wages, courtesy of TT Corporation. Congratulations to you both!" The Professor smiled at his guests and briskly walked to the right of the Stage. "Dear guests," he said graciously, "Thank you for your intelligent participation. We have come to the end of Section Two. Now, I am required to read to you the Draft Legislation on the reorganisation of future time."

Reaching inside the lower shelf of the podium, he opened the book of Draft Legislation and once again began to read aloud. "The Draft Legislation on the subject of reorganizing future time states:

1. Travel will be restricted to safe zones for the protection of our citizens and the citizens of the future.

2. Reorganisation of the future for personal gain is prohibited.

3. Established literature on future laws, regulations, and codes of dress and behaviour will be provided free of charge from public libraries. You must have a certificate to prove you have studied the literature before your travel will be legal.

4.Travellers will be required to be immunised and undergo regular medical screening."

He paused, before continuing, "The next two laws relate specifically to psyche travel.

5. Field generators to repel psyche travellers must be installed to bar unauthorized roaming into restricted areas.

6. Roamers will be required to undergo regular psychiatric health checks."

After finished reading and returning his book to the podium shelf, Professor Doherty became aware of shouting in the Stalls.

"You are blocking our view of the theatre," complained the lady from *Tokyo News*.

"Have some consideration for others!" shouted the slim youth from the *New York Times*.

"You ill-mannered sloth!" criticised the gentleman wearing the terribly expensive suit.

"Please sit down?" asked Faith Firebell, in a raised voice.

After glancing at his audience of Delegates, Professor Doherty immediately recognized a man in his early fifties, presently standing on a seat in the Stalls.

"Ladies and Gentlemen," announced the Professor. "Today we have the pleasure of famous company. The gentleman standing in the centre of the Stalls on his seat - wearing a brown suit - is the esteemed winner of this year's Global Peace Awards. He is Sir Kepplar Holmes!"

Everyone applauded.

"Oops," said the young *New York Times* Reporter.

"You have something to add to the proceedings, Kepplar Holmes?" asked Professor Doherty.

Holmes spoke quietly and deliberately. "I came here today hoping that the Chronoguiser could help me better my life. Now I fear that the new technology laws will actually work against me."

"The new laws will not work against anyone!" retorted the Professor. "However, I realize you have a problem, or you would not have spoken. Please elaborate. For my benefit and for the benefit of our assembly."

"My mother has been medically frozen, awaiting a future cure. I fear that the new legislation will prohibit such procedures because of the risk of contagion."

"With the proper safeguards the risk of infection - "

"Risk infecting a future population? No legislation will ever allow it!" interrupted Holmes.

"Perhaps you are being selfish?" suggested the Professor.

"I am being human," replied Holmes. "Anyone in my position would feel exactly the same. I love my mother. I don't want to lose her. But I love my home as well. I don't want to spoil it for the people of the future."

"I am sorry for your dilemma. Perhaps, by reorganising the past, you could ensure that your mother remains healthy," suggested the Professor. "You could prevent the ailment occurring."

"My mother has always been healthy," replied Holmes anxiously. "The ailment is hereditary - a genetic susceptibility."

"Perhaps we can discuss this later, Holmes. However, we must continue with the Forum. Please sit down."

"The legislation is going to bury my mother!" called Holmes angrily.

"I will not tolerate such stupid ideas!" Professor Doherty said coldly. "You can replace Green in the *Stand of Stupidity*! And you can cool off! Since you *are* a genius, I suggest you that you be the one to come up with a solution as to how to save your mother."

"Holmes, old boy!"

Holmes was surprised to hear the deep baritone voice of TT Vox Populi calling to him. TT was leaning casually over the balcony of his compartment.

"What do you want?" Holmes asked rudely.

"I want to help you," replied TT.

"Sure, you do," said Holmes sarcastically.

"Now, now, don't be like that," said TT. "We can put our heads together after the Forum. We'll see what we can do for you."

Seated on the left of Holmes, a man said shrewdly. "Give it up man. TT's got the people on-side."

Holmes suddenly became aware of the many disapproving faces staring at him. He left his seat and awkwardly approached the Stand of Stupidity. Dismally he climbed the steps onto the Stage and entered the glass booth, brushing shoulders with Green as he passed.

Professor Doherty watched him, then turned back to face his audience, only to be met by another nearby commotion.

An extremely well built woman, wearing a black pleated skirt and a red sweater, was shouting and crying. "I came here today because I believed I would see a real future. All you are offering me is a contrived future - a Theme Park!"

Professor Doherty sighed deeply. "Oh yes, the Theme Park again," he said wearily.

"We can't just go anywhere we like," complained the women. "The past and the future will be restricted. If we stray past the authorized areas, we could be killed, imprisoned, or worse! In order to leisure travel into the past or future safely, the whole trip has to be arranged down to the last little detail. We'll need a Travel Agent!"

In his Balcony compartment, TT keyed a message onto his palmdisk. The tiny screen on the Professor's palmdisk then flashed with the words: *"Shut her up! She's making my planned Tourist Cities sound loathsome, TT!"*

After glancing at the message, the Professor continued speaking to the woman in a calming tone of voice, "I do agree with you in principle, Madam. Of course, a Time Traveller wants to see the real culture, technology and people of a different era. However, I anticipate that a Tourist City - constructed within each Nation - would adequately meet your needs. A Tourist City is a wonderful idea. Don't you agree?"

Most of the Delegates nodded their heads in agreement, but the woman in the red sweater only scowled.

"Everything in the city would truly represent the period," Professor Doherty continued. "There would be absolutely no threat to the future inhabitants or to us. The whole family would be able to enjoy the wonders of the future, in complete safety. Once the cities have been established, and time goes by, we would also be able to visit the past safely."

The woman wearing the red sweater was not listening. She was too upset. "I don't want my travelling to be controlled!" she screamed.

"I'm sorry, Madam, you must compose yourself or Security will be obliged to remove you from the auditorium," the Professor warned.

Standing nearby a man wearing a silver and blue striped suit was tired of the complaining woman. "Shut up!" he shouted rudely.

"I'm going to go to the future *now*," she screamed, "Before you can set up your stupid laws to control everything!"

"How do you propose to do this, Madam?" asked the Professor.

She stared at the Flag fixedly for a moment. Careering forward at pull pelt, she leapt up onto the Stage.

Some minutes had passed. The Delegates were quiet and subdued. The crowd in the Parks were absorbed watching the Mega Screens and those viewing at home kept their eyes fixed to their sets.

The sensitive lady in the front row was crying. Her hands were trembling, and her previous rose coloured complexion was blotched from nerves.

No longer on the Stage, intimidating and glowing, but kneeling in front of her in the Stalls, sympathetic and kindly, was Professor Doherty. He held her hand in his and looked questioningly into her pale, distressed face. The Security Chief stood solidly beside him.

As the auditorium cameras zoomed in on the three, the Professor spoke into the camera for the benefit of the viewers. "The lady I am questioning has lost her memory. Her speedy recovery is contingent on a complete recall of recent events," he said soberly. Then he looked at the sensitive lady enquiringly and with concern. "You fainted," he said gently. "Stop crying. Try to remember what happened."

"The last thing I remember was a woman at the front of the Stalls shouting. I can't remember anything else."

"Yes, you can," coaxed the Professor.

She bowed her head and closed her eyes. She thought carefully, beginning with where she was. She recalled the lively debate and her own participation. She remembered a woman wearing a red sweater shouting, then ... she had been afraid. Blurred images flooded her mind. Feeling as if she had just watched a frightening play, she shook her head absently.

"Did someone get hurt?" the Professor prompted.

"Yes," she replied quietly.

"Who was hurt?"

"The man who won the Global Peace Prize - Sir Kepplar Holmes - he was hurt. I'm a fan - I've followed his work for years." Beginning to cry again, she stifled her sobs.

"Can you tell me what happened?"

"A woman wearing a red sweater got onto the Stage, ran at you, and knocked you down. Then she went at that man there." She pointed at the Chief and paused. "She wrenched his gun off him. The gun landed on the Stage Floor. It accidentally fired."

"Go on," the Professor prompted.

Her eyes welled up. "The glass on the Stand of Stupidity was cracked. Kepplar Holmes just stood there with blood coming out of his side. He was trying to conceal the wound with his hands. He didn't even cry out! I remember I couldn't breathe."

"Sir Holmes been taken to a nearby hospital in Cromwell Road," said the Professor. "His condition isn't critical. The woman who caused the disturbance has been detained."

"I blanked everything out for a little while," said the sensitive lady in explanation. "Today has been so exciting and so much fun. Now it's been spoiled."

"Today's unfortunate accident will soon be a nightmare that you can quickly forget," said the Professor. "You will remember the Forum as a wonderful event that was never marred."

"I can't see how."

Professor Doherty signalled to the Chief who rejoined his men.

"We can reorganize time using the Chronoguiser," said the Professor. Leaning forward, he spoke quietly. "I'll tell you a little secret. The scientists at the Farnborough Research Lab wanted to name the Chronoguiser after the 'Clock of Children'. I sort of agreed. See if you can guess what name I chose. If you guess correctly before the Christening Ceremony, I'll give you a bottle of champagne. If you guess wrong, I'll still give you a bottle of champagne!"

"Thank you," she said.

Standing up, Professor Doherty jumped back onto the Stage and addressed his audience, both in the auditorium and worldwide. "Ladies and Gentlemen. TT Corporation, together with the Natural History Museum, apologise for any distress you may have suffered due to the unfortunate shooting you witnessed - on stage - moments ago. We had planned a practical demonstration of the Chronoguiser. We have decided to cancel that planned demonstration. Instead, we will replace it with something that will mean so much more to all of you. Today, I promise you, our Peace Prize winner - Kepplar Holmes - will be returned to you without a scratch!"

"Fraudsters!" yelled a man in the Balcony.

"Charlatan!" yelled an elderly woman with flaming red, dyed hair.

Ignoring their rude heckling, the Professor continued his address. "The unscheduled break in our debate brings us to Section Three of the Forum. I call the attention of all the viewers at home, all the people in the streets and in the Royal Parks, and all Delegates. It is time to select a volunteer! Those of you who want to reorganize time, please raise your hand!"

Several men and three women raised their hands. Numerous other people from outside the auditorium were ushered into the Hall.

"Excellent!" said the Professor. "Please, come up onto the Stage!"

The volunteers, numbering twenty, moved quickly through the aisles and climbed the Stage steps in single file. They stood in a line across the Stage, well forward of the Flag.

"Call out your surname first, followed by your profession," directed the Professor. "Speak loudly enough for the entire audience to hear, then state why you want to volunteer. After you have had your turn, sit down on the chairs provided for you to the left of the Stage. One at a time, if you please."

Each of the volunteers spoke out, until only two remained standing.

"Firebell, British News Reporter," said the first of the two. "I'm game to try anything new!"

"Green to you all, reformed felon," said the second. "I want to prove that this whole Forum is a load of crock!"

These last two volunteers walked across to the left of the Stage and sat down with the other hopeful candidates.

"Ladies and Gentlemen. Time to choose your volunteer!" shouted the Professor. "When I call out each person's name, indicate your choice by clapping - for those in the auditorium and outside; and by televoting - for the viewers at home."

The Professor called out each name in turn, until again only the last two candidates remained. The response was consistent - with four hundred people voting for each candidate.

"Firebell!" Professor Doherty shouted.

All of the Delegates clapped. As did TT. The worldwide tally registered seven thousand!

"Green!"

Suddenly an immense roar was heard from out in the street.

Subsequently, the Professor's commanding voice flowed out through the Speaker System and over the London crowd, quenching the commotion. "Green is your chosen volunteer!" he shouted above the ruckus. "With a tally of over one million - Green will have the task of reorganizing time! He will bring our Peace Prize winner back to us unharmed!"

Professor Doherty faced the assembly with Green standing proudly at his side. The rejected volunteers trailed across the Forum Stage and stepped down, disappointed.

"Immediately after the unveiling, Green will be asked back onto Stage," the Professor continued. "He will demonstrate how he can reorganise time. Thank you, Green."

Green returned to his seat, amidst much applause from the Delegates and the people outside.

Professor Doherty faced the cameras, the Delegates and his worldwide audience. "We are ready to fly the Flag!" he shouted. "To signal the unveiling of the Chronoguiser - to the World!"

Excited, the seated Delegates reached for their portable cameras. Watching the Mega Screens, the audience outside hushed. At home, the viewers leant forward in their seats expectantly.

The Inventors returned to the Stage and commenced playing the National Anthem, while all the Delegates stood up, as a mark of respect. British people everywhere began to sing proudly. Their voices filled the auditorium, Central London and their homes, and drifted out into the sunny afternoon.

Finishing the Anthem and clapping their hands together in applause, all now watched as the huge National Flag was hoisted out through the domed-roof onto a high flagpole on top of the Museum - revealing to the surprised multitude what had been previously hidden.

"The Chronoguiser is behind that curtain! It is big. It is wonderful! It is most amazing invention that we will ever have the chance to see!" Hundreds of people said these words and millions of minds chanted the same, in silent unison...

Chapter four

...Running from the apartment into the foyer, Zeta called after her dad, only to see him slamming the heavy house door behind him.

"Dad? When will I see-?"

Zeta's voice crackled and stopped in mid-sentence. There was an audible clunk, followed by a mechanical humming and whizzing sound, ending with another loud clunk...

The silence that followed Zeta's cry for her father, on the Forum day, was eerie and frightening. The silence screamed of great damage to the Earth. Many things were gone, and the silence screamed of them all.

Gone was the echo of the transport to which mankind has become so accustomed. The distant roar of a plane and the rumbling of a car engine. The high-pitched whine of a motorbike ferrying its rider forward in the early hours of the morning. The rumbling of a heavy truck and the clatter of a train. The low deep hum of a ship's engine and the soft happy whoosh as the bow slices through the waves. The sound of movement - of intelligent beings working, playing, exploring and living - was no more.

Vanished too were the calls of the animals. The loud bark of a hound and the soft purring of a contented cat. The gay chirping of a bird at the onset of dawn. The furtive squeaking of a delicate mouse, and the dry hoot, hoot of a tawny owl. The whinnying of a horse nearing home and the crowing of a rooster at daybreak. The hurried scurrying of a squirrel bounding up a tree, and the lonely squawk of a crow in the yellow russet outback of a distant land. These and many more familiar, warming sounds were stolen from man's senses, in this strange pervasive silence.

Stillness crept forward, warning of a most disturbing loss. No more were the homely whispers of the plants. No more was the innocent soft hissing, the rustling and whooshing of the wind, as it combs and brushes the leaves of the trees, tossing them topsy-turvy amongst their branches. Silent too, the soft padding on crumpled grass and the gentle rustling of shrubs disturbed by a comforting tepid breeze. Missing was the crunching of the autumn leaves underfoot and the light thud as a ripe apple falls from its bough. Little noises, taken for granted - the sounds of life, of a breathing green Earth - were no more. The trees, and the air that they bring, the plants, and the food they supply were gone, all gone.

Bermuda brushed a short lock of his curly brown hair back from his forehead and tucked it under his chainmail balaclava. Then he switched off the ancient video recording of the TT Forum he had been watching.

Taking a canister from the desk in front of him, he poured clear water into a bowl on the Sitting room floor. Listening, he heard the familiar scampering noise of his Clode, Tri, who suddenly appeared from the adjoining Dining room behind him. Tri bounded towards Bermuda. The animal lapped up the water. Then he sat happily beside Bermuda's desk.

"Keep watchful, Tri," instructed Bermuda sternly. "Earn your keep."

After glancing at his pet, Bermuda stepped past Tri and moved to his left, towards a one-way viewing window. Interested, he looked out at a group of teenage tourists clustered in an airtight, transparent Tubular Walkway directly opposite.

While they discussed the interesting features of his twentieth century cottage hideout - one of the buildings in a Historic Reserve - Bermuda listened to them, by way of a covert Surveillance System.

"Note the reddish, clay bricks on the ground floor combined with the matching tile hangings on the floor above," remarked one of the teenagers, a girl of seventeen - his own age - called Tesla Gosh.

"Yes, Tesla. This is a very pretty cottage. Thoughtfully built, don't you think?" said her friend, a slightly younger girl named Brooklyn Trina.

"Indeed," replied Tesla. "I do like the porch entrance and the high pitched roof. The chimney stack is an *adorable* touch."

"*Rather*," said Brooklyn. "Do you think the ladies of this particular era spilled ash on their gowns?"

"Oh, no," replied Tesla. "It would have been such a fret if they did!"

Tesla patted lovingly at the handsome, ankle-length gown she wore. Rose coloured with gold edging, it had close fitting sleeves, ending just above the elbow, edged with a deep ruffle of lace. Underneath the robe and displayed prettily in a panel at the front was a pink chemise and dome-shaped petticoat.

"You're wearing a new robe, Tesla," remarked Brooklyn admiringly. "The style is reminiscent of a mid-eighteen century Sack Robe, I believe?"

"Yes, indeed, precious. All the rage now. A must-have item. I wouldn't be seen wearing anything else!"

"What do you think of the garden, Tesla? I know it's synthetic now but it must have been truly charming when it was real. Conifers and heathers, a green lawn, roses -"

"Bees," replied Tesla. "Awful little yellow and black striped stinging insects that constantly hovered over blooms, invading proprietor's gardens. I do believe the ladies of this era were forced to wear gauche nets over their heads, protective clothes and thick gloves made of animal skins before they could venture outside."

"Oh!" gasped Brooklyn.

"Oh yes, if they didn't, they would be eaten alive by the bees," continued Tesla. "The neighbours would find dead ladies on their front lawns with their hair full of buzzing bees!" She stroked her long wavy brown hair, beaded throughout with an array of tiny jewels.

"Oh, dear," exclaimed Brooklyn.

"Yes, I can imagine you right now, your long golden hair amass with bees, and your ivory skin all red and blotched from being stung."

Brooklyn nervously touched the roaming-Ring she was wearing.

"You take everything for granted, petal," continued Tesla. "Of course everyone wears a roaming-Ring now, but when this house was built they didn't have the technology. They relied on transport if they wanted to visit each other and they relied on ... let me think... telephones! If they wished to speak to each other that had to dial a series of numbers into a device and talk and listen through that same device! Fancy that!"

"It all sounds a rather impersonal way to communicate," remarked Brooklyn.

"Too impersonal for someone like you, my dear. You just wouldn't have fit in, I'm afraid. You wouldn't have been able to roam and ask for help when the bees were stinging you. Deary me, poor little petal, you would have been lost!"

"What about Pinky?" asked Brooklyn, referring to her artificially pale pink Clode puppy sitting perkily in the pet basket she carried.

"Oh, no! They didn't have Clodes to help them then, Brooklyn. Clodes didn't even exist!"

"They had pets," retorted Brooklyn. "Pets have always helped people."

"Yes, they did have pets. Honestly, I don't know why you go through the fuss and bother of keeping that Clode of yours. Nevertheless, dearest, a pet could have been killed by bees as well. They probably were." She paused for breath. "I imagine all the ladies of the past had pets, and those pets were all horribly killed by bees."

"I would have been done for, then?" stated Brooklyn softly.

"Yes indeed, Miss. The past was a dreadful world really. We have a much better life now dear, and TT Vox Populi is going to make our lives even better." She paused, ascertained that Brooklyn was looking pale, and decided to change the subject. "As you know, I'm hosting a grand Ball, Wednesday fortnight. Remember to bring that gorgeous fellow, Tau, with you as your partner. Make certain his friend Bermuda doesn't tag along. Bermuda is such an honest fellow - but not the type who is appreciated in my circle."

Turning her head, Tesla smiled coquettishly at another teenager in their group, a youth called Miles.

"Miles is wearing the latest in fashion, a frockcoat embellished with embroidery," Tesla continued, leaning closer to Brooklyn and speaking in a softer voice.

"Yes, Miles looks well," agreed Brooklyn, after glancing at the youth.

"Shall we go inside?" Tesla now prompted, calling to her friends. "I can show you what the historic facilities are like. This is my second visit to this house. It's a hobby of mine - history. You'll see that the living conditions the women of the past had to tolerate were - what can I say - appalling. I'll never know how they managed."

She began to walk along the airtight covered path that led to the entrance door of the ancient house, while her group of friends followed close behind, chatting and laughing.

"Oh, wait!" she called, pouting angrily. "We can't go inside! The wretched place has been closed for repairs!"

Bermuda was still staring out of the window, but now he was grinning. He had watched the group walk towards the house and stop.

Now he watched them as they each read the sign he had written and posted on the door.

"We regret that this exhibit is closed for repairs. TT Conglomerate, Global Holiday Consortium."

"Tesla is such a pretentious ninny," he thought. "Good-looking and such a snob. She has a cheek asking Brooklyn to drag Tau to her boring Ball. And she has an even bigger cheek not inviting me!"

He pointed a hand-held device towards them and scanned them for weapons. Clear as expected, he returned the device into a pocket in his jacket. Still grinning, he watched them return to the main Tubular Walkway and move quickly away, with a cross Tesla marching well out in front.

When the group was out of sight Bermuda returned to his desk positioned against the front wall, between the window and the entrance door. Once there, he sat down on the desk chair, with his back to the nearby staircase. He checked his timeband, noting it was 6pm. Then he began tinkering with a spherical device that sat on the desktop. There he remained for the next five hours, rising on the hour to scan the premises for intruders and then returning to his desk. During that time, the outside world darkened. In response to the fading light, the cornices of the room brightly illuminated. Bermuda continued to diligently apply himself to his job, until the end of the sixth hour. Then something happened. He felt a presence. A Psyche Intruder had entered the room.

After glancing tautly at his Martial Arts Fighting-Staff, leaning against the wall to the left of his desk, he scanned the room with his hand-held device.

"Tri, is there danger?" he asked his Clode. "I sense an invisible Roamer - somewhere close."

Tri's large eyes opened wide. The dog tapped twice on the floor with one of his tiny paws.

"That's a no, then. You're never wrong. There is no danger." Bermuda swivelled in his chair and called out into the cosy Sitting room, "I don't know how you got in here with the field generator set to keep you out, but you did. You're not supposed to be in here. We don't take kindly to busybodies, OK. Leave now, Roamer, or you will get hurt!" he warned. He looked around the room but saw no one.

Zeta, however - seriously bemused - saw him. Believing herself to be in her Auntie Marjorie's house in Farnborough, she had no recollection of how she got there. Crouching in the corner under the

Sitting room stairs, she stared out into the hazel eyes of a strangely clad youth, dressed entirely in bronze chainmail. Surprised, she noted the stand-up collar of his jacket, the sleeves that extended over his knuckles - fastening between his thumb and forefinger - and his loose trousers, worn past his ankle and clipped to unusual boots.

The fact that he was he dressed similar to a Medieval Knight was not that unusual, this being England, and Medieval re-enactments being a common leisure pursuit. Neither was the Roaming-Ring that he wore on his head strange, for she knew that thousands of the Rings were sold this very day.

What was puzzling was the elegant creature sitting beside the youth's desk, a type of dog, reminding her instantly of To-do. She marvelled at the dog's skin, smooth and silky like porcelain. She admired its soft, downy coat. Then she noted its silver chest and paws, its tan body, tipped with black and its long, black, droopy ears. Finally, Zeta looked into its large, soft eyes. As she observed the Clode, Tri's eyes widened, dark-brown, sensitive and appreciative. Blinking, he nodded his head sleepily.

"Tri... none of that now!" admonished Bermuda, seeing the little animal begin to doze.

The youth looked straight at Zeta. His eyes narrowed and he made a move to step towards her. Changing his mind, he swivelled his chair back and returned to his tinkering.

Zeta watched him while he worked. Then she let her gaze wander around the familiar Sitting room. She recognized the chintz sofa in the centre. The Display cabinet in the front left corner of the room contained her auntie's collection of dolls and wooden ornaments. She even recognized the five large prints of yachts, framed in black wood, decorating the cream, painted walls. Not familiar, however, were the illuminated cornices filling the room with artificial light.

Zeta suddenly heard a sharp whistle from the rear garden, followed by the slamming of a rear door. She watched a handsome youth of Latin origins enter the Sitting room from the connecting Dining room. Behind him was a smaller boy, with oriental features.

Zeta immediately noted that the youths wore clothes similar to the lad at the desk. Amethyst crystals encircled the Roaming-Ring of the bigger lad, while the latter wore a diadem set at centre front with three gems of Jet.

As they entered the Sitting room, both lads glanced towards Zeta - without seeing her - then quickly approached the youth sitting at the desk.

Finding them daunting, Zeta moved further into the corner, wrapped her arms around her knees and began to listen.

"We have a non-threatening Psyche Intruder," said Bermuda, speaking immediately to the two other lads. "I have given it fair warning."

"Do they mean me?" questioned Zeta silently. "Am I the Psyche Intruder?"

"Do you think we should take action against it, Parsons?" asked Bermuda.

"No," said the smallest boy. "Leave the trespasser to Tau. He can deal with that responsibility when he wakes up."

"What's your opinion, Sebastian?" asked Bermuda of the other lad.

"I agree," said Sebastian. "Tau's the boss."

"Fine," said Bermuda. "The benefits of being a subordinate - no accountability."

"How goes the work on the gravity drive?" asked Parsons, changing the subject and peering inquisitively at the globe on the desk.

"Hey, I thought I recognised that device!" called Zeta angrily. "What are you doing with my dad's invention?"

The youths did not hear her. Tri pricked up his ears.

"Slowly, frustratingly," replied Bermuda. "Professor Doherty kept the secret of the drive well to himself." Pausing, he drummed his fingers onto the desk. "I really need Tau to get the Chronoguiser here as quickly as possible. I need to see Doherty's drive so I can copy it. I *need* that prototype!"

"The Chronoguiser?" exclaimed Zeta, "This is industrial espionage! You can't steal my dad's gravity drive and copy it! We have a patent!" She paused to see their reaction to her outburst, but there was none. "I hate it when people ignore me!" she shouted.

"The first gravity drive that you built functions OK," said Parsons encouragingly.

"No, Parsons, it doesn't."

"It got the Lumpo to Queens Gate, didn't it?" said Sebastian.

"It's merely a Matter Transfer Device," responded Bermuda. "The Lumpo isn't alive, you are. Transporting Space food through space and time is one thing. Carrying *people* is another. My gravity drive would make Lumpo out of you, Sebastian!"

"Tell me, when you roamed and moved Doherty's Tea Party off his table, what did you do with the food?" asked Sebastian.

"I threw everything out the back window," Bermuda replied casually.

Sebastian groaned. "You could have brought the food back here. I wanted to eat it. What a waste."

"I was following Tau's orders."

"Did Tau give you a reason for wrecking the Tea Party?" asked Parsons.

"He wanted Professor Doherty to attend the TT Corporation get-together, knowing it would continue until well after midnight. He was trying to prevent the Professor from going to the TT Showroom."

"Do you think Professor Doherty died on the night of the Forum?" asked Sebastian.

Zeta gasped. "Hey, you're talking about my dad in the past tense," she thought anxiously. Then she clapped her hands together loudly and shouted, "How about listening to me!"

Ignored by the youths, she quickly darted forward. Grabbing a wooden cat from her Auntie's Display cabinet, she threw it at Sebastian. Hastily, she retreated into the corner. The carved ornament sailed through the air and landed with a light thud on the toe of Sebastian's right boot.

"We won't know what happened to Doherty until Tau stops snoring and tells us," replied Bermuda. Then he added sarcastically. "Our unwelcome Roamer seems to like you, Sebastian."

Sebastian raised his eyebrows. "It must be a girl," he remarked casually. Kicking the teak cat across the Sitting room floor, he watched it slide across the shiny planks and hit the opposite wall with a thud.

His action dissuaded Zeta from throwing any more cats. Deciding to keep quiet, she considered her situation and what she had just heard.

"I am sitting in the corner under the stairs, listening to three boys," she thought to herself calmly. "They have obviously broken into my auntie's house and are either blind and deaf, or are cruelly ignoring me - probably the latter. They have admitted to sabotaging my father's Tea Party and they are planning to steal the Dandy Lion. The first thing I'm going to do when I get home is to look in our rear garden and see if Bermuda really did throw the Tea Party out of our back window. Then I'm going straight to my dad to tell him everything I heard."

Suddenly she heard a happy lively jingle, piping through the house. The music was extremely entertaining and the words went as thus:

"*It's Lumpo, its Lumpo. It's lumpy, lumpy, Lumpo.*

It's Lumpo, it's Lumpo, it's Lumpo!"

These lyrics repeated three times, finishing up with a long drawn out happy "*Lump...ooh!*"

When the jingle had finished playing, monitors in the Tubular Walkways outside flashed into life. Advertising images of grey porridge dolloping down and dripping off spoons filled those screens.

The people ambling along in the now brightly lit walkways watched the screens intently until the images faded. Happily, they resumed strolling.

"I hate that annoying jingle!" Sebastian ranted angrily. "It plays night and day, invading everyone's mind with that chirpy music! They never say the benefits of the food - that it's actually good for you! It annoys the stuffing out of me that they never admit that it's taken from the sea, and it's actually a mixture of fish and sea-plants! Of course, they'll not mention that the Lumpo was made two years ago, when the last sea harvest took place. Neither will they declare that there will be none left in a few weeks, except for the stores on the Spaceships!"

"At least you've had food while you were growing up," said Parsons calmly. "The people who attacked us in other nations have been starving since the meteors hit."

"What meteors?" asked Zeta quietly.

"Yes, be glad that TT Conglomerate took you on as a Psychic Knight," said Bermuda sarcastically. "They fed you, educated you, nurtured your psychic ability. Now you are betraying them."

"I was born with my gift," said Sebastian. "TT Conglomerate didn't give it to me. And I'm not betraying anyone. The people are giving up. I believe the Earth is worth fighting for. And I hate quitters."

"*You* think they are giving up. TT's followers believe they are moving on to a better future," said Parsons steadily. "Leaving the Earth has its merits you know."

"Like what?"

"Exploration, freedom. By leaving Earth, we find the home that seemed beyond our grasp. We open our minds."

"Thank you, Parsons. Whose side are you on?" asked Sebastian.

"You need not doubt my support," replied Parsons. "But you are angry with TT Vox Populi and I am not."

"I'm angry because TT doesn't give us any choice. *He* wants to leave the Earth, so every one has to, right or wrong."

"He's not trying to kill us," said Parsons. "He nearly bankrupt his father's Company when he was young, with the Greenhouse Satellite Project. None of our plants are extinct because of him. He funded the research into air-from-water extraction, so we have plenty of air to breathe."

"As long as we stay indoors," said Sebastian sourly.

"You can travel outside along the Tubular Walkways," responded Parsons.

"Wow, I can breath air piped through the ground, whilst being enclosed in a structure. That's what I call life," retorted Sebastian sarcastically.

"I think I preferred you when you were ranting about Lumpo," said Parsons.

All the while they were speaking, Bermuda had been gazing out of the nearby window. Now he swivelled in his chair to face into the room.

"Look outside, chaps," he said, gesturing toward the window and the luminous Tubular Walkway. "There's a child eating Lumpo on an ice cream stick and enjoying it. It's amazing what a bit of imagination can do for your appetite."

Parsons tried to smile, but Sebastian only glowered.

"The populace are certainly making the most of the last three weeks they've been given to live on Earth," remarked Parsons. "It's well past midnight and they're still out revelling."

After listening to their conversation, Zeta was exceedingly interested. "I've never heard of Psychic Knights before," she thought. "Or a Greenhouse Satellite. Or plans to leave the Earth. Neither have I heard of a food called Lumpo."

Prompted by curiosity to come out of her corner, she stood up and walked towards the window. Looking out, she expected to see the local Common - a place where she had walked during each of the seasons, enveloped in a cool hidden world, under a vast canopy of oak boughs. Where the sweet smelling earth had filled her senses, and where in winter, the sun had glistened against snow-topped, bare branches and the morning frost had fashioned a delicate, white blanket over the awakening world.

Instead of this beautiful rustic setting however, she now saw, just past the front lawn, a brightly lit Tubular Walkway that branched off directly to her porch. Strolling through this walkway, many strangely dressed, men, women and children wore Roaming-Rings set with smoky quartz crystals. Shockingly, beyond the airtight walkways, Zeta saw only barren, dust covered earth.

Panicked, she glanced at Bermuda and then back out of the window. She was not in her auntie's house. Of that, she was certain. Neither was she in Farnborough! She was somewhere strange, unfamiliar and frightening.

"Where am I?" she shouted.

Rushing out of the Sitting room and through the Dining room, she flung open the rear door. Then she ran out into the darkness. Halting abruptly, she found herself standing in a synthetic garden surrounded by a black iron barricade. Looking up she saw an awning that blocked the stars from view and extended from the eaves of the house to the iron barricade.

Returning inside, dazed, she slammed the door closed behind her. Entering the Sitting room, she bleakly resumed her place seated in the corner under the stairs.

Tri began an irritating whine and Bermuda felt an anxious sadness slowly pervade the historic room.

"The Roamer has obviously found the outside world to be extremely distressing," he remarked.

"Judging by the hurried exit and return I would surmise so," added Parsons. "The world is rather intimidating when it is an airless desert."

"Is that your prognosis as our resident medical student, Parsons?"

"Yes."

Sebastian frowned. "I don't like these bad vibes. Sing some cheer for us, Bermuda? Sing the peoples' favourite - my favourite!"

Bermuda smiled agreeably. Producing a silver mouth organ from his jacket inner pocket, he played a few bars of a popular, familiar song. Then he threw his mouth organ to Sebastian.

"Here, accompany me," he ordered.

As Sebastian accompanied him, Bermuda sang a winsome, captivating song.

"We deserve a beautiful world. We should sing for all the gifts it will bring.

We should fly into the stars. We should be the best that we are.

Our land, forthright and fair. Our future, all that we dare.

Our hope, all that we dream. Our lives, the finest we deem.

We shall see the summer again, and the beauty that we all yen.

We will breath the fragrance so light. We will soar into the night.

Dearest friends, when you are near, our foes, then they will fear.

Spring will waken out of the cold, for our spirits, loving and bold.

All will find their garden of light. All will leave a world of dearth plight.

Bees will hum their work song again. Bread and honey, food for all men.

We will stroll in forests of green, sheltered by the sublime and unseen.

Yes the Cosmos, given to roam. We will take it thus as our home.

We deserve a beautiful world. We should sing for all the gifts it will bring.

We should fly into the stars. We should be the best that we are."

When he had finished singing, he bowed ceremoniously to his friends. Sebastian grinned, wiped Bermuda's mouth organ and threw it back to him.

A positive ambience filled the room and turned the temper of Tri. Now he sat up with his floppy ears held forward and his eyes shining bright.

Entertained by the song, the three youths settled themselves more comfortably into the room. Parsons sat down on the sofa and Sebastian leant against the wall beside the Display cabinet.

"I'm glad to see you all so casual," said a cross voice coming from the top of the stairs. "We have a deadline to meet, but of course, who gives two figs about that! Let's just sit around nattering like a bunch of girls. Why not cap it all off by singing a pretty song as well, just to ram home the point that you are idle blackguards!"

Walking down and stopping at the foot of the stairs, the owner of the voice stared at Parsons and Bermuda. They in turn promptly stood up. The owner of the voice then glared at Sebastian.

"You've gotten real cranky since you were conferred with your Doctorate of Physics, Tau," said Sebastian derisively.

"He's here!" thought Zeta excitedly. "Tau is the person who knows if my dad is dead or alive. Perhaps he'll be able to hear me? Maybe I'll be able to talk to him and ask him questions."

Tau coughed and scowled. "I worked hard, so I could be productive. Perhaps you should follow my example, John Sebastian?"

"You changed out of your pyjamas before coming down," remarked Bermuda, sensing a forthcoming fight and shifting the subject.

"Yes, I hate those ancient clothes," responded Tau. "I worry that both the shirt and the trousers will disintegrate every time I put them on. However, I have to sleep in them to keep up the charade. It's easy to ignore items like my Roaming-Ring when I mirror, but it's hard to invent clothes."

"You gave yourself a hair cut before you came downstairs. Why?" asked Sebastian.

"I am now part of the Security team working for TT Corporation."

"So TT Vox Populi didn't recognise you?"

Tau grinned. "That's right, Sebastian. TT didn't recognize me without my Knight's Raiment."

"You'll be able to bring me the Chronoguiser soon," said Bermuda. "Once I have the prototype, I can easily replicate the gravity drive."

"Yes," replied Tau confidently. "Now that I have a job working in TT's Research Facility in Farnborough, I will be able to steal the only Chronoguiser in existence, the Dandy Lion, right out from under TT's nose!"

"The TT Showroom is a pile of rubble, then," said Parsons sadly. "What we could have done with four hundred time-machines?"

"We knew that the Showroom and the Chronoguisers were going to be destroyed, so you shouldn't bother being so morose, Parsons."

"Do you know the identity if the saboteurs, Tau?" questioned Parsons.

"No I don't, but I'm interested to find out. The wanton destruction of those time-machines is the reason for all our problems now. Whoever bombed the TT-Showroom has a lot of power. The perpetrator made sure that the Chronoguisers were not built again, not for thousands of years. Not until now, that is!"

"Thousands of years!" exclaimed Zeta to herself.

"Tau and I built ten Chronoguisers," said Bermuda humbly. "Most of them are pretty big."

"Have you finished your recent work, Bermuda?" asked Tau. "Are my time-machines nearly complete?"

"Yes, I've finished, Tau. Your Chronoguisers are complete, with the exception of fully functioning gravity drives."

"Where are these time-machines?" asked Sebastian wonderingly.

"Tau and I hid them where we built them - on Satellite25," replied Bermuda. "We used scrap from old machines, a Replicator, and a lot of elbow grease to assemble them. Plus additional help from quite a few Assembly robots."

"How did you get away with hiding obvious innovative ships in such a public place as a Theme Park?" asked Sebastian, impressed by Bermuda and Tau's inventiveness.

"We were incognito. When the Theme Park visitors saw us they thought we were Maintenance Engineers," replied Bermuda. "They erroneously believed the Chronoguisers were bits of refuse – part of an exhibit of derelict old Spaceships. Once Tau and I had finished the hulls of the vessels, the fact that the Spheres were Spaceships was a little too obvious. After that, we cordoned off the area."

"Will our Chronoguisers fly without hazard?" asked Tau, his face most solemn. "Will they take us through time, to a future Earth?"

"There is no reason why they shouldn't. All I need to do is replicate Professor Doherty's gravity drive into each of them, and hey presto, we're in business!"

"And what of the inventor?" asked Parsons. "Is Professor Doherty dead? Was he killed with the others at the Showroom?"

Zeta, who had been listening attentively all this time, gasped. Her thoughts were in a panic. "What! Is my dad dead? Have people been killed?"

Tri reacted to Zeta's distress. He pricked up his ears, cocked his head to the side and tapped the ground three times with his left paw.

"No one has been killed," replied Tau. Taking two large strides into the room, he suddenly swung around. Crouching down, he stared into the cavity under the stairs.

Zeta, who had been peeping out timidly, trying to catch a glimpse of Tau, found that she was looking straight into the face of - *Dominic*. Except that he wasn't quite the Dominic - she remembered. The colours of his body were intense compared with how he had looked on the afternoon of the Forum, a few hours previous. His hair was short and sandy coloured. His eyes were vividly blue and his complexion was a lightly tanned ivory. Crowning his head, she saw a

Roaming-Ring set with eight quartz crystals. Like the other three youths, he wore a bronze chainmail suit. Additionally she noted that he held his head high, in a proud and confident manner.

"There's someone in here, you slackers," Tau said quietly, standing up and moving to face his friends. "It's in the corner under the stairs."

"It's not dangerous," said Bermuda loudly.

"Didn't you even bother to activate the field generator to stop unwanted Roamers?"

"I did. The Roamer got past it."

"Did you up the frequency?"

"Yes I did," replied Bermuda. "The field generator was ineffective."

"Excellent!" exclaimed Tau. "If the equipment can't keep it out, we might as well throw all caution to the wind!"

"The Psyche Intruder a child, Tau," explained Bermuda in a calming voice. "Otherwise it would have left the moment it saw our Knight's Raiment. Roaming in restricted zones carries heavy penalties. No one wants a visit from the Chronometer Department."

"This area isn't restricted," said Sebastian.

"Any where *we are* is restricted," said Tau coldly. Pausing, he moved over to the window and leant his elbows on the windowsill. Facing into the room, he studied the area under the stairs. "We can't let this spy leave," he continued gravely, glancing away from the corner and winking slyly to his friends.

"It's illegal to imprison spirits," warned Parsons. "You can't."

"It's just a Roamer," said Sebastian, in defence of the entity under the stairs, "in the wrong place at the wrong time."

"I can follow it to see who it is when it returns to its body. I can convince it not to report us," said Tau, his face serious.

The other three exchanged worried glances. Parsons frowned.

Tau stretched out his right arm and plucked a small device off the edge of Bermuda's desk. Leaning back and holding the apparatus pointed threateningly at the corner under the stairs, he spoke deliberately and coldly to the Psyche Intruder.

"In my hand I am holding a particle-gun, Roamer. It fires high-energy heavy electrons in a very pretty way. The electrons pass through a Magnetic Field Transmitter. They arc and spiral inwards before they make contact. Psychic energy is very sensitive to electrical disturbances. You might say that when it hits you, you will feel like you received a very nasty knock on the head."

Moving to his left, he handed the particle-gun to Bermuda.

"Set the stun on high, Bermuda," he ordered.

"Don't do it, Tau," said Bermuda. "The shock can be too great. Look. Tri doesn't want you to do it. He's really stressed."

Tri had begun to whine and paw nervously at the ground.

"Set it on high, I said!"

"Your call, Tau," agreed Bermuda grudgingly, pushing a switch on the device to maximum.

"Fire the gun into the corner the instant the crystals of my Roaming-Ring glow," directed Tau.

Terrified, Zeta huddled in the corner. "They are going to shoot me. How can I get away?" she thought desperately.

Parsons hastily moved back against the wall next to the Display cabinet alongside Sebastian. Tau sat down aggressively on the chintz sofa. Throwing the plump sofa cushions onto the floor, he glared angrily into the corner under the stairs.

"I won't tolerate spies!" he said in a raised menacing voice. Staring into Zeta's frightened eyes, he saw a mere empty space.

"Dominic!" she called. "Can't you see me? Why can't you hear me? It's me, Zeta!" The sound of her own voice rang in her ears, high-pitched and frightened. But the youths in the room with her heard nothing.

Tri scampered forward from his position beside the desk. Bounding onto the chintz sofa, he bit at Tau's sleeve with his small, sharp teeth.

"Tri is distressed," advised Parsons. "Think carefully, Tau, before you continue with your planned course of action."

"Perhaps Tri can hear me?" thought Zeta hopefully. "Dominic doesn't look so mean and angry now. Perhaps he takes heed of the animal's intuition?"

Tau paused to consider the situation. When he next spoke, his voice was cool and decisive. "You can stop trying to bite me, Tri. Go and have your dinner, you little scamp. I'm not predisposed to the cruelty you imagine."

Obeying, Tri jumped down and scampered along the wooden floor, through the connecting Dining room and into the kitchen.

In the kitchen, on a small plate, he found a meal of Lumpo, carefully fashioned into the shape of several small bones. Soon the tiny dog was busy crushing the food between his small, canine jaws.

Tau had watched the antics of the dog with interest. "I've changed my mind, Bermuda," he said. "Set the stun to the lowest charge. I just want this Roamer to wake up. I don't want to give him, or her, palpitations. Do I?"

Bermuda set the device on the lowest setting.

"I'll return when the job is done," said Tau. Settling back into the sofa, he closed his eyes. After the crystals in his Roaming-Ring glowed bright white, he was asleep.

The second he was asleep, Sebastian and Parsons both rushed to join Bermuda.

"Parsons, I don't feel right about this," said Bermuda.

"Quick," Parsons directed. "Give me the particle-gun and get into the corner with the Roamer. I will shoot *you* instead of the Roamer. We won't be disobeying orders. Tau did say *'Fire into the corner'*, did he not? He didn't say precisely *who* should be fired on? When I shoot, you will absorb the bulk of the charge. That way, the child Roamer won't get hurt. I'll fire at your say so."

"There could be anything in that corner!" warned Sebastian.

Bermuda ignored the warning. "I trust my instincts," he said firmly.

"Oh, thank goodness!" thought Zeta, much relieved. "They're not going to hurt me after all!"

Bermuda lurched forward. Crouching down in front of the corner under the stairs, he shielded Zeta with his arms. Sebastian and Parsons watched with respectful interest.

"Fire!" Bermuda shouted.

Zeta closed her eyes.

Parsons fired the gun. A red arc of electron particles spiralled forward.

Zeta felt herself drowning in a blinding anxiety. Seconds later she awoke with a start, in her bed, in her Queens Gate apartment. She felt the warm band of her Roaming-Ring around her head, slightly warmer in the places where the crystals were set. Sitting up, she glanced in her bedroom mirror and saw that the crystals were still glowing white. Then she startled again, for reflected in that mirror, staring at her, she saw the ghostly image of a Knight - Dominic!

She gasped. Her head felt fuzzy. She brushed her hands across her eyes, and like the cobwebs of a dream, the apparition of Dominic abruptly disappeared.

"Just my luck," Tau thought grumpily, standing invisible in Zeta's room. "Of all places Zeta could roam on her very first excursion, she chooses my hideout. I should have anticipated that she would test her Roaming-Ring straight away, and that she would go somewhere familiar, to a familiar person."

Pausing in thought, he looked about the room - at the single white bedstead covered with a rose coloured eiderdown, at To-do, asleep at the foot of the bed and at the Queen Anne style furnishings.

"I didn't predict that anyone from this era would be able to travel quite as far through time as Zeta did," Tau continued in thought. "It explains why she got past the field generator. The settings were wrong." Then he glanced at Zeta. "Zeta either thinks what she saw and heard was a strange dream or she has realized by now that she was roaming. That leaves me with a problem. If she tells any one what she has learnt she may jeopardize my plans. I'll have to speak with her. Now."

Unexpectedly there was a tap on Zeta's bedroom door.

"Zeta, it's Auntie Marjorie," called a voice from outside. "Isabelle is with me. Can we come in?"

Auntie Marjorie and Isabelle entered the bedroom, without waiting for a reply.

"Why are you both here? Auntie? Isabelle?" asked Zeta. "You're wearing your Lab coat, Auntie? Have you come straight from work?"

"Some terrible things have happened tonight," said Auntie Marjorie. "That's why I am here, Zeta. I was working late at the Research Facility when TT Vox Populi rang me. I flew down from Farnborough immediately to collect you. I'm taking you back home with me."

"What's happened?" asked Zeta.

"Isabelle and your father were attacked as they left the TT Corporation party," revealed Marjorie. "Isabelle was thrown to the ground and your father was bundled into a car and taken away. Moments later, the TT Showroom was bombed."

Zeta was incredulous, too shocked to speak.

"No one was hurt in the explosion," Marjorie elaborated. "Apparently, a fair-haired youth cleared the area of people, fifteen minutes before the blast. He managed to convince the people waiting in their flying-cars outside, that the sales plan had changed. He told the customers they would be each offered a free test flight of the Chronoguiser and therefore the venue had been moved to the airfield in Farnborough. The news of the destruction has not yet been broadcast, so right now there is still a flood of flying-cars travelling out to Farnborough, expecting to fly a Chronoguiser. A very convincing lad - he is probably one of the saboteurs."

"What happened to the Security men?" asked Zeta, summoning up the courage to speak. "They are normally stationed inside the building. Some of them are dad's friends."

"The Security men were outside of the building at the time of the explosion, Zeta," replied Isabelle. "Their guard dogs were chasing the fair-haired youth. Luckily, they only received minor scratches from flying debris when the bombs detonated."

"We mustn't talk about this anymore," advised Auntie Marjorie sternly, glancing at Isabelle's grazed knees. "We need to be proactive in a situation like this. Come on Zeta, pack your bags immediately. You are returning to Farnborough with me tonight. My flying-car is waiting outside."

"It's after one in the morning, Marjorie," said Isabelle.

"No sense in waiting," replied Marjorie. "You are coming to live with me now, Zeta." Marjorie paused. "Isabelle dear, you are part of this family," she added. "You're welcome to stay with us."

"Thank you," replied Isabelle softly.

Zeta, who was still sitting in her bed, leant forward and hugged her aunt. "I argued with dad and now I may never see him again," she said, tears welling in her eyes.

"You're being silly thinking that way," responded Marjorie. "Now gather your belongings, like a good girl."

Dressed in an ankle-length, pink nightgown, Zeta climbed from her bed. Quickly she moved about her bedroom, collecting what she needed. Neatly she arranged her possessions into two open suitcases that Marjorie took down from atop her dress closet.

"Damn!" thought Tau crossly, all the while listening. "I bothered to save all those people outside the TT Showroom and the aunt thinks I'm a saboteur. Plus, after my mistake with the particle-gun, Zeta must think I'm a monster. Now she's leaving before I've had a chance to speak to her."

Deliberately he moved outside of the bedroom, up the stairs and into the Sitting room. There he halted, still invisible, before one of the sash windows. Looking out into the street he observed Marjorie's transport - a vintage Morris Minor - modified with a pair of wings fitted to the chassis, and a tail fin mounted on the boot. How this particular flying-car managed to stay together, yet alone fly, was an enigma to many, including Tau. Leaning against the front passenger door of the car was Ret Bourne and inside, at the wheel, sat the younger brother, Eddie.

Finished looking outside, Tau glanced behind him at the cerise and pink balloons still floating where Zeta had left them. Cross - he stared at the two empty gift boxes and the torn packaging scattered on the white fibrous rug.

"It was only yesterday evening that I accompanied Zeta to the TT Showroom to collect her Roaming-Ring," he thought soberly. "She thought I was her friend then. Yesterday seems such a long time ago now. How many years precisely?"

Irritated, he kicked at the bright cerise and pink wrapping paper that had temptingly concealed Zeta's balloon-gifts. Roughly, he booted the two empty gift boxes, so that the whole heap of packaging flew into the air, tumbled behind the claret sofa and clattered softly into the empty fireplace. With that final gesture, his psychic energy field faded quickly from the room.

Downstairs, Zeta's packing was complete and the three females left the pretty bedroom. The two women each lugged a heavy suitcase and Zeta, wearing a dressing gown over her nightdress, hurried behind them holding To-do in her arms.

"Wait. Auntie, Isabelle!" she requested, pausing at the foot of the stairs.

Hurriedly she ran to the French doors that lead to the rear garden and looked out through the clear glass. "I knew it!" she cried, surveying a squished and broken mess. "Bermuda did throw Dad's Tea Party out of the back window. Now I have confirmed that what I experienced wasn't a dream. If my dad was here I'd tell him everything," she thought happily. But an instant later, she remembered the traumatic reality. "Dad's not here. He's been kidnapped, and I don't know who to tell."

Zeta climbed the stairs. Together with the two ladies, she left the apartment, moving out onto the street towards Marjorie's flying-car.

Hurrying forward the instant he saw their approach, Ret ushered the three females into the rear seat of the small, modified car. Zeta, who had not been in the car before, squeezed in between her aunt and Isabelle, feeling like a sad little sardine in a small, metal can. Perched on the edge of her seat, she found her knees jutting between the two front seats, awkwardly brushing against the car's gear stick.

Glancing behind him at this cute little image, Eddie smiled kindly. "Nice Roaming-Ring you're wearing, Zeta," he remarked. When she looked at him sadly, he continued carefully. "You haven't had the... *advantage* of travelling in one of these old modified cars before, have you?"

"No," she replied.

"Sorry if I bump you a bit when I shift gears," he continued. "The stick is connected to the wing flaps." Pushing his left arm through the gap between the bucket seats, he offered Zeta a boiled sweet from a small white paper bag. "To prevent air sickness," he explained. Then he pushed the bag towards Isabelle and Marjorie. Marjorie declined.

When Zeta and Isabelle both had a sweet in their mouths, he continued, "Air sickness is inevitable in a makeshift aircraft such as this, unless you're used to it - like your auntie, here."

When Ret had finished tying the two suitcases securely to the roof of Marjorie's flying-car, he took his place in the front passenger seat.

Tapping him on his shoulder, Marjorie handed him two sets of co-ordinates. "I'd like you to stop off at Isabelle's apartment on the way home, if you please?" she asked. "We need to collect her clothes and her cat. She's also staying with me."

"Very well, Ma'am," he replied, handing the slip of paper to Eddie. "There you are bro," he said, "You have no excuse to get us lost."

"Will you be staying at Farnborough after you take us to my house?" enquired Marjorie.

"Yes Ma'am," replied Ret. "TT Research Facility is our normal posting. We were only here for the Forum."

"Garrett, I'm not familiar with Farnborough," said Isabelle. "Where is the TT Research Facility exactly?"

"The TT Research Facility is smack bang in the middle of Farnborough, Miss Isabelle."

"I'm surprised Hugh didn't take you there to show off his inventions?" interrupted Marjorie.

"I asked him to, on several occasions. He said no."

"Buckle up, now ladies," directed Ret. "If the ride is too rough, just say so and we'll stop for a break at a Sky Café."

Eddie turned the ignition. The doors automatically locked and the small electric engine purred. While London slept, bathed in darkness, the vintage Morris Minor lifted forty metres off the ground, hovered, banked and headed towards Hampshire.

Chapter five

Zeta woke to the cool, sweet fragrance of pine trees, morning roses and fallen blossom. The birds were chirping loudly. The light was filtering through the darkness. It was 5am and she was in Farnborough. She let her eyes wander over her cosy bedroom, with its cream stencilled walls, pine bed and panelled pine door. Then she looked at the empty inbuilt closet, her two unpacked cases and at To-do, curled up on a rug on the shiny, wooden floor. She heard her aunt moving about quietly in the room next to hers, and she listened to the soft calming tones of Isabelle whispering on the landing.

"Marjorie. Let Zeta sleep. We have a busy morning ahead of us. We have so many telephone calls to make and to take - discussions with the police, financial matters to consider. Better that we cope with all the stress and change ourselves. There is no need to involve Zeta in all the enquiries."

"Yes," replied Marjorie, whispering also. "I'll let her sleep. We'll know the worst and the best by the time she awakes."

"They want me to sleep, that's fine with me," thought Zeta. Turning over onto her side to face the window, she closed her eyes. Then she let herself drift away. "Everything is warm," she said to herself, " - the pillow, the soft cream sheets, the blanket tucked around my feet, Isabelle's voice, Auntie Marjorie's eyes, To-do's gentle breathing, everything…"

When Zeta next opened her eyes it was 10am and the sun was already streaming in through the pencil slits in her bedroom curtains. Jumping out of bed she pulled back the drapes, threw open the window and looked out curiously. "There it is," she thought exuberantly, "The forest!"

Situated on a hilly street and neighbouring several other houses of identical design, Auntie Marjorie's house stood bright and cheerful in the early summer sunshine. Zeta's bedroom overlooked the entrance porch, a path bordered by pink carnations, a quiet lane and Farnborough Common - with its massive Oaks and sunny Heathland.

The breeze was warm and Zeta, pleased to be neither dreaming nor roaming, pushed her window open the farthest it would go. A rush of fragrant air filled her room. The breeze woke To-do. Happy and curious, he scampered from corner to corner, sniffed the bed legs and climbed into the empty, open wardrobe.

Throwing her dressing gown over her nightdress - with To-do scampering after her - Zeta ran through the upstairs landing. Walking quickly down the stairs, she entered the cosy Sitting room with its chintz sofa, pine desk and ornament filled Display cabinet. Finding that room empty, she continued through to the Dining room where she found Auntie Marjorie and Isabelle, seated at a rectangular pine dining table.

Marjorie, dressed in a white fluffy sweater, wine trousers and wine shoes, brushed her curly brown hair away from her face and put on her spectacles when she saw Zeta approach. Isabelle, sitting at the right of the table, wearing a blue frock, turned her head and nodded in greeting. Curled on Isabelle's lap, was Leila, Isabelle's fat ginger cat.

"What's happening?" asked Zeta, pulling a chair from the table and sitting down opposite to her aunt. "Any news about dad? Have they found him?"

"There is no news about your father, Zeta," replied Auntie Marjorie soberly. "So far the kidnappers have not made contact and there has been no ransom demand. The police are proceeding with their enquiries, but I very much doubt they are even looking for your father."

"Why wouldn't they be?" asked Zeta, perplexed.

Auntie Marjorie did not immediately reply. Instead, she looked at Isabelle sympathetically. "There is a problem with the kidnapping investigation, Zeta," she continued after a brief interval. "Everyone is blaming your father for the destruction of the Chronoguisers. They are saying that he is one of the saboteurs, because he disappeared just before the Showroom explosion."

"But Auntie! Dad was kidnapped! Isabelle -"

"The police don't trust me, Zeta," Isabelle cut in quietly.

"Are their other witnesses?" asked Zeta, incredulous.

"Yes, but they don't believe them either," replied Isabelle.

Auntie Marjorie took off her spectacles. She placed them on the table, wiped her eyes with her right hand and replaced them again on the bridge of her nose. "I don't know what I'll do if I lose my job because of this," she said anxiously.

"Auntie, I can work."

"Well, that's certainly a good thing, Zeta. But you will also have to learn to economize. From now on, I suggest you exercise more discretion when you shop. Plus I'd prefer it if you didn't wear makeup or jewellery."

"What about my earrings and my timeband -?"

"And the charm bracelet I gave her," cut in Isabelle.

"OK, those few items, but nothing more."

"Fine," replied Zeta softly. "Can I continue to wear my hair slides?"

"Zeta, your hair may create a problem," said Auntie Marjorie.

"My hair is a problem?"

"Yes, a plumbing problem - with the drains. Long hair falls out and blocks up bathroom drains."

"My hair doesn't fall out!" exclaimed Zeta.

"Marjorie? You're not serious?" interjected Isabelle.

"I am serious," replied Auntie Marjorie, in an annoyed tone of voice. "I don't want the expense of a plumber because of excessive vanity. So I insist you cut your hair to a reasonable length, Zeta. And I want you to cut it now!"

"I can wash my hair outside in the garden - in a bucket - if drains are a problem."

"No, you can't do that," responded Auntie Marjorie. "Goodness gracious, what would the neighbours think? They'd imagine we didn't have any sanitation. No, I insist your hair be cut. I have a pair of scissors in my kitchen. I'll get them now."

"No way, Auntie. I refuse."

Auntie Marjorie glared at Zeta through her spectacles. "If you take this attitude with me, Zeta, I won't be responsible for you," she threatened.

Zeta and Isabelle sat in their chairs with their eyes staring wide.

"Marjorie?" Perhaps we can discuss this another time," suggested Isabelle, nudging Leila off her lap onto the floor.

To-do, who had been sitting under the dining table, immediately jumped onto Zeta's lap. The ginger cat, purring and arching her back, walked in rings around Auntie Marjorie's feet.

Marjorie bent forward and stroked the cat affectionately. "Would you like a saucer of milk, precious?" she asked the cat.

Leila continued to purr.

"Yes you do, yes you do," crooned Marjorie. She pushed back her chair, picked up Leila and cuddled the cat in her arms. Holding Leila, she stood up and walked into the kitchen.

"I can't find the scissors so we'll leave the hair cutting business until I return from work tonight." she called out. "And don't think I approve of your ruby hair, Isabelle. The neighbours certainly won't!"

"Shall we go upstairs, Zeta?" Isabelle suggested. "To give your Aunt an easy exit."

When Zeta regarded her quizzically, Isabelle leant closer and whispered very quietly, "She's never acted like this before, has she?"

Zeta mouthed the word silently, "No."

"Well, I expect she's in the kitchen, afraid to come out, embarrassed for coming up with that daft proposal of cutting off your hair."

"Do you really think so?" whispered Zeta.

"Most certainly."

Once again, Auntie Marjorie called out from the kitchen, but this time much more cheerfully. "I'll be leaving for work now! The airways should be clear of the congestion caused by that persuasive boy. Imagine. All those people believing they were going to test fly a Chronoguiser. Well, there's only one of those infernal machines left now - the Dandy Lion - and it's under lock and key, I doubt whether it will ever get an airing again. Not with the way people feel about time travel. Such intense emotions. I would never have thought! Of course, that's why they are behaving so unreasonably with us now." A cupboard door inside the kitchen opened and closed. "I will leave the spare house keys on the dining table, in case either of you wish to go out. Sorry about before, I realize I was a bit harsh."

"It's alright," said Isabelle in a loud voice, so Marjorie could hear.

Zeta looked towards the open kitchen door and dropped To-do off her lap. Pushing back her chair, she stood up.

"Auntie, I'm going upstairs to dress," she said, over the noise of clanking plates. "Have a good day at work. See you tonight. Bye."

Isabelle also stood up. "Bye, Marjorie!" she called.

Both Isabelle and Zeta left the Dining room, moved through the Sitting room, and proceeded to climb the stairs.

"Lets have brunch after your aunt leaves," suggested Isabelle. "After our meal we can explore the Common. Then we can take a tour of the TT Research Facility. You might even see your friend,

Dominic. It's his first day working at the TT Research Facility, isn't it?"

"Dominic?" replied Zeta, frowning slightly. "Yes. It is his first day. A walk through the Common and a tour sounds like a good idea. Better than hanging around here, fretting about dad."

Peeping out from the kitchen, Marjorie heard her niece and Isabelle moving about upstairs and chatting. "Someone has to be tough around here," she said to Leila. "And it certainly won't be those two softies!"

Throwing her Lab coat over her fluffy sweater, she grabbed her car keys and a set of spare house keys from a hook on the side of the wall. She dropped the spare house keys onto the dining table. Checking that the coast was clear, she then dashed for the front door, flung it open and ran down the flowered path. Jumping happily into the familiar seat of her old Morris - parked outside - she coasted that flying-car down the lane until she was airborne. Soaring over the treetops, she headed towards the TT Research Facility.

Leila was curled up asleep on the sofa. The midday sun was high overhead. Wearing a black strappy vest patterned with pink daisies and a low-slung pink pleated skirt - plus boots - Zeta was ready to leave Marjorie's House. Standing beside her, Isabelle placed To-do in the rucksack on Zeta's back. There he peered out curiously. Included in one of the pockets of that rucksack was Dominic's hand-painted miniature.

Stepping outside and locking the front door behind them, Isabelle and Zeta crossed the lane and entered into Farnborough Common. Shaded by Oak trees they walked briskly forward in silence, over the gently undulating paths and bridleways that wound through the forest. As they followed the path to the Research Facility, clumps of high ferns tickled their arms, purple foxgloves swayed over, waving their advance, while dried brown leaves, broken twigs and crumbling acorns were crushed underfoot.

Emerging from the shadowy forest several minutes later, blinking in the bright sunlight, they stepped out onto sunny Heathland. A dense carpet of purple heather stretched out before them, interspersed with small conifers and hardy, pink wildflowers. Drifting slowly overhead, the pale blue sky, wispy with occasional cloud, was empty and undisturbed.

Suddenly, after hearing a loud roar and shielding her eyes from the sun, Zeta looked up at an aircraft flying in the sky overhead. "Look, Isabelle!" she exclaimed. "That's Mr. Vox Populi's antique white helicopter! I've seen it before - when dad took me for a visit to the Research Facility." She paused and smiled at Isabelle. "I don't think Auntie Marjorie will lose her job, as she fears she will - not when she shares TT's passion for noisy antiques."

Isabelle laughed. "Your aunt definitely has an obsession for vintage machines, else she wouldn't keep that old flying-car. Just between you and I, the trip out here was an absolute nightmare. I saw my life flash before my eyes. I really did."

"Me too," agreed Zeta.

Warmed by the sunlight and enjoying the freshness of the Heath, the ladies continued walking for some time, enjoying the atmosphere of the Common, until - tired and thirsty - they halted at the TT Research Facility entrance gate.

"I've changed my mind," said Isabelle. "Let's give the TT Research Facility a miss."

"No way did I walk over five kilometres through the countryside, to turn back now," said Zeta. Surely a monstrous russet robot - with no outer casing, long serrated claws for arms, and eyes that move dreadfully in and out of their sockets isn't going to dissuade you?" she teased. Then she glanced at the horrible robot marching back and forth across the entrance and pretended to shudder.

"Very funny. Let's go home," said Isabelle.

"No, there's Eddie," said Zeta, spotting him standing to the right of the gate, outside of a Sentry Box. Sitting beside Eddie, she also saw two large white dogs, flecked with black.

Eddie smiled amiably as soon as he saw them. Dodging the robot, they hastened their approach.

"Hello? What are the Setters for?" Zeta asked, gesturing admiringly towards the silky haired dogs.

"They're Tracker dogs," replied Eddie. "They impress the tourists."

Zeta smiled, but Isabelle, looking anxiously towards the robot, frowned.

"Don't worry about the robot, Isabelle," said Eddie. "I'll deactivate him, seeing as he frightens you." Taking a slim remote-control from his shirt pocket, he typed in his Security clearance code, the Robot's registration number and the deactivation sequence. A second later, the animated machine was completely still.

"Thank you," said Isabelle. "You're very kind. Not all robots worry me, but I find that particular type plays havoc on my nerves."

"These ones are particularly daunting," sympathized Eddie. "Unfortunately security has been stepped up because of the sabotage at the Showroom, so you'll encounter more of these brutes inside."

He paused and smiled at Zeta. "Well, I didn't anticipate I'd see you two ladies so soon. Are you expected?"

"Yes," answered Isabelle. "We're here to join a Tour Party."

Eddie detached a Radio Transmitter-Receiver from his belt. Holding it close to his mouth, he pressed the transmit button with his forefinger and spoke.

"Hello, Reception. This is the North-East Gate. I have two ladies here - Zeta Doherty and Isabelle - to join a Tour Party." He waited a moment. "Fine, you can go through," he said, looking sternly at Zeta. "But you will have to put the pet you are carrying on a leash."

To-do's golden head poked cheerfully out from the top of Zeta's rucksack. He had become overexcited during the walk through the Common and now he was anxious to run about and play.

"Oops, I didn't bring a lead with me," said Zeta.

"I see he has a collar," said Eddie. "He's only small. A length of string would suffice as a restraint."

Isabelle looked at Zeta's hair, worn up as usual, pinned with several pink slides and decorated with two long lengths of pink ribbon.

"Use you hair ribbons, Zeta," Isabelle suggested.

Grinning, Zeta unpinned the ribbons. Tying them together, she carefully fastened one end around To-do's collar. Making a loop in the free end, she lifted To-do out of her rucksack. Then she placed him gently on the ground. Jumping happily about, he immediately ran forward, stretching the ribbon taut.

"There you are," said Isabelle. "The advantages of having long hair. We can go in now. Thank you, Eddie."

He nodded. "Happy to oblige," he said, wincing at the pink leash and reactivating the robot as soon as they had passed inside.

Once through the gate, the ladies immediately noticed many more russet robots patrolling the perimeter of the large grounds. Isabelle shuddered and Zeta kept a firm grip on To-do's ribbon-leash.

Turning their small, infrared, telescopic eyes inquisitively towards the two newcomers, the ominous robots moved along quickly. Their eyes constantly moved in and out of their sockets and their heads turned slowly up and down, from side to side, and back to front.

Stepping onto a freshly tarred, wide linked road that was busy with traffic, small construction machines and people, Isabelle and Zeta headed for the Reception building. Scientists in white coats, engineers in navy overalls, plant workers in grey jackets and administrative staff in pinstriped suits hurried along with them. Beside them, in the centre of the road, automated trolleys laden with machine parts and electronic components moved slowly along, followed by small automatic Assembly robots and even smaller industrial maintenance and cleaning machines. On the far side of the road, on the left, neat low buggies, seating two, raced by.

Congested by numerous aircraft - undergoing even more numerous tests - the air overhead was just as busy. Looking up they saw strange machines that flew in circles over the Research Facility. Hovering and banking, swooping and diving, many of those vessels suddenly disappeared, to reappear seconds later in different locations.

Nearing the square, multi-storey Reception building with its huge steel pylons and vast expanses of glass, Isabelle and Zeta observed TT's white helicopter landed to the left of the entrance. Beyond this, they saw TT, seated on a large, leather sofa in his sumptuous office, alongside Faith Firebell.

At the same instant, TT saw them. Putting the glass of wine he was holding onto the coffee table in front of him, he spoke quickly to Faith. Then he hurried outside the building towards Isabelle and Zeta.

"Ladies!" he called as they approached him. "So good to have you here! Please, come in."

With that greeting, he ushered them towards the entrance. Entering the building through the massive glass doors, they stepped into a large cool lobby, with a white marbled floor, cream walls and concealed lighting. Modernist paintings adorned the walls and several tall thin brass sculptures stood before the winding stairway. Five large elevators were against the right wall of the entrance area, and beyond that, there was another large room full of scientists at work - one of whom was Zeta's Auntie Marjorie.

"We are obliged to you TT, for allowing two of your Security team to fly us to Marjorie's last night," said Isabelle, quickly and courteously.

"It won't do to have the families of my employees put in any danger," replied TT, sweeping them into his office. "I am sorry, ladies, for the trauma you have had to endure. Rest assured, I am overtly pursuing every possible course of action in an endeavour to find Hugh. Now, please be seated beside Faith." Pausing, he stepped away from them towards an inbuilt Bar. "Would you like a glass of wine Isabelle? Zeta, we have several varieties of sweet non-alcoholic drinks?"

"Yes, we are both very thirsty. Two lemonades would be nice," replied Isabelle, on behalf of them both.

"And you, Faith? I notice that your glass is empty? Would you like another tipple?"

"Yes thanks," she replied, bowing her head in greeting to the newcomers. "Good afternoon, Isabelle, Zeta. I'm sorry about Professor Doherty."

While the ladies sat comfortably on either side of Faith, TT stepped over to a nearby Inbuilt Bar and poured their refreshments.

"Could I have some water for my pet?" asked Zeta, noting To-do tugging impatiently on his ribbon-leash.

TT poured some water into a clean, empty ashtray and placed it in front of To-do, who lapped at it greedily. Returning to the Bar, he put three prepared drinks onto a serving tray. Carrying that tray over, he handing each of the ladies their drinks. Pulling up a nearby armchair, he sat opposite.

"Faith is here because she is preparing a special report for her News programme," he explained to Isabelle and Zeta. "The report will describe the work of TT Corporation and what my Company hopes to achieve for the future. At the end of her broadcast, Faith is going to make a plea to the public for any information that may help us find your father, Zeta."

"We haven't received a ransom demand yet. What happens when we do?" asked Isabelle.

"If a ransom demand is forthcoming, TT Corporation will pay it, Isabelle. We spare no expense when it comes to the lives of our scientists, or for that matter, any of our Staff!"

"The gesture is much appreciated," said Isabelle.

"You're very generous," Zeta added.

"Now, ladies, as your tour of this Facility begins in fifteen minutes, I'll go and organize someone you know to take you around. Garrett is a good chap. Meanwhile, Faith would like to ask you both a few questions for her report. I'll leave you with her, for the time being."

He smiled graciously, stood up and strode from his office.

"Do you realize Zeta, that the sales of the Roaming-Ring have trebled overnight," Faith said enthusiastically, the moment that TT had left his office.

"Oh, why is that?" asked Zeta, surprised at the Reporter's genuinely bubbly nature.

"As soon as people began to use their Roaming-Rings there were several reports of time-slips."

"Time-slips?" asked Isabelle.

"Yes, time-slips," Faith elaborated. "Some people believe the Roaming-Ring brought them to the future, others report slipping through time to the past. The past time-slips have been verified to be true. We have yet to confirm the veracity of the future time-slips."

"Is that going to be in your News programme too?" asked Zeta.

"Yes it is, Zeta. You are going to be a very rich, young lady. TT has told me that your father named you as the inventor when he registered the patent for the Roaming-Ring. That means, when you come of age, you will receive a substantial income. That is, if the Roaming-Ring turns out to a bonafide time-machine for the psyche; *which I'm sure it will!*"

Suddenly Zeta saw Dominic gesturing to her from the doorway of TT's office. "Please excuse me, Faith," she said. Standing up and tugging To-do alongside, she walked towards Dominic.

"Isabelle," Faith asked, her attentions quickly diverted. "What was it like being face to face with kidnappers? Can you describe them? What did they do? What was Professor Doherty's reaction?"

While Faith interviewed Isabelle, Zeta approached Dominic. Noting that he wore the TT Security garb of a blue open-neck short-sleeved shirt, blue trousers and black brogues, she remembered how he had looked the night before, dressed in chainmail. Pinned to the top of his shirt pocket she also noticed a Security tag that bore his name and number, plus a Magnetic entrance key.

When she reached the doorway, Dominic's behaviour was puzzling. Pulling her quickly into the foyer, he marched her behind one of the sculptures. Standing in front of her, he whispered sharply.

"You haven't said anything to TT or Faith about me, have you?"

"What's there to tell?" she answered. "And by the way, thanks for your polite concern about my dad."

"Whisper," he ordered, "The place is full of listening devices."

"Oh, I didn't -"

"Well, have you?" he cut in, growling moodily.

"No. But I should tell someone about the real you. You and your friends are quite the practical jokers, winding me up with your tall tales. I suppose you planned the whole thing last night, right down to the fake picture outside the window and the phoney dog."

Dominic immediately relaxed and trying to be friendly, he bent down and patted To-do. After licking his hand, the little dog ran around his feet in small circles. Dominic straightened up, smiled at Zeta and touched her forearm.

"Sorry about your dad, Zeta. Rotten luck."

Zeta looked away, towards the Laboratory where she saw her aunt working.

"It's a nice day, Zeta," Dominic continued. "I finish work soon. Do you want to go on that zeppelin ride I won? It leaves this airfield at 3pm and returns at 7pm. I want to talk to you. Plus it will cheer you up."

"No, I'm going on a tour of this Facility."

"That only takes an hour. How about joining me afterwards?"

"Sorry, I don't think my aunt would approve."

"How do you know? Have you asked her?"

Zeta shook her head.

"Well, go and ask her now?" Dominic prompted. "It's a good idea. It will help to take your mind off your concerns."

Zeta ignored him and shuffled her feet.

"Why won't you spend the rest of the day with me?" he asked softly. "What's the matter?"

When she refused to answer, Dominic stood silently for a moment. Then his keen eyes caught sight of a tiny, black mushroom at the base of the sculpture. Picking it up, he casually dropped it onto the ground and crushed it into tiny fragments under the heel of his shoe. Crouching down, he replaced it carefully with a blue mushroom of identical size, which he took from behind his Security tag.

Zeta watched him curiously. "I take it we don't have to whisper anymore. Since you've replaced the device with one of your own."

"That's right, we don't have to whisper."

"Well, it doesn't matter anyway, because I have nothing to say to you."

"You're angry with me, Zeta," he said apologetically. "I'm sorry. I've made two mistakes that hurt you. Firstly, I shouldn't have been so insensitive with you just now. As for last night, I sincerely apologize for my behaviour. I honestly didn't know that you were the Psyche Intruder. Where I come from, only spies roam in an invisible state. Standard Roaming-Rings are preset so that everyone is forced to project their true image when they roam, so they appear translucent, like ghosts. It's the law. Besides, roaming invisible is considered the height of rudeness."

"Well, thank you very much for your apology," said Zeta sarcastically. "I'm afraid we can't be friends anymore - now that I know that you play rotten practical jokes on people."

"Do you have your Roaming-Ring with you?" asked Dominic quietly. "Because if you do, I can give it an upgrade."

"Yes, it's in my bag. It's too expensive to leave in Auntie's house." After she spoke, Zeta sulkily looked at the floor.

"Well, give it to me, Zeta?" he prompted. "I can adjust it so you can project and speak audibly when you roam."

"Sure you can."

"All I will be doing is putting an extra electronic chip behind each stone in your Roaming-Ring."

She looked unconvinced.

"Let me explain?" he asked.

"OK explain."

"When a human being wills him or her self to roam, the host's brain produces a tiny electrical spasm or signal. The upgraded Roaming-Ring will detect this signal and translate it into an image of the host. In this case, that will be you. The thoughts that you wish to broadcast will also be translated into audible sound and will be transmitted along with your image. The modification won't harm you, I promise. The end result of the upgrade is that we will all be able to see you as a spectre and hear you, when you want to roam to us."

"Do you think I want to go anywhere near you or your friends again? What you said last night wasn't funny."

"Look Zeta, that house where you roamed to last night is ancient. It is part of a small Historic Reserve, built not far from where you fell asleep. It was originally your aunt's country house in Farnborough but was relocated brick by brick to London when the Reserve was established. My friends and I have commandeered the house - for a while."

"So, you expect me to believe you are a Roamer from the future. That is credible, considering the possibility of time-slips - except for one obvious anomaly. Your ghostly projected image happens to be rather solid and opaque."

"Come on, give me your Roaming-Ring," he asked again.

Zeta dropped her rucksack from her shoulders, removed her Roaming-Ring and handed it to him resentfully. To-do immediately jumped into the open rucksack, curled up and went to sleep.

"You could have always left my place of your own free will, Zeta. You chose to hang around, even though you were asked to leave."

Popping the nine crystals from their settings, Dominic delved into a pocket behind his Security tag. After adding a chip to a circuit in the cavity left by each stone, he replaced the crystals. Then he glanced thoughtfully at Zeta's embarrassed face.

"I was stuck there, if you want to know," she retorted. "I didn't know how to leave."

"If you're roaming and you want to wake up, all you do is wish you were home," he explained. "It helps if there are people at your dwelling who you bond with."

"Gee… thanks," said Zeta sarcastically. "I'll remember that next time someone tries to shoot me while I'm roaming."

"Look, I said I was sorry. Bermuda admitted that he took most of the charge from the particle-gun. He had flashes of light in his eyes for quite a while afterwards."

Zeta still looked sorrowful.

"I wasn't winding you up last night."

"I know you're not a thief, Dominic. You must have been larking around. Otherwise you wouldn't have said all the things you did."

"Come on the zeppelin ride with me after work and I will explain everything. We can speak freely then. OK?"

Zeta looked doubtful, glanced at him, then looked away

"OK?" he repeated.

"Dominic. I'm really worried about my dad. Will you help me? No one is doing anything to find him."

"Everything will be alright. Meet me outside the foyer after your tour. Ask your aunt right now if you can go."

"Dominic, is that a yes?" she called after him, watching him walk away. He turned towards her and nodded his head in affirmation. Then he hurried down a corridor towards the rear of the building.

Chapter six

The sundial outside the Reception building read 2.55pm. The tour was over and Zeta was outside the foyer - standing in front of TT's helicopter - waiting for Dominic.

Underfoot, the ground was baked dry. Scorched and thirsty, the grass on the airfield was yellow. Sticky under a barrage of relentless summer rays, the freshly tarred road, no longer busy with traffic, was hazy, long and indistinct. Under a hot sun that danced wildly off every reflective surface - sparkling, glinting and blinding - Zeta watched Dominic arrive, smiling, still wearing his Security uniform.

"Are those clothes your pyjamas?" Zeta teased. "Are they going to disintegrate from age any second now? How old are your pyjamas? One hundred years, one thousand years, ten thousand years old?"

"First question, answer yes," replied Dominic. "Second question - answer no. Anyhow, I wouldn't care if the clothes did disintegrate. You would be the one to be shocked, not I."

Zeta felt her face flush.

"You only serve to embarrass yourself, trying to unsettle me," remarked Dominic clinically.

"Sorry," apologized Zeta. "But Dominic, you didn't answer my third question. If you are from the future, I want to know when."

"I'll said I'd explain everything once we were onboard the zeppelin. Now come on! I can hear the airship priming its engines from here. Which means we have approximately three minutes before they take off without us!"

Walking briskly, the teenage pair hurried for the orange zeppelin, anchored at the farthest end of the TT Airfield. Several planes looped and dived overhead. A large oddly shaped Assembly robot crossed their path. A group of Security men, also headed in their direction, smiled and nodded.

"Are you and your aunt very close?" Dominic asked. "Will she miss you if you are gone longer than expected?"

"Auntie won't complain as long as I'm home before she is," replied Zeta. "She's taking tea with TT, Faith and Isabelle at TT's mansion in Farnborough. After their supper, TT has another antiquated car to amaze her with - a Ford, built in 1906."

"What sort of radiator grille does it have? Do you know?" asked Dominic. "It isn't a T-Model is it?"

"Not another vintage car enthusiast!"

"No, I'm not, but it was fun to see the expression on your face when you thought I was."

"The question I asked you before, Dominic, about my dad?"

"I'll help you find him, Zeta, but on one condition, I expect you to return the favour."

"What do you want me to do?"

"You already know that answer. Come now, Zeta. Don't look so disappointed. You wouldn't think too badly of a friend who borrowed their dad's car for a bit and then returned it, would you?"

"No I wouldn't. But TT's not your dad."

Reaching the zeppelin, they postponed their discussion and boarded the vessel, taking their seats between the cockpit in the front and the refreshment zone to the rear.

Facing a large floor to ceiling window that stretched along the entire length of the airship, Zeta took To-do, now awake, out of her rucksack. She fastened his makeshift leash to her chair and placed him on the floor at her feet. Then she stared out of the window.

"Enjoying the view so soon?" asked Dominic from his place next to her on the aisle.

"No, I'm watching TT walking this way," replied Zeta. "He's not your most favourite person I gather."

TT did not stop at the zeppelin. He proceeded past the airship to the end of the airfield. There he entered a Hanger heavily guarded by several robots and two Security men.

"That's where they are keeping the Dandy Lion," remarked Dominic, while the zeppelin rose steadily upward until it was floating high in the air.

"You're going to get us into trouble, aren't you Dominic?" Zeta said resignedly.

He smiled at her kindly, but did not reply.

Their vessel airborne and racing away from Farnborough, they now heard the voice of their hostess for the day. Wearing a miniature microphone attached to the lapel of her jacket, her bubbly tones transmitted through a speaker, inset into the armrest of each passenger chair.

"Good afternoon everyone," she called, "We are presently flying over the fabulous South East of England! Our first port of call will be Winchester Cathedral, built in the 11th century, in what was once the Capital of England. Keep your cameras handy; for you will all soon have the chance of seeing, in the Great Hall, the Arthurian Round Table.

Continuing our journey, we will fly over New Forest, a tranquil expanse of ancient woodland and leafy glens. Our Captain will then reduce speed and altitude so that you may film the wild deer and the hundreds of free ranging ponies that trot through the heather or graze with their foals.

The Historic Dockyard in Portsmouth is our second port of call. Once there, you will be all be given the opportunity to board the tall ships, hoist the sails, and for the more adventurous of you, climb the rigging!

Leaving Portsmouth, we will fly over a short stretch of sea to Freshwater Bay, on the coast of the charming Isle of Wight. The island is home to over one thousand species of flora. You will have ample time to swim in the ocean or enjoy a leisurely stroll atop the grassy sheer cliffs.

We will depart from the Bay at exactly 6pm, pass directly over the Hampshire Downs, and as a last treat before we say goodbye, we will visit the Military Museum in Aldershot." She paused and smiled at the relaxed passengers. "In this temperate corner of England, the scenery is fabulous. Directly below us we can all admire the natural beauty of-"

Dominic switched off the speaker on his and Zeta's armrest. "I don't need her to tell me how beautiful it is," he said aggressively. Turning to face Zeta, he continued passionately. "Can you understand Zeta, when you look at the glorious Earth around you, why I want to *stay*." He looked out of the zeppelin window at the scenic splendour of hills and valleys, shielded by cotton wool clouds and the bluest of skies. "A thousand people feel as I do, but they are too afraid to speak out. TT Vox Populi and his Intelligence Officers believe they have them cornered."

"But Dominic, if one thousand are afraid, why aren't you?"

"What's TT going to do to me, Zeta? Lock me in prison for a few months with a field generated so my psyche can't get out? Will he lecture me incessantly on the wisdom of colonizing new worlds? Or will he offer to be my political tutor? Perhaps he will force me to take tea with the relatives - and conform?"

"The relatives?" asked Zeta.

Dominic sniffed. "My mother was Deneisha Vox Populi, TT's granddaughter."

"TT's your great grandfather!" exclaimed Zeta in a whispered voice.

"Yes, I am so honoured," said Dominic dryly, staring out in wonder at the rustic terrain over which their airship soared.

"How old is he? I want to know! Did you all come here in a Chronoguiser? Dominic?"

"TT is one hundred and twenty years old, Zeta. He came here in the Dandy Lion with one of his Intelligence Officers. At home, my home, he gave some contrived story to the media to explain his absence."

"How did you get here, Dominic?" asked Zeta, now oblivious to the spectacular sight of the beautiful Hampshire Downs, flowing past underneath their speeding vessel.

"I have the gift of projecting a solid, spiritual image through time and space. Your guess was reasonably accurate when you said I was roaming. What I do is similar, but it is called mirroring."

"So the sandy haired Dominic, the real flesh and blood you, is asleep in that house in the distant future, and I'm talking to a ghost?"

"You are talking to my spirit," replied Dominic, still gazing out of the window dreamily, obviously in awe of the striking pastoral beauty of the surrounding district.

Zeta sat quietly, joining him in his high altitude observations of the farms, forests and undulating green landscape.

"Dominic? Why didn't TT recognize you, if you're his great grandson, as you say you are?" she asked, a little while later.

"He didn't identify me for lots of reasons, Zeta," Dominic replied. "I wasn't wearing my Knight's Raiment. We haven't been in contact for two years. And as you're already aware, I'm much paler when I mirror."

"From what you've said, TT has never seen you when you are... mirroring?"

"That's right, we don't communicate. We don't see eye to eye. His father, Wiggy, has the gift of mirroring, but he hasn't."

"Dominic? You and your friend's are Psychic Knights. What does that mean exactly?"

"It means that each of us has a finely tuned psychic ability. Mine is mirroring. Parsons has a soporific gift. Sebastian is an Illusionist. Bermuda is a magician. Being a Psychic Knight also means that we are honourable. We maintain a strict spiritual discipline. We are schooled in the arts of self-defence but we are not soldiers. We are disciples of peace." Pausing and staring into her face, Dominic asked her seriously, "Am I telling the truth, Zeta?"

Zeta glanced out at the picturesque terrain far below, remembered his recent passionate reaction to the glorious rural vista and nodded.

"What now?" she asked quietly.

"Have you got a pen and paper in that hold-all of yours?"

"Yes, why?"

"Just give it here?" he asked, holding out his hand insistently.

Zeta pulled her rucksack out from the under-seat compartment, rummaged in one of the pockets, grabbed pen and paper and handed them over.

"Are you wearing your bathing costume?" Dominic asked. "You do enjoy the public exhibition of sun baking."

"Why, do you want the costume too?"

"What I want is for you to go for a swim when we get to the Isle of Wight," he replied. He scribbled some figures on the paper and handed it back to her. "If you haven't a scarf, buy one. Use it to conceal your Roaming-Ring on our return journey. At 6.05pm precisely you are going to roam to your dad, for thirty seconds."

"You're going to follow me?"

"When I upgraded your Roaming-Ring, I put a link between it and mine - a guardian device. It enables me to roam to your location effortlessly. When I follow you, I should be gone for no more than fifteen minutes. Just say I'm in the men's room with a queasy stomach if anyone asks for my whereabouts."

Zeta took a deep breath and looked out of the window. Their zeppelin was losing altitude and the attractive stone cottages of Winchester were coming into view. She looked down at the paper in her hand. "Dominic, what are these notations you have written?"

"They are co-ordinates. You will need them once we have returned to the TT Research Facility. Then it will be your turn to help me. Now come on, we've landed. There's much to see for the time being and soon we'll be at the island!"

Enjoyably spent, the following sixty minutes elapsed quickly. Zeta admired the Cathedral, gazed from her seat on the zeppelin at the New Forest ponies and watched her friend deftly climb the rigging of a tall ship at Portsmouth.

Some time later - when the heat of the afternoon had waned and the light overhead had softened - Zeta sat on a sand and shingle beach with Dominic. Dramatic chalky white cliffs towered behind her. The sea before her was warm. The afternoon was sultry, and small yachts filled Freshwater Bay with triangular white sails.

Zeta, wearing her black two-piece swimsuit, was soaking up the sun. Stretching her legs and pushing her bare toes into the sand, she briefly watched To-do racing happily along the waters edge nearby.

Whilst focusing on the waves breaking gently on the beach and the unique sound of the rolling sea, she smelt the fresh ocean air. Watching a flock of seagulls flying overhead, she listened to their hungry raucous cries. Then she tried to imagine Dominic's world - devoid of plants, and scarce of food and air.

Noting the colours of her surroundings, she admired the blue sea with its frothy white waves, the sand strewn with smooth, tan pebbles and the beautiful seashells, shimmering inside with mother of pearl. Then she glanced behind her at the cliffs on which a rainbow of wildflowers flourished.

Turning towards the youth sitting beside her, she nudged him gently. "About the co-ordinates, Dominic?"

"They are for Satellite25, Zeta."

"And Satellite25 is?"

"The twenty fifth version of the Robotic Theme Park Satellite - the place where you are going to fly the Dandy Lion at 7.15 tonight."

"*You're hopeful.* Sure. I am going to stroll right into the Hanger, past the Security men and the horde of vicious robots and fly away with the only time-machine left in existence! How, pray tell, am I going to achieve that little miracle?"

"I have a plan," said Dominic, grinning. "I'm coming with you, of course. Everything is already sorted."

Zeta looked at him with wide-open eyes. Ready to take her swim, she stood up. Quickly unfastening her charm bracelet and timeband, she threw them into her rucksack. Then one by one she slowly removed the slides in her hair, so that her shiny locks tumbled down the centre of her back in soft, brown waves.

"You're very bossy, Dominic," she remarked. "I have a future of my own and it's not necessarily yours."

Dominic lay down on the sand with his arms crossed behind his head as a pillow. "Do you know that in my era, there is an entire underwater village in this Bay?" he said dreamily. "It's surrounded by a huge net. It's called Aristau. It's my home."

"Are the girls mermaids?"

Dominic laughed. "Sort of. The girls are beautiful and innocent, if that's what you mean by mermaids. My favourite girl is Willow. She has had an aqualung fitted."

"What does she look like?"

"Good hearted, intelligent, someone I can trust."

"So you find that appealing."

Dominic stood up and stared out to sea. "Go and swim now, Zeta," he said coolly. "I don't want anyone to notice my absence. Stay in the water until I return. See you in five minutes."

Zeta ran into the warm shallows, while To-do, waiting at the waters edge, watched her closely. She waded out until the sea was heavy around her thighs. Then she dove forward, disappearing for a few seconds under the salty, blue ocean. When she emerged, she treaded water. Bobbing up and down with the roll of the waves, she waved to Dominic. Then she blinked and looked again, for Dominic, standing on the beach a moment earlier, was gone!

Rushing out of the water to the spot where he had been standing, she looked around, but could not see him anywhere. Picking up To-do, she sat down onto the sand.

"My goodness," she said, quietly amazed - her grey eyes wide and shining.

A short time later, deep shadows filled the valleys and hills on the Isle of Wight. Hazy and warm, the air rose in gentle waves. Incoming, the rolling tide washed high onto the sandy beaches. Inky in parts, aqua in others, the sea was calm. Tinkling the wind chimes hanging over the shop doors, a gentle breeze spun the wheels on the windmill toys, and tossed and turned the edges of the few remaining beach towels, stretched out over the cooling sand.

An hour had passed since Zeta had gone for her swim and had witnessed first hand, Dominic's amazing, mirroring ability. Dressed in a black turtleneck jersey, black trousers and boots, he had returned as promised, after five minutes absence. Reunited, they had visited the Town Centre where Zeta had busied herself thoughtfully shopping, filling her rucksack with many purchases.

Their time on the island almost over, they were presently walking past the Shopping Centre towards their waiting zeppelin. Zeta had teamed her skirt with her bathing costume. Wearing her new pink scarf and sandals and carrying her boots, she was smiling.

"Is all this food really necessary?" Dominic asked. "It weighs a ton. I'm not complaining about carrying your rucksack, but you did buy out half the confectionary store!"

"Of course it's necessary," replied Zeta, keeping an eye on To-do, off his leash and running ahead. "I'm not going to a place where there is only Lumpo to eat without bringing along a few treats. Am I?"

"A few?" he laughed. Then after a moment's silence, he added seriously. "Everything will move quickly once we are onboard the zeppelin, Zeta. So keep your wits about you, Miss."

"Righty oh," replied Zeta.

Reaching their zeppelin a few minutes later, Zeta called her pet to her and picked up To-do. Together with Dominic, she climbed the gangplank and hastily entered the sleepy cabin. Slumping down into her seat, she swept her long hair away from her back. Then she adjusted her pink headscarf, ready to roam. To-do, nestled contentedly at her feet with his head on his paws, went to sleep.

Ringing out, the zeppelin siren gave its last call for passengers. The access door closed. The orange airship rose high into the sky, flying quickly away from the relaxed, tranquil island.

Dominic, having finished stowing Zeta's laden rucksack into the under-seat compartment, glanced at his timeband. "It's 6.03, Zeta. Close your eyes and think of your dad. I've set the timer on your Roaming-Ring. You'll be asleep in two minutes." Then he strode away, heading swiftly towards the corridor at the rear of their zeppelin. As soon as he was shielded from view by that corridor, his mirror image vanished.

Simultaneously his mortal body - asleep in the Historic House in a future world - awoke. Abruptly sitting up, he grabbed a band of interconnecting rings from his bedside table. After slipping the rings onto the fingers of his right hand, he pulled his sleeves down to conceal his fingers. Stretching his turtleneck over his face, he clipped it together at the top so that it formed a close fitting hood, cut with two small eye apertures. Seconds after he had awoken, Dominic let his head fall back onto his pillow. He closed his eyes. The crystals in his Roaming-Ring glowed. Instantly he fell asleep.

Back in the zeppelin, Zeta had also closed her eyes. Mutely glowing under the folds of her pink summer scarf, the crystals in her concealed Roaming-Ring had activated. Asleep and roaming, she floated in a warm, gentle current of waves that lifted her up and bore her deftly forward. Dreaming, she saw her father's face before her, beckoning. Anxiously she ran to greet him. She stopped with a jolt - a fence suddenly barring her way. Then she opened her eyes.

Shaded and shrouded by a dense canopy of dark green leaves, she startled. Finding herself sitting on a forest floor of broken twigs and damp brown earth - a translucent spectre of her former self - she gasped. Looming in front of her was a high, red, painted metal fence. Looking down on her, she saw three hooded, ghostly figures.

"Oh no!" she cried out anxiously, "This is all wrong! Where's Dominic?"

"Hey, I'm here!" called his reassuring tenor voice.

"Dominic!" she exclaimed, in hushed undertones, staring up at one of the hooded, black spectres. "I recognize these surroundings! You need to know - you're outside a disused metal Scrap yard in Farnborough Common, five kilometres North-East of the Research Facility!"

As she spoke, her voice faded. Soft waves gripped her, lifted her up and carried her forward. She saw the small face of To-do, asleep at her feet. She watched the low rolling waves of the deep green sea. Then she opened her eyes. She was in her seat in the zeppelin and she was awake.

"Whoa! This roaming business takes a little getting used to," she thought excitedly. "Moving locations happens so quickly. I guess I found my dad. Dominic obviously has two helpers. Now, I have to wait."

Many miles away from Zeta and the zeppelin - in the Farnborough Common forest - three ghostly black figures backed away from a metal fence, merged into the thick undergrowth and quickly seemed as dark shadows, cast by the thick branches of the overhanging trees.

Around them, the Oaks grew tall and straight, reaching towards the sky, forming a thick canopy of leaves that dimmed the light and closed them in. High ferns, thick and prolific over the forest floor, brushed gently against the trio of dark spectral visitors. Whilst blackberry brambles, coursing haphazardly throughout the wooded glen, coiled underneath their floating feet.

"I'd like to be the real me in a forest like this one day," remarked one of the spectral shadows, looking about him at the abundant flora in this tranquil green copse. "Imagine what a whole world like this would be like?"

"Absolutely beautiful," said the smallest shadow of the three. "Look at the berries on the blackberry bushes. I've never seen berries before. I wonder what they taste like?"

"Sweet, I guess," remarked the first shadow. "As for the forest air, I bet it is crisp and fragrant. If only I could fill my lungs with air like this?"

"Shut up, Sebastian," said Dominic harshly. "You too, Parsons. We're here to rescue Professor Doherty. This is a mission remember. Not a sightseeing excursion."

"Says you, previously off sightseeing with a beautiful girl," remarked Sebastian jealously. Moving slightly away from the others, he floated over a large crumbling log and stared at a squirrel stopped on a low hanging bough.

"What if the kidnappers have already killed Doherty," suggested the shadow of Parsons, spotting a rabbit in a nearby briar and floating towards it. "Then we've wasted our time, Tau."

"Zeta couldn't have brought us here if her dad wasn't alive," cut in Sebastian, moving his transparent hand towards the branch and the squirrel. "You know that, Parsons. What I want to know is: what do I get out of this mission, Tau? Since I'm prohibited from admiring the forest."

When Dominic failed to answer, Parsons drew a deep breath so that the shadow of his chest rose and fell. Then his tone was incredulous. "You are saving a girl's father, Sebastian. I can't believe that you expect gratuitous rewards for-"

"You get a chocolate chip cake," cut in Dominic.

"You're kidding?" said Sebastian, his dark shadow leaning against the grey bark of the tree, beside the amazed grey squirrel. "Is chocolate chip cake nice?" he asked, his voice softened and boyish.

"I believe it is delicious," replied Dominic.

Parsons ghostly figure sat down on the crumbling log. The green fronds of the overhanging ferns brushed the spectral outline of his translucent hunched shoulders. In the slits of his black hood, his brown eyes widened.

"You get marbled fudge chocolate brownies, Parsons," Dominic added quickly.

"Marbled fudge chocolate brownies," repeated Parsons reverently.

"Personally, I wouldn't give you wretches anything," said Dominic gruffly, looking at the strange sight of his friends, furtive shadowy ghosts, lurking in the cool green woods. "Zeta bought the food for you, and she won't travel with me in the Dandy Lion unless her father is safe. So, no father, no Zeta, no cake!" Dominic stood tall and the leaves in the lower branches of a forest tree tickled the black shadow of his frowning forehead. "I expect you to lend a hand, Sebastian," he continued, now growling softly.

"No problem," Sebastian replied, his voice content.

"Good. The remuneration issue is settled," said Dominic. "Let's get the job done."

Peering through the thick undergrowth towards the high metal fence - six metres before him - Dominic coolly observed a series of thin metal rods surrounding the Scrap yard. Newly installed, the rods jutted out from the ground at three metre intervals, forming an impenetrable barrier to Roamers. To his right - he also observed a gravel access road leading up to a high wire mesh entrance gate - chained shut - twelve metres away.

Sebastian floated back to stand beside Dominic, brushing an eerie path through the ferns with his translucent dark form. Leaning his arm against a tall Oak covered in spiralling ivy, he looked around cautiously.

Parsons rose from the crumbling tree log and moved forward to join them. "Those rods are obviously generating the magnetic field that's keeping us out," he remarked. "They're creating a translucent Dome over the whole Scrap yard. I've always been impressed by the field generator, it's a very useful tool to keep psychic busybodies at bay."

"Brilliant Parsons, how *do you do it*?" taunted Sebastian, his eyes gleaming from the slits in his black hood. "Who would have thought *you* were a budding school master. And at such a tender age of fifteen."

"At least I've got a brain," retorted Parsons. "How many brain cells of yours are currently operational? Wait, let me guess? Seventeen, one for each of *your* years!" Floating cautiously away from Sebastian, Parsons shadowy image mingled with those cast by overhanging boughs.

"I'm going over the Scrap yard gate," said Dominic sharply, interrupting their banter. "I'll mirror to get my energy field through the generated magnetic barrier. For the rest of the time I'll stay invisible. With any luck, I'll be quick enough and no one will see my trespass. I'll find the power source that's keeping you two out and I'll shut it down. Then I want you to follow me inside. Until then, keep hidden in this forest." After saying these words, his translucent ghostly image faded until he was invisible to the two other youths. Then he darted away from his shadowy allies.

Leaving no footprints in the fertile forest loam, his psychic energy field promptly swept a curious trail through the thick carpet of trembling ferns. Keeping within the shelter of the undergrowth, he floated to his right until he was diagonal to the Scrap yard gate. Moving out from the darkness of the forest - onto the gravel access road - he floated invisible towards that gate. One metre out from the fence line, as he expected, a force field blocked his psychic progress.

"These fields are usually only half a metre thick," he thought to himself coolly. "That's a half a metre of distance to pass through, mirroring, solid and completely visible, and a half a metre of hope that the men inside the yard aren't watching the gate."

Floating a distance away from the gate, he turned. Rushing at the gate at an incredible speed, he suddenly mirrored. Materialising from thin air, he hurtled forward. Passing through the force field - *visible* - he slammed into the gate. The chain on the gate rattled. Then his mirror image vanished.

Invisible once again, Dominic quickly floated over the gate. Dropping down into the Scrap yard, he moved into the shadows beside the gravel inroad. Initially surprised by the sheer size of the huge, oppressive and dusty yard, he looked around warily.

Strewn throughout the yard were hundreds of shells of wrecked automobiles. Crowded over the stony ground - their paintwork faded and scratched, their windows smashed and their wheels twisted - the cars slowly decayed into the dank hard earth.

Towering over the cars, where the inroad branched to the left, two huge yellow cranes, gutted of their engines, stood forlorn next to a rusted, crushing unit. Farther along, where the road swept away to the right, a large windowless warehouse loomed cold and ramshackle. Although the high, corrugated iron walls of the warehouse were sound, the old flat roof, covered over with a thick layer of decomposing leaves was rusted open in places. Chained closed with rusty links, a pair of huge doors cut a grim picture in the centre of this dilapidated grey building, while next to this, far less daunting, a smaller access door hung partially open. Where the inroad stopped, one hundred metres directly ahead, a yellow workman's shed and a small grubby blue office building - with two smashed windows - sat overlooking this abandoned establishment.

Pools of dried oil formed an uneven pattern of black discs throughout this large graveyard of metal and machine. Shards of broken glass imbedded in between the stones and the earth speckled the yard with unseen hazard and the pervasive smell of grease and dirt hung like a black cloud over the whole compound.

"Shed, office, or warehouse?" Dominic deliberated. "Where is the power source of the field generator most likely to be?"

Instinctively heading for the office, he floated invisible along the gravel inroad. Approaching the office door, he halted. Listening for voices, he turned the door handle slowly. Quietly he slipped inside.

Entering an empty dismal room, interconnected with three others, and furnished with a plastic desk, chair and an old wooden table, he looked around guardedly.

"You beauty!" he exclaimed softly to himself.

Immediately spotting - on the floor by the window - the control unit that generated the field impeding his friends' access, he floated towards that device. Leaving the unit activated, he disconnected the wires that fed power to the outside rods. Looking out from the two broken windows, he patiently waited.

Several seconds elapsed. Suddenly two black spectral images appeared - additional psychic entities in the dilapidated office.

"Very cosy," remarked Sebastian, looking around him at the old furniture and the cracked laminate floor.

"Totally sumptuous," agreed Parsons, watching a small snake crawl across the plastic desk and disappear into a hole in the wall.

"Just the place where I'd like to retire," added Dominic, now also projecting a dark spectral image into the room with them. "Good to see you, chaps," he added, his blue eyes glistening in the slits of his hood. "Now follow me," he instructed quietly, making a super quick exit from the rundown office.

Leading the way - under the shadow of the giant cranes - he floated across the Scrap yard towards the smallest of the warehouse doors. Reaching that door, he slipped inside, followed closely by Sebastian and Parsons. Immediately noticing the gloom, he heard rats scurrying on the grey cement floor. Forty long aisles of scrap filled shelving filled the area. Emanating from the far right of the warehouse - where the shelving aisles stopped ten metres short from the wall - he saw a faint hazy beam of dim yellow light.

Moving cautiously, all three spectres - indiscernible in the large dark warehouse - floated towards the rear of the building where the warehouse was darkest. Racing towards the yellow light, they passed several shelves housing large metal crates.

Approaching the far right side wall, they came to a row of seven small offices fronted with glass. Halting, they observed that while most of these warehouse offices were in darkness, the first one on the far left and the one in the centre, were dimly illuminated and disturbingly occupied.

Outside of the first office and leaning against the glass, Dominic espied a large ugly man, with a huge beer-belly and long black whiskers. Behind this man, inside the office - bound by the hands and feet - was a prisoner. The prisoner wore a grubby purple shirt and matching striped trousers. Concealing the head of the captive was a loose grey sack. The man was barefoot.

"Tau, is the prisoner, Doherty?" asked Sebastian in whispered voice, standing hidden against one of the shelving units alongside Dominic.

"I expect so. Same clothes," responded Dominic coolly and quietly. Glancing down, he looked at a rat's nest and a large rodent that had stopped near his feet. Speaking to Parsons - standing close by - he growled softly, "Use your power, Parsons. Put that beer-bellied brute to sleep! And be quick about it!"

Parsons moved away from the concealing darkness of the shelving aisle and rapidly approached the large, ugly man. Dominic and Sebastian looked on, hidden by the gloom. The unsuspecting man - swiftly overpowered by Parsons' spectral shadow - suddenly fell backwards against the glass wall behind him. His arms dropped as heavy weights by his side. The cigarette in his hand fell onto the grey cement floor. The man's chest rose and fell deeply. Curiously, he began to snore.

Dragged by the shadowy figure of Parsons, his slumbering body then swept the dust of the shelving aisles. Moments later, lifted by Parsons' shadowy hands, he fell neatly into one of the many large metal crates packed on the warehouse shelves.

With Parson's job complete, Dominic briefly pondered. Warily he perceived his surrounds, casting his eye over the high rafters, the dusty shelves and the grubby offices. Frowning slightly, he turned his attention towards the centre office where a group of five men were loudly chatting. Each man held a small glass of whisky in his hand and two of the men were puffing nonchalantly on the butts of their cigarettes.

"Sebastian, it's your turn to use your psychic power. Create an illusion to conceal my approach," instructed Dominic. "Those five in the centre office should not present a problem to you. There isn't a strong mind amongst them."

"They won't present a problem, Tau, but he will," said Sebastian soberly, staring at the last office in the decrepit row.

Dominic scowled to see a very large man, well over seven feet tall, standing in the suddenly illuminated far right office. A Roaming-Ring crowned his dark, short hair. He possessed a square face with a large jaw, broken by a thin, black moustache. His brooding brown eyes were deep set and narrow. Pinned to his collar was a flat, triangular badge marked with his rank, C3, and his name, Kroll.

"That mongrel must have been literally sleeping on the job," said Sebastian scathingly.

"Yes, a Captain, class three. I didn't see him a moment ago," said Dominic. "I expect he has a bed in the office, and was roaming."

"Do you know, what I hate most about his type," whinged Sebastian. "And its not because they reduce the effect of my psychic ability with their oh-so-strong will power. It's their dress sense that I loathe. Those gold flight suits they wear are really ambitious!"

"I had hoped I wasn't going to see him," said Dominic, his worst fear confirmed. Putting his hand out gently, he brushed away a spider web from the steel shelving beside him. Then he watched a large, black, hairy spider scurry away into the darkness. "You can't fool him with an illusion, Sebastian?"

Sebastian shook his head. "Not under these conditions."

"What about you, Parsons?" he asked, as the third shadowy spectre quickly rejoined them. "Can you use your psychic power to put an Intelligence Officer to sleep?"

Parsons looked towards the far right office and the figure of Kroll. Then he also shook his head. "Sorry, Tau. No chance."

"Well, I have no choice," said Dominic. "I have to wake up and switch on my hammer. I'll be back in less than five seconds and then

I'll tuck that simian into bed myself - by using a little old fashioned fisticuffs. That big golden ape is going to get one hour of dreamless beauty sleep, compliments of TT Training Academy!"

After saying these words, his shadow faded away. Where he had been was only darkness.

"Lovely holiday resort," said Sebastian sarcastically. "A smashing clientele."

"Yes," said Parsons. "Very upmarket. The rats make an interesting addition to the uplifting ambiance."

Suddenly Dominic's phantom image returned. When he reappeared, his friends saw that the rings under the cuff of his right sleeve were glowing ominously red.

"How long was I gone? Three seconds?"

Neither of them answered him.

"You're barbaric, Tau," admonished Parsons. "You're not going to use that device, are you? Remember what has been taught for eons? Violence is not the answer."

"You're annoying me, Parsons!" said Dominic angrily. "You know I am more peaceable than all the Psychic Knights combined. What am I supposed to do, attempt to communicate with Kroll and suggest that he is being unkind? Or would you rather I walk away, leave Professor Doherty to his fate and be ashamed of my great grandfather for the rest of my life!"

"Those sparring hammers are expensive," Sebastian interrupted, brashly admiring the shimmering rings below Dominic's knuckles.

"Do what you like, Tau," said Parsons. "But don't blame me if it all goes wrong and Intelligence Officers torture you in a cell for the rest of your life!"

"I haven't got time to argue with you, Parsons!" said Dominic.

Leaving them, he floated back behind the aisles. Under the shelter of darkness, he wove his way towards the right side office. Overhead, the high dusty rafters seemed as thick black bars, closing him inside this large disused warehouse. The only incoming light - shafts of light glowing in through holes in the roof - beamed down on him like pitiful searchlights. Sweeping through the aisles, his fast moving psychic field caused the river of stagnant dust beneath his boots to creep slowly forward. Fragile - spider webs spanning the wide aisles, broke as he advanced.

Snatching a sliver of metal from the floor and holding it over his hand to conceal his glowing rings, he reached the far right office -

seconds after he had left his companions. A dark, discernible amorphous mass outside the illuminated room, he silently opened the office door.

Suddenly mirroring in front of Kroll, he hit the large man smack on the jaw. Then he watched as the body of the Intelligence Officer - almost ten years his senior - slumped slowly onto the office bed. Quickly Dominic grabbed a set of keys from the office desk, switched off the light and exited.

Crouching down to avoid detection - a black shadow again - he floated at lightning speed along the length of offices towards the prisoner's room. Using one of the keys, he entered.

Parsons and Sebastian also moved forward to float outside that same office. Using his psychic gift, Sebastian created an illusion of a whiskered kidnapper and a sorrowful bound captive. Thus, he hid their spectral selves and reality from view.

Around them, all seemed calm. Appearing out from their nests, the rats scratched amongst a pile of rubbish thrown outside of the central office. Settling, the dust coated the cold grey floor. Creaking as a gust of wind rattled the corrugated iron structure, the old warehouse was quiet.

"It's 6.15pm now," whispered Parsons. "You have to keep this illusion up for an hour, Sebastian. At 7.15pm we're free to return to our own time."

"*I can do it,*" replied Sebastian. "If you shut up distracting me!" Then he glanced behind him, noting Dominic - inside the prisoner's room - checking for surveillance devices.

Finding none, Dominic materialized into his solid mirror form. Bending down before the hunched over prisoner, he gently pulled the sack away. When he did so, the eyes of a middle-aged man with dried blood matted in his hair, a swollen lip and a deep blue welt on his ashen face, stared into his own.

"I'm here to help you, Professor Doherty," whispered Dominic aggressively. "Zeta sent me. Be quiet, co-operate, and I'll get you out of here!"

While Professor Doherty blinked against the light, stared at the hooded youth, and looked around him at the grubby bare office, Dominic swiftly untied the man's tight bindings. Glancing at the smashed hand that had previously held the machinery of Doherty's palmdisk, he quickly hauled the Professor up to his feet. Gripping the

Professor's left shoulder, he ran him out the door, past the illusion of the whiskered brute and out of the warehouse.

At the very moment of their departure, the door in the centre office opened. The rats scurried away and a shaft of light shone out into the darkness of the warehouse. Five men stepped out into the gloom. Glancing indifferently towards the mirage of their whiskered colleague, smoking and leaning against the prisoner's door, they grouped together and spoke loudly.

"Dinner break over," said one of them. "Time to circumnavigate this crummy Scrap yard."

"Parsons?" whispered Sebastian. "Tau needs two minutes to clear the yard. Put them to sleep!"

"They are already feeling quite drowsy," whispered Parsons.

One of the men suddenly yawned. "The dinner break was too short," he grumbled.

The man beside him also yawned. "I could do with a coffee," he said pointedly.

"Coffee sounds good," agreed a third man.

The five men filed happily back inside the office. One of them turned on a coffee percolator and the other four slumped into their chairs and rubbed their faces.

"A percolator brewing is a little bit of luxury," remarked one of the seated men. "I like nothing better than the aroma of a good coffee bean!"

"Quite the connoisseur, aren't you?" said the man next to him.

"I will be," he said in reply. "What with the currency I'm getting paid for this job, I'll be able to afford the finest cuisine for the rest of my life."

"He can choke on his gruel," muttered Sebastian quietly, watching the group of rats return.

"They're scum," agreed Parsons in a whispered voice.

Succumbing to Parson's soporific power, all five men suddenly fell asleep.

Meanwhile, outside, Dominic and the Professor were running along the gravel inroad. Reaching the entrance gate, Dominic hastily unlocked the heavy large chain. Pulling the Professor along with him, he ran through the opening. Refastening the chain, he threw the keys far out into the forest. Turning around suddenly, he was just in time to catch Hugh Doherty's arm, as the dazed Professor struck out at him.

"Hold on, Professor!" directed Dominic brusquely, restraining the cultured man.

Once again, he gripped the Professor's shoulder. Pushing him rapidly along in front of him, he ran into the thick undergrowth of the darkening Common. Quickly closing in around them, the tall Oaks hid them from view. Green ferns brushed at their arms and winding brambles caught at their feet. Disturbed by their hasty approach, a grey bushy tailed squirrel scampered up a tree and halted, camouflaged on a coarse, grey bough. Rabbits disappeared down their burrows and hid. Stopped their warbling, the birds of the forest flew back to their nests.

When he was certain that they were well clear of the Scrap yard, Dominic stopped abruptly. "I'm not pushing you all the way out of here, Professor," he stated crossly, his blue eyes flashing in the slits of his black hood. "So air your grievances, now!"

"I do not believe the brute guarding my prison door just let me escape."

"He didn't," said Dominic gruffly. "The thug you speak of is unconscious in a crate, hidden in the warehouse."

"But I saw-"

"An illusion, Professor. Did you smell his cigarette? Did you fear his proximity? Ask your self these questions and then tell me that you *didn't* see an illusion?"

The Professor smelt the leaves in the forest and reflected. "Yes, I concur. I did see an illusion in the warehouse."

"Good. Now, it's my turn for questions, Professor," Dominic asked sternly. "Can you run without aid? Do you know where you are?"

"I can run without aid, yes, and I do recognise my surroundings. I'm not far from my sister's house."

"Which direction is her house?" asked Dominic quickly.

"This way, follow me," replied the Professor, heading towards a grassy clearing

"No, Professor. Stay under cover," instructed Dominic. Grabbing the older man's arm and keeping him at his side, he ran with him through the dense undergrowth. "Try to keep up. Sorry about your feet."

As they ran forward, deeper into the woods, the Professor's bare feet were jabbed and spiked by many sharp broken twigs, small

stones and the coarse bark of the forest floor. His chest heaved from
the exertion of running and he was breathing quickly.

"Professor, time for a few home truths," said Dominic hoarsely.
"Be warned, they are going to hit you hard."

"Go on," said the Professor, slowing his gait in the green, leafy
forest.

"After you were kidnapped, the TT Showroom was bombed. No
one was injured, but all the Chronoguisers were destroyed."

"TT Corporation can build more, now that I'm free," stated the
Professor calmly. "The secret of the gravity drive is mine, you see."

Silent beside him, the hooded black figure of Dominic suggested
there was more to tell.

"What else?" said Professor Doherty after a moment's reflection.

"One of the men who kidnapped you works for TT."

The Professor abruptly halted. Overhanging boughs, thick with
soft green leaves, threw dappled shadows over his incredulous face.
"Why should TT-?"

"TT comes from a future world, Professor, where he does not
consider the Chronoguiser to be a desirable vessel for his populace to
own," said Dominic, cutting the Professor short. "Now keep running.
We can't stop."

"But why? What possible reason could there be for not wanting a
time-machine?" asked Professor Doherty, resuming his stride.

"Imagine a time when colonization of distant planets is desirable,"
said Dominic, helping the Professor over a group of large, fallen logs.
"The Chronoguiser is a neat Spaceship as well as a time-machine.
What effect do you think thousands of small independent Spaceships
would have on immigration control?"

"They would create chaos. But why stop the production of the
time-machine in this era?"

"Hold on a minute," Dominic said, interrupting their conversation.
"There's open Heathland in front of us. We need to skirt around this
section. Keep well concealed in the undergrowth, Professor. Move as
fast as you can!"

Once they were past the open, treeless area and were hidden by the
thick undergrowth of the darkening forest, Dominic spoke freely. "TT
does not consider the Chronoguiser to be an appropriate vessel for the
people of your era to own, given your level of development,
Professor. I am sorry."

"Why did he encourage me to invent it, then?" asked Professor Doherty, grimacing as he stepped on a thorny bramble vine. Stopping, he pulled the thorns from his feet. Then he continued jogging forward.

"It was inevitable that someone was going to invent the time-machine, Professor Doherty. Best for TT to supervise its production."

"Best for TT? He goes to all the expense of producing a time-machine and destroys it."

"Not quite, Professor. He still has the Dandy Lion."

"So, I invented the Chronoguiser for the exclusive use of TT Vox Populi."

"TT wants to ensure that his family retain control of the Chronoguiser, indefinitely," said Dominic coolly, pushing a large low hanging branch out of way and waiting for the Professor to move past.

"I created that machine for the people," said the Professor earnestly. "So mankind would benefit. Instead, I spent years making someone who is powerful, even more powerful. The benefits from my gravity drive will never be realized. I've wasted my life!"

"Professor, stop here!" Dominic cautioned, grabbing the Professor's arm and pulling him to an abrupt halt.

A group of walkers were enjoying a leisurely evening stroll through the forest, chatting and laughing.

"Best to wait until they are out of sight," said Dominic quietly. "And Professor, right now, you need to be concentrating on prolonging your life - not judging its value. The truth is - you're not safe anymore. Not as long as you threaten the plans of the TT Conglomerate Group. That's what they're called where I come from." Dominic paused until a lone rambler had passed out of earshot. "You *will* be pressurized to build more time-machines, Professor. The public will insist. And TT can't allow that to happen."

"So I have to disappear. Is that what you're suggesting?"

"You have no alternative."

"You're also from the future, and Zeta knows you?"

Dominic nodded.

"If I went to the future, to your present, would I be safe?"

Dominic remained silent.

"If I went beyond your present?"

"I can't vouch for what you would find in my future, Professor," responded Dominic. "But that's *my* destination."

"How does your time-machine function?" asked Professor Doherty hopefully. "Does it use my gravity drive?"

"Yes, Professor."

The Professor smiled and a look of delight came into his eyes.

"Come on, Professor. We can move forward now. The ramblers are well clear of our position."

They ran through the forest, but now the Professor was limping and his feet were scratched and bleeding.

"I have two choices, as far as I see it," he said to Dominic, his breath shallow from his physical exertions and his voice hoarsely whispering. "Hide for the rest of my life, stifled and afraid, or journey to the unknown in my own time-machine."

"You have a time-machine?" Dominic asked, hiding his surprise.

"Yes. TT doesn't know it, but I have my own little baby, the *Estrella,* locked away in my sister's garage. She doesn't even know it's there. It's not operational now, but it won't take much work before it is ready to fly. Three or four weeks should do the job."

"Well, good luck, Professor," said Dominic earnestly.

Fifty metres forward of their position, the red brick of several houses peeked teasingly into view.

"You're young. I can hear it in your voice," remarked Professor Doherty.

"I haven't even been born yet, Professor," replied Dominic flatly, looking at the battered visage of a man he admired.

They were now at the edge of the forest. Directly in front of them was Marjorie's house. Professor Doherty hobbled painfully across the road and walked over the front lawn. From under a large pot plant, he withdrew a spare key and inserted it into the white entrance door.

Dominic stood where the Professor had left him - a hooded black figure with two sharp gleaming eyes, in this quaint pretty world of woods and glens and sweet country cottages.

The Professor pushed the door open. "Thank you," he called. "Perhaps we'll meet again!" Stepping inside his sister's charming home - on the outskirts of Farnborough - he closed the door.

Chapter seven

A warm beacon, camouflaged by a burnt orange sky, the returning zeppelin sailed over the Hampshire Downs amidst a party of billowy white clouds.

In tune with the fading light of evening, the colours of the earth had deepened. Lakes were inky blue. Vegetation dozed deep green. The valleys were shaded. The hills - dense with trees - had darkened. Fields were vacant of their chestnut dairy cows, heeding the call of the milking bell, and the chirping song of the birds had ceased, until the morrow.

Aboard the airship, with its large cylindrical balloon and its glass-walled undercarriage, the zeppelin passengers were partaking of a moreish light supper. With their cabin full of the aroma of warm croissants, scones, hot chocolate and tea, everyone was relaxed and content - except for Zeta.

Beside her, the aisle seat was empty. Sitting alone for over twenty minutes, she stared out over the rustic scenery. Holding To-do on her lap, she glanced at her timeband. Then she frowned.

"It's past 6.20pm. Dominic hasn't returned and our hostess has obviously missed him," she fretted. "I hope nothing's gone wrong."

Gazing out of the airship window, down at the sleepy green hills and valleys far below, she focused on the sylvan terrain, smiling up at her in hues of gold, olive and muted browns.

Suddenly the welcoming tune on her palmdisk alerted her to an incoming message. Looking at her palm, she quickly read the communiqué, flashing onto the small circular screen:

Zeta,
You may have been alarmed
at my disappearance, but be
happy in the knowledge that I
am now safe and free.
Dad. 18.22.18

"Dominic did it!" Zeta thought happily. "He rescued my dad!" Admiring the rippling blue water of a picturesque lake over which their zeppelin now travelled, she smiled. "That's wonderful news! How can I celebrate? How can I ever thank-?"

Interrupting her thoughts, a sympathetic voice unexpectedly called out, "Are you alright, young man?"

Abruptly turning her head to her left, Zeta saw Dominic. Stopped in the aisle next to him was their hostess.

"I've had better days," Dominic replied.

Stepping past their hostess, he nodded greeting to Zeta. Slumping down his seat, he stared out over the lake.

"We thought there was a problem. We missed you at dinner. Air sickness was it?" their hostess enquired.

"I couldn't face a meal," came the taut reply.

"Never mind. We'll be landing soon. In the meantime I'll get you a Sports magazine, shall I?" their hostess offered. "Reading may help you forget about the slight air turbulence."

"If you like," replied Dominic.

Quickly moving away, their hostess wove her way through the aisles of their fast moving vessel, smiling and chatting to all the passengers she passed.

"Dominic, you liar!" rebuked Zeta, when their hostess was out of earshot. "Stop staring out over the countryside and look at me! You've mirrored paler and you look so serious. Just as well I know there's nothing wrong with you and you're covering up your absence - else I'd be concerned. Now, tell me everything that has happened."

Choosing to ignore Zeta, Dominic continued to gaze out of the window at the terrain below. He watched a flock of water birds rise gracefully from the lake. Then he looked at the tree-covered hills surrounding that deep, blue basin.

"I had hoped Parsons' worries were unfounded," he thought soberly, glancing at his right hand, now bare of his sparring hammer. "But after seeing the Intelligence Officer, Kroll, I know better. Undoubtedly I will also face imprisonment if I threaten TT's plans."

The lake was now behind him and the zeppelin was flying over undulating pastureland. Staring forward, Dominic's face bore the look of one resigned to be both stalwart and staid.

"There you go again!" exclaimed Zeta. "You can drop the brave face. Our hostess isn't around. Now come on, speak up. I'm itching to know all the details concerning dad's liberation."

Turning towards her, Dominic eyed her steadily. "You call me a liar the minute I arrive back," he said coolly. "Do I deserve such praise?" Then he stared coldly at her, before continuing in a mimicking sarcastic voice, *"Thank you, Dominic. It was very kind of you to face vicious kidnappers and free my father. You are a very good friend."* Resuming his normal voice, he concluded, "You could have said as much to me when I returned, Zeta. However, I know not to expect even a side-ways glance from you - in future."

Zeta was too embarrassed to answer. Dominic stared fixedly before him and Zeta looked through the zeppelin window. Flying at their high altitude, the fenced meadows below seemed to her to be a rustic chequerboard of greens, yellows and hazelnut browns. Gazing out over this lush tended farmland, she pondered as to the reason behind Dominic's unusual outburst.

"Obviously dad's rescue was traumatic. Dominic doesn't want to discuss it and he is genuinely upset," she thought astutely. "Added to that, I was rude for not saying thank you, straightaway. Dominic doesn't know it, but if there were a million different ways to say thanks, it still wouldn't be enough to repay him for what he's done for my me and my dad." Instead of saying what she thought however, Zeta held her palm out, close to the lad. "Look, Dominic, dad sent me a message!" she exclaimed cheerfully.

Without moving, he looked at her little hand. Noticing her long thin fingers and soft white skin, he glanced indifferently at the message. His voice was cold. "That's your dad alright," he remarked, pushing her hand away dismissively. Reminded of the brutal injury to the Professor's hand, Dominic drowned in a flood of disgust towards TT. His face set. "I despise my great grandfather!" he thought. "He shames me in front of *The Zeta*."

Their hostess abruptly returned. "Here you are, lovey," she said, handing him the magazine she had promised. She patted his shoulder comfortingly and hurried back to her hostess stand.

"Dominic?" asked Zeta softly, meaning to say a million things.

"Just be silent, Zeta!" he barked. "I don't want to hear your voice!" Glaring at her, he added, "And put on some clothes. We're not at the beach anymore." He opened his magazine and pretended to read it.

After rummaging in her rucksack under the seat, Zeta put her strappy vest over her swimming top. When she sat back down, she noticed that the zeppelin was losing altitude. Several clusters of country cottages were now visible, nestled amongst grassed green fields.

"Ladies and Gentlemen," said the voice of their hostess, piping out through the armchair speakers. "We are now arriving at Aldershot, the home of the British Army and our final - "

Dominic slammed his hand down on the armrest, cutting off the communication. "I'm staying onboard, Zeta," he said coldly. "Until we get back to the Research Facility." Leaning towards her with an apologetic expression, he whispered hoarsely. "I have to tell you. TT is the one responsible for kidnapping your father."

Zeta stared out of the zeppelin window, initially shocked by his surprising, disquieting revelation. Slowing, their zeppelin skimmed the treetops and Zeta watched the boughs, thick with leaves, swaying in the wind. After briefly deliberating, she rested her hand lightly on his forearm. "Oh, Dominic," she said sympathetically. "I'm sorry."

Less than five kilometres away from Dominic and Zeta, the setting sun threw long shadows across the TT Research Facility. A different world now that the workers had gone home for the night, the Facility was still and quiet. The entry gates were locked. The car parks were empty and the airways above were refreshingly free of their busy air traffic. The blue sky overhead floated serenely. Without turbulence, the air was clear. Flying across the airfield towards Farnborough Common, a flock of wood pigeons headed for the high Oak boughs.

Cooling the now deserted runways and roads, the evening breeze swept through he huge research site - brushing away the aromas of a busy day. Weaving a path around the vacant buildings, the tepid wind streamed into the aircraft hangers and tipped the wings of the residing vessels. Carried by that same wind, a fine layer of dust blew shallow along the empty grounds, tickled the blades of yellowing grass and coated the metal boots of the many russet robots, standing as macabre sentries throughout the Facility. Pausing to benignly ruffle the hair of the four remaining Security men stationed languidly around the site, the wind continued its journey.

Into this environment, a persuasive fair youth entered. Emerging from the Reception building and jogging quickly across the airfield, he headed towards the Dandy Lion's Hanger.

Wearing the TT Security garb, a gun holster and Dominic's Security tag, he stopped several metres back from two men guarding that Hanger. Having the same appearance of the mortal Dominic, he smiled. Brushing his sandy hair back from his face, he casually began singing an enchanting, heartfelt ballad.

Floating in gentle waves across the airfield, his captivating voice entranced the men, compelled to listen. Lifting them up, the song carried them forward on a warm, rolling sea. It rocked them and bathed them. Drawing them into a different world, the song's pervasive melody abandoned them in an enchanting land of calm repose. Leaving them lying stretched out on a warm, white, glistening beach, they listened dreamily to the tumble of the waves on a sandy shore. Awakening from their reverie, minutes later, when the song had come to a gentle close, they stood relaxed at their posts.

Watching them shrewdly, the fair lad resumed his approach. Halting before the two men, he glanced inside the open door of the Dandy Lion's Hanger. Then he greeted one of them cordially. "Salutations brother!" he said, speaking to the heavier of the men, a middle-aged fellow with a round, friendly face.

"Dominic, is it?" asked that man. "You're new. You started today."

"Yes," replied Dominic's impostor. "I'm here to relieve you."

"Thank goodness!" said the other man, grey-haired, in his early sixties. "All I want to do is get home and relax!"

"I wouldn't mind finishing early," said the middle-aged man, staring across the empty runways. "Tonight is too nice an evening to waste working. I'd rather be out on the town, kicking up my heels."

"I can't argue with that," said the impostor.

"You sound different?" remarked the grey-haired man, looking at the blonde youth quizzically. Frowning, he glanced at the photo on the lad's Security tag. "You're hair seems darker and there's more colour in your face." He shook his head. "Anyhow, I thought your shift finished at 3pm?"

"I'm doing a double shift," replied Dominic's impostor.

"Our shift isn't due to finish until 9pm," queried the middle-aged man. "I can't afford to have my pay docked if there's any mix up."

"You're free to return home," said Dominic's effigy, casually regarding the deserted airfield.

The middle-aged man looked doubtful, and the older man - disappointed. Both of them stared across the airfield towards the vacant Reception building. They shuffled their feet.

Dominic's impostor smiled reassuringly. Establishing eye contact with both of them, he held out his open palm.

"See this little mushroom in the palm of my hand," he said, speaking quickly in a rhythmical mesmerising tone of voice. "I plucked it off a sculpture in the Reception building. A strange place to find a mushroom you might ask. Especially one of an inedible variety, like this one in my hand. Nevertheless, it was there. Planted like an Easter egg in a children's treasure hunt. Study it carefully gentlemen - if you dare!"

The Security men moved away from the Dandy Lion's Hanger towards Dominic's double. Keen to inspect the tiny secret device, their faces were inquisitive.

"It is not the listening device you presumed it was?" the impostor encouraged. "It is different - something immensely more powerful!"

Raising their eyebrows in silent response, the two men looked at the impostor's face. Then they looked at each other.

"Who would have thought that this tiny device could establish a portal *and* a cocoon inside a generated field?" the youth confided quietly.

Staring at the blue mushroom in amazement, the men's faces glowed with curiosity. Then they gazed across the airfield dazedly.

"When planted inside any establishment, a blue mushroom is a Roamer's Master key," the impostor continued rapidly. "Making the field generator most ineffective."

The men stared at him, totally impressed, as two small boys might stare at their father, demonstrating a high technology nuclear cannon.

"If you were wearing special glasses," the impostor explained, "you would see an invisible Dome around this whole Research Facility. Look around you. All you see are deserted roads and runways, plus a smattering of vacant buildings. But the generated field exists, I assure you, unseen by your naked eyes. As well as the Dome encompassing you, you would also see - aided by these hypothetical glasses - an invisible tube extending from the outside of the Dome to our current location. Connected to that tube you would see a cocoon the size of a man, also transparent. Inside the cocoon you would see me - Roamer extraordinaire - come to bedazzle you with future science!"

Overwhelmed by the lad's mesmerising voice, combined with this incredible information, the men gazed blankly. Brushing fragments of leaves against their boots - flapping their sleeves and Security tags - a gust of wind blew across the Facility.

"What's even more amazing," continued Dominic's impostor, "is that this little blue mushroom covers my true spectral projection and shows you a real representation of someone else. So, what you see in front of you appears to be a bona fide person." The spurious Dominic grinned genially. "The mimic mushroom doesn't give me the powers of the actual individual - unfortunately. Those endowed with the talent of psychic mirroring are tactile and their psyche carries much of their physical strength. Such are the limits of technology this size. I am but a cruel farce gentlemen, and for this I apologize."

Looking down with mock regret, the impostor peered at the device in his hand. Abruptly he then looked up, to stare intensely into the eyes of the Security men. They in turn, stared back at him, totally bewildered.

"Aha!" he continued rapidly. "You are totally bamboozled, my brothers. But no matter. I cannot tell a lie! I cannot project anything other that myself. So, a device with no conscience and no moral fortitude is required to do the job for me. Of course, in order for all of this to happen, the Roamer - yours truly - needed to have someone on the inside this Facility to plant the devilish device. TT's flesh! TT's blood! Am I making myself clear?"

The two men's minds were struggling. The mention of TT and his family frightened them, so they replied habitually and politely.

"Without doubt," replied the grey-haired man.

"Yes certainly," agreed the middle-aged man.

"Well, what are you doing standing around here, gaping at me like I just hypnotized you! Get away to your leisure pursuits. Now!" ordered the garrulous youth.

As the men began to walk away, Dominic's impostor shouted after them, "Hey, what about shutting down the six russet robots circling this Hanger! We're not in the House of Horrors, you know!"

"Sure," replied the oldest man.

Using a remote-control device that he retrieved from his shirt pocket, he keyed in the deactivation codes for the robots. They instantly halted. Their heads became stationary and their eyes withdrew back into their sockets. Adding to the quiet picture of the closed establishment, the robots stood around the perimeter of the Hanger, like ugly decorative monoliths. Hurrying across the airfield, the Security men, jumping into their flying-cars, were soon airborne and away.

The time was almost 7pm. In the sky over the TT Research Facility, the orange zeppelin was floating into view.

Dominic's impostor stood with his back towards the open Hanger and heaved a satisfied sigh of relief. Keenly watching the airship's rapid approach, he thought soberly, "After Tau has appropriated the time-machine - the Dandy Lion - I will have to put in another two hours of this charade."

Observing the smoothly gliding zeppelin as it passed slowly over the Hanger, he saw a girl onboard - Zeta - staring at him. Moving back into the shadows of the Hanger, he kept partially hidden.

Sitting forward in her seat in the zeppelin, Zeta nervously appraised Dominic's impostor, the Hanger and the surrounding airfield. Noting that the breeze had picked up, she observed a steady stream of small dried leaves blowing haphazardly across the flat, empty field. Giving way to the wind, she saw the grass bend. On the roof of the deserted Reception building, she noticed several coloured pennants flying.

"Hey Dominic!" she whispered. "When we left on the zeppelin, I remember seeing two Security men and several russet coloured robots surrounding the Hanger of the Dandy Lion. There is only one Security man now, but the disgusting shredding mechinoids are still there. Look at them. I saw one of them up close. It had serrated arms, a revolving skull that bobbed up and down and red telescopic eyes that distended out on stalks. What do you think of them? Horrible eh?"

Dominic cocked his head. "I don't consider robots a threat."

"The more I see of these particular ones, the less I want to go to Satellite25," she admitted.

"I can understand why you have changed your mind... after what I told you about TT.

"No, that's not it," she replied nervously. "Can't you see how ghastly those mechinoids are?"

"Robots are a lot different where I come from," he assured her calmly. "Satellite25 will be fun. I guarantee." Then he whispered, "If you look carefully, Zeta, you will notice that the robots you fear are deactivated. See, they're not making the even the slightest movement."

Leaning further forward in her seat, Zeta peered down at the six russet robots beneath the zeppelin. "Yes, you're right. But what about the Security man at his station? He can reactivate the robots. I can't see him well from this distance, but from what I can see, he looks really reserved and frosty. Just the type to enjoy watching us being torn to shreds by those robotic claw arms!"

Dominic's reaction surprised her. He chuckled and grinned.

"You certainly lack guile," he remarked incisively.

"I don't know what you mean by that remark," she responded. "And I definitely don't understand your casual attitude. Why on earth are you laughing?" She moved closer to him and whispered even more softly. "We'll never get past that snowman at the front!"

Dominic continued grinning, but did not respond. Sitting relaxed in his seat, waiting for their zeppelin to land, he looked out calmly over the quiet Research Facility.

When their vessel landed - minutes later - some twenty metres diagonal to the Dandy Lion's Hanger, the zeppelin passengers disembarked. Grabbing Zeta's heavy rucksack from the under-seat compartment, Dominic helped her fasten it onto her back. Gesturing with his head towards the exit, he made his way down the departure ramp. Holding both the loop of To-do's leash and her walking boots in her left hand, Zeta followed close behind.

Once outside, Dominic glanced at the Hanger and its retractable domed-roof. Striding towards the Hanger, he kept his eyes fixed on the wide entrance. "You're still here?" he said after awhile, staggered to see Zeta walking behind him.

"Why shouldn't I be?" she said, smiling back at him.

He grinned. "Remember what I previously told you. We are just going to walk straight inside, like welcome guests. I don't want anybody watching us imagining there is anything untoward about our behaviour. Don't get nervous on me, will you?"

Zeta however was very nervous. Moving forward with her head bent down, her eyes watched each step she took over the smooth, grey tarmac. Counting her steps to distract her from her destination, she feared not only the robots, but also the consequences if Dominic took the Dandy Lion.

Suddenly she froze.

"Dominic!" she exclaimed. "The TT Security man? He's the real flesh and blood you!"

"He's not me, he's Bermuda. He's roaming. Now quit stalling! Don't look so surprised, Zeta. You knew I had a plan."

Zeta was even more distressed. Quickening her pace, she walked at Dominic's side. "Dominic, I thought that when a person roamed they projected their own ghostly image. Otherwise, they had a psychic gift and mirrored - appearing solid, like you. How can Bermuda-?"

"Bermuda is covering his own true spectral image with a secondary projection," Dominic replied, without turning his head away from the Hanger. "The blue mushroom I planted is doing all the work."

Continuing walking forward, they drew level with his counterfeit twin.

"Halt!" the Security man ordered gruffly, with the voice of Bermuda. Opening his gun holster, he withdrew a small pouch. This he handed to Dominic. "You won't be going anywhere without these," he said.

"At least the Security guy doesn't have Dominic's voice as well as his face," thought Zeta with relief. "I would hate to have such an uncertain friendship, wondering all the time whether I was talking to the real Dominic, or to an *impostor*!"

"Everything I need is here?" asked Dominic brusquely, closing his fist around the pouch.

"They're my best tools, Tau. So don't leave them behind," responded Bermuda. "And Tau? The Professor's liberation - were your suspicions correct?"

"Yes," replied Dominic gruffly.

Bermuda grasped his friend's shoulder and nodded courteously to Zeta. Then he waved them both forward, through the wide Hanger door into the recess of the dim aircraft bay.

Blinking as darkness quickly enveloped them, they listened to the light tapping of their footsteps on the red cement floor. Silently walking forward through the centre aisle - alongside rows of recently designed airships, aeroplanes and compact Spacecraft - they gazed about them.

"Some of these ships are amazing," remarked Zeta, her voice more relaxed and her heartbeat slowing.

"It's no wonder the Chronoguiser came out of this establishment," commented Dominic wryly, glancing with interest at the range of innovative vessels. "They certainly have the cream of Engineers and Designers working for them." Proceeding further into the depths of the Hanger, he kept a vigilant watch for a glimpse of the Dandy Lion.

"Glad you came?" he asked, smiling at Zeta in the semi-darkness.

"Yes," she said - quietly impressed.

Suddenly spotting a blue glow emanating from deep within the Hanger, Dominic ran forward. Then he stopped. Floating silently, tantalizingly, three metres above the ground, the silver Dandy Lion radiated soft blue light beams into the gloomy surrounds.

"Your blood made this!" he called, glancing back at Zeta.

Running towards the craft, he then bounded up the boarding steps and disappeared inside the Dandy Lion.

Zeta scooped To-do up in her arms and slowly followed. "There's no turning back now, To-do," she said resolutely. "We're going into the unknown. So I'm warning you, you had better behave, or you won't get any of the dog biscuits I've brought for you."

Taking one last look around her at the array of innovative vessels inside the large Hanger, she took a deep breath. Bravely climbing the boarding steps of the Dandy Lion, she hesitantly entered the silver Sphere.

Once inside, Zeta surveyed the cabin with genuine interest. "I see they finally decided on a plush navy fabric for the seats and a matt padded beige for the interior walls," she thought approvingly.

Glancing at Dominic, she saw that he sat in the passenger's seat, keying information into the onboard computer.

"I'm sorry to see they left the floor as ugly steel grating," she continued in thought. "I don't like the safety belts either - thick ugly black nylon. Dad said the Chronoguiser is a slightly rough ride, especially over long distances. Perhaps the belts are necessary."

"Zeta?" Dominic asked abruptly. Finished imputing flight data into the computer, he stooped his head as he moved into the centre of the Sphere. "I need to stow your belongings and get you strapped in."

Pulling her rucksack from her shoulders, he opened a concealed under-floor storage compartment and threw the sack and her boots inside.

"Go on, throw your dog in," he prompted.

"You can't put To-do in the floor as well?"

"Have to, Zeta, and no arguments. If you keep him out here and lose a grip on him when the time-machine function activates, he'll be thrown against the cabin walls by the pressure of opposing gravity vectors. The hull of this vessel is amazingly strong to withstand such pressures. I found out just how strong, when Bermuda and I tried to build such a machine. All my inheritance money has gone into moulding the hulls of *my* Chronoguisers."

Zeta looked down unhappily into the under-floor recess. Then she glanced at the gravity drive, the onboard computer, the Flight Controls and finally at the padded beige walls of the Dandy Lion. She placed To-do in the compartment. Dominic closed and fastened the lid.

"Get into the front passenger seat, Zeta, and I'll strap you in," he instructed, gently pushing her into that chair. Fitting the safety harness securely over her shoulders, he fastened it in the centre of her chest. Swiftly he secured the lower safety belts around her ankles. "With your permission?" he asked. Removing the scarf concealing her Roaming-Ring, he finally fastened a thin, soft band around her head.

"I feel like you're strapping me into an electric chair," she remarked. Glancing casually at the onboard computer before her, she saw the destination date. Then she gasped.

"What were you doing with the onboard computer when I came into the Dandy Lion, Dominic?"

"I input the co-ordinates of Satellite25 and the time we wish to arrive - which I gather you have just seen. I also double-checked the Star charts, to ensure the astronomical co-ordinates of the Galaxy are accurate, for the period we wish our craft to enter. They have to be precise or we'd end up somewhere we don't want to be. "

"How clever are you, Dominic?"

He smiled. "I have to alter the Dandy Lion's automatic pilot," he said, ignoring her question. "I will be deactivating TT's remote control ability and replacing it with my own."

"Where is your remote-control?"

"Upstairs, in the Historic House. I'll use it once I wake up."

"What about the homing mechanism?" asked Zeta. "Dad said it can't be disengaged."

"The homing mechanism is incorporated into the automatic pilot," replied Dominic confidently. "Anything can be disengaged with the right tools." He grinned at her. "Now I'm busy. I won't take too long."

Squatting in front of the Flight Control panel, he pulled it out of its housing. Using the delicate tools that Bermuda had provided, he began working on the circuits of the automatic pilot.

Zeta watched him for a short while. She let her eyes roam over the simple instrument panel on the dashboard of the Chronoguiser. She looked out of the viewing window into the dark Hanger outside. Then she glanced at her timeband.

Resting her head back against the plush navy fabric of her chair, she closed her eyes. "Dominic will be done soon," she thought. "It's gone past 7.12pm and he said we'd be leaving at a quarter past the hour. I wonder what will happen after we're gone? Nobody will realize until a few hours from now, that I've actually disappeared. Then they'll start looking for me. They'll assume incorrectly that I left Dominic, when they see his twin, working a second shift outside. They'll probably search the forest. Dad will worry. Perhaps if I roam to dad right now and explain." She felt warm and sleepy and her mind began to drift into a secure stable slumber. "It would be so easy to fall asleep," she thought calmly. Suddenly, however, she jumped - startled by an angry, threatening voice.

"It's very handy having a double, isn't it Dominic?" said Eddie, unexpectedly jumping into the cabin of the Dandy Lion. "I thought you were a bit too smooth for a Security man," he continued in an antagonistic tone of voice, from where he stood to the right of the hatch, behind Zeta's seat. "I had you pegged from the moment I saw you. He's one of those toffy nosed University types, I thought. More like the boss's son than the boss's lackey. Now, where are the two Security men who are supposed to be on duty? What have you done with them?"

Dominic moved forward. Stepping between the two front seats, he brushed Zeta's shoulder as he passed. With his back close to the pilot's chair, he cautiously faced Eddie. "I haven't touched them," he replied truthfully. "They went home early."

Eddie's eyes narrowed. After glancing nervously at the hatch opening and the boarding steps beneath, he looked searchingly through the viewing window. Then he noticed the displayed co-ordinates on the onboard computer, and the Flight Control panel - out of its housing. Using a standard electronic wristband he wore, he pointed his hand at the computer, deleting those co-ordinates. Then he stared at Dominic coldly. When he spoke, his voice was gruff.

"Your twin brother waiting outside fed me some piffle, when I asked him to explain why the robots were deactivated, and why he was the only one on duty," Eddie said coldly. "You're expecting him to appear through that hatch any minute now, aren't you? To help you out? That's why you're so cool. Am I right?"

Dominic stared at Eddie guardedly, but did not reply.

Eddie removed a slim remote-control from his shirt pocket and held it up gloatingly for Dominic to see. "Do you know what this is, Dominic?" he said, swivelling the device in his hand. "This is a *big* sign that says you are wasting your time trying to steal this vessel. I've already reactivated the six robots surrounding this Hanger. I've programmed them to enter in five minutes time, to assist with your capture. If you give me any trouble, I'll ask them to shake hands with you. So, you might as well give up now. Trundle down the boarding steps, like a good fellow."

Zeta was watching Dominic. "Dominic, please do as Eddie asks! It's too late. We're in trouble. Plus I can't bear the thought of those robots coming anywhere near me!"

"I see the glib cad has involved you in his plans, Zeta," said Eddie, glancing quickly towards the back of her seat.

Suddenly a loud thud resonated throughout the cabin of the Dandy Lion. The remote-control, previously held in Eddie's hand, was knocked roughly from his grasp. Flying up in the air and bouncing off the cabin ceiling, it tumbled down.

Simultaneously Dominic rushed aft. Briefly losing sight of him, Zeta strained against her Safety harness, but the stern of the vessel was beyond her range of vision. Pushing against the harness and leaning forward, she eventually saw him.

Determined and cool, he had Eddie pinned roughly against the fastened rear seats. Out of the corner of her eye, Zeta also saw another figure, standing close behind her seat, in the compact silver Sphere.

"Your brother isn't half as much of a pansy as you are!" growled Eddie, speaking to Dominic. Then he glowered menacingly at Dominic's impostor. "I was watching the hatch the whole time. Where in the hell did you come from?" he asked Bermuda.

Bermuda glanced at Eddie's nametag. Establishing eye contact with the captive youth, he stared at him fixedly, in the same hypnotic fashion as he had previously stared at the two Security men.

"I just floated up the boarding steps, Eddie, as an invisible Roamer, he replied quickly and rhythmically in a nonchalant, friendly manner. "So of course, you didn't see me. As is proven by the rather awkward predicament you are in right now. You've probably roamed invisible yourself - so you are familiar with the concept. However, those ancient Roaming-Rings available to you now, are outdated and outlawed where I come from. We are always required to show some good form. Therefore, I was rather rude! Very naughty of me, I confess, to be invisible and catch you off guard. I'm just one of those undesirable spectres that thwart the lives of many - or so my enemies believe. But I'd rather have *you* as a friend, Eddie. You'd make a fine member of our team. You're just what we need. Possessing such an intransigent brain, you are a useful commodity. Anyways, I caught you out by being wicked, Eddie. I am *so sorry*."

Struggling violently under Dominic's grip, Eddie growled, "Sure you are, you sarcastic smart mouthed-"

"Mind your manners. We have a lady present," Bermuda reminded him. "Now, I am truly sorry, Eddie, and I have a second apology to make to you. I deeply regret hitting you just now. It was ill mannered of me I admit, but unfortunately necessary under these circumstances. Being able to throw an opponent against the stern of the Dandy Lion is just another little bonus of the delightful blue mushroom that I carry in my hand. Bear in mind, Eddie, it's a very tiring exercise. I believe I could only repeat it three or four times without feeling a tad tired."

"You're very amusing - to a crone!" retorted Eddie acidly.

"Do you realize," continued Bermuda, "that you were actually hit by psychic energy, not muscle and bone?"

"Shut your stupid face!" growled Eddie, trying his best to break free from Dominic's vicelike hold. He pushed against the stern wall of the Dandy Lion's cabin with his shoulders and he braced his feet against the steel grating, trying to pull free.

"Bermuda?" scowled Dominic impatiently. "We're running out of time! Five minutes remember!"

Bermuda broke eye contact with Eddie. Replying to Dominic his voice was sober. "I'm sorry Tau. As you can see, Eddie has amazing will power. Dogmatic is his middle name. I couldn't distract him when we were outside. Neither could I convince him of anything. I had to let him just stroll into the Hanger, and into the Dandy Lion."

Eddie looked from one adversary to the other and his expression grew dark.

"My mistake," declared Dominic. "I thought I had accounted for all the Security men. Eddie was supposed to go off duty at 7pm."

"Well you got your accounting wrong, you sop," interrupted Eddie. "I was waiting at the North-East gate to let the zeppelin passengers out. You and Zeta weren't with them. After I locked up, I came looking for you both."

"And you found them, clever you!" taunted Bermuda sarcastically, taking a step towards Eddie in the crowded cabin.

Eddie glared at Bermuda hatefully and began to utter an oath.

"Now gentlemen, we have more pressing matters to attend to, so you will have to continue your little tête-à-tête some other time," interrupted Dominic, glancing searchingly over the vessel's steel floor. "Bermuda, can you see where the robot's remote-control landed?"

"I've got it!" piped up Zeta, who had been listening attentively the entire time. "It fell into my lap."

Still strapped tightly into her chair she held it up between the seats for Dominic to see.

"Thank you Zeta, you splendid girl," said Bermuda, moving towards her seat and plucking the device from her grasp.

"It's no use to you," growled Eddie, staring fiercely from Dominic to Bermuda and back again. "Your five minutes is up! The six robots will be on to you - any second now. Have you seen their serrated arms. Before you know it, they will be tearing you limb from limb."

"How melodramatic," replied Bermuda sarcastically, glancing happily at the gravity drive mounted on the curved ceiling. "I doubt very much if they will all fit into this cosy little cabin, Eddie. Now, tell me your security clearance code. I want the registration number of each robot and the deactivation sequence."

"Drop dead," snarled Eddie.

"Dominic?" Zeta called out in a frightened voice, whilst staring out of the viewing window. "The robots have just entered the Hanger and are moving along the centre aisle towards us."

"You can manage without him, Bermuda," growled Dominic, tightening his hold on Eddie.

"Since you remain obstinate, Eddie," said Bermuda casually. Quickly he attached the little blue mushroom he held in his hand onto the display panel of the remote-control device. "I'm just looking up your previous data input, Eddie," he explained. "Here we go. Five minutes fifteen seconds ago, you keyed in six registration numbers, your security code and the reactivation sequence." The tips of Bermuda's fingers tapped rapidly onto the small keys. "A little bit of this and a little bit of that, combined to make... no problems! All done!"

Zeta, staring out of the viewing window, saw the six robots suddenly freeze. "They're turned off," she said, her voice relieved.

Dominic looked towards his comrade and smiled. "I want you back at your post, Bermuda," he said calmly. "Any further absence from your station will arouse suspicion. But before you go, push the Flight Control panel back into its housing, will you?"

In the blink of an eye, Bermuda had moved in between the front seats, done the job and was standing near the open hatch, ready to leave. Solemnly he looked from Dominic's face to the belligerent angry face of Eddie, still pinned against the stern wall.

"I can handle him," assured Dominic. "And I'm a lamb in company, remember. Thanks for the tools. Now go!"

Bermuda quickly retreated through the hatch of the Dandy Lion and ran down the boarding steps. Jogging through the large aircraft hanger, he reactivated the robots with the remote-control. After watching them march back to their original stations outside, he returned to his own post outside the Hanger entrance.

Back in the cabin of the Dandy Lion, Eddie continued his struggle to break free. The beige cabin walls of the compact Sphere closed him in, the steel grating felt hard under his feet and the navy rear seats dug into his back. Looking up at the gravity drive, he thought of the enormous value of the Dandy Lion. Then he glanced at the Flight Control panel now back in its housing.

"Once I'm free, I'm going to smash your head like a piñata," he threatened Dominic.

"We can continue this discussion later, in private," replied Dominic coldly. "But for now, I'd like to talk to Zeta."

"Zeta, are you all right?" he asked hoarsely.

"I'm alright," she replied. Still strapped into her Safety harness, she peered around the edge of her chair at Dominic. "What are we going to do now? What are you going to do about Eddie?"

"Eddie is going to make an unwilling time jump into the future," replied Dominic coolly.

Following that remark, Eddie renewed his efforts to break free. "That's right, talk about me like I'm not here," he grizzled.

"We can't bring Eddie with us. It's wrong," Zeta said anxiously.

"At least there's someone in here with a conscience," remarked Eddie.

"I have no choice, Zeta," said Dominic. "Eddie's not going to keep quiet and I'm not having him tell the whole world we commandeered the Dandy Lion."

Zeta was troubled, and her eyes widened.

"Is that your fancy word for stealing, Dominic?" remarked Eddie gratingly. "You're not going to get away with this."

Dominic tightened his grip on Eddie but otherwise chose to ignore him. Glancing in between the front seats, towards the dashboard of the Dandy Lion, he spoke earnestly to Zeta.

"Zeta, I want you to fly the Dandy Lion to Satellite25. Will you do that for me?"

"Don't do anything for him!" shouted Eddie.

"I decided to help him when he saved my dad," thought Zeta. "And I promised. Yes," she replied softly. "What do I do?"

"Input our destination co-ordinates back into the computer, for starters."

After glancing at a piece of paper retrieved from her pocket, Zeta quickly completed that task.

"What next?"

"Set the automatic pilot and the Flight Controls in front of the pilot's seat. Stretch forward as far as you can. No, don't undo your Safety harness! Don't even think about it, you'll give me a heart attack! Just stretch."

Zeta pulled forward against the strap on her head and those around her shoulders. She stretched out her right arm until her hand touched the Flight Control panel.

"What now?"

"There are two levers on the right hand side of the panel - a black one and a white one. Push them both down."

"Don't do it, Zeta!" called out Eddie.

After pushing the levers, Zeta heard a light clunking noise of gears and hydraulic arms. The boarding steps immediately withdrew into the vessel and the hatch closed. Overhead, the three arms of the gravity drive stretched down and locked into position. The drive hummed expectantly in the centre of the craft. Instantly flooded with hundreds of blue light beams that all emitted from the apex of the drive, the cabin was filled with soft, strange, lulling music.

"The journey into Outer Space will take approximately two minutes, Zeta," Dominic continued in a cool calming voice. "The journey through time will take thirty seconds."

"Thirty seconds!" exclaimed Eddie gruffly. "Are you mad? The Dandy Lion travels one thousand years every-"

"I don't enjoy being interrupted," cut in Dominic. Glancing at Eddie, he jabbed him discreetly in the ribs. "So keep your little calculations to yourself, please?" Turning back to face Zeta, Dominic quickly continued his instructions. "Look at the Flight Control panel again, Zeta. There is a column of six switches on the far left, closest to you. Those switches set the functions we require. I want you to flick indigo, violet, red, orange and yellow, in that order."

He paused and waited for her to flick the switches. When she did, a small circle of matching coloured light illuminated underneath each one.

"That's good. Now that you've set the functions, you need to activate them. Focus on the next column in the centre of the panel. Those buttons activate the functions you have just set. I want you to press indigo, violet-"

"You're not going to steal the Dandy Lion!" Eddie raucously interrupted. Then he began to struggle with all his might.

Distracted from Zeta, Dominic now put an immense effort into keeping his prisoner still.

"You've asked for a beating and now you're going to get one!" Eddie growled.

Lurching forward, and with a massive heave of his shoulders, Eddie suddenly wrestled free. He came at Dominic violently. Punching him in the face, he hurled him against the pilot's chair. Hearing the thud and turning away, Zeta listened unhappily to the noises of the fight.

"Fight back!" shouted Eddie angrily, above the melodious waves from the gravity drive.

"Just listen to me for a minute?" retorted Dominic, also shouting but his voice calm. "I don't want to fight you, Eddie. I'm not stealing this ship. Believe me. I'm going to return it as soon as I replic-"

"Shut up!" shouted Eddie. "I'm not your granny who you can feed with codswallop!"

"I can't cope with any of this," Zeta thought nonplussed, as the dull hollow thuds of the youths' fighting continued. Trying to focus her thoughts, she stared at the Flight Control panel. "The buttons activate the functions. Which buttons am I supposed to press? Everything's colour coded. That's the solution! I flicked violet, indigo, red, orange and yellow on the function switches. So all I have to do is press the same colours in the centre column to activate those functions! And then we're away!"

Zeta stretched her right arm forward and in sequence, she pressed the five buttons. Each illuminated with bright colour. "The indigo is the prettiest," Zeta decided. "That's the invisibility button."

Abruptly the Dandy Lion began to move, rising slowly at first. Zeta watched through the viewing window as the other ships in the Hanger seemed to sink quickly from view, noting with interest that her own ship threw no reflection off the shiny hulls of the other vessels. She saw light flood into the cool Hanger as the domed-roof above, automatically opened. Seconds later, she gazed out at the beautiful blue sky as the invisible Dandy Lion - quickly clearing the building - ascended into the stratosphere.

Fully alert, Zeta's eyes fixed on the viewing window in front of her. Behind her seat, the shuffling, the thwacking and thumping, the hollow thuds, and the bumping of the back of her chair continued. All this fighting kafuffle was intermingled with the mellow music of the gravity drive.

The Dandy Lion climbed higher through the Earth's upper atmosphere, speedily moving towards the vacuum of Space. She felt a quick uncomfortable pressure on her body. Promptly breaking free of the Earth's gravitational field, the Sphere shot out quickly into the black, eerie void. Zeta looked out in awe at the enthralling regions of Space - a charcoal vista speckled with twinkling stars.

"Oh, rats!" exclaimed the bitter voice of Eddie. Stopped dead centre to the viewing window - in front of the gravity drive - he gazed transfixed at his home planet, Earth.

"Good. They've stopped fighting," surmised Zeta, quickly glancing at Eddie.

Looking back through the viewing window, entranced, she fell into euphoric thought. "I haven't been in the Spacebus for two years, not since I went to the Satellite Gardens," she reflected. "I had forgotten what it was like to see everything from an entirely different perspective. Looking up to the heavens at night from the Earth, I thought of the stars in the Milky Way Galaxy as a collection of countless twinkling lights, dotted higgledy-piggledy over a huge black canvas - a speckled painting of a realm beyond my reach.

Now, all of a sudden, I'm part of that realm. I see before me coloured marbled globes of different sizes - suspended in the blackness - illuminated by the Sun. Beyond them, the small, glowing white globes of distant stars are surprisingly tangible." Spotting a vessel in orbit she stared out excitedly. "Hey, I can see a satellite coming into view! It must be the new one - the Robotic Theme Park - because I've seen the other two satellites and it's not either of *them*. I remember the Satellite Aquarium and Satellite Gardens as remarkable achievements. A collection of robots may be even better!" The viewing window began to close before Zeta's eyes and a large silver panel quickly took its place. "A few seconds and the show's all over," she thought regretfully. "Just when I was enjoying myself."

Startled from her reverie, she heard Dominic's urgent voice.

"Eddie! Don't just stand there day-dreaming!" he yelled harshly. "The Dandy Lion is about to travel through time! Hold fast! Hang on to something!"

Awoken from his trance by Dominic's commanding tone, Eddie instinctively obeyed. He gripped the back of Zeta's chair and braced his feet securely against the struts on the floor.

Suddenly, all in the Dandy Lion's cabin were bathed with intense blue light and their ears were awash with thousands of musical notes.

"I'm listening to the music of the Universe," thought Zeta, lulled by the enchanting complex sound. "Dominic told me that the time jump would take thirty seconds, so it's probably a good idea if I start counting. Then I'll know when we've arrived at our future destination." She started to count to herself, backwards from thirty. "Thirty, twenty-nine, twenty-eight, twenty-seven..." She felt the Dandy Lion increase speed. Then she gripped the sides of her chair as the vessel began to rock violently in all directions. Tilting from side to side, it bucked back and forth erratically.

Behind her - holding fast onto the back of her seat - Eddie had already lost his foothold. Wrenching at her chair he was thrown chaotically from side to side. The muscles in his forearms strained from his efforts. Placing his feet slightly apart, he tried to retain an upright position, while determined to hang on, his young face set stubbornly.

Briefly glancing towards the stern of their vessel, Eddie suddenly and unexpectedly began to grin. Watching with cruel interest, he was astonished to see Dominic's mirror image - strapped into a seat at the rear - begin to glimmer, then fade. Eddie blinked, not believing his eyes.

"Dominic's been roaming all this while," he concluded astutely. "But in a solid state! Roaming into a fast moving time-machine must be a little difficult, I gather." Then he gaped in amazement and smiled, as his foe suddenly and swiftly - before his widened eyes - vanished.

"I'll buy one of these beauties myself," Eddie thought happily, beginning to enjoy the violent chaotic pitching of their vessel. "If that's what it takes to get rid of that well-spoken aristocrat. Who would have thought that all this time he was roaming. I'll be darned!"

Eddie was not long pleased though. Losing his grip on Zeta's chair that same instant - due to the jerky wild bucking - he was hurtled behind the ship's drive. Swiftly seized by the gravity vectors, he was dashed against the stern. As he felt a blow to the back of his head, the intense blue light of the Dandy Lion's cabin faded from his eyes. Knocked unconscious by the impact, he remained pinned in an ungainly fashion against the Dandy Lion's back wall.

Zeta, having heard the thud at the rear of the Dandy Lion's cabin, followed by a groan, was still counting, "nineteen, eighteen, seventeen..."

Unexpectedly she felt herself in pain. Her ankles throbbed and she felt a tight aching band across her chest and shoulders. "A giant hand is trying to pull me mercilessly from my seat!" she thought, beginning to panic. "My legs are being pulled out of their sockets, and my head is being wrenched off my neck!"

Enveloping her, the cabin was filled with thousands of shafts of blue light, all emitting from the gravity drive and all creating a conglomeration of directional forces within the amazing Sphere. Forces which tugged at her body, cruelly and relentlessly, from all possible directions, and gave her pain. Forces that dragged at the ship and pulled it through time, to the point of equilibrium required by the craft's Star charts.

Continuing to play, the orchestra of planets from which this power source emitted, created a cacophony of sound that bathed Zeta and Eddie within a deity of glowing azure waves. Waves that filled the craft with the voice of the galaxy.

"Ten, nine, eight... Where is Dominic?" Zeta thought suddenly. "I'm sure he's not in the Dandy Lion anymore. He was in the rear of the vessel, but now he's gone. I'm scared. Dominic!"

Emitted from her Roaming-Ring - projected a metre above her head - a thin, silvery ring of translucent light suddenly appeared. Simultaneously, Dominic's mirror image materialized into the pilot's seat beside her.

Watching him activate the manual pilot console - housed above the Flight Controls - she saw him terminate four of the flight functions, leaving only the orange. Then she watched him type swiftly into the onboard computer. "I wonder what he's doing?" she thought. "I believe I've asked him this already, but have I? I'm not sure?"

Beginning to drift out of consciousness, she closed her eyes and counted against the pain. "It will be over soon," she thought hopefully. "If I can *just* hang on for a few more seconds. Four, three, two..." She grimaced. She heard herself faintly cry out. "I'm in the Dandy Lion," she remembered, "and I'm in Outer Space." Then she realized thankfully, "The rocking of the ship has stopped, in fact, the whole ship has stopped! We must have landed. But oh! The pain is still there!" She sighed. "I feel so tired. I can't even open my eyes."

Dreamily she fell sideways, curled up in her blue velvet seat, which, to Zeta's sleepy mind, had magically reclined. Enveloping her body, she thought she saw purple mist caressing her with frosty, light tentacles - chilling her instantly and making her shudder. Wincing as a stinging band of cold wrapped around her ankles she felt that same band of cold tap curiously against her shoulders.

Suddenly all her pain was gone. Warming rapidly against a light fabric that benevolently drifted over her, like a soothing weightless balm, her body relaxed. A warm hand rested softly on her cheek and pressed tentatively against the side of her neck. Singing cheerfully to her tired ears, she heard the happy yapping of To-do. Left to rest by Dominic, Zeta fell into an innate chasm of peaceful slumber.

Chapter eight

Marbled blue and grey, covered in wispy white clouds and tilted on its axis, the planet Earth zoomed through Space. Vast and black, the Space vacuum, twinkling with stars, did nothing to impede its progress, while the turbulent Sun, shining forth, lit the face of this habitable globe with benign stellar rays.

Orbiting the Earth - the moon, Space telescopes, and a variety of man-made satellites - also hastened forth, but on much shorter journeys. Especially so did Satelliet25, the venue for tonight's Satellite Cup.

Spinning gracefully, the two colossal grey tubular wheels of Satellite25 revolved without sound, without friction, in the daunting black void. Joined together by a hollow axle that served as a multi-tiered Spaceport, the revolving wheels - banded by hundreds of illuminated portholes - stared unblinkingly out into the mysterious Cosmos.

Crowned by a large gold and red neon sign - mounted atop the vertical extended hub - this monstrous satellite shouted out visually, *'Welcome! Robotic Theme Park! Open 24 hours a day!'* A further two illuminated billboards, one on each of the rotating wheels, blazoned out in gold and blue with the words, *'Science Level One'* and *'Fun Fair Level Two'*. Completing the picture, thousands of brightly coloured decorative disks attached to the double-wheeled satellite, caused the vessel to sparkle attractively.

Thus, Satellite25 shone welcome like a happy beacon to all of its eager visitors - except for one. She had slept during her vessels approach and landing to this popular Theme Park. Now just awakening within a secret landing-bay - on the highest deck of the multi-tiered Spaceport - she opened her eyes.

Surprised to see Eddie in Dominic's seat in the stationary Dandy Lion, Zeta, previously asleep, sat bolt upright. The cream blanket covering her slipped down onto the floor. Automatically, her chair returned to its upright position. Chilling, the cabin air pressed in around her. Glancing down at her summer clothes, her eyes rested fearfully on her purple shoulders and ankles.

"What's happened to my skin!" she gasped.

"Don't worry, it's first aid treatment powder," remarked Eddie, his expression dark. Turning his head, he showed her the large red swelling on the back of his skull - recently sprayed over with a purple film.

"I hit my head on the stern during the time jump," he explained. "That thirty seconds of time travel really packed a wallop, even with padded walls."

When he turned back to face her, she was blushing with embarrassment.

"The purple stuff is a cooling analgesic, Zeta," he added. "So I expect you won't find any bruising when you brush it off."

Zeta touched her shoulder. The fine purple dust fell quickly away onto the cabin floor, revealing clear undamaged skin.

"All that pain, and I'm not injured," she thought to herself. "It slipped my mind that the icy mist was purple." Kneeling up in her chair, she looked to the stern, hoping to see Dominic. Sitting back down, disappointed, she reached for the blanket and wrapped it around her. "Eddie?" she asked. "What are you doing in the pilot's seat?"

"Nothing," he replied. "I want to do something, but I can't. If I could fly the Dandy Lion back to the TT Research Facility, I'd be the hero. However, as you can see, by a quick look around you - that is impossible. The gravity drive has returned to its position locked onto the ceiling and the dashboard lamps are all out, except for... one." He paused, stared at her and continued slowly. "The *one* functioning lamp indicates that this vessel is on *remote pilot*, Zeta. Does that mean anything to you? Do the words ring any alarm bells in your pure, sweet mind?" Suddenly he thumped the Flight Control panel with his fist in a deliberate attempt to frighten her. Then he glanced furtively at her uneasy expression. "The controls are *completely dead,* Zeta!" he shouted. "The onboard computer has been shutdown and I can't even get the hatch to open!"

Zeta stared at him, then watched him scan the bottom edge of the dashboard searchingly, looking for any controls that he might have accidentally missed in his previous perusal.

"There will be a manual override somewhere," he muttered crossly to himself. "All I have to do is find it."

"Don't even try to open the hatch before we know what's outside," cautioned Zeta. "It's too dangerous. We could be floating in Space!" She paused. "You could open the viewing window. That would be smarter." Glancing at Eddie's face, she frowned. "I don't know why you are in such a strop, Eddie. We are going to return the Dandy Lion soon. Dominic is only borrowing it from his gre-"

"What sort of a nincompoop do you think I am?" Eddie's voice boomed out angrily within the Dandy Lion's small cabin.

"I don't know. How many sorts are there?"

"Don't even think about talking back to me," Eddie growled. "I won't put up with any defiance. Next time you might do your homework before opening your mouth. We are obviously in a landing-bay at the Robotic Theme Park, sitting under an Air-conditioning System! Why else do you think your pretty, blonde friend covered you up with a blanket. I noticed we were close to the Park just before the time jump. I'm certain that's where we are. Dominic didn't have enough time to take us anywhere else."

"Time?" she whispered questioningly to herself, not intending him to hear.

Eddie however did hear her, and he responded brusquely but in a quieter, cooler voice. "I regained consciousness a couple of minutes after the time jump, Zeta, and the Dandy Lion's power had already been shut down. For simplicities sake, the Navigational System of this Chronoguiser has been based on the Earth's position in the Milky Way Galaxy, on any given day and year. Time jumps land us in the same location, following the same 24hour clock."

"Oh. I didn't know," apologized Zeta, deciding it would be better for her to avoid any further discussion. "I never meant to imply that you weren't capable."

"Who's got the remote-control of the Dandy Lion, Zeta? Eddie asked, resting his left hand on the edge of her seat and leaning towards her. "Have you got it?"

"No," she replied softly. She looked down at the folds of blanket in her lap. "Dominic has the remote-control of this ship. It's not in this cabin. And I'd rather not talk for a while, please."

"We'll try another tack, Zeta," he continued, ignoring her request for silence. "Maybe if I approach this problem from a different angle, you will help *me*. Do you know where Dominic put the tools that I saw him using?"

As Zeta shook her head, To-do, quiet until now in the under-floor compartment, began to scratch irritatingly at the metal grating over his head.

"I should let To-do out, Eddie," Zeta said. "He's been in there…" She glanced at her timeband. "For half an hour now."

"Leave the dog where he is!" Eddie growled, piqued at the obvious planned diversion from his questioning. "Now then," he continued in a gentler quiet voice. "If you won't help me, perhaps you could explain to me why you helped Dominic steal the Dandy Lion?"

Zeta turned to face him. She looked from his Adam's apple and his strong chin, to his high cheekbones, his large ears and his wavy brown hair. She even noticed the small scar above one of his eyebrows. In fact she managed to look everywhere on his face except for his eyes. These deep-green absorbing orbs she avoided. When she spoke, her voice was earnest.

"When my dad was kidnapped, Eddie," she explained, "everyone except for Dominic gave him up for dead, turned on him, or pretended they were helping when they were doing the opposite." At the memory of her father's abduction, her dreamy grey eyes misted. She brushed her hand across her face.

Eddie regarded her sternly. "And?" he prompted.

"Dominic saved my dad!" Zeta blurted out emotionally. "That's why I'm helping him!"

"I see," said Eddie sceptically. "How come I was on duty until after 7pm and I didn't hear any reports about your dad being rescued?"

"Dad sent me a message on my palmdisk at 6.22pm this evening, to say he was free. I can show you if you like."

"I'd rather not see the phoney message, Zeta."

"It's not a bogus message!"

Eddie shook his head incredulously. "Zeta, you are so *gullible*. That message could have been from anyone."

"No, the communication was from my dad," she insisted stubbornly.

"Oh yes?"

"I roamed to my dad's location so they could free him," she said quietly.

"They?" asked Eddie curiously, glancing behind him at the closed hatch.

"Dominic has friends who help him."

Eddie frowned. "Look," he suggested. "Why don't you make use of that expensive piece of equipment around your head and roam to your father right now? If your pal, Dominic, did in fact save your Pop, Professor Doherty will be at home in your apartment in Queens Gate with his feet up, sipping an aperitif and enjoying hors d'oeuvres. Go and see him. Prove me wrong?"

"OK, I will," she responded, accepting the challenge confidently. "I'll roam this instant!"

Settling back in her seat, she put her hand to her forehead, activated her Roaming-Ring and closed her eyes. As the quartz crystals began to glow, she quickly fell asleep.

Shifting sideways in his chair, Eddie let his eyes wander over all the expensive equipment in the Dandy Lion. He looked at the defunct controls in front of his pilot's seat and he glanced sadly up at the silent gravity drive. A few moments later, he saw Zeta's grey eyes open.

"I couldn't roam to my dad," she cried. "I just went to sleep and I didn't go anywhere. I tried to get to Queens Gate where I thought my father would be - but nothing happened."

"So your Pop wasn't rescued," remarked Eddie coldly.

Zeta only shook her head stubbornly. "I believe everything Dominic told me. Dad is safe. I'm just not practised at using my Roaming-Ring. That must be the reason why the roaming didn't work."

Eddie gritted his teeth, hating himself for what he was about to say. "You believe Dominic just like you believe your dad," he stated slowly and acidly.

Zeta held her arms around her knees and huddled under her blanket. The cabin of the Dandy Lion had become much colder and the bright interior lights shone harshly over her anxious face. "What are you talking about now, Eddie?" she scolded. "Why don't you just go away? Sit back properly in the pilot's seat and stop leaning over me!"

"Sorry, I can't oblige and I have news for you, Zeta. Your dad lied to you when he told you that your mum went missing."

"You don't know anything Eddie. Mum went missing five years ago. You weren't even around then. Just be quiet, will you?"

Zeta edged to the left of her chair. Turning her face away from Eddie, she pretended to be interested in the equipment lining the cabin walls.

"Ah, but I do know everything, Zeta. I know what happened to your mum. The TT Research Facility operate a 24hour Surveillance System and they archive the surveillance recordings for *ten* years. Your mother went missing while she was visiting the Facility and the whole scenario is recorded on film, *seen by me*!"

Zeta turned back to face him.

"You *are* going to help me, Zeta," he continued, leaning further towards her. "I want you to get the remote-control for the Dandy Lion from Dominic, whenever the opportunity presents itself. Once I have that, I can fly this craft home. When we are back at the Research Facility I will show you what is on the surveillance tape, so you will know what happened to your mother. I won't get you into trouble. I won't even mention you helped *commandeer* the Dandy Lion for your friend. We can keep that a secret between ourselves. Well?"

When she failed to respond, Eddie grabbed her arm.

"Come on, make up your mind, Zeta. Do you want to see the tape or not?"

"Let go of me!" she exclaimed indignantly, pulling away from his grip. "Dominic will be here soon and you can discuss your grievances with him."

"You're incredible," Eddie said coldly. Seeing her upset, he moved back into his seat.

After sitting in silence for some minutes, they both suddenly heard a loud click, followed by an audible faint hum. The onboard computer illuminated, accompanied by the sound of a tinkling bell. On the Flight Control panel, the black lever moved automatically to the up position.

Spurned into action by the obvious return of power to the ship, Eddie tried to activate the manual pilot, housed neatly above the Flight Control panel. To his paramount displeasure, however, he heard the familiar clunking sound of gears and hydraulics activating. The hatch quickly opened. The boarding steps slid down. Outside, below the Dandy Lion, he heard someone call his name.

Glancing at Zeta, he jumped from the pilot's chair. Motioning with his head for her to follow him, he made quickly for the open hatch. After a hasty glimpse downward, he jumped through the opening.

Alone, Zeta sighed and settled back in her chair. Even though the cabin was warmer due to the power restoration, she pulled the blanket close around her.

"My mum disappeared at the TT Research Facility five years ago," she thought pensively. "Dad should have told me the truth back then." Stretching out her fingers, she observed that her hands were shaking. "I really need to talk to Dominic about the surveillance tape. I have to see it."

Bending her head forward, she covered her face with her hands. The beige walls of the Dandy Lion's cabin curved around her. The illuminated equipment on the dashboard blinked at her warmly. She heard the soft murmuring of several voices coming from outside.

"That boy who ran out of here made you cry, didn't he?" asked a sympathetic voice, suddenly quite close.

Zeta uncovered her face and looked up. A girl of her age - with oriental features, waist length hair and a thin Roaming-Ring - stood in front of the pilot's seat. The girl wore a maroon, ankle length, dome-shaped dress with a blue checked band at the skirt hem.

Surprised to hear the hatch door closing, Zeta rested her head back against her chair.

"Never mind," continued the girl. "He's gone now." Smiling at Zeta, she introduced herself. "My name is Felicity Parsons and I'm very glad to meet you, Zeta. My brother Joseph sent me in here to deliver your gown." She looked at a zipped bag recently draped over the cushioned backrest of the pilot's chair. Then at a smaller holdall on the front of that seat. "Your gown is from Terence Tau. You're not allowed to come out before you've put it on."

"Felicity, could you tell me where we are?" asked Zeta, glancing at the viewing window, still closed. "Also, what does Terence Tau look like?"

"We're on the highest deck of a multi-tiered Spaceport on Satellite25," replied Felicity. Tau has blonde hair, he's serious and he's a mirror."

Zeta couldn't help a little smile.

"Would you like to see your attire?" prompted Felicity. "Because I would."

When Zeta nodded, Felicity quickly unzipped the largest bag and pulled out three items of clothing. Firstly - a wine chemise, threaded with a thin bronze ribbon at the décolleté. Secondly - a full length, dome-shaped wine skirt with a bronze band stitched to the gathered hem. Lastly - a stately open robe made of a matt-brown fine woollen fabric, stitched with the same wide bronze band as the skirt, at the hem and at the sleeve.

"The set is exquisite, Felicity. An elegant light coat with a feminine skirt and blouse underneath."

"Yes, it *is* a rather nice combination. The three items together, function as one complete and beautiful gown. The brown robe will look very stylish with the wine chemise slightly visible and the front panel of the skirt displayed."

"Is that how I'm supposed to wear it?"

"Yes," replied Felicity, passing Zeta the clothes. "There are tiny fastenings on the inside of the coat that attach to the sides of the skirt to keep the outfit in the right shape. The robe is always worn buttoned up from just below the chemise to the hip line."

Admiring the clothes, Zeta discovered a pink tulle petticoat underneath the wine skirt. "What's inside the other bag, Felicity?" she asked. "Open it now."

As Felicity opened the holdall and placed the contents, one by one on the pilot's seat, Zeta looked on with a mild expression of interest. The first article was a timeband similar to the one Felicity wore. The next items were brown slippers, and stockings - the same shade as her robe. Several assorted slides and combs - coloured plum, chestnut and brown - were included in the bag. Plus, an aerosol can of hairspray, a hairbrush and a small mirror.

Felicity smiled. "You'll like the spray, Zeta It's the newest fashion."

The last item Felicity extracted from the bag was a small dog collar and a matching leash.

Zeta beamed.

"You have a pet?" asked Felicity.

"Yes. His name is To-do. He's sleeping in the compartment under the cabin floor. Do you want to see him?"

"Yes, I do. I want a pet but my aunt doesn't like animals. What colour is To-do?"

"Golden," replied Zeta.

Rising, she quickly stepped through the space between the seats. Felicity followed. Promptly she opened the under-floor compartment lid. To-do jumped out happily, straight into her arms.

"Oh, he's a big Clode!" exclaimed Felicity. "You're so lucky to have him. The large ones are much better at blocking bad thought waves than the smaller ones, but they're not as clever."

Zeta crouched on the grating and hugged To-do. "I thought you were special, you little scamp," she said to him. Standing up, she pushed To-do into Felicity's arms. "Here, hold him for a while."

"Sure," replied Felicity. To-do immediately licked Felicity's hand and blinked his eyes.

Grabbing her boots, Zeta pulled her rucksack from the compartment and dropped the lid closed.

After watching Felicity gently pet and fuss over To-do, she solemnly asked, "If you can't roam... to someone you love... it means they are dead. Doesn't it, Felicity?"

"Oh, no!" exclaimed Felicity swiftly. "Lots of times I've tried to roam to Joseph and I couldn't. He wasn't dead. He was just too far away. My home is with my auntie and uncle," she further explained. "Until recently we lived ten thousand miles away from Joseph, on the other side of the world. I couldn't roam to him by myself however hard I tried. I had to get my aunt to roam with me. Hardly anyone can roam such long distances by themselves." Felicity, now thoughtful, absently stroked To-do's golden coat.

"Felicity, is it really hard to roam long distances through time?" Zeta asked, respectfully glancing up at the gravity drive. "Or is it easy?"

"Why Zeta. It's very hard - impossible for most people. They can roam backwards or forwards through time two or three hundred years at most, and they are very happy to do so." Felicity was surprised. "Didn't you know?"

Zeta shook her head.

Felicity put To-do onto the cabin floor and touched Zeta's hand. "Do you want to roam to someone? Would you like me to help you?"

"It's a terribly long way in the past."

"We might get there for a few moments," advised Felicity. "If we do, be ready to say what you have to say quickly, before we disappear and awaken. All we have to do is to sit down, activate our Roaming-Rings, hold hands and close our eyes. Then it's your job, to wish with all your might that you can see your..."

"My father. Should I picture him in my mind's eye? At home, for example? Would that help?"

"No, don't do that Zeta. If he wasn't at your dwelling, you would go nowhere. Just picture his face, if that helps. More important is to concentrate on how you feel about him."

Zeta took a deep breath. She noted the pile of clothes that she had left on her own seat, and the items from the holdall neatly arranged on the pilot's cushion. Then she unfastened the Dandy Lion's rear seats. They both sat down.

"One question before we roam?" asked Felicity. "Joseph has told me that you are *The Zeta* and you have travelled from the past in this time-machine."

"And?" prompted Zeta, surprised to hear herself referred to as *The Zeta*.

"I appreciate that your social customs may be different from ours," Felicity cautiously continued, "and I don't mean to be rude. But, is your father comfortable seeing you in your current state of undress? You're hardly covered, Zeta. He may be of ill humour when he sees you wearing those pauper's clothes. Perhaps it would be better if you wrapped yourself in your blanket. For propriety?"

Zeta was astonished at first. She glanced at her pink pleated skirt and her black vest top covered in daisies. Then she was amused.

"No, it's OK, Felicity, I don't need to cover myself with a blanket. My father is very liberal. And you haven't offended me. I'm just surprised, that's all. Dominic... he didn't..." She smiled, decided not to finish the sentence and lightly thought to herself instead. "Dominic didn't tell me he considered me to be in a state of undress all the time. It never occurred to me that we might have cultural differences."

"Dominic?" asked Felicity.

"Dominic is the name I call Terence Tau," replied Zeta. "But I can tell you about that later. Come on, let's roam to my dad. He will be worried about me because I should have been home at my Auntie Marjorie's by now."

Both girls activated their Roaming-Rings, held hands and closed their eyes. As the quartz crystals began to glow brightly, Zeta thought confidently, "The first night I owned my Ring, I roamed nearly three thousand years forward in time to Dominic. Now I just have to roam the same number of years backwards in time to see dad."

Seated with Felicity in the sealed cabin of the Dandy Lion, she closed her eyes and concentrated on thoughts of her father. She remembered with gratitude his consideration towards her and she thought proudly of his many achievements. But most of all she longed to see his kindly responsible face again. As Professor Doherty's face became clearer and clearer in her mind's eye, his daughter, Zeta, quickly fell into a deep purposeful sleep.

Seconds later she opened her eyes. "Oh!" she gasped excitedly.

Together with Felicity, she now stood inside a spacious garage-shed. The central overhead light shone bright sharp rays through her now translucent roaming image and her ghostly face was aglow with the triumph of a successful journey. Moreover, she had opened her eyes to see - floating directly before her - a gleaming silver Chronoguiser, christened the *Estrella*.

The garage-shed into which she and Felicity had psyche travelled was an extremely large, well-lit structure with tawny brick walls, a grey cement floor and a high corrugated iron roof. Immediately recognising her whereabouts as the interior of her Auntie Marjorie's garage, Zeta looked hastily about for her father.

"So that's why dad has been spending every weekend in Farnborough!" she deduced. "He's has been building his very own Chronoguiser!"

Glancing past the *Estrella* towards the front of the garage-shed and the double, metal access doors, Zeta swiftly detected the presence of a modified robot, similar to the russet security mechinoids used by the TT Research Facility. Operational and curious, its eyes extended on stalks and it stared at the ghostly spectres of the girls. Not programmed to respond to visible psychic energy fields, it remained stationary, guarding the entrance.

Unperturbed by the robot and turning quickly to look behind her, Zeta saw her father, sitting before a long workbench at the rear of the garage-shed. Observing that he wore an old leather jacket, black trousers and boots, she noted his devotion to his task. Tinkering with a gravity drive, he rested his forearms on his bench, while occasionally glancing at a notepad full of complicated mathematical formulae.

"Dad!" she called quietly so as not to startle him. "It's me, Zeta! I'm only here for seconds, maybe, and I'm roaming with Felicity. Don't get a shock when you turn around, but you'll see us both as visible Roamers. Dominic added some extra components to my Roaming-Ring, and the upgrade means that I no longer roam invisible. He is the one who orchestrated your escape, Dad. Don't worry. I'll be safe with him. He took me to the future!"

"I surmised as such," said the Professor. Calmly he swivelled around to face her. "Without a doubt, Zeta, your friend is a young man - *full* of surprises! I see you have a companion. Hello, Felicity."

As Felicity nodded greeting, Professor Doherty noted the two spectres standing before him, Felicity's strange attire and the glowing Roaming-Rings that both girls wore.

"You've been hurt," remarked Zeta, saddened to see the deep blue welt on her father's face, his swollen lip and his injured right hand - now bandaged.

"Superficial or already on the mend," he replied. "Don't concern yourself."

Glancing to her side, Zeta noticed that Felicity's image was beginning to shimmer. "Eddie Bourne is also with us in the future," she called out hurriedly. "His voyage was accidental." Seeing the garage-shed waning before her eyes, she added urgently, "I'm glad you're safe, Dad! The *Estrella*? Will you join us soon?"

Before he had time to answer his daughter's last question, both apparitions disappeared from the garage-shed.

Leaning back against his workbench, Professor Doherty gazed at the stark shed around him and at his Chronoguiser, *Estrella,* floating promisingly a metre above the hard grey floor.

"Seeing my daughter in spirit is certainly a psychological *experience*, especially for a man of science like myself," he reflected earnestly. "Most girls send their dad's a palm-disk message to say they'll be out for an extra hour or two with their friends. My daughter turns up as a spectre and tells me she's gone to the future." Chuckling and with renewed zeal, he turned back to his workbench and to his task.

Professor Doherty remained occupied fine-tuning his gravity drive until the numerals on his time-band indicated it was 11.00pm. Switching on his worktop computer, he began to watch a televised News programme, compiled and introduced by Faith Firebell - concerning the TT Research Facility.

Resolved to remain indifferent, he observed, on his small screen, the opulent blue and gold lobby of TT's Farnborough mansion. Hanging from the high ornate ceiling was an attractive chandelier. Four huge vases full of red and cream genetically engineered gladioli stood elegantly in each corner. Within the branches of a dwarf Australian gum tree, near the front door, TT's pet koala, *Snookums*, munched contentedly on a sprig of eucalyptus leaves. Faith Firebell - keen to address her viewers - stood in the centre of the lobby.

"I am Faith Firebell, speaking to you live from the home of Mr. TT. Vox Populi, Chief Controller, in Farnborough, Hampshire," she said, as her cameraman zoomed in on a close up of her face. "Professor Hugh Doherty, distinguished employee of the TT Corporation was recently abducted after attending a farewell party at the TT Offices in London. We have just this moment received news that terrorists have again struck at the notable Doherty family.

At 11pm tonight, Miss Zeta Doherty, daughter of the kidnap victim, failed to return to her home. Her disappearance has been construed as a further abduction committed by an underground faction, intent on thwarting the advent of time travel in our society today.

Sadly, with all but one of the Chronoguisers destroyed, and their inventor and daughter most likely murdered, it seems this covert group of antagonists have certainly achieved their aim."

"They write both our obituaries with no remorse," reflected Professor Doherty angrily. "I'm glad Zeta was responsible and roamed to see me tonight, else I would possibly have gone insane with worry after hearing such news!" He sighed. "So much for my decision to stay indifferent."

An awful photograph of Zeta flashed up onto his computer screen. She was eight years old. She was wearing a big yellow party dress. Atop her head was a polka dot bow. The Professor laughed scornfully. "A very nice memorial for Zeta, I must say!"

With the screen once again showing images of TT's lobby, he now saw Isabelle and Marjorie standing beside Faith.

Holding her microphone close to Marjorie, Faith asked, "Tell me, Miss Doherty, when did you last see your niece, Zeta?"

Marjorie took a deep breath and removed her spectacles. Her face was pale and she was obviously distraught. "I last saw Zeta just before 2pm this afternoon," she replied.

"And how was her frame of mind after her father's abduction? Did you envisage that she was in any danger of being kidnapped - or murdered? Do you think she may have run away from home as a reaction to the loss of her father and her changed circumstances?"

"Zeta was coping with her father's abduction as well as could be expected," Marjorie replied. Then she briefly glanced away from the camera towards a person standing at the lobby front door. "And no, I didn't presume her to be in any danger. As for the last question, no, I doubt very much that Zeta has run away from home. She is far too sensible to let minor differences of opinion prompt her to that unlikely course of action."

Finished questioning Marjorie, Faith turned her microphone towards Isabelle. "Miss Isabelle Peaton, you have known Zeta for four years. Are you close with her? Have any ideas as to where she may be?"

Isabelle's brown eyes were puffy and red from crying. "I have become very fond of Zeta over the last four years," she replied sincerely, clutching a crumpled handkerchief tightly in one of her hands. "And I would like to believe that we had become close. But no Faith, I haven't the faintest inkling of where she might be?"

"When did you last see her, Isabelle?" prompted Faith.

"I last saw Zeta at 3pm this afternoon. She was going touring with a friend and they were due back at seven. We know she arrived back at the TT Research Facility after the tour at 7pm. We also know that the friend she was with worked an extended shift that started at 7pm. We presume she decided to walk home through the Common alone. Unfortunately…"

The distress Isabelle felt meant that she could not continue. Faith patted her arm and the ladies moved away to sit on a gold settee at the rear of the lobby.

Standing alone in front of her cameraman, Faith continued solemnly, "Police patrols have been notified of Zeta Doherty's unexplained absence. They are also looking for Eddie Bourne. He was stationed at the Research Facility's gate at 7pm and may have been the last person to see Zeta before her disappearance."

Drawing back from Faith the cameraman focused on TT Vox Populi, who had been standing in his lobby all the while - in front of his grand entrance door - quietly watching the filming.

"Tell the viewers at home, Mr. Vox Populi," prompted Faith, moving towards the door to stand beside him. "What is your reaction to the news of Zeta Doherty's disappearance? What is being done to help the Doherty family deal with the trauma of a double abduction? And what measures are TT Corporation going to take, to deal with the anti time travel faction that has targeted your organisation?"

Looking benignly into the camera, TT's large green eyes were thoughtful and intent. "Well Faith, as the viewers are already aware, TT Corporation have already offered a substantial reward for anyone who comes forward with any information leading to the safe return of one of our most highly valued employees, Professor Hugh Doherty. This reward also applies to his daughter, Zeta. I am personally not pleased that such a worthwhile young girl has disappeared, and I have my own men out looking for her on North-East Farnborough Common. We have a good team of Tracker dogs and if she is on the Common, they will find her. In addition to that, to safeguard against any further trauma imposed upon the Doherty family, I have asked Miss Marjorie Doherty, Professor Doherty's sister, and Isabelle Peaton, his dear friend, to stay with me, under my protection, here in my home." TT glanced across his lobby at those two ladies, seated opposite on the gold settee. "They have agreed, and will remain with me until it is deemed safe for them to return to their homes."

"Oh, great! Isn't that just dandy!" grumbled Professor Doherty, seated in his garage-shed, watching. "Now TT has my sister and my girlfriend in custody. How the dickens am I going to get them out of there!"

Meanwhile TT paused and the cameraman zoomed in on a flattering close up. "As to your last question, Faith, concerning the anti time travel faction, I would like to say that TT Corporation is specifically a travel and aviation company with hundreds of branches worldwide. It is beyond our means or jurisdiction to deal with terrorism. That job rests with the authorities responsible for preventing crime in our society. However, we have dramatically tightened our own security procedures and we have instructed our people to remain vigilant at all times."

"Thank you Mr. Vox Populi," said Faith sombrely.

The cameraman now filmed a wide-angled view of Faith. Seen by millions of viewers, she stood in the large lobby of TT's mansion, next to the man himself, with the wide imposing entrance several metres behind her.

"That completes my special report on the TT Corporation," she concluded. "The unexpected bombing of their Showroom in London, the abduction last night of their most valued employee, Professor Hugh Doherty, and the disappearance of his young daughter this evening have all struck mammoth blows to a responsible, innovative company. I will return with a further update, following tomorrow's six o'clock News Broadcast. This is Faith Firebell of the British News Team, bidding you goodnight."

Professor Doherty turned off his worktop computer screen and crossed his arms. "When my *Estrella* is ready, I will join Zeta in the future," he decided. "I will bring Marjorie and Isabelle with me, if they care to come."

Taking his robots remote-control from one of the wall shelves, he spent several minutes rapidly keying instructions into the complex keypad. Then he watched his robot quit its post at the entrance doors and deftly begin work on his Chronoguiser. Assured that the work adhered to his exacting standards, he slipped the remote-control inside his jacket, opened the panel on the gravity drive in front of him, and slowly and deliberately continued his work.

Heedless of the many hours he had been working, the sun was beginning to peep over the horizon when Professor Doherty heard a light tapping outside his garage-shed doors, followed by furtive whispering. Stiff and aching slightly from his habit of remaining in the one posture for far too long, he stood up and pushed back his chair.

Taking the robot's remote-control device from his inner jacket pocket, he switched the robot's function from assembly to defence. Using a voice activated command he instructed the robot back to its post at the doors, while he himself moved cautiously to the front of the garage and listened.

"Professor Doherty, it's Kepplar Holmes," murmured a voice from outside.

"Professor Holmes," whispered a second voice.

"Ret," whispered the last voice. "We mean you no harm and we may be able to help. We know you're in there, Professor. Kepplar has registered your thought waves. Let us in."

"Robot, complete three scans within a radius of one kilometre," the Professor instructed his mechinoid urgently. "Scan for robots. Scan for clusters of over two human beings, weighing a minimum of seventy kilograms each. Scan for weapons."

A second later the rasping voice of the robot replied. "Scans complete Professor D. Robot scan: nil. Human cluster scan: Three human beings weighing over seventy kilograms each at three metres. Weapons scan: nil."

"Robot, scan the area for vehicular heat sources, within a range of five hundred metres."

"Two flying-cars at fifteen metres, Professor D.," the robot instantly replied.

"Well, I have two scientists of my calibre, plus one of TT's Security men waiting outside," the Professor thought. "Ret seeks his brother, perhaps? As for the other two, they may remain committed to their cause of saving, mother of one, and wife of the other. If so, they could be useful intermediaries between Marjorie, Isabelle and myself."

Deciding to take a chance and let them in, he placed the robots remote-control in the side pocket of his jacket. Then he called to the men waiting outside, in a smooth unharried voice, "Come in, gentlemen!" After which he ordered curtly, "Robot, open doors, sixty second delay, close doors."

His robot speedily unlocked the garage-shed doors and then swiftly locked them again after the last of the three visitors, the portly Ret, had entered.

"I hope that one of you has brought me a stiff drink," said Professor Doherty, addressing them coolly. "I could do with a little pick me up right now."

The three men, all dressed casually in blue jeans and jerseys, regarded the Professor's battered face grimly. They glanced at the robot respectfully. Then they gaped in amazement at the shining floating *Estrella*.

"Who knocked you about?" asked Kepplar Holmes.

"TT Corporation," came Professor Doherty's guarded reply.

Kepplar remained impassive, but Ret frowned. Taking a hip flask containing whisky from his jacket pocket, he handed it to Professor Doherty apologetically. Accepting the flask, the recipient placed the open cap to his lips and swallowed a welcome mouthful of the smooth warming beverage.

"Professor?" asked Ret. "Zeta? Eddie? Do you know-?"

"They have both done a spot of time travelling," replied the Professor calmly.

"Thank goodness!" said Ret. Holding out his hand for the return of his flask, he too took a long swig of the warming draught. "I honestly didn't know that TT Corporation were behind your abduction, Professor Doherty. When Eddie didn't return home after his shift, I feared the kidnappers had got him as well."

"He's safe. Lucky him, he gets to see the future," said the Professor. Pausing, he observed the look of envy that flashed across Ret's face. Then he glanced quickly in the direction of Professor Holmes and Kepplar, "How did you meet up with these two scholars?"

"When I went to the Research Facility looking for my brother, they were waiting outside, Professor. I had secretly hoped that Eddie and Zeta had borrowed the Dandy Lion and had used it to time travel. But the ship was still in the aircraft hanger. The onboard log doesn't register any activity, since she was flown in from London. I had to find you, Sir. Kepplar and his dad wanted to find you as well. We teamed up. We've been searching for you since midnight."

"You didn't take long to close in on my location," remarked Professor Doherty. "Is my workshop that distinct?"

"No, quite the opposite. No one would have thought to look for you here."

"Well, how did you find me so easily?"

"Kepplar has a gadget he invented that sweeps for high intensity human thought waves. He set the device to search for individuals with your registered intelligence quotient. It brought us to you."

"I call it my hate scanner," interrupted Kepplar. "I developed it for the Correction Facilities. Its primary purpose is to calibrate hateful thoughts. That way the authorities can predict with reasonable accuracy the probability of criminals re-offending, just by taking a measure of the inmates thought waves before they are released back into society. It works well."

"So I'm full of hateful thoughts," laughed the Professor.

"No, it measures intensity of thought as well. Most of the scientific community rate a high score."

"Ingenious. You are congratulated. However, let me get to the point of your visit. You want to time travel, do you not?"

Kepplar nodded. His father looked anxiously at the *Estrella*, floating promisingly in the centre of the brightly lit garage-shed.

"This is the deal," said Professor Doherty quickly. "Kepplar - the *Estrella* is non operational. I want you to help me change that. Professor Holmes, I would like you to visit TT's mansion. I want you to tell Marjorie and Isabelle who was behind my abduction. Let them know that Zeta is safe. It is essential that you keep my whereabouts strictly hush-hush. Ask them both if they want to travel with me into the future; permanently. If they say yes, you need to get them out of the mansion."

"You'll take us with you in your time-machine?" asked Kepplar eagerly. "We can bring back a cure for my mother?"

"I'll take you, not your father. The absence of you both would raise questions and cause alarm. It is also best that Professor Holmes remains here to watch over your mother."

"We accept the contract," said Professor Holmes. "I'll arrange to take tea with Marjorie and Isabelle this afternoon, Hugh. I'll return this evening to let you know their reply." He turned to leave.

"I'll stay here to help Professor Doherty work on the *Estrella*, father," said Kepplar, already moving towards the workbench.

"I can help," offered Ret hastily, as Professor Doherty instructed his robot to open the garage doors. "I can assist with the plan to get the two ladies out of TT's mansion. For that, Professor Doherty, I'd like to join my brother in the future."

"It will be a tight squeeze with you in my ship as well, Ret. The *Estrella* is smaller than the Dandy Lion. However, I gratefully accept your offer. With the addition of your help, I am guaranteed of the ladies swift liberation!"

Outside, a cockerel crowed. Tiny shafts of morning light filtered into the garage-shed. The dawn air was crisp and fresh and the dust of anxiety settled onto the cold, cement floor. Ret and Professor Holmes, cautious of the robot, swiftly departed. Kepplar and Hugh Doherty, of singular purpose, shook hands. As the day broke certainly upon them, the two scientists began working in tandem, applying themselves to their arduous commission, the preparation of the *Estrella* for her vital maiden voyage.

Chapter nine

Soberly considering the group assembled in Satellite25's topmost landing-bay - all waiting for Zeta and Felicity to disembark from the Dandy Lion - Sebastian glanced towards Dominic.

"For no good reason Aristotle has banned Tau from seeing *The Zeta*?" he growled.

"Tau does have a fine murderous stare as a result," remarked his brother, Joshua. "Needless restrictions certainly work wonders for group morale."

"You know the rules," said Parsons. "He is prohibited from going anywhere near *The Zeta* until Aristotle has her father's permission that he may do so."

Cutting a handsome figure as he stood in front of the Dandy Lion, Aristotle glanced their way. Forefather of Dominic Tau, architect and governor of the undersea City, *Aristau*, he looked no less noble and imposing in these dusty ochre surrounds than he did while he waved to his people - on the balcony of the government palace - within his own Marine City.

Matching his demeanour, his clothes were stately and refined. His height, his thinning ash blonde hair crowned by his Roaming-Ring and his lean body, all combined to complement his mellow features. Obviously well read by the mode of his speech, and cultured, by the form of his thoughts, he was in précis, a fine distinguished gentleman.

Grouped behind him in the huge circular and windowless landing-bay, his gathered retinue of friends and family chattered eagerly. Each member of his fifty strong party wore their Roaming-Ring artlessly. Occasionally one of their set would close his or her eyes, their lips would move in sleep and absorbed in their art of psychic communication - they would briefly roam.

To the right of Aristotle stood an engaging group of females each wearing an elegant demure gown, edged with lace or ribbon. With satisfaction, he noted that all of their pastel frocks carried a wide bronze band - his family colour - at the skirt hem. Five of these ladies

however differed, for these young women wore the practical flight
suits commensurate with their status as pilots.

Aware of Aristotle's discerning gaze, these five ladies smiled
confidently at their grandfather. Staring past him, engrossed with the
splendid sight of two rows of gigantic russet Chronoguisers floating
next to the silver Dandy Lion, they grinned happily.

Following their example, Aristotle also looked hopefully towards
those ten russet Spheres. Firstly at the huge vessels of the *One to
Eight* Fleet, the *Alpha, Beta, Gamma, Delta, Epsilon, Zeta, Eta and
Theta,* and finally at the two smaller vessels at the end of the inner
row, against the rear wall of the Bay, the *Heritage* and the *Warrior.*

On the opposite side of Aristotle stood a ring of his male
descendents, his sons, his grandsons, and his great grandsons.
Finished admiring the Chronoguisers, it was towards one of these
males, Terence Dominic 'Tau', cordoned off in the centre of this
group, that he now stared severely.

Distinct from the rest of the males in his family who each wore a
brocade frockcoat with a wide band of bronze on the lower sleeve,
plus trousers, Tau was dressed in his full Knight's Raiment. A
prisoner in the centre of his family circle, he glared sulkily at his
great grandfather.

"I am better than this treatment, Aristotle," he called.

Aristotle, of steady resolve, silently returned the lad's angry gaze.

Ignored by his great grandfather, Dominic turned to the two men,
presently gripping his arms in detainment.

"Unhand me before *The Zeta* disembarks, uncles," he cautioned.
"Or this will not make for a good first impression - of you."

Listening to Dominic's remarks and positioned between the male
and female counterparts of the Tau family stood a line of four
additional young men. Three wore chainmail - John 'Sebastian' and
his two older brothers, Samuel and Joshua. Sebastian and Samuel
wore bronze. Joshua wore grey - the uniform of the Aristau Guards.
To the right of Joshua, wearing casual dress, stood Joseph Parsons.

After nodding politely to Aristotle - who had previously overheard
his name mentioned by them - Samuel glanced sternly at his younger
brothers.

"We have enough of a job to do piloting the *Zeta, Eta* and *Theta*
for the next sixteen days, without concerning ourselves with social
formalities," he said flatly. "It's no mean feat to ship seeds, saplings

and Botanical robots to silos all around the world - especially when we have to travel fifty years forward in time to do so."

"We do have attractive help, though. Don't we?" teased Joshua. "Tau's five aunts over there will fly the other five vessels of the *One to Eight* Fleet. You will have a chance to talk to the youngest one, Samuel. Mutual admiration, isn't it?"

"Don't try to change the subject, Smarty," said Samuel, his tone of voice compelling those around to listen. "I was about to remind you of the satellite shipments. TT Vox Populi has already emptied the Zoo, Aquarium and Greenhouse Satellites for his Transport Fleet, so will have the additional task of restocking those vessels."

"I presume we will get the fauna and fish - to restock - from Aristau," said Joshua.

"Yes," replied Samuel.

"Because of our efforts over the next few days we will have three satellites of flora and fauna orbiting the Earth waiting for our tri-centennial return," said Parsons.

All three brothers and Parsons, very much aware of the secret landing-bay around them, looked enthusiastically towards the *One to Eight* Fleet.

"I expect the Greenhouse Satellite will be our top priority," said Joshua. "Where are all the seeds and saplings we are going to transport? Samuel?"

"Read it in the cargo manifests," replied Samuel curtly.

"That means he doesn't know," said Sebastian. "But I know. The saplings are in a tree nursery hidden in Aristau."

"And the seedlings?" asked Joshua.

"See those twenty huge derelict rockets in the landing-bay behind us," replied Sebastian. "Besides making this place look like a Spaceship mortuary, *and* acting as brilliant camouflage for our small Armada of Chronoguisers, those wrecks contain billions of seeds. Plus ten thousand Botanical robots, two hundred Agricultural robots, twelve Construction robots and twenty Multi-tasking robots - also to be shipped to the future."

"The Tau family have invested in a lot of robots," remarked Joshua.

"Fifty years henceforth - when the soil is free of pathogens - the Botanical robots will seed the Earth. Then they will tend to the burgeoning plant life," interrupted Parsons enthusiastically.

"And the other mechinoids?"

"The Agricultural and Construction robots will build us a new city, on the River Thames, Joshua, in readiness for our tri-centennial return."

"Great. I'll enjoy some fresh accommodation. What about the Multi-tasking robots?

"Initially the Multi-tasking robots will erect containment structures inside the *One to Eight* Fleet and will assist with the loading. Then they will be taken to the future to be distributed around the world - to each of the major cultural centres. Tau wants to retain the Earth's cultural heritage as far as is feasible during our absence, so the primary programming of the Multi-tasking robots is to ensure that our beautiful historical buildings are maintained."

"Smart lad, he's got my vote," said Samuel, intrigued by all these details.

Suddenly, after glancing at the Dandy Lion, Parsons stiffened.

"The hatch of the Dandy Lion is opening," he warned. "Felicity and Zeta are coming out. Tau has asked that you three brothers remain behind after the formal greeting. You are to use your time to study your flight plans and to assist Bermuda when he returns at 9pm. Tau will brief you and answer any pertinent questions at 10pm, just before your first time jump."

The line of four lads now watched the goings on before the Dandy Lion. Already disembarked, Felicity stood at the bottom of the boarding steps with Governor Aristotle at her side. To-do, after running down the steps unfettered - with his new lead trailing behind him - yapped happily at her feet. Zeta, wearing her wine and brown gown, was midway down the stairs.

"*The Zeta* is lovely!" remarked fourteen-year old Mandy. Standing at the front of the group of females, she was absorbed by the sight of the first female time traveller in their history. "Look at her hair - pinned up and sprayed with a fine veil of the tiniest sparkling bronze gems. Do you know she's thousands of years old!"

"Hush," said Cynthia, a cousin, standing beside her. A poised young girl with dark sandy hair, worn in a chignon, Cynthia paused. Then she continued. "Great grandfather will be giving a short convivial speech explaining us to Zeta. Then we will be spending time with her enjoying the Theme Park."

While they were speaking, Zeta neared the bottom of the boarding steps.

"Dominic's looking a bit peeved," she thought calmly. "Probably because he is still at odds with Eddie." After glancing around the landing-bay, she further pondered. "Where is Eddie, anyway? He's definitely not amongst all of these people. I hope he isn't hiding somewhere, ready to jump out suddenly and cause another fight." Looking up, she noticed two large overhead pipes that were drawing freezing air over the top of the Dandy Lion. "Eddie is stubborn and refuses to listen," she thought. "But he was right about one thing. We *were* parked right underneath an Air-conditioning System."

She had now reached the bottom of the steps and Aristotle bowed courteously.

"Greetings Zeta Doherty!" he exclaimed loudly, in an affable tenor voice. "My name is Aristotle Tau, and I am the Governor of Aristau. My family and I are delighted to have you with us. Your accommodation is in our Aquatic City and I hope that your stay with us will be pleasant. Shortly, our whole party will be entering the Robotic Theme Park via the elevator that you can see in the centre of this landing bay." He paused and in a slightly raised voice, continued. "As a token of our respect, please let me present you with the key to Aristau!"

Holding a small key pendant on a long gold necklace, he placed it carefully around her neck. The assemblage applauded. Zeta, tongue-tied, smiled bashfully.

"Zeta, let me introduce you to my family and friends," said Aristotle, now turning to face the gathering. "Immediately in front of us are the three Sebastian brothers, and Joseph Parsons - in the brown suit. Joseph will take you and his sister Felicity home after you tire of your recreation here. To my right are all my male descendents. In the centre of the group, is Tau, who you have met in mirror form. He is forbidden from seeing you, pending your father's permission."

Oblivious to her amused reaction, Aristotle faced the opposite side of the assembly. "To my left, is my life partner Miriam," he said proudly. "My great granddaughters are standing in front of her. Mandy is in pink. Cynthia in peach is sixteen."

Clapping his hands together for attention and facing the assembly, Aristotle now spoke loudly, "Thank you all for your attendance! You are all aware that against the consensus, we plan to remain on the Earth, but move our group to a future epoch. The work undertaken by all of you during the next sixteen days is a vital part of that plan.

Fundamentally, we will be laying the groundwork for the regeneration of the Earth by shipping resources fifty years forward in time to the empty satellites and to agricultural silos. These resources include robots, wildlife, livestock, saplings and seeds." Aristotle's face was happy and hopeful as he looked thoughtfully at the people standing before him. "I would like everyone to return here at 10pm to help with the consignments. Please disperse down to the Amusement Park in your separate groups as promptly as you can!"

Zeta watched the gathering withdraw. Following the ladies, Aristotle and his male descendents moved swiftly towards the yellow shaft of the satellite's central elevator housing. Felicity quickly moved to stand beside Zeta. Sebastian ran up the boarding steps of the Dandy Lion to retrieve Zeta's luggage. Parsons discreetly approached, while Mandy and Cynthia hesitantly stepped forward.

Suddenly To-do, quiet and sitting complacent at Felicity's feet until now, began barking. Darting away, he ran between the two rows of russet Chronoguisers and disappeared out of sight.

"I'll have to go after him, Felicity," Zeta said, abruptly making to run after her pet.

"No wait," said Parsons. "I am Joseph Parsons, Felicity's brother. Your pet is safe within this enclosed area. There are only two exits in this landing-bay, the central lift shaft and a double airlock for Spacecraft. Your Clode can't escape."

"I would prefer to search for To-do immediately, if you don't mind," said Zeta.

Sebastian, now returned with her rucksack and holdall, handed them to Zeta and smiled.

"I've seen you before," he said. "Outside the Scrap-yard when Parsons and I helped your dad escape."

"Yes," said Zeta quickly. "I'm usually forgetting my manners." Turning to face both lads, she unfastened her rucksack. "I'd like you to each accept a small gift."

Retrieving a chocolate chip cake in a small white box from her rucksack, she handed this gift to Sebastian.

"If you've got more like this, you're carrying a little gold mine!" he said, beaming and accepting the cake.

Zeta handed a smiling Parsons his gift of marbled fudge chocolate brownies. "Thank you both for helping my father," she said quickly. "My dad means a lot to me."

Donning her rucksack and carrying her holdall - which now contained her boots and summer clothes - Zeta turned away. Making her way alone through the area at the rear of the landing-bay, she explored the strange dark aisle between the large floating Spheres, searching for To-do.

Dwarfed by the high ochre roof and the floating russet Chronoguisers on either side, Zeta smelt the dusty stale air. Listening to the sound of her footsteps tapping on the black metal-ridged floor, she gazed about curiously.

All the while, she called for To-do. "To-do! Come out, boy. I'll give you a dog biscuit," she promised.

On her left, she passed the *Alpha*, which was the closest Spaceship to the Dandy Lion, then the *Beta*. By the time she had reached the *Epsilon*, she had come to the end of that row. Glancing across to the adjacent row to her right - the one against the rear wall - she saw two much smaller vessels alongside the larger, *Zeta, Eta and Theta*. The first one, the *Warrior*, was twice the diameter of the Dandy Lion, but the last Sphere - the *Heritage* - was only moderately larger.

Shocked and surprised, she now discovered the whereabouts of Eddie.

Dressed in a navy brocade frockcoat and trousers, a plain maroon shirt and a bronze cravat, he was handcuffed to the lower railing of the *Heritage* boarding stairs. On his head, he wore a slim Roaming-Ring set with five quartz crystals.

"Eddie?" she asked, approaching him quickly. "Who imprisoned you this way?"

"I'm not exactly imprisoned, Zeta. I'm just being kept out of the way in a rather robust fashion."

"What happened when you left the Dandy Lion?"

"A minor scrimmage, but everything is sorted now. The bronze cravat means that I am a guest." He paused and glanced at her laden rucksack. "Hey, you wouldn't have any food in that bag of yours, would you?"

"Yes, I have food."

Dropping her holdall, Zeta let her rucksack fall from her shoulders onto the ground. Swiftly finding a small sealed white bag inside, she handed that bag to Eddie. "I wasn't hungry at tea time on the zeppelin, so I saved my dinner for later."

Eddie smiled. Opening the bag, he bit into a buttery croissant.

"Forgive me for asking," she enquired, watching Eddie eat. "But when I was touring the TT Research Facility, I overheard your brother Garrett telling Isabelle that you have a progress conviction. Do you mind telling me what you did wrong?"

"I played truant, Zeta," Eddie admitted. "I have a progress conviction for missing too much school. It doesn't pay to have an entire population of dunderheads. But I was otherwise occupied, hanging around the TT Research Facility learning how to fly. School and I didn't make for a favourable mix. As you are now well aware, I find it hard to listen. But sitting still - well that is a feat I find near impossible!"

"I see," she responded quietly. "That's alright then. I had to ask, since we ended up onboard this satellite together."

"You'd better go up and see his Lordship now, before he gets impatient and decides to mirror to you," Eddie advised between mouthfuls of food.

"His Lordship?" asked Zeta. "Who *are* you talking about Eddie?"

"Tau."

Zeta was confounded. "You've had words with Dominic?"

"Yes." He paused. Then he grinned. "I confess, Zeta, that it was quite a shock for me to meet the mortal Dominic for the first time, but he's quite a solid chap. I take back all that rubbish about him stealing the Dandy Lion. Once I saw all the amazing high-tech equipment in the *Heritage*, I knew he wasn't going to confiscate our archaic technology.

The onboard computer in that vessel is simply amazing! You see, the *Heritage* is only camouflaged with rust paint, Zeta. It sparkles underneath. Contrary to how it looks, it already functions perfectly well as a time-machine. There is just a small glitch in the gravity drive, which their engineer, Bermuda, needs to rectify. It causes terminal cell damage over long time jumps, but over short journeys, the injury is negligible."

Zeta looked away. Silent, she stared at the derelict rockets in the dusty landing-bay.

"What's wrong?" he asked, already guessing the reason behind her withdrawn expression. "You don't want to see Tau?"

She shook her head in reply, declining to speak.

"Why not?"

She didn't reply.

Eddie smiled. "You have to face his Lordship. Now go. Up the stairs with you."

Leaving him and climbing the boarding steps, she hesitantly entered the Sphere, stepping onto a curved white floor. Glancing around, she saw a cabin lined with equipment. Underneath the viewing window and crammed with a mass of baffling instruments, a high dashboard stretched across the entire front of the vessel. The silver front seats were small and light. The gravity drive was fitted into a shaft in the centre of the craft. Plus, there were many intriguing calibration devices. Daunting, the Flight Control panel and the manual controls were complex.

Observing Dominic sitting in the pilot's seat with his back to her, she immediately noticed the broad bronze sash around his waist - a cummerbund - his brown trousers, shoes, and his smart cream shirt.

Hearing her enter and turning his chair around, he greeted her in a strange perfunctory manner.

"Hello Miss," he said. "It is pleasant to see you dressed in something apt, rather than your customary dishabille. Take off that key to Aristau city. Bow. Then approach me."

Surprised in equal measure by his attitude, his unfamiliar mortal appearance and by his request, Zeta moved away towards the stern. To-do, inside the *Heritage* since the time he had run away, peeped out from under the co-pilots chair. Running forward, he sat by her side.

"You're joking?" she said quietly.

"No, you bow to me. It is our social custom."

"Social custom!" she exclaimed. "I meet the mortal you for the first time and I find you are uncivilized! You do not behave like any friend of mine. How could you bring Eddie along to this Space satellite, then handcuff him to the boarding stairs of this ship? It was wrong to take him with us as we did. I would have objected if I'd known you were going to mistreat him!"

Dominic's expression darkened. "Well, thank you," he growled. "I do immensely appreciate your comment about us not being friends. Obviously, our camaraderie is one-sided and I am naïve." Pausing, he flicked a switch on the dashboard of the *Heritage*. "Zeta, go downstairs and wait with Eddie," he ordered brusquely, "Who is now free of his manacles."

Zeta hesitated. "I'm sorry Tau," she quickly apologised. "I didn't like seeing Eddie detained, that's all. He hasn't done anything wrong.

But you've freed him now. I didn't mean to imply that you aren't my friend. That just fell out accidentally. Everything is so different, you see. The Dominic I know and feel comfortable with has pale blonde hair, light blue eyes, pale skin and ... "

"And what?" he asked gruffly.

After having broke off in mid-sentence, she stood silently.

"You left out handsome, with a good physique," he said quietly. Stepping quickly out of his chair, he grabbed her arm.

"Let go of me, Tau," she scolded, trying to pull away.

"No, I won't let go of you," he stated coolly. Settling back down in his chair, he left her standing indignant before him. "I have to detach your palmdisk, in case the kidnappers use it to track you. I am going to include an ornament on the bracelet you wear, to keep you safe. I also want you to either remove that key necklace, or conceal it under your blouse."

Without further ado, Dominic used a small precise tool that he retrieved from his shirt pocket, to attach a tiny gold mushroom to her lucky charm bracelet.

"The ornament is a key device, Zeta. It stops anyone who is using a field generator from barring my psychic energy field. As long as you wear the bracelet, I can roam to your location unimpeded. I'll only roam invisible if absolutely necessary." Peeling the palmdisk from her hand, he crushed it under his heel. "Sorry, Zeta, I know it was expensive."

Studying her face, Dominic noted her blushing. "I discomfit you," he stated sympathetically. "You no longer call me Dominic. My appearance is unfamiliar."

Zeta nodded and looked away.

"What if I dye my hair a lighter shade, wear pale blue contact lenses and put white powder on my face?" he suggested. "Then, once I've run a hundred kilometre marathon, I will be totally de-energised and will be exactly the same as the friend you remember!"

"You can't run a hundred kilometre marathon," she contradicted. "Where would you get the energy?"

"Where did I get the stamina to mirror a solid image, two thousand nine hundred years into the past, for so many hours a day, Zeta? I do have a certain magnetic vitality, my dear, and a very long life span - two hundred and sixty years. Give or take a day. Are you impressed?"

Zeta was wide-eyed and he grinned charmingly. His large deep blue eyes sparkled with vivacity and Zeta noticed his prominent chin, full mouth and charismatic profile.

"The longevity comes with my gift of mirroring, Zeta. Roaming is very healthy for the body. It gives one's cells and vital organs a rest from all that invasive psychic power naturally within. My body gets even more of a rest than most, because mirroring is more potent than roaming."

"Tau?" Zeta blurted out quickly. "On the topic of roaming, I roamed to see my dad, with Felicity's help."

"You spoke to your father?"

"Yes, I told him I'm safe with you, and Eddie is with us. I had an exciting surprise too. Dad's building his own Chronoguiser! Also, I saw that he was injured - you didn't tell me." She paused and for the first time since she had entered the cabin of the *Heritage*, she looked directly into Dominic's eyes. "I know this sounds terrible, but my dad lied to me," she confided. "My mum disappeared five years ago, on June 14th. Dad said he didn't know what happened to her. But I found out from Eddie that she vanished while she was visiting the TT Research Facility. Her disappearance is recorded on a surveillance tape, kept in their archives. I want to see it."

"I'll be working my four hour shift at the Facility as long as TT remains in Farnborough. If you like, Zeta, I'll copy the tape and bring it to this era using Bermuda's Matter Transfer Device."

Zeta's face brightened. "If you would do that for me, it would be tremendous."

"Consider it done, Zeta. Sometime after 8pm tomorrow, I'll have time to mirror inside Willow's apartment in Aristau, into your room. I'll have the surveillance tape for you by then."

"Willow? I'll be staying with the mermaid?"

Dominic laughed. "Willow has offered to be your guide to help you make the most of your time with us. Unfortunately, because I am committed to helping Aristotle with our consignments to the future, I won't be able to spend much time with you. But I can mirror mid-week and weekends, to visit."

"Who says I want to see you at all?" Zeta remarked sulkily, suddenly realizing that although Dominic's mortal self was intense with vitality and a much darker hue that his spiritual mirror form, his voice, the voice of her friend, was all too familiar.

"You do," he replied affably. "But we must observe the social customs. There are simple formalities to be upheld, Zeta. You need to understand that I am not allowed to see you in my mortal form until your father gives his permission, in person, to Aristotle. I'm breaking the rules right now."

Zeta smiled. "What Aristotle doesn't know won't hurt him. Now, can we go and see the Robotic Theme Park? I didn't come all this way to stay stuck here in a landing-bay. If the robots in the Park are anything like the inside of your ship, they will be absolutely fantastic!"

"Sure," he replied happily. "I'll close the *Heritage* in a few minutes and we can go down to the Funfair Level - the lower of the rotating wheels. The upper wheel is the Science Level. My cousins, Felicity, Eddie and Parsons are already waiting outside this ship to join us."

Zeta looked at him shyly. "You mirrored in the landing-bay. Did Sebastian create an illusion? Is that why everyone imagined they saw your mortal self?"

"Everyone except you, Zeta. You saw the truth, didn't you?"

"I wasn't sure," she answered evasively.

Considering her thoughtfully, he smiled. "I'm one of the finalists in the Satellite Cup," he revealed proudly. "It's an annual race being held here tonight from 9pm until 10. The contestants have to traverse physical obstacles, escape from the clutches of robots and prove themselves against an array of Illusionists, Hypnotists and Magicians. The race ends with a hundred-metre sprint to the finish line. Bermuda was my team-mate for the qualifying heats. He agrees that I have a better chance of winning if Eddie replaces him for the race final."

"Do you think you'll win?"

Dominic grinned.

"That's a yes, then."

"After the race I have to return to this landing-bay, Zeta, to fly our gun ship, the *Warrior* and supervise the time jumps of my *One to Eight* Fleet. You of course, may remain with Felicity to peruse the Park at your leisure. With one proviso, I insist you avoid the Fun-fortress."

"The Fun-fortress?"

"The Funfair Level is constructed as a hundred-metre long showgrounds, Zeta, coupled with a lengthy one-way enclosed Fun-fortress, in the shape of a horseshoe. The fortress is the venue for the race. You'll be able to see it through the spectator screens in the showgrounds, once we're there."

"You haven't said why I have to avoid it?"

"It's too rough a place for girls. And before you open your mouth to complain, forget it. The answer will always be no!"

Zeta smiled. "Well, you're still as bossy as I remembered, but I do hope you win," she said sincerely.

Seated in his pilot's chair, Dominic looked at the girl before him, suddenly noting her changed expression. "What?" he asked casually.

"About Eddie? You mentioned that he would be your aide during the race. Afterwards, where will he be lodging?"

"Do you suspect I will keep him in custody Zeta? Is that why you are asking?"

"No, that's not it," she replied, embarrassed. "I just wondered where he might be. He's a stranger here too and he will naturally appreciate how bewildered I may feel."

Dominic glanced quickly away. When he turned back to face her, he replied coolly, "Eddie's quarters will be in Aristau, Zeta, in the same building complex as Willow's apartment. But tonight, after the race, you won't see him, because he remains on Satellite25 to help with our evacuation plans. In return he gets the chance to fly our Chronoguisers."

"One last question?" Zeta asked, doubling up the chain on her necklace and hiding the pendant under her chemise. "Can I be sure to see you tomorrow evening? I know it'll only be Tuesday, but..."

Rising from his chair, Dominic stepped briskly forward and yelled coarsely down the open hatchway, "Hey Eddie, throw Zeta's bags up here will you, so I can stow them away! We're heading off for the Funfair Level!" After catching her rucksack and holdall and putting them aside, he turned to Zeta and answered her in a cool but gentler tone, "You will see the surveillance tape tomorrow night, Zeta. Now grab To-do. Let's go!"

Minutes later, after a brief trip in the central elevator and a brisk walk through the busy level two access spoke, Zeta stood happily with her party - against the right wall - just inside the entrance of the Satellite Showgrounds on the Funfair Level.

The atmosphere fizzed with gaiety and excitement. Decorated huts, built on the longest and left side of the circular deck - signposted as robotic stables, shops, stalls, a cafeteria and an adjudicator's hut - bid her a most cheerful welcome. Twinkling star-shaped white lights encrusted on the surface of the curved pale-blue ceiling overhead, glistened. While sure underfoot, the royal-blue ceramic floor of the fifty metre wide tubular showgrounds gleamed.

Stylishly dressed young people - the ladies wearing gowns and the gents, frockcoats and trousers - amassed genially about her. She listened to their bubbly laughter, intermingling with the showground music in these warm pleasant surrounds. Then she glanced a distance of fifty metres across to her left, where every five metres - inside the open huts - a round porthole reminded her that she was indeed onboard Satellite25 many miles above, and orbiting the Earth.

Currently outside a small closed door - the rear exit of the horseshoe shaped Fun-fortress - Zeta waited while Dominic, Eddie and Parsons scrutinized a scarlet running track. Extending from the fortress exit and stretching away to the high red gates of the Fun-fortress entrance, the track ran along the inner right side of the tubular showgrounds - against the wall.

"Will the Satellite Cup be good?" Zeta asked Felicity.

"The Satellite Cup is a big, big deal to everyone here," Felicity revealed. "You will understand once you have watched the contestants race. We don't often get to see mind powers demonstrated with such zeal. When it starts, Satellite25 will exude non-stop excitement. Be warned - it starts very soon."

The lads finished perusing the running track. Zeta, along with the rest of her party, now walked amongst the exuberant horde of Robotic Theme Park visitors - through the showgrounds, past the stables, towards the shops.

To-do ran happily around her feet and Zeta grinned widely. Robotic pets and miniature mechinoids of immense variety, airborne or pedestrian, bustled around her. Deliberately designed so as not to mimic human beings in countenance or other organic life forms in texture, she found the robots to be nothing short of delightful.

Talking pot plants filled with perky chatty animated flowers, trundled along cheerfully. Sunny speaking sunflowers stepped gingerly through the crowd on delicate green stalks. Flying robot fairies filled the air. Occasionally landing daintily on visitors to exchange small pleasantries, they flitted away gracefully on gossamer wings. Tiny robot pixies sat on the sides of the amusement stalls, adding mirth to the games of chance and skill. While small interactive cartoon characters with buoyant amusing personalities, tugged at skirt hems or trouser legs timidly, offering hints on how to traverse the Level's main attraction - the eight, fifty-metre long chambers of the satellite's Fun-fortress.

"Oh!" exclaimed Zeta, as a flock of strange flying birds with extraordinary heads flew by. Startled, she laughed as a knee high robotic monster gently grabbed her skirt with its long thin hands, then looked up beseechingly with purple oval eyes.

Dominic pulled its hands away. "Off you go, machine," he said. "Zeta doesn't want to play."

Moving on to explore the shops, Zeta was fascinated by the array of wares on display. Gazing admiringly into a colourful aquarium, she saw golden lights blinking out from the windows of a tiny undersea city. In that same aquarium, she smiled happily at the sight of miniature robotic mermaids swimming alongside dancing robotic seahorses. In response to her mirth, robotic starfish - nestling in the sand - winked, blew bubbles and waved.

Noticing how taken she was with one particular piece of merchandise, Dominic stood by her side. In her hand, she held a wonderful robotic doll. Twenty-four centimetres tall, the high-technology mechinoid functioned as an interactive tutorial system with projected graphics. Additionally, the doll was adept at finding all those little lost belongings that one is invariably always losing.

"Dominic, can I buy this?" Zeta asked.

"Sure," he replied. Stepping towards the shop counter, he allowed the assistant to scan his Roaming-Ring.

After purchasing the doll, Zeta's group moved eagerly towards the amusement stalls.

"Hey!" said Eddie, calling to Dominic and Parsons. "Give this chap in the stalls some money so we can have a shooting contest!"

While the lads used strange guns to shoot at ghastly holographic monsters, the girls walked over to a stall featuring a large saltwater tank. The interesting tank contained sand, seaweed, faux coral and a huge mechanical oyster. Contestants at this stall were required to roam inside the tank and snatch a large pearl from the oyster - before it closed.

"Let's each have a go," suggested Cynthia. "My treat."

A short time later and after much jollity, they were reunited with the lads.

"Dominic, who won the shooting contest?" Zeta asked.

"Parsons," replied Dominic. "What about you girls?"

"I won," said Mandy proudly. She held up her prize - a robotic fairy.

All hungry and thirsty, they now visited the cafeteria - the chosen gathering place for most of the robotic pets in the Park. Sitting on the tables, chairs, even on the serving counters, the talking robotic pets, of many different breeds, chatted unassumingly to all of the guests.

While Felicity, Mandy and Cynthia ate their meal of Lumpo, and Eddie and Parsons discussed the forthcoming race, Dominic and Zeta sat close by, at a small round café table near the cafeteria entrance.

Lounged back in his chair, Dominic was smiling. Zeta sipped cool sweetened water. Staring thoughtfully at the enormous array of faultlessly engineered robotic pets, she noted the delight of both adults and children alike when the programmed mechinoids conversed with the patrons in an attentive and helpful manner.

Overawed, her face shone with enthusiasm. "Today I have chosen my career," she declared. "I will be a Robot Designer!" Then she moved to rush away, to further scrutinize more amazing and amusing machines.

"A very worthy vocation, Zeta, but please remain seated and stay with our group," Dominic insisted, tugging her back into her seat. Glancing across the cafeteria towards a group of teenagers staring out of the portholes into the darkness of Space, he was thoughtful.

"But why do I have to remain?" questioned Zeta impatiently. "There is so much to see. I want to see everything. *Right now*!"

Dominic laughed. "Well, one thing I want you to see is that scarlet race avenue outside of the cafeteria, the one on the inner side of the wheel. Yes, that's right. You've spotted it correctly. You saw me checking it out when we first arrived. At the end of the race, I have to sprint through the showgrounds along that track for the last hundred-metre dash, finishing at the Betting-hut, situated to the right of the Fun-fortress gates. Don't forget the race begins anytime now." Then he smiled, noting her distant expression as she stared off across the cafeteria at an interesting collection of robots.

"Dominic, do robots work in all fields? Will I find them in every occupation?" Zeta asked, turning back to face him.

"No, Zeta. Mechinoids function in most occupations, but not all. Animated computers are excluded from five important categories. It is illegal for anyone but human beings to work in the Military, the Judiciary System, the Law Enforcement Agency and Medicine. It is also illegal to design a robot that resembles a human being or is stronger than a man."

"What about animal robots?" she asked, checking To-do, still restrained by his leash and sitting quietly under their café table. "I know robot pets can never replace the real thing, but they are still fun and functional."

"Robots can be modelled as animals, birds, reptiles, spiders and insects," Dominic clarified. "But they must not have realistic casings. With the exception of robots fashioned to resemble wild animals. Those mechinoids are restricted for special exhibits and are not available for private sale."

"Dominic, this may seem presumptuous, but could I borrow some books on introductory robotics?" she asked hesitantly. "And buy a tutorial disk on the subject for my robotic doll?"

Dominic leant further back in his chair. "Do you know what you are asking, Zeta? We still have many roaming, time travelling tourists who visit the TT Theme Parks throughout the world and the laws restrict their access to data. Many of those regulations also apply to you. I am forbidden from providing you with concentrated scientific facts without due regard for the time travel edicts. If I give you the books and the disk, you can never go back to your old life."

"I'm not asking you to break any rules, Dominic. I have decided I want to stay in the future," she replied sincerely. "Please get me the books."

He sat back in his chair and studied her face keenly. Then he smiled. "You make such a weighty decision so quickly. Perhaps it's the excitement of being on this satellite, or the showgrounds. Or perhaps you are tired."

"Excuse me, but it's an obvious decision. Now, about those books?"

"No," Dominic replied, his eyes fixed firmly on her face. "You must discuss this with your father first. If he gives his permission, I will confer with him. Only then will I bring you the disk and books."

Zeta was piqued. "Well, I can't ask him in private," she said huffily. "Because I can't roam to him by myself. I told you, I can't."

Dominic only smiled. "I intend to buy you different gems for your Roaming-Ring. With the jewels I buy, you'll be able to roam unaccompanied to see your father. Until that time, you will have to exercise patience."

"I can't see the harm in my learning, but you've obviously made your mind up, Dominic, so there's no point arguing." She paused, picked up To-do from under the table and held him in her arms. Then trying not to offend, she spoke quietly. "Thanks for offering to buy me better gems, Dominic, but I prefer not to accept any more of your gifts. It's not proper. I will find a way of repaying you for my clothes and my doll. Sebastian gave me the impression that I could trade the sweets I brought with me for money. Is that right? If I gave them to you, could you swap them over for some cash?"

Dominic looked away from her and focused on a group of familiar people chatting at the far end of the cafeteria. He nodded politely to three he recognized, Tesla Gosh, Brooklyn Trina and Miles Sturgeon. Then he cursorily glanced across the room, through one of the porthole windows and out into the black Space vacuum. When he turned back to face Zeta, he replied coolly.

"Sure, if that's what you want. Your haversack is still in the *Heritage*. I'll take your food and exchange it for currency."

Zeta was pleased. "Thanks," she said appreciatively, "How much do you think I'll get?"

"Possibly a months salary."

"Great! Oh, and make sure you don't sell the jar of honey. I bought that for Bermuda. Could you give it to him?"

"I'm glad *someone* made a good impression," responded Dominic. Glancing at his timeband, he rose from his chair, gesturing with his hands for his group to arise. Just as he did so, an urgent voice piped shrilly through the cafeteria Loudspeaker System.

"All contestants for the Satellite Cup; please report to the adjudicator's hut! All contestants; please report to the adjudicator's hut. Thank you!"

"Eddie and I have been summoned!" Dominic declared, bowing to his female cousins and the petite Felicity. "So my chums and I must bid all you lovely ladies au revoir!" Grabbing Zeta by her shoulders, he pulled her gently from her chair. "Except for you, Miss. You are my responsibility while you are here. Before I compete, I must hire you a robotic pony. Once I have you settled on a steed, you can comfortably watch me vie for the Cup, without fear of being jostled by the crowd." Hurrying her away he said patiently in his young tenor lilt, "Just because I look different, doesn't mean I'm not the same inside. I still want us to be friends, Zeta."

Her response was honest and well thought. "I can't manage to roam to my dad without help, Dominic, and then it's only for a few seconds at most. I roamed to your hideout for over an hour. I guess that means that we'll always be friends."

Outside the cafeteria, the crowd pressed around them. Filling the wide tubular deck, cheerful young children, many with brightly coloured hair, laughed and played gaily underneath the twinkling ceiling. Quiet thoughtful teenagers, keen for the Satellite Cup to begin, casually moved through the gathering and nodded recognition to Dominic. The many adults present smiled and chatted happily.

As the teenage pair wove their way quickly towards the riding stables at the entrance to the showgrounds, delightful talking cartoon character mechinoids skipped merrily about their knees, wishing them prosperity. Round-winged robotic sprites with button faces, cute acorn hats and rustic olive green garbs flitted around Zeta's head and sang quiet harmonies. While To-do, now let down on the ground, strained on his leash, sniffed everything in his path, and ran curiously forward.

The rest of the girls, leaving the cafeteria, followed leisurely behind. Disappearing in the opposite direction, Eddie and Parsons ran for the adjudicator's hut, located to the left of the Fun-fortress entrance.

All the while, sheltering Zeta and all its cheerful patrons, the two massive wheels of Satellite25 gently revolved in the realm of Space. Excited visitors, specifically stopping over to enjoy the Satellite Cup continued to dock their Space Shuttles in the multi-tiered Spaceport. With the Cup due to begin any moment now, the atmosphere in the huge orbiting Park - sizzled.

Chapter ten

Electric - a current of excitement filled the satellite showgrounds. Elation lit up the faces of the eager patrons and their laughter spilled like a flowing concourse. Wonderful feminine ladies wearing stately domed gowns and gleaming metallic diadems swished through the crowd in colours that were warm rich and vibrant. Whilst gentleman in fine brocade jackets and smart tailored trousers waited patiently and respectfully within their genial fold.

Excited to witness the event of the day - the Satellite Cup - many cheerful spectators had gathered in the now packed showgrounds. Mutually with them, Zeta waited twenty metres from the red Fun-fortress gates for the race to begin. Sitting on a mechanical palomino pony near the scarlet race avenue, To-do peered inquisitively from one of her saddlebags and her new robotic doll peeped prettily from the other. With her new friends keeping her company - Felicity to her left on a roan pony and Cynthia and Mandy to her right on skewbald and chestnut steeds - she gazed curiously towards the fortress entrance.

Parsons, she saw, was queued at the sparkling white Betting-hut, along with hordes of other punters. While Eddie and Dominic had taken their places with the eight other challengers for the Cup, at the yellow starting hurdle, five metres in front of the Fun-fortress gates. Each of the challengers, she noted, wore knee length sorrel running shorts, a brown short sleeve jersey vest, a black belt and black racing slippers. Dominic it seemed was the youngest.

"What do you think of the calibre of our athletes, Zeta?" asked Cynthia, looking over the group of contenders and measuring her cousin, Tau's, chances of success. "The race numbers stamped on the back of their shirts are certainly big enough."

"They look like they mean business, Cynthia. How old are they?"

"I have the race guide here," butted in Mandy, holding up a leaflet with a purple logo. "The lads in the other four teams are between seventeen and nineteen and weigh... a lot more than Tau." She laughed. "In contrast my cousin is-"

"Quite lean," interrupted Cynthia.

"The other lads are much stronger?" asked Zeta.

"Physically stronger, yes," replied Cynthia.

"Look!" exclaimed Felicity, interrupting. "The Cup is about to begin! It's fast, non stop action all the way from here, Zeta!"

Transmitting images onto eight wall mounted telescreens in both the Funfair and the Science levels, the cameras in the fortress flashed into life. Concurrently the Cup-adjudicator climbed up onto the chequered podium outside his hut. Smartly dressed, with a neat haircut and an efficient manner, he smiled at the crowd.

"Thank you all for joining us for our Tenth annual staging of the Satellite Cup," he announced. "Our five teams this evening are: Team 200, 42, 87, 95 and Team 128. In one minute, I will fire my starting pistol five times at two-minute intervals. Team 200 will run first. Team 128 with the highest handicap will run last. Please put your hands together for our challengers!"

Eddie was most impressed. "We run last," he said firmly, his voice stifled by enthusiastic clapping.

Suddenly a gun's loud report echoed through the showgrounds. "Team 200, led by Sangria, is away!" the adjudicator shouted.

As the race enthusiasts clapped, the first pair of lads leapt over the starting hurdle. Rushing forward at a generous pace towards the fortress entrance, they ran through the gates and out of sight.

Measuring the speed in which those two fit lads had easily sprinted away, Eddie groaned, "Hell, Tau, no way can I run as fast as that!"

"Strength of mind is equally as important as physical prowess in this contest," responded Dominic coolly. "The winner's purse is large, Eddie - keep focused on your share. But, just so you don't pike out on me, I give you fair warning - there will be some ugly faces if we do lose. Parsons has placed a very large bet on behalf of my work mates." Aware of the concern behind Eddie's sober expression, Dominic added. "With your unique dogmatism, Eddie, our odds are excellent for a win."

The starting gun fired again. The second pair of lads jumped the hurdle and dashed forward.

"Team 42, led by Hanepoot, is away!" shouted the smiling adjudicator and the assemblage cheered.

"How many work mates are risking their money, Tau?"

"Twenty eight, Eddie. And I bet a months salary on myself."

"Thanks for that."

The gun fired for a third time.

"Team 87, led by Mahoney, is away!" shouted the adjudicator above the noise of applause and cheering. The next pair of contestants sprang forward over the hurdle, promptly disappearing through the red fortress gates.

Glancing shrewdly behind him at the crowd, many waving 128 pennons, Eddie remarked, "Our race number 128 imitates your Fleet, Tau. Why?"

"Advertising," replied Dominic, also glancing behind him at the flock of young people, most of them in their late teens. "The more people I can persuade to join me from different occupations the better off my splinter group will be - when we leave."

"You've told me why you needed to borrow the Dandy Lion, Tau. Aren't you afraid of retaliation from your current world leader?"

A look of apprehension flitted across Dominic's face.

The starting pistol fired its fourth shot and as the crowd yelled delightedly, the fourth team literally flew over the hurdle, to be swallowed-up almost immediately by the waiting fortress.

"Team 95, led by Keating is away!" shouted the grinning adjudicator, belatedly.

"If anyone beats us, Keating will," said Dominic, crouching down at the starting line ready to spring away at the next firing.

Lean and fair, his noble face set with calm determination. Eddie of heavier, shorter physique and with more moderate, but still pleasing features, followed suit humbly.

"About your previous question, Eddie," Dominic now replied. "Yes. I am afraid of the repercussions if TT catches me."

Eddie gaped. "TT Vox Populi?"

"Yes. TT is my great-grandfather," Dominic replied soberly.

"By jingoes!" exclaimed Eddie, grinning widely. "One of your kin is the Governor of an undersea city, the other is your world leader. No wonder you're so -"

"Appealing," cut in Dominic, his blue eyes flashing. He glanced away quickly. Then he looked sternly back at Eddie. "They are signalling me. Get ready!"

A loud report from the starting pistol split the air.

"Team 128, lead by Tau, is away!" the adjudicator shouted.

Amidst a deafening roar of applause, both lads leapt the hurdle and darted swiftly towards the fortress gates. Dominic took the lead with Eddie running not far behind.

"My cousin is very popular, Zeta," remarked Mandy proudly, watching them both disappear inside the fortress.

Via their telescreens, the showground spectators now enjoyed coverage of the competitors racing through the fortress. Eagerly they watched as Dominic and Eddie raced down a dark inclined tunnel, heading for the first of the eight, fifty-metre square, fortress chambers.

"The first chamber is called the Antigravity Room, Zeta," explained Felicity. "There is no gravity, of course. And little light. It is designed to make any visitor feel as if they were floating in Space, amidst the stars."

"How beautiful," remarked Zeta, able to see the room herself on her telescreen. "It's like the Milky Way Galaxy inside."

"Hey you two! Watch the contestants," said Mandy, her eyes fixed firstly on her cousin and then on Eddie. "Tau is just about to dive through the Antigravity Room. I've seen him do this once before in a previous heat. They've changed the room around this time. Keep your eyes glued to your telescreen. The dive looks really good and will be over in less than a minute."

As Mandy spoke, Eddie, rounding a sharp bend, not far behind Dominic, was just in time to see his team-mate dive through a specially designed access tube. Once Dominic was through that tube and into the simulated Outer Space environment of the Antigravity Room, he flew weightless across the chamber.

Realistically fashioned to mimic familiar constellations, the room around him was Space at its best - enchanting, beautiful and enticing. Shooting gleaming light forward from distant celestial bodies, glistening particles speckled the chamber. Predominately a black and white vista, the constellations were also coloured with hues of blue, gold, pink and aqua.

Appearing in the middle of the chamber - part of a holographic light show - the blue planet, Neptune, suddenly shone brightly. Dominic floated quickly through its centre. Following in quick succession, he saw images of Saturn and Jupiter - marbled white and peach. Golden and arid, Mars appeared before him, followed by the tranquil blue-grey Earth. The fiery red Venus and Mercury - grey, bleak and pocked with craters - completed the planetary show.

Forty metres through the room, still in weightless flight, Dominic now enjoyed the searing golden vista of Earth's star - the Sun - around which all the other planets previously witnessed, now revolved. Flying through its apex, golden light beams stuck fast to his body and for an instant, he seemed to be a gleaming arrow, blazing in the darkness.

Bringing a cheerful finale to this holographic light show of the Earth's Solar System, several miniature mechanical comets, glowing brilliantly in the darkness, whizzed playfully around him. Darting away, they left a trail of sparkles.

Not taken in by the brief amusing light show and expecting trouble, Dominic glanced to his right, left, and as far behind him as he could practically see. Alerted to movement over on the far right of the chamber, he peered intently through the darkness. Spotting five model asteroids approaching fast, he took sombre note of their heading.

Still flying forward, he reached the rear wall of the Antigravity Room, hitting that wall with a light thud. Hanging fast onto an attached railing, he watched Eddie dive into the chamber. Surprisingly the crystals in his Roaming-Ring began to glow. A split second later, he was asleep.

"What's he doing?" asked Zeta, not taking her eyes from the closest telescreen.

"He's roaming. He's going to help Eddie," Felicity replied.

"Roaming?"

"See those dimly shining model asteroids, Zeta," explained Mandy. "The ones flying towards Eddie. They're really Space robots. It's obvious they intend to intercept Eddie. If they catch him, they're both out of the race."

One minute behind Dominic, Eddie had indeed just dived into the Antigravity Room. Rather than following through with his dive however, the peaceful ambiance of the room immediately overtook him. Opening out his arms, he leant backwards. Floating serenely within the simulated Cosmos, he marvelled at the detailed constellations in the distance. Far away across the chamber, he vaguely noticed the quartz crystals in Dominic's Roaming-Ring gleaming in the darkness. Cocooned by this enchanting Outer Space environment, he lost all sense of urgency.

"Eddie, look out!" Dominic warned, suddenly appearing as a ghostly image by his side. "Sports robots - a metre to your right!"

Eddie, startled from his languid state, hurriedly tried to move away from the robots. Failing that, the robots stretched out their mechanical arms to grab him. Just as the pincers of all five robots commenced to close on his arms and legs, however, he felt a strange force seize him. Consequently, Dominic's psyche hurtled him across the room. A moment later, he hit the rear wall with a thud. Holding fast onto the wall railing, he hauled himself upwards and climbed through the exit tube. After which he fell out into a purple shaft that connected chambers one and two.

Dominic, now conscious, quickly followed. Also climbing through the tube, he emerged out into the purple shaft. As they both ran forward, he placed his hand on Eddie's back. Aggressively, he increased his gait.

"Too slow, uh?" shouted Eddie.

"Yes!"

"Your psyche threw me almost fifty metres across that room!" exclaimed Eddie. "Is strength of spirit the key? Or can anyone do that with enough practice? I wouldn't mind having that knack when I roam. If you're ever offering any pointers, Tau, I'm listening."

"We lost valuable time in the Antigravity Room," responded Dominic. "If we win, I'll offer up a few useful tips. Now, pick up the pace! Inside the next chamber will be a human obstacle - a chamber guardian. When we enter that chamber, the guardian will focus on me. Distract him or her. Give me a chance to get clear of the room. As soon as I'm near the exit, run as fast as you can!"

All of a sudden, outside in the showgrounds, the spectators cheered.

"They're cheering for Matthew Keating, Zeta," said Felicity, noting the questioning expression on Zeta's face.

"Look at the telescreen over to your left," suggested Cynthia, "at the lad with the dark hair. He's just used his mind powers in quite a remarkable way."

"I missed it. What did he do?" asked Zeta.

"He has the gift of telekinesis. He just reversed the trajectory of a whole heap of baseballs that were being pelted at himself and his team-mate - by Sports robots."

"Shush. I'm watching my cousin," interrupted Mandy. "Tau and Eddie will soon enter the Soporific Room."

"The Soporific Room is the first of four chambers guarded by a person with a psychic gift," whispered Cynthia, moving her pony closer to Zeta's. "The chamber guardians try to trap the lads. This promises to be most exciting."

Via their telescreen, the girls watched Dominic and Eddie racing through the wide purple shaft towards the Soporific Room. The shaft was so steep that by the time the lads had reached the chamber entrance, Eddie was struggling for breath. Standing in the chamber doorway - two metres above the floor below - the lads hastily jumped down.

As soon as their feet hit the floor, the dark chamber around them softly illuminated. Plush, a comfortable hall stretched out before them. Warm, a burgundy carpet lay thick underfoot. Long mahogany occasional tables placed throughout the room offered carafes of fruity mellow wine and appetising hors d'oeuvres. Big brown leather sofas promised relaxation, while muted lighting from rose-shaded lamps created an easy ambience. Completing the luxurious decor, creamy sheepskin rugs scattered over the floor guaranteed deep restful slumber.

"Tau, I can smell the aroma of freshly baked bread and percolated coffee in here," remarked Eddie. "I thought you only have Lumpo to eat."

"That's right," replied Dominic. "We do."

Unexpectedly, the relaxing strains of fine music suddenly filled the chamber. Simultaneously a pedestal theatrically rose up from a nearby floor cavity. Sensationally Goth, an exotic raven-haired young woman - barely twenty - stood on that pedestal. With a beguiling smile, her eyes set on Dominic.

"Welcome, Tau," she said in a most alluring woman's voice. "Look at me, darling."

Dominic's eyes met hers. Staring at her beautiful face, he was unable to look away.

"Rest for a little while, Tau," she continued enticingly. "Enjoy the comfort. There is food and wine. I have much to offer." Moving off her pedestal she stepped down a flight of stairs - all the while keeping her eyes fixed firmly on Dominic's face. "Join me," she said. Sitting down on an adjacent rug, she smiled up enchantingly.

Succumbing to her soporific gift, Dominic took one step forward. Then he stumbled.

"We'll have none of that, your Lordship!" shouted Eddie. Grabbing Dominic's arm, he shook him roughly. "Wake up, boy-o. Remember the competition. All that money?"

Failing to break the intense stupor overwhelming his team-mate, Eddie lurched threateningly towards the girl.

"Excuse me, poppet!" he shouted. "Do you mind?"

Unnerved by Eddie's behaviour, the girl broke eye contact with Dominic. The psychic connection was shattered and the fair lad dashed away.

When he was only half way across the chamber, Mandy, watching him on her telescreen, began to exclaim, "What's Tau doing? He's stopped at one of the tables! The food is really Lumpo and water. Oh. Don't stop there, Tau. You don't know what's behind that sofa - only a metre away. If you knew, you wouldn't stop!"

"He can't hear you, Mandy," said Cynthia.

"I want him to win," Mandy said sulkily.

Dominic indeed, had stopped at a table, but his interest was not in food. Reaching down, he grabbed a sharp knife from the tabletop. Wrapping the knife in a cloth table napkin, he shoved it into his belt. After which he ran for the exit.

"What do you think he wants the knife for?" asked Felicity.

"I don't know. He likes collecting things in his travels," replied Cynthia, grinning at Zeta as she spoke.

"Oh dear," remarked a nearby spectator, watching a different telescreen. "The lads of the Hanepoot team are lying unconscious behind one of those sofas. One of them is my brother."

Mandy glanced at the speaker. Then she exclaimed, "Look Zeta! Hordes of knee-high Housekeeping robots have scuttled out from a hole in the floor and are chasing Tau. Aren't they nasty - speeding towards him with their arms outstretched and their claws snapping!"

"They have so many hands," said Zeta quietly. "They're like huge upright silver centipedes with oval heads. I hope Dominic gets away. I don't think I could bear to watch dozens of those things jumping on him."

Mandy however, was now watching the chamber guardian. Arising from where she had languished on her sheepskin rug, she moved towards Eddie.

"My, my, you are a strong lad," she said in a cool, throaty drawl. "You have such striking deep green eyes. Give me your name and please, sit down. Drink. Indulge your appetite. Rest and enjoy the comfortable lifestyle. You are tired."

Stubbornly turning away from the young guardian, Eddie focused on Dominic, escaping from robots in the distance. Glancing back to look at her, he responded genially, "You have extravagant tastes, Miss, and an extraordinary hair style. Thank you for your hospitality, but I must abstain, for my health! Goodbye!"

Observing his team-mate rush through the exit, Eddie ran as fast as he could. Striking forward past the girl, his feet thudded lightly on the soft burgundy carpet. Swerving to avoid the clutches of several busy Housekeeping robots, he headed for the distant red exit door.

Meanwhile - many metres away - stopped outside the door of the next chamber, three, Dominic activated his Roaming-Ring.

"Watch this, Zeta," said Cynthia, not taking her eyes from the telescreen. "Eddie's not half way through chamber two, right?"

After she spoke, the crowd in the showgrounds gasped. Dominic's gleaming phantom had suddenly appeared in the centre of chamber two. Sensationally his psyche - flying at Eddie's back - pushed his team-mate forward at an incredible speed.

Recognizing Dominic's ghost behind him, Eddie threw much of his own energy into running faster. Aided by Dominic's driving advance, he crossed the remaining thirty-metres of the room - in seconds. Applauded by the showground spectators outside, he burst energetically through the exit door.

Unfortunately for Eddie, however, he tripped. Accompanied by a startled oath, he tumbled down the next short interconnecting duct between chambers two and three. Falling awkwardly outside the wide blue door to chamber three, next to the mortal awakening Dominic, he grimaced.

Rubbing his bruised knees, he glowered. "You're not half rough!"

"Just as well no-one outside can hear you, Eddie. They might just think you were a little girl, complaining," Dominic said coolly, yanking Eddie quickly to his feet.

"Well, since they can't hear me," said Eddie. Facing away from the camera and judging Dominic's reaction, he said something quite coarse. Met with a determined unflustered look by his team-mate, he grinned resignedly. With the air cleared of any previous pent up hostility, Eddie pushed open the next door. United, they ran into the warm humid environs of chamber three.

Strikingly pleasant with a calm atmosphere, the colours of this chamber were golden, blue and bamboo brown. Mimicking a sunny day, the overhead lighting shone warm rays over a curved beach covered in soft yellow sand. Decorating the beach, the umbrellas of palm trees cast strong shadows over that sand. Central to the chamber, the waters of a deep circular lagoon lapped gently over shiny white rocks bordering the shoreline.

Abruptly stopping before the lagoon, Eddie started to laugh. "Good gracious, the lagoon's full of piranhas and giant snapping oysters!"

Constantly jumping out of the water, sporting jagged teeth, the robotic piranhas fascinated Eddie. As he watched them briefly, he also listened to the strange sound of large mechanical oysters that rose up close to the surface, opened and shut their vice-like clams and stared at him with robotic eyes.

"Tau, what's this room called?"

"It's the Confusion Room, Eddie," replied Dominic, whilst cautiously glancing at their only avenue across the lagoon - a bamboo-bridge, suspended by ropes from the fortress ceiling.

Eddie also focused on the bridge, the sandy beach on the other side of the lagoon and the ochre exit door. Then he made to run for the bridge.

"Wait a tick," warned Dominic, listening to something and holding him back. "This is all too easy."

They both now heard the sound of wheels briefly turning, disturbing the otherwise quiet chamber. Without warning, the bamboo-bridge - an innocent link to the exit - groaned and pitched. Moments later, it snapped into ten uniform segments. Swinging violently away from its neighbouring segments, each piece of bridge stopped in the centre of the lagoon, many metres from the shore.

"The experience will only get better. Believe me," remarked Dominic. Noting Eddie's appalled expression, he grinned.

Unexpectedly, the waters of the lagoon began to bubble. An underwater door opened at the bottom of the lagoon. Thereafter, ten creatures swam out of that door, leapt out of the water and landed, one apiece, on each of the ten bridge segments. There they sat, grinning puckishly - metre-high, blue-haired, silver-bodied robots. Each robot had a scaly blue fish tail, a scantily clad, but modest torso, a triangular head and a unique designer face. As Eddie gazed at the little mechanical creatures, one of them began to sing to him in a synthesized sweet voice.

While Eddie listened to the song, Dominic surveyed the water, the bridge segments and the robots.

"Roaming-time, Eddie," he advised.

Gripping Eddie by the shoulder, the crystals in his Roaming-Ring glowed. Simultaneously his spectre appeared on the closest bridge. In less than sixty seconds, he had swept all the bridges clean of robots. Awakening with a memento in his hand - a small circuit board confiscated from one of the robots cranial electronic systems - he smiled.

The aquatic mechinoids, thrown from their seats, swam amongst the snapping piranha, swept back their long blue hair and grinned at Eddie impishly.

"Not sentimental about the mechanical mermaids, I see," remarked Eddie.

"Fitted to the right side railing on each of the bridge segments is a small electronic device - a keypad and screen," explained Dominic curtly, ignoring the previous comment. "I'm expecting the closest bridge to swing this way, any time now. When it does, jump on and don't get between me and the railing device."

A harsh wind suddenly began to blow through their tranquil chamber. The blue lagoon instantly became choppy. Sirens fitted to the chamber walls began to sound. Dazzling stroboscopic lights beamed from all directions. The bridge segments shuddered and rocked. Previously calm, the mermaids leapt and dived.

"Get ready!" shouted Dominic above the dissonance of sound.

As he had anticipated, the closest bridge segment abruptly swung towards the shore, then stopped.

Springing forward and landing on that bridge segment, Dominic immediately read a legible sequence of seven numbers, displayed on the railing device. Three seconds later he watched those numbers disappear, to be replaced by a clock, counting down from twenty.

Joined by Eddie, Dominic swiftly keyed the seven memorized numbers into the railing device. Two seconds later, their bridge segment lurched forward across the lagoon and adjoined itself to another.

"Jump!" he yelled, above the noise of the sirens.

The two lads leapt forward onto the next pitching bridge segment.

Watching as the bridge behind them collapsed heavily into the pool, Eddie shouted, "What now, your Lordship?"

"The next series of numbers will flash up on the railing device on this bridge segment any moment now," advised Dominic. "I repeat the process of keying the memorized numbers into the keypad and we jump from bridge to bridge, ten times. I have twenty seconds to key in the numbers before the bridge underneath us collapses."

"There's more to this than just keying in numbers?" shouted Eddie as a leaping diving mermaid deliberately splashed him with a high wave of water.

"I don't suppose cricket is your game?" responded Dominic, spotting two little black robots with round orange wings flying into their chamber.

"Crikey. Each of those robots is loaded with a bag of cricket balls!" Eddie exclaimed.

Approximately one metre tall and half of that wide, Eddie observed that these particular robots each had four eyes, a large oval head, two hands similar to baseball mitts and spindly dangling legs.

"Best kick one of the balustrades free of this bridge and arm yourself with a bat, Eddie!" shouted Dominic. "You're looking at Sports robots and they're lining us up as targets!"

As Dominic spoke these words, the next series of nine numbers flashed up onto the railing device. After the black numerals faded, Dominic keyed in the retained information. Then he readied to jump to the next bridge segment.

Meanwhile Eddie kicked roughly at the bridge balustrade, snapping off one of the club-shaped pins at the base. Twisting it upwards, the pin broke free in his hand. Hanging on while their bridge swung to join another - armed with his crude bat - Eddie leapt onto the third pitching structure, with Dominic by his side.

"More Sports robots!" shouted Eddie, spotting two additional robots flying into the chamber. Then he batted away several fast-bowled balls, pitched by those robots. "We get two more every time we jump onto a new bridge, right?"

"Right. And watch you don't brain me!" warned Dominic, ducking to avoid a swing of Eddie's bat.

Buffeted by the strong wind, Dominic continued to key in remembered numerals while Eddie deftly batted away an ever-increasing number of cricket balls. All the while, they leapt from one quickly collapsing bridge segment to another.

By the time they had reached the ninth bridge segment, the sequence of numbers displayed on the railing device had grown to twenty-three. Eighteen Sports robots buzzed around their heads, pitching countless cricket balls. The sirens blared. The stroboscopic lights flashed and eight collapsed bridge segments, half submerged, floated sorrowfully in the choppy lagoon.

Finished keying in the ninth set of numerals Dominic shouted urgently, "Be ready to jump, Eddie!"

Swinging across the lagoon, the ninth bridge segment joined itself to the tenth - the last piece of bridge.

The lads jumped, landing on the tenth bridge. A fraction of a second later, they heard a loud snap. Giving way beneath their feet the entire bamboo decking collapsed. Accompanied by the disappointed cries of the watching spectators outside, both lads fell awkwardly through the bridge, into the choppy lagoon.

One school of piranha rapidly swam towards them. Several giant cream oyster shells rose up out of the water to snap at them. Fast approaching, the blue-haired mermaids grinned cheekily and splashed them. Flitting overhead, the Sports robots offered to fish them out.

"I am not impressed. Twenty seconds, baloney," grumbled Dominic. Yelling coarse instructions to Eddie, and irritated by small bruises from tiny fish nips, he scrambled up onto the tenth bridge segment. There he clung tenaciously to the slippery bamboo railing.

As Eddie heaved himself out of the water onto that same bridge, the final black numerals flashed up onto the railing device. Dominic committed the numbers to memory. Then he keyed the last twenty-five digits into the keypad. Instantly their bridge segment departed the centre of the chaotic lagoon, swinging towards the sandy beach.

Deliberately breaking the railing device from the last bridge segment, Dominic shoved it into his belt. When the tenth bridge segment hit the shore with a thud, he flung himself off, landing drenched and dishevelled on the warm beach sand. Eddie, landing beside him, ran straight for the exit.

"No, wait!" Dominic shouted, drawing him back.

"I thought time was of the essence?"

"Not so - in this instance. Stand guard over me, Eddie. I'm going to roam and collect two of those ropes left hanging from the ceiling. We'll need them. Make sure the Sports robots don't whack me in the face with their cricket balls - while I am asleep!" Seeing Eddie grinning divisively, Dominic added in warning. "If I don't get to go to any parties because I have a black eye, you'll fare the same."

After which he closed his eyes, the crystals in his Roaming-Ring glowed, and his ghostly image appeared in front of his mortal self. Taking his knife from his belt, his spectral self flew swiftly to the ceiling. Once there he cut down the requisite ropes. Returning promptly, he dropped his booty onto the floor before his waiting team-mate and his sleeping body.

Eddie observed, just at that moment, that the sirens ceased to sound, the wind ceased to blow and the lights in the Confusion Room returned to normal. The Sports robots and robotic mermaids disappeared through a hidden door. The mechanical oysters sank down to the bottom of the lagoon and closed.

Ready to run, Eddie was surprised when Dominic's spectre turned towards the surveillance camera mounted on their chamber wall - and waved.

"My cousin is very polite, isn't he, Zeta?" said Cynthia proudly, glancing around her at the pleased showground spectators.

"Hey. Wake up," muttered Eddie, back in the Confusion Room. Shaking Dominic's mortal self rudely from slumber, he growled. "I thought we were in a hurry!"

"Just the once," said Dominic, now awake and his spectre vanished. "We won't be delaying again." Grinning, he stowed his knife carefully into his belt and hastily coiled the two lengths of lightweight rope. Tossing one length to Eddie, he slung the other diagonally across his own chest.

"How much cable have we got?" asked Eddie.

"One hundred and twenty metres between us," replied Dominic coolly. "Now, let's go!" Together with Eddie, he summarily departed the now tranquil blue lagoon of the Confusion Room.

Running through a steep red corridor between chambers three and four, Dominic with strong stride, once again aided Eddie's progress.

"Tau, any clues on what's next?"

"The next room is called the Illusion Room, Eddie. We will be up against another guardian. This will be another chance for you to demonstrate the merits of your fine intransigent mind."

Reaching the top of the corridor, they heaved open the heavy access door to chamber four. A gust of freezing air embraced them, fastened icy tentacles onto their wet clothes and made them shiver.

Stepping out onto a high landing, a large white frozen hall glistened beneath them. Bitterly cold, stalagmites smattered the icy floor. Snowdrifts banked up against the sides of the chamber gleamed powdery soft. While realistic snowmen scattered throughout the room blinked at the lads with robotic eyes. Central to the room a structure of descending and ascending stairs crossed over to the high exit platform on the other side. Flowing underneath those stairs an icy stream bubbled over mossy rocks.

Glancing towards the exit platform they saw a stout old lady wrapped in a blood red cape. Whipping her loose dark grey hair about her face, the glacial wind in the chamber chilled her bones. Standing stock still, she coldly met their gaze.

While Eddie regarded the guardian indifferently, Dominic cast a discerning eye over the rest of the chamber. He peered at the icy stream. Believing he spotted Team 87 - led by Mahoney - standing in the water beside a tall silver rock, he frowned. Looking over the small landings connecting the stairs, his eyes then narrowed. For on the nearest landing, dressed in her pink skirt and black vest, he imagined he saw Zeta. She was crying. Scowling, but now on terms with his mendacious surrounds, Dominic turned to Eddie.

"How many people can you see besides me?" he asked.

"Three," replied Eddie. "The guardian on the exit platform and the two youths of Team 87, under the stairs. They have been captured by a snowman robot. There's one more robot, standing on the landing closest to us?"

"What does it look like, Eddie?"

"That particular robot resembles a mini recycling skip, your Lordship," warned Eddie.

Dominic soberly studied the chamber ceiling. "We can forget the icy stairs, Eddie," he said. "We'll get through here fastest by shimmying along a rope that I will fix to the ceiling rings. We can climb up one rope to the top, crawl our way across the ceiling and drop down on the final length of rope. Stay here and guard me while I roam."

"It's a fifty metre drop if I fall," said Eddie, throwing his rope uneasily towards Dominic.

"Well *don't* fall!"

Hastily throwing off his own coil of rope and tossing it in front of him together with Eddie's cable, Dominic gripped his team-mate's shoulder. Closing his eyes, the crystals in his Roaming-Ring glowed. An instant later, his flying phantom was soaring towards the ceiling.

Eddie watched Dominic's spectre secure the lightweight rope through loops on the ceiling. Once the lad's spectre had fastened the spare ends to the stair railings at the entrance and exit point, it vanished.

Awake and jumping up onto the stair railing - with Eddie temporarily leading - Dominic climbed the rope to the ceiling.

"Great suggestion. It's definitely more comfortable up here," remarked Eddie, when they had both reached the ceiling. "I'm drying off nicely with the warm breeze. However," he continued cheekily, "if this is your idea of a date, Tau, I'm obliged to tell you now that I'd prefer any company other than yours!"

"I'm devastated!" retorted Dominic, entwining his legs around the rope and moving quickly across the ceiling, until Eddie blocked his progress. "I'm not hanging upside down, *static*, clinging to a cable that's cutting into my hands, because I want to listen to your romantic petulance. What do you want, Eddie?"

"No one looks at me?" replied Eddie quietly.

"If you want someone mild to suit, I can make the introduction. She looks OK, is about 160cm tall and weighs approximately fifty kilos. Interested?"

"Sure I am. When?"

"After the race," Dominic replied cursorily. "Now you're sorted, Eddie. No excuses. Get moving!"

"Wait!" asked Eddie. "What about Mahoney and his team mate. You can't just leave them. They'll freeze down there."

"Any contestants who fail are released as soon as the last team passes them - which means us. Now I'm tired of hanging around," Dominic shouted. "Go!"

Smartly moving forward, Eddie slithered across the ceiling. Dominic followed close behind. After several minutes of strenuous exertion, the lads reached the far side of the chamber. There they dropped down the last length of rope onto the exit platform, next to the Illusionist.

Dominic glanced at the rope still fastened to the railing, nodded to her coldly and spoke quickly, "Eddie, you're on guard duty again while I roam and recover our ropes. Then we're out of here!"

Gripping Eddie's shoulder he was instantly asleep - flying in spectral form up to the high chamber ceiling. Moments later, with their ropes slung across their chests, Dominic grinned roguishly. "You'll enjoy the fifth chamber, Eddie. It's an assault course, and it's called the Jungle Room!"

Running hastily from the Illusion Room, watched by the spectators outside the fortress, the lads slid speedily down an almost vertical shaft into chamber five.

Their descent into the Jungle Room was swift. Dominic landed on his feet at the bottom of the shaft. Eddie hit the ground faster, tumbling forward.

Jumping hastily onto his feet, Eddie discovered that they were now in the small lush green clearing of a virtual Amazon rainforest. Edged by a thick barrier of undergrowth and trees, a murky green stream pushed its way through the forest, from their clearing to the distant exit. Lounging on the banks of that stream several crocodiles blinked at the newcomers. Overhanging the stream, coiled on a low hanging tree bough, a large green anaconda opened its mouth in a horrible smile.

Within moments of their arrival, Eddie saw the cold staring eyes of a band of guerrillas, camouflaged within the forest, looking their way.

"Tau, what do those apes want?" he asked.

"I told you this was an assault course, Eddie," replied Dominic, coolly standing by his side. "They're here to assault you."

Unexpectedly a flock of red parrots, perched in the branches of a nearby tree, squawked raucously, flew up to the curved satellite ceiling, and landed on a length of overhead piping.

"You're kidding, right?" growled Eddie.

"It's rather humid in here," remarked Dominic, preoccupied with a necessary electronics challenge - that of fixing the mermaid's circuit board into the bridge railing device.

"When you've finished, just let me know, won't you?" said Eddie sarcastically, fitfully eyeing the approaching guerrillas.

Blinking coldly, the crocodiles slid down the banks into the stream. Floating just underneath the surface, they began swimming towards the clearing.

"*Hello*? Your Lordship?" Eddie asked nervously, measuring his words slowly. "Have you got your toy working? I'm no squib, but there are five *big* guys, only a few metres away, who are going to remind us both of what the word *pain* means."

Dominic remained unresponsive. Keying in a final code and setting a frequency on his makeshift remote-control, he stared past the guerrillas, into the jungle.

Suddenly there was a loud bellow. Startling all in the clearing, something large and unseen came crashing through the trees. Underneath them, the chamber floor shook. Swishing and rustling, the jungle foliage fell, trampled down by a heavy beast. Seconds later, the source of the disturbance burst into the clearing. Trumpeting loudly, waving its head and tusks menacingly, an African elephant stomped and thumped about the clearing, forcing the guerrillas back into the trees.

"Give it a rest, Tau, that beast is dangerous!" yelled one of the guerrillas, a large young man, aged twenty, called Blake.

Dominic keyed another code into his makeshift remote-control and grinned. Abruptly the elephant stopped stomping. Walking towards him, it swung its trunk benignly. Then it knelt down.

"The elephant's a robot!" shouted Eddie.

Dominic's response was urgent. "All the wild beasts in here are robots, except for those guerrillas. Jump onto the elephant quickly, Eddie, before the five brutes over there get brave enough to charge the elephant."

Dominic easily leapt up onto the elephant's back. Hauling Eddie up roughly behind him, he hastily typed more instructions into his electronic keypad. "Once I combined the mermaid's integrated circuit with the keypad, Eddie," he hastily explained, "I was able to tune into the elephant's remote function frequency. Then, hey presto!"

Instantly their elephant rose. Turning towards the exit it shook its head and tusks at the guerrillas, dissuading their cautious advance. Stomping heavily from the clearing, through the dense undergrowth, it trumpeted again.

"Tau, you pusillanimous amoeba!" called Blake, disgruntled to see the lads escape so easily. "Get off that beast! Come back! I challenge you to combat!"

Dominic yelled back swiftly. "For reasons of decorum, Blake, I decline your challenge! Today, I am gentle and refrain from all barbaric forms of combat."

"Where's your best buddy, Tau? Are you afraid to fight without that Herculean magician by your side!" Blake shouted.

"You're missing Bermuda?" shouted Dominic sarcastically, his elephant now fading from view amongst the thick jungle foliage. "How sad for you, Blake, that your only recreation is fighting."

Without expression, all the belligerent guerrillas watched the lads leave.

"Tau obviously planned to get out of here as quickly as possible," Blake said sourly. "I had hoped this jungle would detain him and possibly beat him. Now I'm left disappointed." Darkly scrutinizing his four, pokerfaced comrades, now lolling casually about in the grassy jungle clearing, Blake's eyes narrowed shrewdly. "Tau is certainly on his best behaviour today. Who's he trying to impress?"

When one of the other guerrillas silently mouthed a name, Blake glared at them all nastily.

"Thanks a bunch! Why didn't any of you galumphing galahs tell me the little lady was here?" Respectfully he brushed his hand against his Roaming-Ring. "Just because I adhere to Tau's endeavours doesn't mean that I judged him to take *this race*. I placed my bet on Keating to win, and now I've wasted all my money!"

Blake watched Dominic and Eddie, now in a raised clearing at the rear of the chamber, leap from their elephant and disappear through the vine-covered exit.

"You pack of bludgers!" he shouted at his four comrades in final reproach. Then he too dropped down to lounge in the clearing, all the while keeping his eye on the nearby crocodiles.

Meanwhile, the lads had stopped in the vertical access duct between chambers five and six. With no easy way to climb up the narrow duct, Dominic once again chose roaming as a solution.

"I'll fly up to the top of the duct and tie my rope off, Eddie," he briefly stated. "The lads through before us have confiscated the supplied ropes for this duct. I'll be back in a tick. Be nice to our showground audience while I'm asleep. Your soon to be new friend is amongst them."

Eddie watched the crystals in Dominic's Roaming-Ring glow. The fair lad's subsequent apparition flew upwards, armed with the rope. Eddie waited, looked at the camera and smiled. Moments later, he saw the end of the rope drop down through the duct and fall at his feet. Simultaneously, Dominic awoke.

"How far is it to the top?" Eddie asked soberly.

"Sorry, forty metres."

Eddie glanced at his hands. Taking the lead, conscious of the cameras, he grabbed the rope and began his ascent.

By the time they had both climbed through the duct to the platform at the top, both their vests were wet with perspiration and their hands were chafed. While Dominic wrenched at the heavy grey steel door that blocked their progress into chamber six, Eddie, feeling tired, slumped down onto the platform.

"Tau? What's this chamber called and what can we expect?"

Dominic shook his head soberly, "I honestly don't know what to expect, Eddie. And you don't want to know what this chamber is called."

Suddenly, giving way to Dominic's persistent tugging, the steel door swung open violently, accompanied by a noisy echoing bang. Glancing through the doorway, Dominic saw a pitch-black chamber inside. Seeping from that chamber towards him, he felt a cold chill.

"Get up, Eddie!" he shouted. "After this chamber, there are only two more to traverse, then we're through the fortress. Come on!"

While Eddie jumped to his feet, Dominic rushed through the door, to stop a moment later on a small square balcony. Below and above him he could see only darkness. The chamber smelt damp and the air was stale. The atmosphere was ominous and he could detect a strange odour of engine oil far down below. Cautiously leaning forward over the balcony, he peered down into the blackness. Then he carefully listened but heard not a sound. A moment later, Eddie was by his side.

"There's a metal ladder fastened to the wall next to the balcony, Eddie. I'll go down first. If all seems favourable, I'll call you." Climbing over the balcony, Dominic jumped for the ladder. Catching the ladder railings, he quickly found a foothold. "The wall is greasy, Eddie," he advised. "Try not to get any of the stuff on your hands."

Holding onto the side rails of the ladder in a controlled descent, Dominic slid quickly downwards. "I'm at the bottom of what seems to be a well," he shouted upwards, a short time later. "Your turn Eddie!"

In the darkness and keeping a measured distance away from the ladder, he waited until Eddie had completed the thirty-metre descent. When Eddie landed beside him, he heard the entrance door slam shut with a bang, leaving them in total darkness.

"Light certainly took a holiday from this chamber," remarked Eddie, standing warily by his team-mate's side. "I have to admit that I don't like it in here - one little bit."

Deprived of his vision, Eddie's other senses came into play. His hearing and his tactile senses coming to the forefront, he became aware of two distinct factors. Firstly, that he was standing on something that was hard, slippery and slanted. Secondly, that he could hear a strange sound coming from somewhere close - that noise being an irritating combination of tearing, scratching, and scurrying, intermingled with horrible high pitched squeals.

"Just in case there's a remote chance, Tau - are any light switches in here?" he asked. "So we can see what's making that disturbing racket."

Glancing at a high-tech night vision camera against the wall behind them, Dominic answered coolly, "The spectators in the showground can see what's going on. We obviously are going to be left in the dark."

"Oh, lovely. They'll get to see me being eaten and I'll miss it."

Suddenly the scurrying noise became louder and Eddie felt something brush against his leg. "There's something in here," he said quietly.

"Yes," replied Dominic, thumping his boots down on the hard metal surface underfoot. "Crawling on your legs, no doubt, as they are on mine."

"Tau, you wouldn't perchance to have snatched a torch in your travels, would you?" asked Eddie, his voice nervous.

"Yes and no," replied Dominic quietly. "The display screen on the railing device will cast a bright light for us. A small illumination, but it will have to do."

"Well, we might as well know the worst," said Eddie. "Light up the chamber, your Lordship!"

Dominic searched in his belt for the railing device. Activating it in the darkness, he quickly illuminated their dank musty surrounds.

Cast by his light, creepy muted shadows danced ominously over the chamber walls and the structures within. Looming large before Dominic and Eddie, fifteen pivot-mounted metal disks of increasing height filled what was indeed a cylindrical well. Ascending from where they stood on the first disk, to the last disk located in front of the now faintly illuminated blue exit, the disks were large, green, oblique and metal. On each of these facing disks, a strange shadowy figure sat in the gloom, watching them with red gleaming eyes.

"What are they?" asked Eddie.

"Human-shaped, stocky, with square metal heads and square hands. I'd hazard a guess that they are Agricultural robots," said Dominic. When we get closer, I'll be able to tell for sure. If I'm right they'll each be dressed in a flannel shirt, black dungarees and Wellington boots."

"Friendly then?"

"Not to us, today. Make sure they don't grab you."

While speaking, Dominic watched a large shadowy black mass that was moving nearby. When he stepped towards it, the mass rushed away, disappearing over the edge of their disk.

"Right. I need to check out what's underneath the disks, Eddie. Don't go anywhere."

Stepping cautiously forward towards the edge of their disk and looking over, Dominic saw a huge creeping shadow. Holding out his light, he discovered the source of the worrying noise. Scurrying across long thin floating logs, over an oily pool - one metre below - were hundreds of large black rats.

Returning to Eddie, he ordered him brusquely, "Don't ask questions, Eddie. Just co-operate. Raise your arms!"

When Eddie obeyed, Dominic tied one end of his rope around Eddie's chest and the other end around his own.

"I'm tough, and I'm asking?" enquired Eddie. "What did you see underneath the disk? Why the rope?"

"Rodents," came the taut reply. "We jump from one disk to another, one at a time, Eddie. If one of us doesn't make the gap, the other has the job of hauling him up. Right."

Eddie, frowning in the chilly gloom, was glad that Dominic had turned away and could not see his pale troubled face. "Rodents, no problem!" he remarked bravely. "I assume they are mechanical?"

"Yes, but they still bite."

Suddenly, over the squeaking and scurrying noise of the rats, they both heard a distinctive hum. Abruptly all of the slanting disks in the vast room began to spin sporadically, at a slow but ever increasing rate.

"Quick!" Dominic yelled urgently, seizing Eddie's arm and roughly impelling him forward. "In a few minutes time the disks will be spinning so fast we'll never get out! Make for the exit!"

With their one small torch, fastened to Dominic's belt, lighting their way, they both ran forward in the chilling darkness. With as much haste as they could chance, they ran across the first rotating disk, jumped the gap, then ran across the second spinning disk, swerving to avoid the Agricultural robot. They repeated this process - of running forward, jumping the gap, sometimes catching a much higher disk by its rim and climbing upwards - many times over.

On two occasions, Eddie stumbled as the disks revolved in fits and jerks. Accompanied by unheard 'oohs' and 'ahhs' from the showground spectators, he fell onto his knees. There to be hauled roughly to his feet by his disgruntled team-mate.

Suddenly, while jumping the last gap between disks fifteen and sixteen, Eddie lost his handhold on the higher disk. Falling a distance of ten metres, he landed atop the jet-black, grey-tailed robotic rats in the greasy slimy sludge beneath. Simultaneously disk sixteen stopped spinning.

"Ooh, poor Eddie!" said Zeta, watching him on her telescreen. "That's so horrible - falling in with the rats." Then she shuddered.

"My cousin is on the final disk," said Cynthia. "Look now!"

The Agricultural robot on disk sixteen had just lurched towards Dominic. With its square hands outstretched, it attempted to seize him. Dominic ducked and ran, luring the robot to the edge of the disk. Once there, he kicked at the mechinoid forcefully. It tottered and swayed. Then it toppled over the edge into the oil beneath.

Using the rope that connected both the lads, he then hauled Eddie back onto the last of the disks. Resulting from this alarming mishap, the lads were covered in greasy black oil. The only team-number visible was the 128 on Dominic's back.

Now the spectators watched the lads dash through the blue exit door. There they stopped at the top of a dim, black, inclined shaft between chambers six and seven.

"I'm slowing you down!" said Eddie, bruised, bitten and fatigued.

Dominic wiped the sweat from his brow. His brown vest was soaked. His hair was tousled. Between the smudges of oil on his body, his tanned skin gleamed with beads of perspiration.

"Agreed, you are slowing me down," Dominic replied. "But you'll prove your worth in the next chamber."

"Why?"

"Because it's the Enchantment Room - notoriously impassable. The guardian will be a magician."

"Hey, you might as well let me know what the last chamber was called, now that it's behind us?"

"Chamber six was called the Contusion Room."

"That figures," said Eddie, wryly laughing.

Without further discourse, they both hurtled down the next access shaft, into the warm, heady and fragrant realm of chamber seven.

Sliding behind Dominic, Eddie landed on his feet inside a four-metre square glass booth, the entrance to chamber seven. Glancing to his left, he spotted the magician seated on a corner chair - wearing a cream suit and a white broad brimmed hat. Exceedingly tall, the man was lean. His hair was silvery white. Above his upper lip, he wore a fine white moustache. Whilst chanting, he stared at the youths with piercing grey eyes.

Beyond the booth, on a lower level, Eddie quickly scrutinized the main portion of the chamber - a gigantic garden maze - entwined throughout with thick jasmine blossoms. Green and dense, the narrow maze corridors were dim and unusually misty. Covered over with a thick layer of mulch, grey twigs, dried golden leaves and dark loam, the maze floor gave off the pungent aroma of a winter forest.

Whilst staring incredulously at something he had just seen in the maze, Eddie was jostled by the youth at his side.

"Quick! Tell me, Eddie; what's in this chamber?"

"We're in a glass booth with the magician, Tau," Eddie answered. "An open door, four metres in front of us, leads down steps into a huge garden maze. Ten robots that look like large garden gnomes are marching through the maze. And," he continued, his voice agitated, "Team 95 and 200 are in there. They appear to be blind."

When Dominic did not immediately respond, Eddie turned to face his team-mate. Quickly he noted Dominic's unusual pallor.

"Not you too?"

"Yes. The magician has made me temporarily blind, Eddie," Dominic whispered angrily. "I'll have to roam. Stand guard over me. Give me one minute to reconnoitre the maze. Then I'll awake."

Stoically, Eddie stood guard while the crystals in Dominic's Roaming-Ring began to glow. After watching his team-mate's anguished face relax into sleep, he saw the spectral image of Dominic fly high over the fifty metre long maze. Dominic's spectre circled once, then disappeared through the rear wall of the chamber.

The magician stood up and walked towards the youths - one sleeping, one awake.

"Hello Eddie," his persuasive voice oozed in greeting. "Did you fall in with the rats? Your black greasy clothes suggest you did. Your friend Tau - his spirit has left him. His psyche won't return. He thinks he's lost, you see. He's given up. When you spoke to him, you could read his defeat in his face, couldn't you? Did he tell you he was blind? You certainly don't want to attach yourself to a loser, do you? You are tired. Defeated. Why don't you admit it, Eddie? This sort of challenge isn't really your cup of tea. Is it?"

Eddie put his palm up to his forehead, brushed a lock of his brown hair away from his eyes and felt the smooth metal of his platinum Roaming-Ring under the palm of his hand. Glancing toward his teammate, he saw Dominic waken.

"Eddie! Twenty, twenty vision is mine! Run! Fast as you can!" shouted Dominic commandingly. "And ditch your rope!"

Throwing off his own coil of rope and pushing past the magician, Dominic ran for the door.

Dumping his cable, Eddie also raced forward. Side-stepping the magician, he ran down several steps out into the green leafy maze. Golden leaves crunched underfoot as he ran and grey twigs snapped. His feet sank into the soft dark spongy earth and he smelt the strong warm melange of jasmine, bark and thick sweet loam. Rounding the first corner of the maze, behind Dominic, he brushed past the other four temporarily blind contestants. Rounding another, he leapt over three small trundling mechinoids with gardening tools for hands, yellow and red pointed heads and large brown leather aprons with pockets full of seedlings. Three metres away from the robots, Eddie had cause to stop.

"What's happening?" he asked between breaths. "What's the hold up?"

"I need one of those Botanical robots," replied Dominic, halted before him in the narrow maze.

Unclipping his makeshift remote-control from his belt, Dominic promptly deactivated the closest robot. Grabbing the machine and carrying it under his arm, he jogged forward hastily, with Eddie close behind. Navigating the maze, he turned several times to the left, then his right. Finally, Dominic ran down an extended corridor and stopped, at a gloomy dead end.

Halting abruptly behind him, Eddie groaned, "I can't believe you made a mistake memorizing the exit route. All I can see is a thick wall of shrubbery!"

"I didn't make a mistake. There isn't an exit."

Putting down the machine, Dominic opened a plate in its yellow, pointed hat. After keying instructions into the tiny computer located within the base of its skull, he closed the plate. Then he stood back and waited.

Activated and using hands that functioned as gardening shears, the small robot cut a hole in the green maze wall.

"Is the aperture to your satisfaction Sir? Do you require any further assistance?" it asked.

"Your work is satisfactory. You are dismissed," replied Dominic. As the little machine trundled away, he threw off his belt. "Your door to the chamber eight has been opened, Eddie," he said cheerfully. "The Hallucination Room awaits!"

Eddie peered through the newly cut aperture, straight into the huge hall of chamber eight. He grinned. "No connecting shaft," he said. Then he paused and asked. "Tau? The magician made you blind. What changed when you woke up?"

"I focused on someone I care about, Eddie. His tricks are shallow weapons. Now get through that hedge. I thrive on competition and I want to shout something to the other two teams in here."

As ordered, Eddie promptly disappeared through the hedge. Now, as the Theme Park spectators watched curiously, the charismatic lad, Tau, whistled piercingly for attention.

"Remember who you love!" he shouted in a raucous voice. After which he dove through the hedge opening into chamber eight, somersaulted forward into an upright position and broke into an immediate run.

Grabbing his team-mate by the arm, and hurtling forward, he headed for the exit in the diagonal corner. "The other teams will be behind us any second now and they'll pass us smartly!" he shouted. "An Illusionist controls this room, Eddie, so I can't trust my eyes. What can you see?"

Grey mist blanketed the damp earthen floor of the chamber before them. Reminiscent of a bleak wintry evening, small cold veils of shadow hung hither and thither. Close on their left stood a small grey twelfth century castle, complete with a dank grey drawbridge. Winding past that castle and through a graveyard in the centre of the chamber, a narrow, red, slippery path led to the exit. Completing the picture, several dilapidated wooden huts on the far right of the chamber leant against each other, smacking of decay. Drizzling down, cold rain drenched everything in sight.

Scanning the area hastily as he ran alongside Dominic, Eddie hoarsely replied. "I can see big robots, each with five round eyes on stalks, four arms and lots of claws, lining the winding path to the exit. Stone coffins are strewn throughout the area. Also, there is one teenage girl, seventeen years of age, I'd guess, wearing a gauzy tattered orange frock. She is standing up on the parapet of a castle to our left."

"The robots are Construction mechinoids," responded Dominic hoarsely, sprinting along at a faster pace. "The girl's the Illusionist. Everyone who steps into this room hallucinates, Eddie. She makes demons, monsters and ghouls sneer in our faces. Keep pace with me! I'm going to push you to the limit. Parsons will resuscitate you at the end, if necessary. And nav-"

Suddenly three Construction robots, flying at them, tried to grab Dominic. Pushing Dominic sideways to avoid the robots, Eddie sharply changed course. Still heading for the exit, he and his team-mate vaulted over several coffins.

"That's right, good show!" shouted Dominic encouragingly, when they were clear of the mechinoids. "Navigate us away from those robots, Eddie! Try to run the straightest path possible. Give it your all, and we'll win!"

Keating's Team 95 and Sangria's Team 200 were now behind them and were gaining fast.

"They'll pass us soon!" Eddie shouted.

Dominic ran faster, but on his face, Eddie saw a strange faraway expression.

"You're hallucinating! What are you seeing?" Eddie yelled, whilst they continued to race forward at breakneck speed.

Dominic's words were wrought, "Nefarids! Monsters from another planet! The loathsome things that killed my parents! All I'm seeing right now are Nefarids." Then his words were stoic. "The Illusionist uses grief to thwart me, Eddie! But the soles of my feet are light! Run faster. Help me win!"

Eddie had never run so fast in his whole life. His feet were flying underneath him. His heart was pounding in his chest and his lungs felt like they were going to burst. But for some uncanny reason he had never felt so determined in all of his life. He kept pace with the fair lean youth, guided Dominic away from the approaching robots and leapt over obstacles.

Suddenly he saw Team 95 and 200 overtaking them and he felt a painful bolt of disappointment urging him to give his all. The other two teams shot through the exit gate before them and Eddie's vision began to blur. He was running blindly now but he refused to stop. Seconds later, they dashed through the exit and Dominic released his arm. Gratefully he fell forward, breathless onto the showground race avenue, with his chest heaving painfully and his lungs fighting for air. He heard the spectators screaming and yelling. Parsons was putting an oxygen mask over his face and was helping him up. Up ahead, the team leaders - Keating, Sangria and Tau - were hurtling apace along the curved race avenue.

Charged with excitement, these changed surroundings were bright and warm. The showground ceiling twinkled overhead. The shiny blue floor underfoot gleamed and the coloured lights on the amusement stalls blinked gaily.

With so many people packed together, all keenly watching the finale of the Satellite Cup - the last hundred-metre sprint - the air was abuzz with excited calls. Now as the lively crowd pressed against the barrier alongside the race avenue, they cheered and hollered, urging their favourite sprinter on, to give his very best.

Seconds into the finale, Keating was well in the lead, ten metres ahead of Sangria and fifteen metres ahead of Dominic.

Dominic however was quickly gaining ground. Now running alone, the fair-haired youth lengthened his stride. Agile and swift as a wild elk, he sped forward at lightning speed, for the last frantic and exciting dash. Unlike the other two tidy athletes, he was covered with black oil. His hair was tousled and his face gleamed with perspiration. But, like them, he was a practiced sprinter.

Fleet of foot, he flew artlessly around the curved scarlet track. With a natural stride, he drove himself hard. In less than one minute, he had overtaken Sangria. Lining the race avenue, his fans screamed with delight.

Running fifty metres from the finish line, Keating was still fifteen metres in front. Twenty-metres from the finish line, Dominic had caught up.

Racing fiercely, he was close on his competitor's heels. Mad with excitement the showground crowd yelled and screamed. The two sprinters raced forward, with only seconds to the finish.

"Tau! Tau!" screamed Mandy and Cynthia in unison, as their cousin rushed by.

The Betting-hut loomed up quickly in front of the two strong sprinters. Only five metres remained before the race was run.

Suddenly, with a surprising burst of speed, Dominic darted quickly around Keating. Taking the lead amidst the noise of deafening applause, he dashed forward. Breaking through the red-ribboned finish line, he threw up his arms in victory, to the elated cries of the exuberant race goers.

Wildly dancing around, the showground crowd blew whistles and threw streamers. Some of them hugged each other. Others, grinning, tore up their betting slips good-naturedly - then tossed those pieces high in the air.

Dominic halted and stood with his hands on his knees while he caught his breath. Wiping his face with cloth a nearby race steward provided, he rubbed the oil off his arms and legs. Then he grinned.

Eddie, recovered, ran over and slapped him hard on the back. "Good one, Tau. I've never seen anyone move so fast!"

Parsons, joining them, also grinned. He waved his betting slips excitedly. "You've got cash to splash now, Eddie. We all have!"

"Clean yourself up a bit, mate," advised Dominic, throwing Eddie a clean cloth. "Get the oil off your face, so Brooklyn can see you properly."

"That's her name?"

"After the crowd dies down, she'll probably come over with her friend. When I introduce you, call her Miss Trina for the first few sentences. And don't say too much."

Eddie hardly had time to comply before the Teams 200, 42, 87 and 95 surrounded him. Jostled and congratulated by these boisterous lads, he was quickly hoisted up onto the shoulders of Sangria and Mahoney.

Similar treatment was vetted out to Dominic. He was lifted onto the shoulders of Keating and Hanepoot. Carried triumphantly to the chequered winner's podium, the lads waved happily to the satisfied crowd.

"We won!" shouted Dominic, whistling and waving to Zeta, Felicity and his cousins.

Moments later, standing on the chequered race podium with Eddie, he accepted a large gold trophy from the race adjudicator. Smiling charmingly and facing the showground crowd, he addressed them briefly.

"Greetings! Salutations! Thank you, our organisers, other contestants and especially our patrons! You followed the brief journey of our teams today with great enthusiasm, and I'm glad you all enjoyed the show. Citizens of Earth! Live long and prosper! Thank you!"

While Dominic and Eddie held the large gold winner's cup between them, the crowd in the showgrounds cheered happily. Completely chuffed, Eddie shook hands with many showground patrons, reaching up to him on the high chequered podium.

Conclusively accepted as the people's champion, Dominic held the trophy and looked on happily. His race for the Satellite Cup had answered all his follower's unspoken questions and had quelled all their doubts. He valued them, as he valued Eddie. As he had worked hard to bring Eddie through the fortress, he would work hard to bring them to their new home. He gave equal opportunity to Eddie standing on the high podium, sharing the Cup with him. So too would he offer them equality. Moreover, as he had included the moderate Eddie in his life journey, he would include them. Dominic's victory was not merely over the fortress, for today, by demonstrating his warmth and his compassion he had won the most valued prize of all, his follower's confidence and trust.

Suddenly the garrulous crowd hushed, their revelry interrupted, for a band of roaming young men had suddenly appeared on the chequered podium. Surrounding Eddie, they immediately began to heckle the lad.

"How do you think this grubby Neanderthal managed to win the Cup?" taunted the first ghostly young man.

"Beats me?" said the second, stepping closer.

"You supplanted an excellent contestant, you know," said the first young man. "Such a shame."

Eddie looked at the four large spectres standing around him, all wearing chainmail, three in bronze and one in grey. Then he glanced at his oil covered clothes and his assortment of scratches and bruises. "Tough monkeys," he retorted.

"That you are," said the first young man. "A very tough monkey."

While the second and third of the band, both grinned, Eddie felt his feet lift from the podium. All around him, rather than the showground crowd, he saw a pride of lions stalking him in an arid desert.

"The little intruder needs to be taught a lesson," threatened the fourth young man, wearing grey chainmail. Floating upwards, he pushed his ghostly face close to Eddie. Then he realistically growled like a lion.

"I don't know how I'm going to fight you pack of jokers," said Eddie hoarsely, his feet dangling in midair. "But I'm going to try.

Tau!" he called to Dominic, "Any suggestions on how to get rid of pests?"

Dominic, also suspended a metre above the podium, outside the ring of ghosts, glanced at Eddie. "You can roam to their true location and… jostle them rudely awake, if you like!"

Immediately the crystals in Eddie's Roaming-Ring began to glow.

Suddenly the first ghostly Roamer grinned. Along with Dominic, Eddie found his feet firmly on the podium.

"You put on a splendid show during the Cup," said the first young man. "Congratulations, Eddie. I'm Bermuda."

"I'm Sebastian," said the second young man. "Still seeing lions? I'll stop that now. How about a field of flowers instead?"

"Samuel," said the third phantom in introduction. "Any time you need a lift - just ask."

"Joshua," said the fourth, growling lion-like again. Then grinning.

Now the showground crowd were also grinning, all temporarily seeing a field of flowers blossoming around them.

Bermuda turned towards Dominic. Thumping him zealously on the back in congratulations, he pushed him over the edge of the podium onto the eight other contestants.

"Thanks," said Dominic, as he was lifted back up onto the chequered stand by three of those lads. "By the way, Bermuda," he said, moving astutely away from the edge. "There's a jar of honey in the haversack in my ship. Take it. The delicacy is for you. Compliments of our visiting celebrity, seated on the palomino pony over there."

Bermuda waved to Zeta, then to the three other girls. Together with his band of three ghostly roamers, he bowed to the showground crowd, many of whom recognized him. After which the four benign roamers and the illusion of acres of flowers instantly disappeared from the Satellite Showgrounds.

Chapter eleven

Spirits were high and emotions were warm. Reopened to sell their wares, the Funfair Level's shops were busy. Colourful amusement stalls once again delighted patrons young and old. Lively robotic pets tempered the showgrounds with their ingenuous presence and the cafeteria was serving sweetened water and Lumpo.

Ten minutes had elapsed since the winners of the Satellite Cup had claimed their trophy and the crowd was slowly thinning around the chequered podium.

"Zeta, we must go," prompted Felicity, astutely observing the warm happy gaze of Dominic - triumphant on the winner's podium - as he quietly looked their way. "Governor Aristotle has arrived to congratulate the winners. Added to that, I can see Tesla Gosh and her friend Brooklyn walking towards the podium. You don't want to meet Tesla on your first day here. Come on. Dominic's cousins have returned to the landing-bay. We should make our way up to the Science Level. Now."

"But I'd like to congratulate Dominic and Eddie first," said Zeta. "Look. The two girls you mentioned are talking to them."

"Sorry, no," advised Felicity. Seated on her robotic roan pony she fastidiously adjusted her maroon frock. "Governor Aristotle strictly follows protocol. You heard what he said to you in the landing-bay."

Zeta smiled and waved to Dominic shyly. Reluctantly she turned her pony away from the Fun-fortress and the triumphant winners. Together with Felicity, she then rode through the crowd - their heading - the elevator near the showground entrance.

They passed the cafeteria, the amusement stalls and the shops. Reaching the stables and turning a sharp left into the level two access spoke, they cantered their steeds down an artificial turf bridleway. Their ponies' hooves thudded lightly on the simulated green grass underfoot. Long silky manes flapped against their steeds' sleek shiny necks, and the ankle length tails of the small robotic horses swished gaily.

Approaching the elevator, the girls trotted their ponies inside. After their ascent and subsequent arrival on the Science Level, they rode down another access spoke and bridleway.

Entering a bright cheerful domain, crowded with people and filled with amazing exhibits, Zeta stopped her pony. Delighted, she gasped. Then she beamed. Spanning a length of five hundred metres and presenting twelve spacious Halls of interest, the Science Level offered Zeta the most intriguing outing she had ever imagined.

Overhead, the star-shaped lighting shone brightly. Underfoot, the cream tiles gleamed. Fresh, reminiscent of the seaside, the air was invigorating, while the temperate climate of the satellite remained pleasantly mild. Through the many portholes on the outer wall of the wheel, distanced behind the exhibits, Zeta glimpsed the blackness of Space. Then with sparkling grey eyes she looked at those congregated around her - other visitors to the satellite - equally delighted by the remarkable displays.

Fifteen metres wide, with a bridleway along the inner wall, the corridor into which the girls had just ridden curved tantalizingly away, hiding all but the closest Hall. Trotting her pony onto that bridleway, Zeta signalled that she was about to stop. Halting in front of a detailed guide board, she waited for Felicity's pony to draw up beside her.

"Let's view the twelve Halls starting from here and travelling to our right," she suggested cheerfully. "The guide board says that we're presently outside Hall 1 - an exhibit of Designer robots. In Hall 2, we will see a modern miniature village. The remaining ten Halls are demonstration environments. If we need a rest, there is a lounge area between Halls 5 and 6. Oh, there are stables as well. That means we don't have to go back down to the lower wheel when we've finished with our ponies."

Felicity nodded. Then she smiled. "I'll be the timekeeper, Zeta. Joseph will turn up at midnight to take us home. That gives us ten minutes maximum to see each Hall. OK?"

"I'm not bothered with time," Zeta replied.

Breaking off, she moved across the bridleway and the tiled floor, to halt her pony before the Designer robots exhibit. Felicity followed, halting her pony behind a low glass barrier alongside Zeta and many other visitors.

Behind the barrier, a sizeable plush room stretched out before them. The lighting was soft and elegant. Rich warm textiles in hues of red and brown coloured the room. Gilt-edged glass occasional tables sat luxuriously on a deep white carpet. Next to those, several velvet settees invited leisure. Topping off the lavish decorations, numerous wall paintings provided an excellent cultural display.

Superb on a raised white and black marbled platform - central to the room and the obvious highlight - twenty elegant shimmering statues stood in a variety of graceful postures. Delicate and striking in appearance the statues were each two metres tall, had long thin limbs, ivory outer casings and were partly transparent. Inside their shells, their aesthetic inner organs glowed a muted golden pink and all around them, the air blushed the softest violet. Two beautiful almond shaped eyes looked out from their elegant non-human pointed faces. Each statue had a nose and a painted mouth. While their hands - also pointed - had a thumb but no fingers.

"Where are the robots, Felicity?" Zeta asked, unable to take her eyes off the beautiful statues. "I can't see them. Are they tiny?"

"I'll call them for you, shall I?" offered Felicity. Moving her pony closer to the barrier, her sweet voice sang out into the lavish room, "Robots, come closer and meet my friend!"

Suddenly, to Zeta's astonishment, the statues began to move. Bearing their weight on large round feet, they stepped gracefully down from the platform. Moments later, they all stood behind the low glass wall only a metre away.

"Good evening, ladies," one statue said sweetly, through a small gold speaker in its tapered thin neck. "My name is Stanza. Would you like to converse? Please? Name your topic. Perhaps the great composers take your interest? Or painters from the twenty-ninth century?"

"I would like to discuss Fine Art in the twenty-first century," said Zeta. Gazing admiringly at the stunningly robot, she was soon engaged in a short but informative discussion.

Soon the robots were chatting to many of the other visitors waiting alongside the barrier.

"The Designer robots are beautiful moving sculptures, completely non-threatening and well shown by their designers," summarized Felicity, when the robots began to move back to their platform.

"I had no idea robots could ever be constructed so artistically," responded Zeta.

Speaking softly to their ponies, commanding them to proceed, the girls moved quietly ahead along the curved wide passageway to the next attraction, a very large Hall, thirty-five metres square and brightly lit.

Zeta smiled. Cobbled with red paths and open for their ponies to enter, the scenic setting before her featured a scaled-down valley. Carpeted in brown loam and surrounded by a purple mountain range, the valley was realistic in minute detail. Winding its way through the centre of the valley, a blue river coursed sedately through the feature of the exhibit - an exquisite miniature village.

Glancing excitedly towards that village, Zeta hurried her pony forward. Careful not to jostle any of the many visitors, who were casually strolling through the exhibit, she kept her steed moving ahead at a slow canter. Dismounting, she tethered her pony to a rail. Quickly running along a narrow pathway into the centre of the miniature village, she abruptly halted.

Gazing down at an arrangement of large translucent globes sitting on tall curved columns around her, her eyes widened. Kneeling down and peering inside one of those globes, she was amazed to discover it was a home.

"Felicity, your homes look like crystal balls; sitting atop beautiful curved vases!" Zeta exclaimed, when Felicity caught up.

"Yes, in miniature they do," agreed Felicity. "Our homes have been like this for hundreds of years. Have you looked inside?"

Zeta had, but took this opportunity to look again.

"Inside each crystal ball I can see a beautifully constructed house," she whispered quietly. "Amazing. Simply stunning." Then she glanced questioningly at a ground level network of tubing that connected the homes.

"The Earth hasn't much air, Zeta," said Felicity. "That tubing represents our sealed oxygen-filled walkways."

"Why are the homes on columns far above the ground?" asked Zeta, her expression bright and curious.

"Because it is easier to land on something that is elevated, plus the support is functional and pleasing to the eye."

"Your homes float and fly?" exclaimed Zeta excitedly.

"Yes," Felicity replied. "Our dwellings are buoyant aircraft. They are all privately owned mobile homes."

"Mobile? You mean if you want to leave an area you just float away in your house?"

"Yes," replied Felicity, laughing. "We just release the clamps holding our Globe Home secure to its column and start the propeller.

When we want to land, we pass over a vacant column and activate our magnetic anchor. There is one drawback though. The Globe Homes only have a top speed of one hundred and fifty kilometres per hour, so it can take a little while to complete a voyage.

"Only?" said Zeta, starting to grin.

"My auntie and uncle whom I live with flew our Globe Home to London just recently," Felicity continued quietly. "We came here because we are going to journey forward in time with Tau's group, to a new city he is building for us. We travel in the '*Gamma*' of the *One to Eight* Fleet."

"A new city?"

"Yes. Tau has told me a little about the city. A transparent circular Dome - with a radius of five kilometres and open to the air - will cover our *Garden* city. We will all have new Globe Homes of course. You may be familiar with the area. The entrance to the Dome will pass over the River Thames. Do you know it?"

"Yes, I know the area very well," replied Zeta. Finding all this new information suddenly overwhelming, she distracted herself by leaning forward and peering inside one particular house within a model globe. For a little while she watched a tiny robotic doll moving about inside the house. Then she whispered seriously, "You are happy to go with Tau's group?"

"Why yes," declared Felicity quietly. "Tau is similar to TT Vox Populi, but he is better, because he has a psychic mirror gift, and is most humane."

"Is that what everyone thinks?"

"Certainly. Now that he has returned with you and the craft you travelled in, one thousand people will definitely join him on his journey. Joseph told me this, immediately after the race. Many more would come, but they are too afraid to offend his great grandfather, TT. Plus they consider it to be an exciting achievement to colonize five alien planets."

As a large group of people approached the centre of the miniature village, Felicity pulled Zeta back towards their ponies. "Come on, Zeta! Let's hurry on to the next exhibit."

Hastening towards their waiting tethered ponies, Felicity easily mounted her steed. Zeta however, troubled by her gown, found the process rather more difficult.

Startled by the sound of a strange youth's voice behind her, she turned around, finding herself facing a handsome lad. Dressed in a pale blue frockcoat with a navy band extending from the wrist to elbow, teamed with navy trousers, he stood casually at the front of a close group of friends.

"Would you like help to get back onto your pony?" he asked politely.

Zeta only stared at him with her big dreamy grey eyes, curious to be face to face with one of the challengers for the recent Cup.

"I note by your clothes that you are a member of Tau's family," he continued, when she failed to offer a response. "My name is Matthew Keating."

"Thank you. If you wouldn't mind," Zeta finally responded, remembering, that like Felicity, she too was keen to continue their tour.

Keating smiled. Stepping forward, he easily lifted her onto her saddle. After handing her the pony's reins, he stepped away.

"He's seventeen," remarked Felicity when he was well out of earshot.

"Do you know him?" asked Zeta, taking one last admiring look at the miniature village.

"Sort of," answered Felicity casually, while they trotted their steeds back out into the crowded satellite corridor. "Joseph went to his birthday party last week. Come on. Hall 3 is the first of the ten demonstration environments. I've heard it's a popular attraction."

"It features Sports robots," added Zeta.

Trotting her pony forward, with Felicity alongside, Zeta rode carefully through the sea of happy patrons. Stopping outside a low, glass wall lined with spectators - the fence fronting Hall 3 - she was immediately distracted by the amusing antics of the robots within.

The huge Hall before her was an area full of mirth and recreation. Badminton, volleyball, table tennis and basketball, played in courts to the left of the Hall, were games of boisterous fun. In the billiard's room in the centre front of the Hall, an intense game of snooker was proceeding nicely - the results followed by many eager spectators. While at the back of the Hall on a green playing field, a group of robots were playing baseball. Tiled blue and inviting, a large rectangular pool on the right of the Hall, full of swimming mermaids completed the happy, fun picture.

Zeta halted her pony in front of the volleyball court. "Every one of the players on the courts and all the swimmers in the pool are robots!" she exclaimed. "Listen to them. They are so merry."

"I know," said Felicity. "Terrible isn't it - especially for a couch potato like myself. All the Sports robots are programmed with bubbly personalities, to encourage a healthy lifestyle."

Suddenly in the tennis court, the girls heard a loud commotion. Whilst flying towards the tennis net at full speed - trying to thwack a yellow tennis ball - a Sports robot had failed to stop. Hitting the white net with its body, it had bounced spectacularly into the air. Presently it was hurtling across the Hall with its orange wings madly buzzing.

Moments later, on the baseball field, the girls witnessed another outstanding sports misadventure. While attempting to hit a fast-bowled ball, another robot, playing baseball, batted with such a mighty swing, that it spiralled like a top for at least a minute. Then it flew dizzily away.

"The Sports robots aren't very good at Sports," remarked Zeta curiously.

"They play around like that for a lark," said Felicity.

Proving her point, in the middle of an exciting game of basketball, the star player of the winning team - a robot with a large grin - abruptly sat down on the court and began reading a book.

"The robots are serious when they have to be," said Felicity. "Look over at the pool."

Looking where directed, Zeta was surprised, along with the other spectators, to see a mermaid drowning. Splashing frantically about in the pool and quickly going under, she was calling out anxiously in a mechanical voice.

Four Sports robots - on duty around the pool - were at the trauma scene in seconds. Buzzing calmly over the mermaid, they fished her out of the water. Then they carried her over to a robot ambulance that had quickly appeared from a concealed side entrance.

"They are good little lifeguards, aren't they, Felicity?"

"Yes. They are worthwhile machines, Zeta," agreed Felicity. "Many people who keep larger homes own one of them. They are the perfect aides to keeping fit."

Along with many other visitors, Zeta watched the robots as they continued to play their games with enthusiasm and good cheer. For a while she listened to the little machines as they yelled out their scores, amiable taunts and constructive encouragement.

When Felicity tapped at her timeband, indicating that they must move on, Zeta reluctantly moved her pony away from the fence.

Trotting their ponies side by side, they quickly followed the curved satellite corridor around to the next attraction, careful lest they bump anyone in the busy corridor.

Both girls were soon peering through a thick glass wall into the black environs of Hall 4 - an antigravity chamber, titled *Space Robots*.

Beside them, three large groups of friendly people chatted and laughed. Farther away, one dark-haired little boy, wearing a short-sleeved brown shirt and standing on his own, glanced at Zeta. Then he stared transfixed at the Space exhibit.

Providing a beautiful backdrop to the hundreds of twinkling stars floating throughout the large area, a realistic study of the Milky Way Galaxy was projected on the rear wall of the Hall. High in the air, the Earth's Solar System in miniature - the Sun and its orbiting planets - revolved constantly. Floating in the centre of the large antigravity room, a damaged Spaceship of small proportions drifted next to a chunk of asteroid.

Completing the picture of a ship disabled in the depths of Outer Space, the large model of an unfamiliar planet loomed large on the left of the Hall, close to Zeta. Orbited by two crimson moons and surrounded by three azure rings, the blue and purple marbled world was strangely beautiful.

"That planet is beyond Earth's Solar System," Zeta remarked, turning towards Felicity. "I've never seen it before."

"Yes. It's Nefaria," responded Felicity. "Beautiful on the outside, not so beautiful on the inside. Can you see that sliding door built flush on the side of the planet? I expect it will open soon. Watch to see what comes out."

While Zeta kept her eyes focused on the large door, Felicity busied herself observing the Space robots repairing the smashed hull of the Spaceship. All looking like huge headless beetles, with their large complement of arms and legs, they fascinated her.

Surprising Zeta, and causing many of the crowd to startle, the door in Nefaria suddenly opened.

With mouths already open to bite and devour, a gaggle of disgusting slimy grey monsters flew out. Rushing viciously at the thick glass wall where the visitors stood, they suckered onto that glass with long tentacled limbs. Loathsome, the things slid sickeningly along, eyeing the humans hungrily.

Horrified by the sight of the diabolical creatures, Zeta stared - aghast. Her chest tightened. Her breath shortened and she shuddered. Many of the spectators, also nauseated by the sight of the monsters, stood back.

"You're a strong girl, remaining so close to the glass," remarked a lady standing nearby. "I can't bear to even look at the ghastly things."

"I think I'm too scared to move," said Zeta, grinning bravely. "They're robots, right?"

"They are robots, but they're too realistic for me," said the lady.

Looking back towards the antigravity chamber, Zeta observed the creatures more closely. Three metres long and akin to large upright squids, each monster had a white puckered face on a large helmeted head. Two black walnut-shaped eyes, a pencil thin nose, a long narrow pointed chin and jagged white teeth formed the basis of the creature's facial structure. Complemented by a horrible red leering mouth, each monster's visage was indeed horrible. Counting their limbs, Zeta also observed that these obvious cephalopods each had a minimum of ten tentacles and their long suckered appendages functioned as both arms and legs.

While she looked on, several Space robots emerged from the hull of the Spaceship and sped towards the obnoxious creatures. Using a set of arms that functioned as cattle prods, they jabbed at the monsters until the creatures released their grip on the glass. When the visitors moved back against the glass barrier for a closer look, the Space robots herded the monsters back inside their planet.

"Good, eh?" said Felicity. "The display is certainly worthy of note, don't you agree?"

Zeta stared. "Do those monsters I just saw, really exist?"

"Of course," replied Felicity. "We have found many dangerous and bizarre organisms during our exploration of Space. Those ones you just saw - the Nefarids - are the most evil we have discovered. They are gliding, swimming cannibal predators that walk upright on their tentacles. Surviving by benumbing the thought processes of their prey, they eat their captives alive. If a human being encounters even one of them, that person becomes immediately inert. Once a person has no power of action or resistance, you can imagine what happens! Dreadful!"

"I see," said Zeta, her face paling.

"They'll come out of their planet again in a few moments," said Felicity. "It's all part of the show."

Preferring to move away from the scene of these ghastly replicated carnivores, Zeta indicated to her friend that she wished to move on, by trotting briskly away.

"I guess we ran overtime at the last exhibit," said Felicity, quickly catching up.

Shortly after, they stopped next to many other visitors, before the next small Hall, titled *Educational Robots.*

The Hall, divided into four sections and partitioned off by a low glass wall, featured a classroom with yellow desks, a rustic Children's Playground, a Sitting room, and a Technical workshop.

In each of these sections simply dressed mechinoids with square heads and hands taught formal classes, supervised nursery playground fun, guided home-school pupils and directed practical applications. For demonstration purposes, all of the pupils were robots.

"Felicity?" Zeta asked. "Have Educational robots replaced human teachers?"

"Hardly," replied Felicity. "Imagine a teacher who can take his or her class roaming to an Egyptian Sphinx - in the blink of an eye."

"That teacher would very popular where I come from," said Zeta.

"They're popular here, Zeta." Glancing at her timeband, Felicity continued, "We're between Halls 5 and 6, Zeta. Unless you need to stop at the lounge, I suggest we ride our ponies onto the bridleway. That way we can have some fun galloping around to the next Hall and save time in the bargain."

"Sounds good to me."

Trotting their ponies over to the bridleway, Felicity immediately urged her steed into a fast gallop. With Zeta following close behind, they rode quickly along beside the vibrant crowd.

Small children with their parents smiled and waved to them. Other riders, further ahead, moved over to the left to allow them passage. While their ponies' hooves thudded on the turf, the girls hung on tightly to their saddles and their reins. Riding past the robotic stables and the comfortable lounge area, they saw hundreds of visitors lolling on sofas and chatting. Then, all too soon for Zeta, they came to the next presentation.

"I'd like to do that again," she said excitedly. "To-do certainly enjoyed it. Look at his face!"

"I'd almost forgotten he was with us," said Felicity. "He's a well behaved tenacious animal. Remarkably he clung on inside his saddlebag without falling out."

Halted across the way from Hall 6, both girls were beaming, having immensely enjoyed their ride. Moving their ponies off the bridleway they trotted slowly on to the cream tiled area in front of the next peculiar exhibit.

Titled *Waste Management Robots,* the display - partitioned behind a high mesh wire fence - was reminiscent of a small garbage refuse dump, divided into zones, by type of refuse. Food waste, hovered over by a heavy swarm of robotic flies lay heaped in the left corner of the Hall. Other types of discarded material filled the rest of the area.

In this demonstration, along with a group of quiet families, Zeta watched robots shamelessly rummage through rubbish. Scooping up items speedily with their six flexible tubular arms and vice-like curved claws, they sorted paper, plastics and metal containers. These they consumed through three distinct cavities in their square massive frames. The robots gurgled and clanked, digesting the refuse. While Zeta looked on, slightly disgusted, the metal contraptions regurgitated the crushed and liquefied remains into recycling bins, from their large square mouths.

"Gross!" she remarked to Felicity. "But essential drudgery, I suppose. I bet humans are glad they don't have to do that sort of work anymore."

Felicity laughed. "Yes, we stopped regurgitating rubbish long ago!"

Looking eagerly ahead, Felicity moved her pony forward. "Come on," she prompted. "Let's go and see the next exhibit. It features Food Processing robots. You'll get the inside information on how our Lumpo is made. I gather by your behaviour in the cafeteria that you haven't tasted Lumpo yet."

"What behaviour?"

"You were a bit too eager to part with your sweets."

Slightly embarrassed at being overhead earlier that evening, Zeta quietly trotted her pony along next to Felicity's steed. Soon they halted outside a low glass barrier. Behind that barrier, Zeta observed a clean, busy, white space - Hall 7.

Linked by conveyer belts, an array of stoves covered the central floor area. Large vats of seaweed and fresh fish were stored on the left. Rows of empty refrigerated containers stood on the right.

Leaning forward on her pony for a closer inspection, Zeta observed three separate groups of industrious mechinoids. Tall, tin, with bodies made of shiny stainless steel, each robot had a long rectangular head and two large eyes - the size of teacup saucers. Additionally each wore an orange coat and a high, lime-green Chef's hat.

Curious to see how the food was processed, Zeta watched a group of robots empty a vat of fresh ingredients into a cooking machine, together with herbs, spices and minerals. A second quality-control group checked the cooked food on its journey along the conveyer belts. The third group of robots loaded the final processed product - the cellophane wrapped Lumpo - into refrigerated containers for shipping.

"What does Lumpo taste like?" asked Zeta, remembering Felicity's remark and suddenly regretting giving up all her sweets for sale.

"Lumpo isn't tasty, Zeta. But it's an OK food," replied Felicity honestly. "It's nutritious and healthy. You just wouldn't want to pig out on it, that's all. Let's move on. There are five more Halls left out of the twelve to see, and we've fifty minutes left. The two coming up feature Home Management robots and Construction robots."

Moving alongside Felicity, Zeta trotted her pony forward along the busy corridor. The hooves of the ponies clicked on the cream tiled floor. Their long tails swished and the robotic animals pricked forward their ears.

Moments later, after weaving their way through the crowd, the girls halted their ponies in front of Hall 8, a beautifully designed Showroom, titled *Home Management Robots*. Alongside the girls, a group of ladies also stopped. Grouped behind the low glass wall, they all looked admiringly into the colourful Hall.

"Oh!" exclaimed Zeta. "I didn't expect I'd be looking inside the tiered interior of a giant doll's house! The house is full of knee-high toys wearing white frilled aprons and ribboned caps."

Felicity couldn't help laughing. "It isn't a doll's house, Zeta. It's a life-sized reproduction of the interior of a modern home. And they're not toys. They are industrious Housekeeping robots of the standard variety that you saw in the Fun-fortress - the type that everyone owns."

"But the ones in the fortress looked like giant silver centipedes," said Zeta.

"These do too, once they're moving, with every single one of their arms extended. Clothes make a big difference."

"Can I see these robots at work?"

"I can see a keypad mounted on the glass wall in front of you," replied Felicity. "Press a few keys. See what happens."

Fascinated, Zeta quickly urged her pony towards the keypad. After studying the keys, she pressed every one. Instantly the whole house was alive with busy mechinoids. They made beds, plumped cushions, and stacked away clean dishes. After folding clean laundry, they placed it neatly into cupboards. Completing their demonstration, the robots excelled by dressing a superb dining table for twenty guests.

The ladies watching were most impressed.

"All of those robots are on my list of must haves," Zeta heard one of them remark.

Pleased with that show, Zeta was keen to move on. "Come on pony, trot forward to the next display!" she instructed her robotic steed.

Carefully trotting their ponies through the crowd, the girls soon came to Hall 9. Cordoned off behind a high mesh fence, this large building site, aptly titled *Construction Robots,* demonstrated the four stages of house production to interested spectators. Behind the fence, Zeta observed four small Globe Homes, each at a different stage of production. Additionally she noted that all the workers on the Globes were robots. Each robot had four eyes on stalks, plus four arms.

Along with hundreds of other visitors, Zeta was privy to see the beginnings of a transparent Globe Home, currently being set in a huge cast. Discovering how the aeronautical equipment, solar powered engine and elevator were incorporated into a second small Globe Home, she was most impressed. Observing, she saw the Water, Air and Sewerage Systems fitted below the floor line of another home. Capping off the demonstration she watched intrigued as an internal dwelling was constructed quickly within the fourth Globe.

"Are you ready to move onto the next attraction?" asked Felicity, conscious that the clock was ticking.

Suddenly Zeta's pony shuddered. Jolted sideways, she slipped in her saddle. Regaining her seating, she looked about for the source of the impact.

Standing beside her pony's left flank, she saw a small dark-haired boy, dressed in a short-sleeved brown shirt. Having just whacked into Zeta's steed after a flat-out run along the satellite corridor, he stared at her boldly. He glanced at the doll in her saddlebag. Holding a thirty centimetre robotic Nefarid monster doll in his hand, he then shook the toy and growled, as he expected the monster would growl.

Ruffled, Zeta stared back silently. Quickly he ran away, disappearing back into the crowd from which he came.

Felicity, watching Zeta, was thoughtful. "Zeta," she said quietly. "While we were in the cafeteria, I overhead that you wanted to learn a few things. Tau didn't tell you, but that terrific doll in your saddlebag can dial into our free Telecommunication System. She will access lots of information for you. Once you are in the System just ask her anything you like. She will even project large visual displays for you into the air. No screen is required. When you switch her on just ask her to dial 'Freeteleworld'. In no time at all, you will be au fait with all the latest data. If you wish to contact me without roaming, ask your doll to dial *Felicity Parsons*. I will set my doll at home to accept your messages. Your doll is call-signed *The Zeta Waves*."

"*The Zeta Waves*?" repeated Zeta, a puzzled expression on her face. "How do you know my doll's call-sign Felicity? I didn't even know she had one."

"I found out accidentally when we were shopping. I was leaning on the counter playing with a robotic chameleon doll. When Tau bought your doll for you, I saw him register that name. Sorry for snooping, Zeta."

Zeta was surprised at the revelation, but happy to have access to a bountiful supply of information.

"Shall we move on to Hall 10?" suggested Felicity, commanding her pony forward.

Directing her palomino pony along the curved satellite corridor, Zeta followed closely behind Felicity's roan steed. Soon after, along with at least one hundred other visitors, Zeta stopped behind a low synthetic privet hedge before the next large Hall.

Titled *Botanical robots* and built along the lines of a neat presentation garden, the Hall featured a lawn of real green grass edged with real cobalt cornflowers, white geraniums and small weeping willows. A compact open greenhouse, stocked with beautiful orchids of all varieties, stood to the left of the display, while on the right, a lovely fountain with a pink flamingo statue at centre, bubbled pleasantly.

Breathing in a blended sweet fragrance from the freshly cut lawn, combined with the aroma of flowers, Zeta, together with the other visitors, couldn't help but smile.

Caring over this pleasant setting, three small robots with pointed yellow heads trundled along underneath the willows. Watched with pleasure by the visitors they went about their duties - planting seedlings, aerating turf, pruning and seeding.

"The plants in this display are all real," remarked Zeta, very conscious of the wafting floral aroma. "I thought the Earth was infertile, Felicity. Where do these plants come from?"

"They're borrowed from the Greenhouse Satellite, I expect," replied Felicity, dreamily gazing at the flowers and trees. "None of our plants are extinct, Zeta. The Greenhouse Satellite contains every plant that existed on the Earth, before the devastation caused by the meteors. TT Vox Populi stocked it eighty years ago."

"What are you thinking?" asked Zeta, noting Felicity's rapt expression.

"I'm thinking that one day soon I'll have a garden like this outside my very own home." Taking one last look at the charming garden, Felicity reluctantly moved her steed away from that exhibit.

Trotting their ponies briskly along, the girls soon stopped at the next large Hall - a realistic setting partitioned behind a low white wooden fence. Titled *Agricultural Robots*, the setting featured an open farmyard with stables to the left, a pigsty and sheep field at the rear, and a chicken coup and run built neatly on the right.

"The farmyard creatures seem real," said Zeta.

"They are. Borrowed from reserves on the Earth," responded Felicity. "I just read that on a sign over there."

Tending over the animals and birds, Zeta saw four stocky robots, each dressed in a yellow flannel shirt, black dungarees and yellow Wellington boots. As she watched approvingly, these Agricultural robots mucked out stables, fed chickens, herded sheep and chased swine. While they worked, she saw their square mouths move, as they spoke softly to the farmyard animals.

"Ready to see the last Hall?" suggested Felicity.

Zeta laughed. "Let me guess? It's Hall 12, titled *Marine Robots*."

Minutes later, they halted their ponies next to hundreds of other visitors, outside a massive, deep, glass-fronted aquarium. Measuring thirty-five square metres, the saltwater aquarium was full of real sea plants, growing between beds of colourful coral on the sandy base.

Everything inside the aquarium was to scale and everything was miniature.

Enchantingly beautiful, built in the centre and covering a third of the aquarium's floor area, Zeta was astonished to see a modern castle of exquisite design. Many towers ringed the castle's perimeter with further towers of varying heights at its core. The building fabric was metallic gold. The architecture was faultless. Gently diffusing into the surrounding water, the city lights caused the castle to shimmer.

Above the marine city and feeding the castle its power, an array of solar plates floated on the surface. Inside the city an extraction plant removed air and freshwater from the surrounding seawater.

"That's Aristau, Zeta," said Felicity quietly. "Tau's home - where you'll be staying."

"I saw the best last," said Zeta. Mesmerized and silent, she stared admiringly at the castle before her.

"A Marine robot demonstration is starting now," said Felicity, nudging her pony gently into Zeta's steed. "There's a model undersea farm located on the far right of this exhibit. "Go on, look."

Three miniature robotic dolphins with gold coloured snouts swam out from the farm. A school of robotic mackerel also appeared - spiralling in a glinting. silvery tornado in the depths of the tank. Chased by the dolphins, the mackerel broke into a rectangular stream, then darted quickly past the thick glass window.

Three pale-blue robotic turtles then emerged from the undersea farm. Towing a large grey net between them, the turtles headed speedily for the school of mackerel. Dropping their net over the fish, they returned their catch to the farm.

After the fishing display, Felicity checked her timeband. "It is time to go home now, Zeta," she advised. "As I said previously, I'm staying in London. I'd like to visit you in Aristau?"

"Please do," responded Zeta.

As Felicity moved her roan pony away from the exhibit, the spectral image of Parsons silently appeared.

Standing transparent before her pony, he enquired genially, "Sister Felicity, Zeta. Have you enjoyed your recreation? Are you ready to go home?"

"Yes thank you, Joseph," Felicity replied on behalf of them both. "We have enjoyed our tour and we are ready to return to Earth."

"Wait for me at the entrance to this wheel, in front of the guide board. I will collect you both in five or ten minutes," he advised. Bowing politely, his ghostly image vanished.

After he had gone, Zeta yawned sleepily. "Felicity, do you know the girl I will be staying with. I know her name is Willow. Is she Dom-, I mean Tau's best friend?"

"Willow Tau is his grandmother, Zeta," replied Felicity. "She looked after him when his parents were killed and he lived with her until he entered the Training Academy. She still looks very girlish and he affectionately calls her 'his girl'. Joseph talks about his friends sometimes. He told me."

Heeding Parsons, Zeta and Felicity rode their ponies away from the final exhibit. They trotted onto the bridleway and stopped in front of the guide board. There they dismounted. Zeta regarded her palomino pony for one last time. She took her doll from one saddlebag and her well-behaved puppy from the other. She cuddled To-do for a moment and spoke softly to him. Then she placed him on the ground at her feet, firmly holding his leash in her hand. Both girls said goodbye to their cute little ponies and sadly watched the animals trot away to the riding stables.

Parsons was slow to arrive. To-do, doggedly straining on his leash, tugged a tired and dreamy Zeta away from Felicity and the bridleway. Happily yapping he pulled her through the crowd and across the curved corridor, towards one of the few accessible portholes.

"Zeta, don't go over there!" shouted Felicity, trying to see Zeta through the crowd. "Tau mentioned to me that it's not such a good idea for you to see outside - not just yet anyway!"

Shocked, Zeta was already staring through the satellite porthole. Through that window, she saw the Earth.

No longer did the oceans kiss against the shores - tinted aquamarine, blue and navy. Neither was her Earth marbled emerald, lime and jade. Misty and opaque, a blanket of cloud replaced swirling wispy white billows that had once flowed gently through an azure benign sky. Beneath that cloud, a sandy infertile desert stretched a hard hand over the entire planet.

"Is this really Earth?" Zeta said to herself in a sad whisper.

Brought on by the sudden realization that everything Dominic had told her was true, Zeta's face paled. Her eyes widened. Her heart began to beat quickly and her breath became shallow.

Staring through the window with To-do flopped sadly at her feet, her dreamy grey eyes misted. Silent teardrops trickled slowly down her cheeks. Consequently, above her head, a translucent silvery ring of light appeared.

"The sparkling ring over that girl's head is beautiful, Daddy. What is it?" asked a little girl, stopped amongst a large group of visitors, now watching Zeta.

"She has a mirror's Guardian Ring," her father replied soberly. "Rare, even in our cultured society."

"Perhaps I should go over and help," said his partner, a warm plump lady. Taking one step forward, however, she abruptly stopped. Staring, like others, she moved back. Then she focused on the air space that now shimmered and glowed beside Zeta.

Impressing all present, the mirror image of Dominic dramatically materialized. Standing determined at the porthole, dressed in his Knight's Raiment, he immediately glanced at the grey planet - Earth. Compassionately he pulled his friend around to face him. As he did so, the silvery ring glowing above Zeta's head faded.

"I see you're on foot, Miss," he commented lightly in his gentle tenor lilt. The crystals in his Roaming-Ring glinted and threw needles of light into the corridor, while around his head the air still shimmered. "If you're that upset about giving up your pony," he continued, "we'll have to see about buying you one of your own." He paused. "Now let me see?" he mused aloud in moderate tone. "What is the market price of a pony these days? A half a month's salary, I'd guess. That should equate to about five large chocolate bars in your haversack. What do you say, Zeta? Shall we place an order at the manufacturers for your very own pony?"

"You're so stupid, Dominic," said Zeta. "You know full well what upset me. Anyhow, why didn't you tell me about my doll's call-sign?"

Glancing behind him at Felicity and the halted gathering, Dominic nodded greeting. As the curious crowd continued quietly on their way, he turned back to face Zeta.

"I was going to surprise you, Zeta, by calling you with my Psychic Knight doll," he casually replied.

"You've really got a Psychic Knight doll?" she asked him innocently.

He chuckled cheekily. "*No.* But I *am* going to call you."

"I can access information with my doll, Dominic," she said, seeking approval.

"Sure, there's no problem with you knowing general information, Zeta. Only concentrated scientific data is restricted to time travellers."

Unexpectedly she moved closer to him and nervously whispered. "I saw some horrible creatures in one of the displays. They were called Nefarids. Are you afraid of monsters?"

"Keep this a secret, just between you and I," he whispered sincerely in return. "I'm not afraid of Nefarids, Zeta. They are afraid of me."

Noting the arrival of Parsons, plus Felicity's approach, he put his arm reassuringly around Zeta's shoulders. Then he walked with the small group through the busy level one access spoke towards the elevator.

"I thought you'd like to know Zeta," said Dominic. "I have returned the Dandy Lion. No-one will ever know it was gone."

"You've replicated my dad's gravity drive; that quickly?"

"Ten times over, for ten Chronoguisers," he replied proudly.

Now, as they approached the elevator, Dominic looked towards Felicity. "Goodbye Felicity," he said.

"Goodbye Tau," she replied, stepping into the open elevator.

"Parsons!" Dominic called, as Joseph Parsons also entered. "An instruction for you. Fly the Space Shuttle home to Aristau using instruments alone, and close all the ports. I don't want any of TT's pilots seeing Zeta arrive."

When Parsons nodded his compliance, Dominic ushered Zeta into the elevator. Once inside, she turned to face him.

"Hey!" she called. "Congratulations on your victory."

Dominic beamed. Bowing theatrically and with a practised flourish of his arm, his mirror image began to glow, then to shimmer. Seconds later, where he had been standing, Zeta saw only air. Startled, she then heard his voice calling out, resonating gently through the satellite corridors, "Goodbye from the winner of the Satellite Cup! Goodbye, Zeta!"

Chapter twelve

As the invisible *Heritage* swooped down out of the clouds over the English Channel, the grey sky thundered. Slave to ocean currents, the powerful sea rolled harsh, deep and green. Between the sea and the sky, the blustery wind blew cold. Rain began to fall. In heavy droplets, it spattered the sea with small transient circles. Filling the air with fine sheets of water, it tumbled down onto the low flying vessel, insistently drumming on the silver hull, thud-a-dud, thud-a-dud.

Warm inside the bright, dry cabin - with its gleaming silver dashboard and its impressive array of instruments - the pilot, unperturbed by the stormy environment, listened to the sounds outside. Then he glanced at his radar.

Studying nine moving red blips that had suddenly appeared on the screen before him, his thoughts remained steady. "Good, the approaching craft are all Chronoguisers," he quickly surmised. Ascertaining the location of the blips, he checked his timeband against the clock on the *Heritage*. "The *Warrior* and my *One to Eight* Fleet have just entered the Earth's atmosphere," he reflected attentively. "Cloaked invisible and travelling at their current velocity they are approximately five minutes behind me - their heading - also Aristau."

Warily he scrutinized various other blips of different colours on his radar, taking dutiful log of the rest of the air and sea traffic. Satisfied that the area was clear of threatening vessels, he transmitted a coded message to his nine Chronoguiser Captains, advising them to proceed with caution.

The mouth of Freshwater Bay now rushed into view. Land loomed close. The rough sea began to subside. Plaintiff, the cries of white-winged seagulls - hovering over these shallower waters - heralded his swift approach. Advancing through the Bay, he surveyed the tranquil inlet. He glimpsed a flock of cormorants bobbing up and down nonchalantly on the cradling waves. Then he smiled. Abruptly he then dived - plunging the *Heritage* into the salty green depths.

Exploding high into the air in exclamation to his sudden dive, a great ring of water burst forth from the sea. Now underneath the rolling waves - the *Heritage* made its quiet, invisible descent.

Quickly reaching Aristau, the pilot moved beyond the city's perimeter. Settling the *Heritage* on the seabed, beside a Submarine Bay - cut into the thick rock foundations of the castle - he waited. Around his vessel, long sheaves of purple and dark green seaweed swayed gently with the tide. Startled by his ship, a black Manta Ray rose up out of the sand and hurriedly sidled away.

Minutes later, he monitored eight invisible ships - the *Alpha* through to the *Theta* - until they had all moved inside the Submarine Bay. When his instruments told him that the *Warrior* had set down on the seabed on the opposite side of the gate to him, he closed his eyes and began to mirror.

Subsequently he materialized into a neat room inside the Marine City. Illuminated by under-floor lighting and cleverly decorated by coloured cornices, the room was cheerful and bright. On his left was a holographic pre-disaster Earth globe adjacent to a cobalt divan. In the front corner on his right sat Zeta, on a bean-shaped cobalt settee. Dressed in her wine skirt and long sleeved chemise, she smiled at him warmly. On her lap, she held a large jewel box containing nine amethyst gems and a small cream handwritten card, which read:

'To Zeta,
Please indulge me by accepting this gift. Every time I see these amethysts in your Roaming-Ring, I'll remember the time when I was fifteen and I won the Satellite Cup.
Your friend,
Dominic.'

Behind Zeta he recognised a length of shelving containing his books, running trophies *and* the miniature 'Constable' painting that he had received from the TT Corporation on the Forum day. Before Zeta, he saw To-do - fast asleep - curled at her feet.

Finding all familiar and checking the closed door behind him, the young man - dressed in Knight's Raiment - stepped towards Zeta.

"Good evening, Miss," he whispered furtively, putting his forefinger to his lips to beg for her silence. "I'm not allowed to be in here with you. Remember Aristotle's rules. Not a word, or Willow will hear us."

"But how did you manage to get in, Dominic? There's a field generated around all the private rooms to keep out roamers - plus visiting time in the Reception room is over for the day?"

"I gave you a little golden mushroom to add to the charms on the bracelet you wear, didn't I? That's how I broke through the Security System," Dominic explained, moving closer. "Now, give me your Roaming-Ring and I'll replace the quartz crystals with the amethyst?"

Zeta lifted her Roaming-Ring carefully from her head.

Prizing the quartz crystals from their settings, using a tool from the shelf behind, Dominic fitted the amethysts. Silently he returned her platinum band.

Delighted by the gift, she briefly stared at her Roaming-Ring.

"Thanks," she whispered, placing the beautiful diadem back onto her head.

Dominic's expression was strangely distant. Glancing away from Zeta, he reached his hand forward and withdrew an envelope and pen from the shelf behind her. After addressing the envelope to - *Angle, C/O Francis Bermuda, Psychic Forces, Aristau* - he placed the nine quartz crystals inside. Zeta watched his eyes twinkle as he then posted the envelope through a narrow duct in the wall.

"What's that all about?" she asked.

"Mind your business, Miss," he replied. Casually he flicked an array of switches at the back of the shelving unit. Then he added amiably, "Get ready for a change of scene, Zeta."

Altering from a cobalt and grey colour scheme, the room around Zeta softened with a more feminine decor. The divan and the settee were pastel pink. The shelving units, cupboards and globe pedestal were a pleasing violet. The Earth globe activated. Tilting on its axis, it slowly rotated. The terrain seemed real and the waves on the seas, now discernible, rolled with the tides. In addition, modern popular music quietly filled the room.

Finished personalizing her quarters, Dominic adopted his most harmless expression. Squeezing in next to Zeta on the right of the small settee, he spoke hastily.

"I just made your room a little bit more homely. We can't talk above a whisper yet. Willow still might hear us above the music." Pausing, he bent his head closer to Zeta's and whispered even more softly. "I've arrived to take you roaming, Zeta. But before we go, I'll quickly explain your room. When you wish to retire for the night, you need to command, 'Lights off, globe off, music off,' OK?"

Zeta nodded and he hurriedly continued.

"On the subject of music, Zeta. Just briefly. The Psychic Forces run a Pirate Radio Station. I broadcast Tuesday and Friday nights from 11pm until midnight. If you want to listen to the show when it's on, command 'Pirate live'. Otherwise, you can preset the sound equipment to record it by commanding 'Pirate record' then 'Pirate playback,' for a later replay. We share the same taste in music so you will probably enjoy my selection of tunes. The listener chats are also very entertaining."

Zeta smiled. "OK, I'll make sure I don't miss your show," she whispered. "Now when and where are we going to roam? How much time have we got?"

Dominic grinned. "We haven't much time. The three stages of our journey will be interesting, amazing and enlightening. First stop, the *Heritage*, parked seventy metres below your room on the sea floor. Second stop - a surprise. Last stop - a polite visit to see your father. Bermuda and I are going to offer him engineering assistance while he prepares his Chronoguiser for flight. Our help will shave weeks off his departure time. After I have a brief word with him, I'll return to my ship. You will want to remain to speak to him privately. With your new gems, you'll be able to see your dad for as long as you like. Now activate your Roaming-Ring, Zeta. We go."

Immediately sparkling and glowing violet-blue and pink, the beautiful amethyst jewels in her Zeta's Roaming-Ring activated. Conscious of a faint and unusual tugging sensation within her chest, she was instantly asleep.

A moment later Zeta opened her spiritual eyes. She was sitting - a transparent ghostly Roamer - in the co-pilot's seat in the *Heritage*. Beside her sat Dominic, awake and mortal in his pilot's chair.

"I have the TT Surveillance film you wanted to see, Zeta," he said. Glancing at her, he slipped a tiny disk into a slot on the *Heritage* console. "I reformatted it into something more compact."

Leaning forward in her seat, Zeta immediately began viewing the short surveillance film, projected onto the now closed viewing window.

After seeing images of her father and mother - as they had looked five years earlier - she felt tearful. She gazed at her mum's pretty, motherly face. Then she saw a close up of her father - his hair much less grey - his face much less weary. Her mother and father were happily touring the TT Research Facility and she watched them entering a sealed laboratory.

Disconsolate, five minutes later, she sat back in her chair. Speaking to Dominic, her voice was raised and angry.

"This is my summary of that film, Dominic," she began quickly. "And before I start, I can say I'm not pleased."

"Fire away, Zeta."

"My mum climbed into a Test-Chronoguiser. The lights blinked. The Chronoguiser disappeared. Sixty seconds later it reappeared - without my mum onboard. End of summary. Conclusion - the Chronoguiser dumped mum somewhere in another time. Maybe even on another planet." Pausing, Zeta looked away from Dominic. Not wanting him to see her face, she stared fixedly at a point on the cabin wall. "What did dad think he was doing letting mum climb into a test machine?" she continued vehemently. "What happened to make the vessel activate all of a sudden? A power failure? That would explain the blinking lights. Followed by what? A power surge?" Stopping, she stared back at Dominic. "Confounded Chronoguiser! The dodgy makeshift machine wasn't even finished and just switched itself on like a toaster when the power came on! That's what happened! I can see it now."

After saying this, Zeta gazed around her at all the high technology equipment lining the walls of the *Heritage.*

"The Test-Chronoguiser was the Dandy Lion," revealed Dominic quietly.

Zeta looked at him with widened eyes.

"Where did mum go, Dominic?" she asked.

Dominic's expression was sober. "The test ship's co-ordinates revealed that your mother was dropped at the Research Facility site on June 14th, 1890. These details were registered in the Facility's records."

"She's not lost?"

He shook his head. "I wouldn't think so."

"Dad always knew what happened to mum."

"Seems that way, Zeta."

"Why didn't dad go and search for her then?

Dominic was silent.

"Come on, out with it!" she prompted. "I know you're holding back."

"I'd rather not upset you any more than you already are."

"You're making excuses, Dominic. I want you to tell me what you know. I would have expected dad to search for my mum. I thought he cared about us."

"He does, Zeta. I talked to Ret about the accident to your mum. After that, I checked the laboratory journals. Your dad is a responsible man, Zeta. He did search for your mother - every day for six months. When he wasn't searching, he was scouring the computer archives of old newspapers. He thought your mother might leave some clues in the papers as to her whereabouts. But your father never found anything, and he never found your mother. Ret told me that every year on June the 14th, Professor Doherty takes a Chronoguiser to the spot where your mum landed and waits for her to return. Even though his life moved on with Isabelle, he knew you wanted your mum back."

"Do you believe what Ret told you?" asked Zeta, her face astounded at this sudden emotional news.

"Yes I do, Zeta. He's an honest chap."

"So dad was telling me the truth when he said mum ran away. I shouldn't have argued with him. Now I feel guilty. I guess the lies and the fear of being harmed were too much for my mother to handle."

Dominic was incredulous. "Lies and fear of being harmed?" Leaning towards her, he studied her face closely.

"Yes," she replied coolly and primly, oblivious to his proximity. "There has been so much intrigue surrounding the production of the Chronoguiser that my mum must have sensed there was something amiss. She is a very perceptive person. I can understand why she didn't want to return to such an uncertain environment. Dad too, was obviously aware of subterfuge, because he built his own Chronoguiser."

Dominic settled back in his seat. "We can't be sure of the reason why your mum failed to return to the site where the Chronoguiser dropped her, Zeta. Not until we find her and ask her ourselves."

"We can find her?" sparked up Zeta, suddenly enthusiastic.

Dominic smiled at her sudden change of temper. "Sure we can, by roaming."

"Wonderful!" she exclaimed. "When can we begin searching?"

"Once my splinter group are settled three hundred years into our future, I'll help you search for your mother. I'll give the matter top priority." Dominic said this kindly, trying to weigh her disappointment. "I apologize that we can't start the search immediately."

"No, that's great, Dominic. I didn't expect we could search straight away. I know you are very busy right now. Thank you. I'm happy to wait. It will give me time to think of what I'm going to say when I meet mum again."

Keenly watching her face, he noted she was troubled.

"If you're upset about waiting I could try -"

"The thing is," interrupted Zeta, "I always thought that mum was alive. What if my feelings are wrong? What if-?"

"You know how I mentioned that your dad searched through computer archives of old newspapers," said Dominic, cutting her short. "Well, he wasn't thinking big enough. Look what I found!"

Dominic flicked a switch on the console of his ship. A portrait, painted in 1895, appeared projected onto the closed viewing window.

"I checked. The lady in the portrait was alive and well at the time of the sitting. She is your mum, Zeta. Am I right?"

"Yes, that's mum."

"Good. That's sorted," he said amiably, abruptly changing the subject. "Let's roam to see that alien planet. Close your eyes. Count to three. When you reopen your eyes we will be there - and flying!"

"No wait! What alien planet? Flying you say? I need to mentally prepare." A few seconds later, she closed her eyes. "Ready now. One, two, three!" she called aloud.

As her roaming spirit left the ship - travelling at the speed of light to a distant planet - Zeta once again felt, in her chest, a strange tugging sensation.

Opening her eyes to discover she was indeed flying over a colourful world in a vastly different location, she gasped. Soaring high over the rugged terrain of an exotic planet - with the spectral image of Dominic flying close by her side - she stared in amazement.

Crimson moons shone brilliantly in a violet night sky. Twinkling stars married with gentle moonlight, illuminated a dry purple landscape that was both vivid and striking. Underneath the teenage pair's transparent flying forms, huge black craters pocketed the landscape. Deep green salty pools at the base of those craters rippled slightly under a crisp breeze. While skirting the pools, a narrow sandy beach, marked with thousands of strange footprints, lapped the shoreline. Additionally at the base of each of those craters, accessed via the shoreline, a multitude of dark forbidding caves cut into the sheer rock face.

Between the clusters of craters, scoring the surface of the planet in almost parallel lines, deep purple canyons plunged kilometres downward. On the floor of the canyons, bathed in night shadow, hundreds of silvery trees flourished - their boughs heavy with large scented orange blossoms and pods of small white seeds. Moreover, at the base of those canyons, further caves - subterranean caverns - linked by tunnels, stretched far down into the core of the planet.

"Why on Earth did we roam here?" asked Zeta, immediately recognizing the planet by the colours of the landscape and the two crimson moons.

"What do you think of this world, Zeta?" asked Dominic, ignoring her question. "It certainly looks harmless enough, with its violet sky and purple terrain. Rugged, arid and uninhabited is the first impression. The later is not so positive."

With Dominic now speeding along the length of one of the largest deepest canyons, Zeta wanted to shout. Needing all her concentration to remain flying by his side, however, she remained silent, waiting for an opportunity to speak further. Several minutes later, after diving into the canyon, Dominic slowed his rapid flight.

"As I was saying, Zeta. This planet looks reasonably benign," he continued. "Later this evening, however, everything will change. At 1.15am the orange Sun will rise. The planet will scorch under the sun's blistering onslaught. The temperature will climb to 50 degrees Celsius and the sky will sear white. Best of all, the creatures that are now hiding within the caves at the sides of those black craters or are presently swimming in the tepid crater pools, will come forth. They will hang on the canyon and crater walls by the thousand, basking their disgusting selves in the sun. Six hours later, just before sunset, the surface of the planet will be hell - a dry, airless place full of happy sun-baked demons."

"Dominic," said Zeta, her tone exasperated. "This is Nefaria. You might humour me by being the tiniest bit concerned for our safety. Now, if you don't mind, could you answer my question? Why are we here?"

"There is a particular subterranean cavern I want you to see, Zeta," he replied coolly. "We're nearly there. Follow me."

As they swooped down to fly deeper into the canyon, the rugged walls loomed high around their spectral forms. Looking below her,

Zeta could see silvery orange trees profuse over the canyon floor. Landing in a large clearing, moments later, she faced the lad.

"I can see you are blasé about being here, Dominic. But for the record - are we in danger?"

"Even if it was Sun-up, together, Zeta, we would not be in any danger. The Nefarids find my thought processes painful to them - blinding by observation. They will not approach."

"But I thought Nefarids were dangerous to humans."

"They are. I am proud to be the exception. Since I gained my pilot's license, I have paid regular respectful visits to my parent's graves. They were killed and are buried here. As a result, I have spent a lot of time staring the monsters out. A potent immunity to their paralysing powers has developed."

Zeta looked at him kindly. "Dominic. Sorry about your parents."

Trusting him, she glanced around at the forest of silvery trees. Underneath those trees, contentedly eating seeds that had fallen onto the coarse blue sand, she saw hundreds of blue fluffy animals, similar to dwarf rabbits.

"The Nefarids are asleep now?" she asked, thinking about the calm blue animals.

"They're resting. They don't like the cold. Or the dark. Or me. Come on," he prompted, striding away.

Concealed by large and leafy purple ferns, the entrance to the subterranean cavern that Dominic sought was several metres away. Crossing the clearing and entering the cavern, Zeta followed the lad inside.

The mouth of the cavern was small. Walls that were wet, black and cold quickly closed in around her. Obliged to take the lead at Dominic's insistence, Zeta discovered a steep and narrow rock stairway. Hesitantly descending that stairway, with Dominic close behind, she stepped down into darkness.

Soon the glowing forms of the spectral teenagers provided the only source of light within the dark steep cave. Finding it extremely difficult to see where she stepped, Zeta felt compelled to halt and speak out.

"Dominic, it's growing so dark in here. In a few moments, I won't be able to see the steps at all! In fact, I won't be able to see a thing! Let's go back."

"Don't worry. You can't fall, Zeta, even if you miss a step. You're a roaming entity, remember. Besides, as soon as all the surface light has been deprived from this particular rock face, the steps will start to glow of their own accord. In a matter of seconds it will be stunningly bright in here!"

Zeta glanced quickly around at his transparent image and his confident face. Then she continued her tentative descent into the pitch-black cavern. As the last semblance of exterior light faded around her, the steps did indeed begin to glow. Zeta, pleased to be able to see clearly, continued in silence.

Eventually, standing beside Dominic outside the entrance to a vast illuminated rock chamber, she gazed inside. First, up at the high curved chamber roof, then down at a floor strewn with grey flint and smooth shiny white pebbles. Glancing quickly to her left, she also discovered the entrance to a further smaller cavern.

"What's in there, Dominic?"

"My parent's graves."

Guiding her inside the larger chamber and through it, he advanced towards a further narrower tunnel. Walking beside him, Zeta abruptly halted, surprised to hear the tinkling, splashing sound of falling water coming from that tunnel.

"Come on, Zeta," Dominic said impatiently. "You dithered so long, mincing your way down the rock steps that I only have five minutes left before I have to check on my ships. You won't have time to see the cavern I mentioned, if you don't get a move on."

Startling her, he suddenly mirrored. His form became solid and he grinned. "Quit stalling," he said. "I know you're not keen to go into the next tunnel. But I insist."

"Just because little things like rats don't bother you, you presume everyone else is equally as robust."

Resigned to cooperate, she quickly moved inside the faintly glowing tunnel. Immediately she discovered that the curved walls were dry and encrusted with iridescent shells. Underfoot, the blue sand was warm. The temperature had risen. Additionally, the atmosphere was strangely cheerful - even exciting.

Listening to the water sounds, now much louder, she guessed that there was a subterranean stream up ahead. Further splashing suggested that there were live creatures swimming in that stream - possibly fish.

"You're not into a spot of angling, are you?" she asked, glancing suspiciously at Dominic. "I'm not going to find two fishing rods plus a bucket of maggots waiting up ahead, am I?

"Drat. My secrets out. Don't say you won't be in it!"

Discounting the prospect of fishing and rapidly walking ahead for several metres, Zeta laughed with relief. Then she gasped with delight. The passageway had suddenly widened. Before her was a beautiful glistening cavern - sparkling in soft hues of silver, pink and blue.

Spanning the wall at the rear of the cavern, the most amazing waterfall spilled a high, wide stream of silvery water over its white glossy face. Cascading over three distinct tiers, the water bubbled and glistened. Then fell in fine showers. Filling the air with a rainbow of colours, a fine hazy spray lingered close to the falls. A tranquil melody, dispelled by the tinkling water, resonated throughout the cavern.

Around the falls, Zeta watched the water tumble and fall into a deep curved pool, where it mingled with calmer waters over a blue sandy base. Shiny white boulders beaded the pool - a natural half circle. While fronting the pool and speckled through with thousands of tiny orange gems, an expanse of clear blue sand stretched out invitingly.

"I could easily spend an hour in here, sitting on the sand, gazing at that glorious waterfall," Zeta said, turning towards Dominic. "The sound of the tinkling water as it cascades down the falls is spellbinding. I regret dithering now. Can we stay a little longer? Or come back another time perhaps?"

"Oh this is good," said Dominic. "You're asking me if you can come back to *Nefaria*."

Zeta grinned. Leaving Dominic standing a few metres behind her, she walked gladly into the centre of the expanse of sand. Inside the cavern, the atmosphere was fresh and natural. Drinking in the enchanting aura and the refreshing surrounds, she gazed about dreamily.

Suddenly startled, she gasped. She cried out. Then she stared wide-eyed at the falls. Six metres in front of Zeta, close to the tumbling waters, seven large bubbles had suddenly appeared. Inside each of those bubbles sat an ethereal alien creature. Draped around the shoulders of each of these alien beings, a cape of silver iridescent gauze fell in gentle folds. Each creature had a cream body, head and limbs and was of similar size and appearance to a human toddler. The hair on their heads was white and each was dressed in a demure white shift.

"Dominic, can you see them?" Zeta called softly. "They're floating near the waterfall. What are they? Are they dangerous?"

"Yes, I can see them, Zeta," Dominic replied. Quickly he moved to stand by her side. "They are Salubes. There are over one hundred Salubes living in these subterranean caverns. From what I can conjecture, they have been here for thousands of years. They are not dangerous. But they are cheeky."

"How do you mean?"

"The first time I brought a Spaceship here, and saw them, those same seven picked me up and dropped me in the pool."

"Are they the reason we are here - you wanted me to see them?"

"Yes and more." Pausing he smiled. "I want you to do something for me, Miss. The Salubes have the capacity to endow a long life to any living creature they touch. I want you to keep very still. Don't be frightened."

"Why should I be frightened?"

Dominic glanced at her calm happy face. "Right you are, then," he said. Moving back a discreet distance from Zeta, he carefully watched the Salubes.

While six of the Salubes formed a floating ring in front of the waterfall, the seventh approached Zeta.

Unable to take her eyes off the Salube, Zeta discovered that what she had previously believed to be a gauzy, metre-long cape was actually a pair of folded wings. When the Salube was only two metres away, its bubble disappeared. Materializing, it stretched wide its silver wings. Flying high in the air, Zeta observed it in its new form - no longer a ghostly floating spectre - but a tangible flying entity.

Swooping down, it hovered in front of her. While her eyes widened in pleased astonishment, it gently landed on the warm blue sand.

The Salube stared at Zeta and she stared back.

Gulping in amazement, she spoke to the creature in a very soft voice. "My name is Zeta," she said quietly. "Behind me is my friend, Dominic. What's your name?"

The Salube stopped staring. Smiling, it knelt down before her. Stretching out its small pretty hand, the alien creature drew eight marks in the sand. Zeta read those eight letters. Then she laughed.

"Hello, Temerity," she said cheerfully.

Temerity nodded greeting. Zeta grinned with delight.

Shyly whispering she enquired, "I hope you don't mind me asking, but the name you have just written in the sand indicates you may be a male. Are you a boy, Temerity?"

When the Salube again nodded, Zeta turned to glance at Dominic. He smiled at her kindly.

Resuming her discussion with Temerity she further enquired, "I can see that you can write, Temerity. How do you normally communicate?"

Temerity stretched out his hand and this time he wrote nine letters in the sand. A few seconds later, Zeta was reading the word 'Telepathy,' written in deep grooves into the coarse blue sand.

"Oh my!" she thought to herself happily. "We can hear each others thoughts!" Then her eyes welled with tears of amazement.

Dominic, watching, was both interested and pleased. Realizing that their leisure time was exhausted, however, he glanced at his timeband. Then he quickly moved forward.

"Sorry, Zeta. We have to go now. I need to return to my ship."

"Goodbye, Temerity," Zeta said wistfully. Then she felt a strange tugging sensation in her chest.

In the blink of an eye, she had returned to the *Heritage*. Dominic was awake - his assertive mortal self. She was translucent - a roaming spectre.

Zeta laughed. "Back in your ship - and you're already busy checking the instruments on your console."

"I'm in the middle of supervising a sapling consignment," he admitted. "Now, I'm going to mirror to all my Chronoguiser Captains. You are going to wait here until I return. I won't be long. Don't touch anything."

"Wait! Before you go? I have a question to ask. I feel a strange tugging sensation in my chest when I'm roaming with you. I didn't feel it when I roamed with Felicity. Do you think there may be something wrong with my Roaming-Ring?"

"Your Roaming-Ring is functioning perfectly, Zeta. The amethysts are ideally suited to your psychic projection." He paused briefly and was thoughtful. "I believe you are feeling a slight pull on your spirit because I mirror, rather than roam. There is a lot more energy applied when mirroring. Plus, there is a bond between us, as demonstrated by your functioning Guardian Ring." After saying all this, however, Dominic regarded her with genuine concern. "The tugging sensation doesn't hurt, does it?" he asked quietly.

"No," she replied. "There isn't any pain. I just feel it, that's all."

"Good," he said quickly. "I'll be back soon."

"No wait!"

"What now?"

"I never thought I'd be thanking anyone for taking me to a planet full of Nefarids. But seeing the Salubes will have to go down as the ultimate experience of my whole life. This evening has been much appreciated."

Dominic grinned. The quartz crystals in his Roaming-Ring glowed. Two seconds later, he was asleep.

Sitting quietly and. resisting the temptation to close her eyes, Zeta decided to leave her seat. Standing up, she moved towards the rear of the ship. She glanced with scientific curiosity at the newly installed gravity drive and at the array of amazing scientific equipment set into the curved walls of the Sphere. Wary of Dominic soon wakening, she hurriedly moved back towards her seat.

In her haste, she brushed against a Martial Arts Fighting Staff fastened to the rear wall of the vessel. The Staff, dislodged from its fastenings, toppled. Then fell with a clatter.

Recognizing the weapon as similar to one she had seen during her first roaming excursion, she stretched out her ghostly hands, bent down and picked it up.

After glancing around to see whether the noise had startled Dominic from sleep, she studied the weapon. She noted its length - one hundred and twenty centimetres. And its colour - matte gold with black bands and black etching. She counted the number of amber stones and the pieces of jet imbedded into the centre portion. Then she looked closely at the exquisite artistic etchings, which covered the Staff from the handholds, to within ten centimetres of each end. Finally, she gazed at the shiny thick bands of black casing that tipped both ends of the Staff.

Holding the Staff by the handholds, Zeta pushed it back between a set of clasps. Feeling an electrical surge coursing through her hands, she jumped. "Oh!" she exclaimed quietly, quickly pulling her hands away. "There's something quite unusual about this weapon." Glancing at her timeband, she returned to her seat.

A few minutes later, Dominic awoke.

"My ships will be ready to leave shortly, Zeta," he informed her quickly. "We must visit your father now. After that, you will wake up in your room and I will go back to work. Are you ready to leave?"

"Sure."

Keen to ask Professor Doherty if she could stay in this amazing future world, Zeta closed her eyes and counted aloud, "One, two, three!"

Awake in her cosy pink and violet bedroom, ten minutes later, Zeta lifted her Roaming-Ring from her head. After placing it in the recessed headboard of the divan, she let down her hair. Changing into her nightclothes, she gratefully climbed under her bedcovers. With the details of her visit to Professor Doherty still fresh in her mind, she rested her head back on her pillow. Then she smiled.

Pleased, she had discovered that her father planned a permanent visit to the future. Additionally she had learnt that Isabelle, Ret and Kepplar Holmes wished to join him.

Zeta had also heard how Isabelle and Auntie Marjorie had managed to escape from TT's mansion. While Ret had turned a blind eye, they had simply strolled through the gates, unchallenged. Later, when a frosty TT had contacted Marjorie, she had explained that while his offer of protection was appreciated, the ladies preferred the quiet quaint ambience of Marjorie's cottage.

Time now to sleep and dream, Zeta settled back into her warm bed.

"Good night, To-do!" she called softly.

The puppy, happily dozing on the pink settee, blinked and yawned.

"Lights off, music off, globe off," Zeta commanded. "Oh. Pirate record," she added.

The room became dark and quiet. Pulling the pink coverlet over her shoulders, she reflected on the amazing roaming experience of this evening. She wondered at the strange planet with orange blossom trees and fluffy blue animals. Dreamily she then pondered over the Salube she had encountered. Picturing 'Temerity' in her minds eye, she softly whispered his name.

Unexpectedly a small round light suddenly appeared in the mid-point of her room. The light grew bigger. Glowing and benign - an alien creature - the focus of her thoughts, suddenly materialized.

Kept buoyant by two gossamer wings, Temerity smiled. Flying slowly towards Zeta, he landed gently on her divan coverlet. Moving forward, he threw his arms innocently around her neck.

Zeta wondered why, instead of alarm, she felt happiness. Her chest rose and fell under the slight weight of the small alien. As time passed, he seemed to lighten. Seconds later, she felt no weight at all.

Temerity kissed her forehead. Inhaling deeply, Zeta discovered that the air in her bedroom now smelt like the air of the subterranean cavern - natural, fresh and sweet. Her eyelids were heavy. Drifting off to sleep, the last sight she saw for that evening was Temerity, flying in midair - with silver wings outstretched - lighting up the darkness.

Chapter thirteen

Around the *Estrella,* needles of light pierced the golden sea. Never halting their constant advance, those needles spread, faded, but always they reached searchingly forward. Sometimes when the needles refracted and splintered, a spectrum of colours painted the Deep. Beams of the finest red, orange, yellow and blue neighboured parallel streams of indigo, green and violet. Forming millions of strange images, those paintings hung transient in the dense salty water, swaying while the sea rolled.

Seated in the *Estrella,* behind the pilot's chair, next to Ret, Isabelle glanced around the small glowing blue cabin. She listened to the soft gentle melody emitted from the gravity drive, central to their Spartan silver Sphere. Out of the viewing window, she looked through the deep, gold water, at the beautiful Marine City of Aristau. Several moments later, when their invisible vessel had reached and passed over that city, she turned to Ret.

"You look fine, Garrett," she remarked, in response to his previously expressed concerns. "Svelte and handsome. In fact, we all look remarkable in the outfits that Dominic sent us to wear. No one will be able to tell us apart from the locals."

"Thank you, Isabelle," responded Ret, pleased at the reference to his trimmer appearance. After which he looked towards Professor Doherty and Kepplar Holmes to join in the conversation.

The famous inventor and the Global Peace Prize Winner, seated in the pilot and co-pilot's seat up front were too absorbed in their own intelligent thoughts, however, and so remained silent.

Descending to the seabed, their vessel entered a Submarine Bay - located in the rock bed under the city.

"I'm disengaging the invisibility function now," said Professor Doherty.

"Yes. Best that our welcoming committee can actually *see* us arrive," agreed Kepplar.

Rising up into a large white and blue marina, underneath one of Aristau's perimeter turrets, sheets of water cascaded off the Sphere's silver hull. When the Sphere was floating clear of the water, the occupants of the *Estrella* curiously looked out.

The marina was bright and warm. Edging the marina, a wide brown platform provided four access points into the city above. Many vessels were moored alongside that platform, including several bathyspheres. Lamps set into the walls of the marina caused the water to sparkle and coloured directional signs added a friendly ambience to this welcoming area.

Standing on the otherwise empty platform waiting to greet them were four males. Aristotle stood smartly, wearing his Governor's sash over a fine frockcoat and matching trousers. Two Psychic Knights - Dominic and Sebastian - stood on his left. Eddie, dressed casually in a brown shirt and comfortable cotton taupe trousers, stood on his right.

Recognizing the lads, Professor Doherty moved the *Estrella* forward to hover over the platform. He opened the hatch, dropped the boarding steps, and the occupants of the small time-machine all filed out.

Ret, first to disembark, rushed forward. After embracing his brother, he thumped Eddie hard on the back.

"Good to see you bro!" he growled happily.

The rest of the travellers - also excited, but not quite so exubrant - quietly approached the three indigenous males. Governor Aristotle greeted Kepplar and Isabelle. Professor Doherty stepped briskly towards Dominic. He clasped the fair lad's hand and shook it warmly.

"Good afternoon. Nice to finally meet you in the flesh, young man," he said in his cultured deep voice. "A fine specimen of manhood you are, too. You have vivid blue eyes and sandy coloured hair. You are assertive *and* strong. I'm guessing your life span is double mine. Am I right?"

"Yes, Professor Doherty," replied Dominic. "Your observations are accurate. But I wish to ask you. Was your journey without trouble? Is the *Estrella* an adequate ship?"

"She's an exceptional ship - thanks to Bermuda's engineering help. Plus your own and Sebastian's input. I have learnt more in the last twelve days, working with you and your friends than I have learnt in the last ten years. Toiling alongside three ghosts is an eye opening experience."

"We were honoured to be of assistance Professor," responded Dominic frankly. Glancing towards the buoyant *Warrior*, also docked in the marina, Dominic's expression darkened and he abruptly changed the subject. "Professor Doherty, TT Vox Populi arrived back last night," he revealed sombrely. "We have tightened the security around Aristau as a necessary precaution. We have also brought forward our departure date. We will be leaving tomorrow night."

"My small party are ready to travel further forward through time - on your say so," responded the Professor quickly.

After noticing Aristotle nodding politely to him, the inventor of the Chronoguiser shook Sebastian's hand. Then he began to move towards Aristotle.

"Wait! One last thing, something you ought to know, Professor," added Dominic hastily. "Although I do not share mutual goals with him, TT Vox Populi is my great grandfather - on my mother's side. I'm sorry for what he did to you."

Professor Doherty took the revelation well. "Even more reason why I am in your debt, lad. Now let me meet Governor Aristotle, who I also believe is a relative of yours."

Dominic nodded. Smiling at Isabelle politely, he left her to chat with Sebastian. Stepping quickly towards Kepplar Holmes he grabbed the Peace Prize Winner by the arm. Taking him aside out of earshot of the others, Dominic at once began a furtive exchange with the accomplished scientist. His expression was cool and his voice was quiet. An intriguing device was passed from one to the other, which Dominic hid in the inner pocket of his chainmail jacket. Then the lad's tone of voice and attitude fell into kindness.

"I am aware Kepplar, that you wish to find a cure for your mother's hereditary ailment," Dominic said thoughtfully. "She is presently being kept unconscious in a state of suspended animation?"

"Yes, that is correct," replied Kepplar.

"After you have settled into your quarters, Governor Aristotle will take you to Aristau hospital," Dominic advised. "Doctor Marie at the hospital already has a copy of your mother's medical file. She will provide you with the best solution to manage your mother's condition. We are fine to send any equipment and medication required - back to your father."

"Are saying there is a cure?"

"Yes, there is a cure. Your mother will be well in a matter of months."

Kepplar Holmes gripped Dominic by the shoulder and shook him heartily. "I couldn't be more pleased," he said excitedly. Wiping a tear from one of his eyes with the back of his hand, he looked appreciatively at the *Estrella* and then curiously at the *Warrior*.

"The others are waiting for you to enter Aristau City with them. You best go," said Dominic, guiding the scientist towards his great grandfather, Isabelle and Professor Doherty.

Before leaving the marina, Professor Doherty retrieved a remote-control from his pocket and pressed a switch. Consequently the boarding steps of the *Estrella* withdrew, the hatch closed and the vessel - with its invisibility function now activated - appeared to disappear.

After the older party had left, Dominic spoke to the three lads remaining with him on the marina.

"We have a mission," he growled.

Gesturing with his head for the lads to follow, he walked briskly towards the *Warrior*. Once inside that ship, he slipped the device he had previously concealed in his jacket into a locked compartment. After which he took his position in the pilot's seat.

Underfoot, the silver metal floor gleamed. Cocooning him, the walls - fitted with equipment - sparkled with specks of colour from the many illuminated switches and dials. The seats, fastened to the floor in rows of six were small, white and slightly padded. Fitted into the central shaft - the gravity drive - a sphere of small size, sat polished silver, quietly glistening.

When the other three lads entered the Sphere, Dominic closed the hatch, quickly submerging the *Warrior* into the Submarine Bay. Then he piloted the vessel through the illuminated water to the exit gate. Activating the invisibility function of his ship, he took her out into the deep waters surrounding Aristau.

"Strap yourselves in tightly, lads," Dominic advised. "Tough flying is required on this particular mission. Be warned. At times you may feel very uncomfortable."

Rising quickly to the surface, bursting out of the sea amidst a cloud of white foamy spray, the *Warrior* headed for the stratosphere - at an extremely high velocity.

"One thousand TT Space Transports are presently orbiting the Earth, Ret, Eddie," Dominic explained, glancing at the Bourne brothers, seated beside Sebastian on his left. "They are empty of passengers now, but in one weeks time they will take our entire

planet's population to five distant worlds. Flying guard beside them -
on the far side of the Transports, hidden from view to Earth's
telescopes - are five squadrons of Space Fighters. Today we are going
to pay those squadrons a furtive visit."

Reaching under his seat, Dominic pulled out two black electronic
boards - Radar Grid Tablets. These he handed to the Bourne brothers.
Eddie and Ret quickly acquainted themselves with the light, thirty
centimetre square boards.

"The Tablets you both have in front of you are capable of
registering - at close range - the unique communication frequency of
every vessel ever manufactured," Dominic further explained. "This
afternoon, you are both going to register the frequency of one
hundred Space Fighters. Once we have that information, we will
know where every enemy vessel is - even at long range. Without that
information, the Fighter's stealth capability makes our radar
equipment ineffective."

"I know the Tablet is a Radar *and* Battle System," said Eddie.
"Can you explain the functions of the Battle System?"

Ret nodded in enthusiastic agreement.

Dominic increased speed. The *Warrior* shot like a ball of blue
light, out of the Earth's atmosphere into the darkness of Space.
Blackness instantly enveloped the vessel. Leaving a whispery blue
wake, trailing kilometres behind, the invisible Spaceship hurtled
forward. An infinite number of stars sparkled around the ship and the
brothers, forgetting themselves - stared childlike through the viewing
window - out into the vast realm of Space. They observed the Earth
shining, a massive brown and blue globe. They saw and somehow felt
the darkness that surrounded their ship. Peering out at the white
glowing stars twinkling in the distance, they marvelled. Then they
surveyed the huge functional beacons - the Earth Satellites - slowly
revolving in the vacuum, like tiny oddly shaped moons.

"Fill them in on the pertinent details of the Battle System, will you,
Sebastian," requested Dominic, jolting them from their reverie.

Eddie nodded enthusiastically and the brothers looked away from
the viewing window.

"The Radar Grid Tablet has been designed to plug into any ship's
console," Sebastian explained. "With the use of the attached pointer, a
wall of combat strategies can be quickly selected. The whole
dashboard in front of you is the *Warrior's* wall of combat strategies.
That's right, Ret. You are looking at this ship's Defence System. The

socket where the Radar Grid Tablet gets plugged into is below all the manual control switches."

Eddie and Ret looked at the switches that controlled the Weapons System of the *Warrior* with eager interest, while Sebastian continued to explain all the different combat capabilities in detail.

Shortly after, when the brothers were again gazing into Outer Space, Ret enquired, "Where are the TT Space Transports, Sebastian? Shouldn't I be able to see them by now?"

"Earth's Space perimeter has been divided into four sections," said Sebastian. "The Transports are orbiting in the fourth, restricted quadrant - which we are fast approaching. The Satellites orbit in the first quadrant. The second quadrant is for exiting Spaceships. The third is for entry."

The *Warrior* suddenly surged forward. The Fleet of silver Space Transports - aligned in five rectangular Contingents of two hundred - immediately came into view. Filling the heavens as far as the four lads could see, the Fleet stretched out over many kilometres. Gleaming out into the darkness, the light shining from their many portholes, swathed the Fleet with a hazy aura.

Ret let out a deep breath.

"The sight gets me too," said Sebastian. "You can't hep feeling proud."

"Look at the design of those Spaceships!" exclaimed Eddie, quite impressed. "What's in the centre of each vessel? Tau? Explain?"

"At the centre of each vessel is a square Habitation Block," Dominic replied. "A rectangular open frame box-wing, made from thousands of adjoining triangles, is attached on either side of that Block. The wingtips are permanently illuminated - as is the perimeter of the Habitation Block. Furthermore, each vessel is marked with a coat of arms - an emblem of a shield with a planet at centre - on the front and rear of each Block."

"What's with the coat of arms on each ship, Tau?"

"Although they will all travel to the same Solar System, Eddie, each Contingent of two hundred ships has their own planet to go to, and each has their own motto. The symbol on the first Contingent is a two masted, fore-and-aft rigged wooden sailing vessel painted in the core of a planet. Their motto underneath - you can read yourself."

"*Exploration champions freedom*," Eddie read aloud, his keen vision seeing the first Contingent, far up ahead.

"My eyes aren't that great. I wear contact lenses," admitted Ret. "Go on reading the axioms, bro."

"Contingent two have an open book inside of the planet logo," Eddie continued. "Underneath the logo is the axiom: *Knowledge furthers prosperity.* Contingent three have a set of gold weighing scales. Their motto is: *Law promotes peace.*"

"The fourth group's emblem features a harp at the core of the planet," interrupted Sebastian. "Their maxim is: *Music fosters tranquillity.* My favourite."

"I can read the fifth group's emblem myself," said Ret, "now that we are closer to the rear of the Fleet. It features a paintbrush stretched diagonally across a planet. Right? Their motto is: *Art ennobles progress.*"

"Ready now. Hang onto your seats!" Dominic warned. "Fast erratic flying is mandatory. The Intelligence Officers flying guard over these Transports have good instincts. Even though their radar is ineffective against *us*, they will know we are here if we linger any longer than necessary. If they guess we are here - invisible or not - they will blow us out of this airless black void."

"On my first day, too," said Ret quietly.

Dominic now stretched his spatial abilities of configuring speed, distance and angles to the limit, cleverly weaving the *Warrior* between the rows of ships in the rear group of Transports. His heading - the opposite side of the Fleet - where the Space Fighters lurked. Flung back in their seats, his crew were heaved in every direction. Swerving in a zigzag pattern, their vessel pitched up and down.

Nervously observing the wings of the Transports looming very close, at times, Eddie growled, "How dangerous is this? You could slow down a little, Tau. You're flying way too -"

"How fast are the Transport Ships, Tau?" Ret interrupted.

"The Transports were constructed in Space as comfortable secure passenger ships, Ret," explained Dominic coolly, after a brief pause, "not for speed or manoeuvrability. They are slow ships compared to the TT Space Fighters."

"I expected the Space Transports to be larger, since they are taking the entire Earth's population onboard," remarked Ret. "You say they are comfortable?"

"Their size adequately reflects the amount of cargo each of them is expected to carry," Dominic responded, "- one thousand passengers and provisions for five years."

"One thousand passengers!" exclaimed Eddie, who had, until now been busy keeping his eye on Dominic's flying. "One thousand passengers multiplied by one thousand Space Transports, equals only one million passengers. I thought the entire Earth's population was being evacuated!"

Dominic glanced quickly to his left at Eddie's baffled expression. Concentrating on his course and continuing to weave his ship erratically between two hundred vessels, he replied sympathetically. "One million *is* the entire Earth's population, Eddie. The meteors that bombarded our planet seventeen years ago caused mass devastation. The famine that followed, brought death, disease, and civil unrest."

"Wars?" asked Eddie.

"Fighting over scarce resources. Yes," replied Dominic coolly.

"So you two have spent your whole lives fighting?" asked Ret quietly, glancing at both Sebastian and Dominic.

"We've spent our time studying and learning how to fight," replied Sebastian. "Our actual combat experience is negligible."

While Ret mused on this information, Eddie continued his line of questioning regarding the colonists. "If only one million people are travelling into Outer Space, Tau, that means that only two hundred thousand people will inhabit each of the five planets. Two hundred thousand citizens isn't much." Then he gave voice to his concerns. "The colonists could be easily wiped out. Especially if there were unforeseen natural disasters on these new planets, or even worse - plagues or hidden monsters!"

Dominic glanced at Eddie. "I can be sure that Mother Earth hasn't got any nasty surprises waiting in store for my group," he remarked gruffly.

"How can you be so sure, Tau?" asked Ret.

"Tell him, Sebastian."

"We've taken the *Heritage* on a reconnaissance mission three hundred years into our future," answered Sebastian candidly.

Just at the moment, Dominic increased speed.

Eddie coughed and grumbled, "Sure - fly even faster, why don't you, Tau. I suppose you were just warming up before. Who cares that my bones are being crushed against my seat."

Ignoring Eddie and readying to fly out from between the Transports into open Space - just behind the rear squadron of TT Space Fighters - Dominic spoke sternly.

"Here we find the black hornets nest! There are twenty Space Fighters to a squadron, five squadrons, and one hundred frequencies to register. We've five minutes to complete this job and get safely away. Fast as you can now, boys! Begin your registrations now!"

Further increasing speed, the *Warrior* flew behind, and then along the far flank of the rear Space Fighter squadron.

"Wow!" exclaimed Eddie, hurriedly glancing through the viewing window at that squadron, flying in triangular formation. "Those Space Fighters are beautiful! This is the first time I've seen them up close. They are streamlined, sleek and aeronautically perfect. They have great bodywork -"

"Eddie! Get back to your job!" chastised Dominic in a gruff whisper, cutting him off, but at the same time suppressing a smile.

Sebastian, aware how vital these registrations were to their security, quickly assisted the two overawed brothers.

"Those Space Fighters are impressive," he remarked quickly to the brothers. "Their manoeuvrability is unsurpassed and their Weapon System is state of the art. The equilateral triangular body shape of the Fighter allows the vessel to slip sideways and dive on its prey in an instant. Modelled after ancient jet fighter planes, but flatter and more compact, the TT Space Fighter is a highly desirable vessel. The vessel even has a neat escape capsule incorporated into the back. Who in the Psychic Forces doesn't want one?"

"What is the top speed of the Fighter?" asked Ret, keen to know.

"Not half as fast as we're going now, I bet," grumbled Eddie.

"Very, very fast," whispered Sebastian.

"Sebastian? Can you persuade his Lordship to slow down?" said Eddie. "I know we are all going to die in the next few seconds."

With all the registrations now complete, he glanced hurriedly out into Space at the lead Fighter squadron.

"Heck no!" he suddenly cried out.

Panicked after spotting a Shuttle - high and wide at the rear, and pointed and flat at the cockpit in front - ten metres away, he held fast to his seat.

A split second later, his body and the bodies of the others in the *Warrior* were thrown violently back. Pulling his ship into a fast vertical climb to avoid impact with that grey, cone-shaped Shuttle,

Dominic gritted his teeth. Meanwhile the other lads beside him - fearing the worst - braced for collision.

Seconds later, the *Warrior* was back on a horizontal course and Dominic was grinning.

"That Shuttle just cut across our prow!" exclaimed Ret in a relieved low voice. "I can't believe we missed it! I thought a collision was -"

"Imminent," cut in Dominic, brusquely and quietly.

"Managing to avoid that Shuttle must mean that we were travelling at close to the speed of light," thought Eddie. With his heart still thumping from the physical shock of the steep climb, he watched while Dominic piloted the *Warrior,* in an arc, back behind the Shuttle they had just avoided.

"What's an Aristau Shuttle doing in this restricted area, Tau?" he asked, recognising the insignia of Aristau - a blue whale - painted on the side.

"The pilot is attending an interview with regard to his compulsory five year Commission onboard a Space Transport. Plus, he is delivering a secret package - on my orders."

Dominic now listened - via his Surveillance System - to a message from the Squadron leader to the pilot of the Aristau Shuttle.

"Aristau Shuttle - you have deviated from the authorized flight path for visitors. Identify yourself and your business?"

"Francis Bermuda, reporting to Transport 0002 - to see Captain Brussels for interview," the Shuttle pilot responded.

Looking through his viewing window, Dominic observed the Squadron leader break formation and fly towards the Shuttle.

Suddenly, without provocation, the Space Fighter fired! A loud explosion resonated through the dark emptiness. An instant later, all in the cabin of the *Warrior* witnessed the startling and jarring eventuality of the Shuttle - all ablaze! Orange and blue flames licked out from the rear of that vessel. Smoke billowed into the darkness in a large cloudy ball. Simultaneously vibrations from the blast flowed forth like a rough river through the black vacuum, rocking the *Warrior*.

"Destroyed?" asked Ret quietly.

Speeding ahead towards the site of blanketing smoke, flames and partial debris, Dominic hovered the invisible *Warrior* over the site of destruction. He checked his instruments. Suddenly he mirrored. One tense moment later, he awoke.

"Bermuda has suffered no harm," he quickly revealed. "The reserve engine in the prow of the Shuttle is still fully functional, so the vessel will be able to dock in the Transport landing-bay and return to Earth unaided."

Sebastian watched the smoke clear. What remained of the Shuttle's rear engine was charred and black. Nonetheless, the airtight hull was undamaged. Speaking, Sebastian's tone was angry.

"Since when did TT Vox Populi apply such heavy handed tactics?" he growled.

Dominic frowned, replying in an extremely quiet voice - which only Sebastian could hear. "These hostilities need to be managed, Sebastian. I am TT's great grandson and a thorn in his side. I will press this agitation to our advantage."

From the safety of the invisible *Warrior,* all three of Dominic's crew now watched as the Aristau Shuttle turned and limped towards Transport Ship 0002. Dwarfed by the thousand strong Fleet and intimidated by the hostile squadrons, the cone-shaped vessel floated like a speck of dust in a lightless world. Seeming very small and defenceless, it slowly entered the landing-bay - on the bottom deck - at the rear of Transport 0002's Habitation Block.

Dominic, his face thoughtful, watched the Shuttle until it was out of sight. Turning his ship about, he headed on a fast course back towards the first orbital quadrant.

With Dominic flying at a moderate pace, all those in the *Warrior's* cabin now had the chance to appreciate the sparkling stars in the heavens and the breath-taking vista of the planet below them. Space was especially tranquil after the threatening atmosphere around the Transport Fleet. Staring out at the awesome environment around them, their spirits calmed.

With the Transports well at their backs, the Earth loomed large in their viewing window. The Earth Satellites came into view and they entered the first orbital quadrant.

"I take it our espionage is out of the way for the day," said Eddie. "What now your Lordship? A spot of deserved recreation wouldn't go amiss."

"We're going to stop at Satellite25 and transfer to an Aristau Shuttle. We'll then travel through the third quadrant and return to Aristau."

"I don't think that an Aristau Shuttle is quite my choice as the ultimate form of transport right now, your Lordship," remarked Eddie.

"I could always leave you on Satellite25, if you like," responded Dominic. "You could keep company with the robots and the tourists. Of course, you would then miss the opportunity of watching the tournament."

"What tournament?"

"Sebastian and I are due to compete in a Martial Arts Staff-Fighting tournament at the Aristau Sports Stadium. We fight for thirty minutes. Aristau versus London. So that's where we're all going – except for maybe you, Eddie."

"The tournaments are always dynamic, challenging and skilful," said Sebastian.

"We're going," said Ret. He grinned at his brother. There after, both their faces lit up at the prospect of some violent sports.

Several minutes later, after transferring to the Aristau Shuttle and resuming their journey, they reached the third quadrant. Leaving the black vacuum of Space behind them, they breached Earth's atmosphere. Descending through the clouds over Britain, their Shuttle was soon plunging into the sea over Aristau.

Travelling through the deep waters, Eddie and Ret quickly spotted the golden Marine City.

"That's the Sports Stadium, Ret," said Dominic, pointing out a structure built on the top of one of the higher Towers in the City centre.

Looking towards that Tower, Ret admired the stadium - an impressive round white building, modelled on the Roman Coliseums of old. The architecture was brilliant and imposing. High Corinthian columns stood massive and tall around its perimeter. The windows were arched - as were the doorways. Whilst the entire structure, built over several levels, had an eager prosperous ambiance that virtually oozed from the walls.

Blazing out from the stadium, shooting forth in long shafts into the surrounding seawater, the light was dazzling. While inside the brightly illuminated building, Ret could see almost everything - from the circular arena covered with artificial turf to the crowd of ten thousand spectators, already seated in the tiered Stands. Dominic circled the stadium once. Returning to the Submarine Bay, he moored their Shuttle alongside many similar vessels.

Out of his seat and standing next to Sebastian, Dominic presently addressed the Bourne brothers, still seated placidly in their chairs.

"Come on!" he directed them gruffly.

Taking note of their contented expressions, he ushered the two males promptly from their seats. Both Knights grabbed their Fighting-Staffs from the stern. Dominic unlocked the Shuttle door. As he heaved it open, it slid, grating noisily. He and his three companions jumped out onto the marina. Then the fair lad heaved the heavy clanking door shut behind them.

Striding out from the marina into the City proper, the lads took a connecting elevator to the Sports Stadium Tower. Minutes later, they entered that large amphitheatre. Spotlights shone down from high in the Stands over the centre of the promising circular arena. A huge scoreboard, hanging up on the opposite side of the stadium, shone brightly with the words: *Aristau Vs London*. Tiered red seats, ascending steeply, were full of eager spectators, crowned with Roaming-Rings. The aisles were packed. Completing the vibrant picture, several large groups of boisterous young men - crowding the thoroughfares - were excitedly placing bets on the outcome of the tournament.

"Tau, are ladies not admitted?" asked Ret, noticing that every single one of the spectators was male.

"Who cares - let's quickly make our bets - before the Tournament begins," said Eddie.

Counting the money tokens he had in his pockets, he and his brother left the two Knights, to hastily join a queue of punters.

Sebastian and Dominic exchanged knowing glances. Purposefully walking out from the Stands onto the far left of the arena - they strode straight into the midst of the London Team.

All ten members of that team - standing strong and intimidating - glared at them. Each wore a red armband and each was holding his Fighting-Staff boldly. Amongst them, Dominic recognized four members of the Psychic Forces - Matthew Keating, Mahoney, Sangria and the sandy haired Hanepoot. These four all wore their bronze Knight's Raiment. Amongst the other six members of the London Team - all wearing the black chainmail of the London Guards - he saw Blake.

Politely he acknowledged the four members of his elitist group. Sebastian repeated the courtesy. Both young men then moved to the right of the arena where their team - also comprised of four Psychic Knights and six Guards - was assembled.

Samuel and Parsons grinned as they approached.

"You're late, Sebastian," harped Joshua, looking fine in his grey chainmail.

"John. Tau," said Samuel. Thumping both newcomers on the back, he handed each of them a blue armband.

"Are you ready to give London a thrashing?" asked Dominic, speaking to Parsons.

The smallest and youngest member of their team merely grinned in reply.

"What about you lot!" Dominic asked loudly, turning towards the Aristau Guards. "Are you all ready to do Aristau proud?"

The resounding answer was nothing short of a definite roar.

Suddenly the voice of the Master of Ceremonies boomed out of the stadium's loudspeakers.

"Thank you for joining us! You are all asked to take your seats. The combatants for the Martial Arts Staff-Fighting Tournament - Psychic Forces division - are just about to move out into the centre of the arena. The battle will begin on the sound of the horn."

Naturally, following this announcement, all the males, young and old, in the encircling Stands, cheered enthusiastically. Some of them waved pennants carrying the colours of their team, blue for Aristau and red for London. While others, wearing clothing accessories bearing their team's insignia, immediately began yelling and whistling.

Meanwhile the two umpires, assigned to mediate the tournament, instructed both teams to commence a warm up drill.

Along with his team, Dominic stepped out surely into the spotlight in front of the large crowd. As did the London Team - captained by Keating. Taking up his allocated position in the field, four metres from his closest neighbour, he glanced at the thousands of spectators in the amphitheatre around him. He looked at his Fighting-Staff. Made from an excellent conducting material, it felt light, sure and familiar in his hands. Then in exercise, like those around him, the fair lad began a careful sequence of combat actions. Watching him admiringly, his fans saw that all his manoeuvres were completed swiftly, smoothly and gracefully.

Sudden and booming, the starting horn blared out welcomingly. Instantly the arena was excitingly alive with the figures of twenty combatants all energetically fighting.

With their eyes fixed on those combatants, the rowdy spectators immensely enjoyed the spectacle of such controlled hostility. Happily, they listened to the continuous sound of twenty Fighting-Staffs - wielded by the fighters - whooshing through the air and striking forcefully. Eagerly they observed the contestants as they leapt and spun aggressively using their weapons for both defensive, and attack. They groaned too, when their favourite contestant was struck forcibly. Only to discover the strength of that Combatant, who unconcerned, continued relentlessly fighting.

With the action so furious, time slid away. Twenty minutes into the dynamic competition already, the scoreboard above the arena indicated that Aristau was winning with 200 points to London's 180.

Dominic, fighting on the left of the field, was currently battling against five assailants - Keating and four London Guards - one of them Blake. While the remaining action proceeded in the centre and right of the field - with five combatants of the London Team, fighting against nine of the Aristau side.

With the odds mounting against their champion, the confident Aristau supporters, keenly watching Dominic, were becoming unusually edgy. Sitting amongst them with his brother, Eddie was watching Dominic *and* all the other combatants he knew.

Sebastian, he saw, was engaged in an extremely fast moving and taxing battle with Mahoney. Samuel, striking out with his Fighting-Staff every few seconds was fighting Sangria. While Parsons, fighting on the right of the field, a few metres from Sebastian and Samuel, was blocking Hanepoot's persistent and grating attack. Joshua, Eddie observed, fought a good fight with the rest of his teammates against two extremely tough and fast London fighters.

Dominic, currently the main interest of the tournament, was leaping and spinning with great energy - fending off five assailants. Blocking their many strikes, he brandished his Staff so skilfully that rather than finding their task easy, his opponents were all working hard to keep him contained.

"Five against one! No problem!" yelled out Eddie, enjoying the games immensely. "His Lordship rises to the challenge! This match is a foregone conclusion - Aristau wins!"

Listening, a small nearby group of London spectators exchanged furtive glances.

"Watch this," said one of them, a practised Illusionist.

Unexpectedly, at a time when spirits were most high and the battle was at its height, Dominic, puzzled, suddenly heard the rowdy crowd quieten. Glancing towards the Stands, he was further surprised to see two males dashing out onto the far left of the arena.

Running in a blind panic - imagining that the ground was falling away beneath him - Ret was dashing across the field into the throes of battle. A few metres behind him ran Eddie - shouting his lungs out for his brother to stop.

"What the Dickens? Cease fighting! Cease fighting!" Dominic yelled in his loudest voice.

His own team - Aristau - fighting in the centre and on the right of the arena, lowered their weapons and questioningly glanced his way.

"No, all combatants continue fighting! I outrank you, Tau, and my order stands!" yelled Keating. Countermanding Dominic's wishes, he and his four helpers persisted in their attack.

"Order your men to desist, Keating!" shouted Dominic vehemently. Observing as he bellowed, that Ret was now standing dazed amidst the fray. Keating however, remained obstinate.

Eddie, reaching his brother, listening and most pro-active, decided to deal with this debate in his own particular way. Aggressively hurtling himself onto Keating's back, he tried to bring the strong lad down.

Retaliating, Keating threw Eddie away from him. While Blake - moving towards them both - swung his Staff high in the air, ready to bring it down like a club across Eddie's shoulders.

Those in the Stands who recognized Eddie from the Satellite Cup, gasped. The umpires, running across the field and reluctant to blow their whistles and halt the tournament, scowled. While the remaining fourteen combatants, standing still in the centre and far right of the field looked on with interest.

Dominic thought fast and acted fast. Not given over to panic, he focused on using his Fighting-Staff to his best advantage. Whilst he concentrated thus, the crystals in his Roaming-Ring instantly began to glow - not white - but deep blood-red.

Exercising perfect balance he crouched, jumped high into the air, swivelled a complete 360-degree circle and struck Keating hard with his Staff, knocking him sideways. A split second later, he swung his Staff towards Blake, determined to prevent the assault on Eddie.

The crowd were watching him intently - their eyes widened at the extraordinary sight of his Roaming-Ring and the glowing red crystals.

Suddenly, while all eyes in the crowd were literally glued on him, a beam of blinding white light shot out from Dominic's Staff, arced and hit Blake directly in the chest. Lifted off his feet by that psychic energy beam, Blake was thrown three metres backwards. There he fell with a thud, landing on his back on the artificial turf.

The entire audience stood up. Seconds later the whole stadium of spectators let out a mighty roar, "Tau! Tau! Tau!"

Still stunned by the gripping spectacle of the beam of dazzling white light, they watched Dominic run towards Eddie and Ret. Reaching them, Dominic pushed them roughly out of his fighting circle.

"Get back to the Stands!" he yelled hoarsely. "I dearly hope you bet on me to win - for your sake!"

Ret, freed from his trance, stared at the red glowing crystals in Dominic's Roaming-Ring with a puzzled expression.

"Come on bro," said Eddie, pulling his brother away. "I'll fill you in later."

Meanwhile the two umpires had reached the scene of the debacle. They conferred briefly with the two team Captains - Dominic and Keating. Then one of them briefly roamed to the judges' office, high in the Stands. Moments later, the finishing horn sounded. Simultaneously the Stadium's Communications System crackled into life.

"Aristau has been disqualified for using psychic power during this match," said the loud, officious voice of the judge. "London wins by default."

Exploding in an avalanche of protest, the stadium walls resonated with the sound of yelling from the incredulous Aristau supporters.

"Well fought, Tau," said Keating, still standing in the arena beside Dominic. "Bad luck about the disqualification."

Dominic glanced at his Fighting-Staff. "There was a lot of bragging about the super conductor incorporated into the alloy of my particular style of weapon when it was first manufactured. Now I know why. It turns out it's a nice little transmitter of psychic energy. Pity the discovery cost me the match."

"Their game - their rules," remarked Keating.

"Obviously," said Dominic grinning.

Keating regarded the fair lad thoughtfully, "I wouldn't mind a few pointers on how to knock down an opponent using a psychic energy beam. If you're amenable, Tau?"

"Only if you agree to join my Splinter Faction and travel with my Fleet into the future."

Matthew Keating stared at the fair young protagonist. Then he held out his hand in friendship. "Without question - I would be honoured," he replied.

Chapter fourteen

The atmosphere was harsh and eerie. The location was the highest deck on Satellite25 and the area was restricted. No breath stirred the air within this large solitary space. No sound disturbed the sleep of this shadowy cold site. Littered with many derelict Spaceships, the deck was untrodden. The secret Fleet of Chronoguisers floated dark and silent. Spider webs blanketed the site. Whilst veiling the black metal deck, a thick layer of dust hung suspended in the stale dry air.

Undisturbed from the earliest hours of the day, to a time when the sun was high over the Northern Hemisphere, the deck remained tranquil. The tools of intrigue would not lay quiet long, however, and everything was about to change.

Blown away in thick streams, the dusty veil overhanging the deck suddenly tumbled and swirled. Before a chilling airstream, the spider webs shivered. Whooshing and whistling a chaotic wind swept the deck, rushed amongst the Spaceships and filled the area with disquieting sound.

Hardly visible in the darkness, many vaporous amorphous creatures had just entered this contained secretive space. They were congregating. They were ominous and they were angry.

Flitting and darting around the gloomy locale, the amorphous creatures tattered the cobwebs. Whizzing through the dusty derelict Spaceships they threw debris hither and thither. Twisting like many miniature whirlwinds in a frightening storm, they circled the Chronoguisers. Finally, hovering over the deck, they blew the dust high in murky, twirling clouds.

Just as suddenly as they had appeared, the creatures amassed in a loose midair circle, metres above the cluttered deck. Consequently, the sound of rushing airstreams ceased.

Shockingly, the formless transparent clouds then began to take on ghostly human shapes. Seconds later, many aggrieved male faces stared out solemnly over the derelict vessels in this covert landing-bay.

Deep, low and belligerent, grumbling phantom voices echoed through the place. As their wraithlike number increased to forty, the aura of this quarter grew tense. All palpably agitated, the spectral eyes of these beings smouldered with intense suppressed anger. When they uttered words, the sounds that came forth were hoarse low growls. When they glanced around, their resentful expressions were guarded.

No astute observer would have ever expected to see such a sight as a federation of angry ghosts assembling within a Space Satellite. For all historical accounts have deemed ghosts to belay in haunted shady woods, large crumbling mansions, or in some other earthly place. Rightly so, the judicious observer's presumptions would stand true. For these spectres, all aged between fifteen and twenty-two and all dressed in metal suits of bronze, grey or black chainmail were definitely not ghosts – they were Roamers. Congregated in this secluded place and incensed by recent events - they were all attending an emergency meeting.

Dominic, the host of this urgent Roaming convention was already floating in the centre of the gathering. Addressing his assembly - many of them friends - he spoke in a clear, precise and steady manner.

"Thank you, Knights and Guards, for attending this meeting at such short notice. I'm glad to see that half of you managed to be scheduled off duty, as made obvious by your vests, chainmail trousers and distinct lack of footwear. As for the other half of you, presently on duty, congratulations on having the knack of keeping your eyes open - even in sleep."

Those dressed properly chuckled softly at this remark.

Dominic continued, "One hour ago, all of you received notification to immediately take up your five-year Space Transport Commissions. Am I correct?"

Unexpectedly none of them replied. They only stared angrily out over the derelict Spaceships crumbling on the deck beneath them.

"Failure to report for duty will earn you arrest, an armed guard to your ship - followed by a fortnight's incarceration," Dominic said evenly.

Again, he was met with angry stares.

"Can I deduce by your rude silence that the TT Transport Fleet will sorely miss us all?" he questioned. His own voice now gruff and deliberate.

"Too right," they all growled.

"This is an order, Knights and Guards," Dominic said commandingly. "You will be pleased to make yourselves scarce on the auspicious occasion of your transfer to the Transports. I want you all in our Fleet of Chronoguisers - ready to lead our group to a prosperous future!"

In response, all of the spectres shouted out in hearty accord.

"I called you here," Dominic continued assertively, "to charge each of you with a Charter you desire. The three terms of your Charter are:

You will escort one thousand of our citizens to their new homes in London, three hundred years into our future. You will protect our citizens from all danger during the term of your office. You will safeguard and conserve all the natural resources of our Earth.

As reward for your services, you will have dominion over the Earth, and ample resources on a familiar planet. What do you say? Do you accept your Charter?"

"Yes!" came the unanimous reply of all the spectres floating around him.

Dominic's voice changed to a quieter and more private tone. "I have known each of you personally for eight years," he continued sincerely, "and some of you, like Bermuda, I have known from early childhood. The Charter is not just a job - it is a commitment. Therefore, I ask each of you earnestly, and I expect an honest undertaking from you all: *Look after our people to your best ability*."

"I will!" each replied loyally.

"What about *The Zeta*?" called one of the Roamers.

Dominic smiled, following up with a sarcastic reply. "Lucky you, Blake. She's not your problem."

The urgent address now turned to logistics.

"Listen up lads!" Dominic said. "I am calling out the names of the co-pilots and pilots required to fly the *One to Eight* Fleet at the time of our departure. The co-pilots are:

Keating - the *Alpha*,

Hanepoot - the *Beta*,

Mahoney - the *Gamma*,

Parsons - the *Delta,* and

Sangria - the *Epsilon*. You five will assist my Aunts. All clear!"

"Yes, Sir!" the five phantom figures responded.

"John, Samuel and Joshua Sebastian will pilot the *Zeta*, *Eta*, and the *Theta*. All clear on your orders!"

"Yes, Sir!" the three brothers replied proudly.

"The remaining Knights and Guards will ride in the *Warrior* and function as a combat team. Bermuda will Captain that vessel. All clear!"

"Yes sir!" responded his allies in one vigorous voice.

"Have any of you any problems with your assignments?" Dominic finished sternly, casting a shrewd eye over all those floating around him.

"I have a problem, Tau. I'm still in jail?" said the spectral image of Hanepoot.

"Governor Aristotle is arranging your probation as we speak, Hanepoot," replied Dominic encouragingly. "You'll be released within the hour."

Hanepoot's face brightened.

"Keating, Sebastian - please remain. Everyone else, if you haven't any further questions - disappear!" instructed Dominic, terminating their ghostly conference.

"Additional orders, Tau?" Sebastian asked calmly, when all but three floating spectres remained.

"Not quite," replied Dominic evenly. "This request is of a personal nature. Sebastian, I want you to collect Zeta from Willow's place tonight and escort her, along with your own dancing partner to Tesla's Ball. I may not be able to attend."

"Sure, no problem," replied Sebastian, his face suspicious. "Is there anything you would like to share?"

"I received my Commission Papers two days ago," Dominic admitted. After a pause, he added gruffly. "Behave yourself with my cousin, Cynthia. Now, go."

Nodding, Sebastian's spectral image promptly disappeared. Keating, who had been floating a distance away, moved forward. In a conversation that lasted scarcely a minute, Dominic spoke to him in a hushed, barely audible voice. Keating nodded. Both then vanished.

Empty of all life except for the smallest eight-legged creatures, the dust settled over the deck of the covert landing-bay. The spiders began the delicate task of rebuilding their webs. The derelict Spaceships lay waste - once again, unseen relics of days gone by. Whilst constantly spinning, the shining Satellite - home of Dominic's secret Fleet - continued its smooth routine orbit.

Clocks moved forward with slow rhythmic constancy. The warm afternoon hours were spent. Twilight settled over the higher regions of the Earth's Northern Hemisphere and as the light dwindled, the sky glowed pink and peach. Then darkened.

The tide turned. Strong ocean currents swept a calm rolling sea over the sandy beaches on the Isle of Wight. Freshwater Bay - one of the island's many inlets - was calm. Usually seen bobbing up and down on the waves, the cormorants had returned to their nests. So too, the seagulls habitually hovering around the cliff face had ceased their raucous calls. Standing settled in rows on the high cliff shelves, they looked searchingly over the Bay.

Fathoms below the waters of that Bay, the sea around Aristau had dimmed and cooled. Ever glowing golden, the marine towers reached up to a now darker sky. Bathed by the light from those towers, sea creatures cruised languidly amongst the seabed's rocks and seaweed. Quiet in her bedroom within one of those Towers, Zeta was readying herself for her first ever Ball.

Wearing a long sleeved white organdie dress, edged at the high neck, hem, and wrists with artificial feathers, she stood before a large cheval mirror. Brushing her freshly washed hair, she glanced easily at her surrounds. To-do was curled up asleep on the bean-shaped sofa in the corner opposite. Her white satin dancing slippers were tossed on her bed. In front of her closed door was a large white bag - placed there lest she forget it when she left for Tesla's Ball. Opposite the door was a porthole, through which she gazed at the sea outside.

"Pirate playback," she called out into her quiet room. Deciding, whilst dressing, to listen to the previous night's Pirate Radio Broadcast.

"This is Francis Bermuda, guest host for our Tuesday late night show," said a smooth young voice, as the broadcast began. "All you listeners - hello from me to you! I'll imagine you shouted 'hello' back, just to keep my confidence bubbling. Alternatively, you could all immediately use your transmission devices and key in our call-code, just to make me feel doubly secure. I'm waiting. I'm wait...ing. Wow! Five hundred people accessed our call-code in just those few seconds! How popular is that? I certainly make a good first impression! You all love my interesting musical voice - no doubt."

All noise from Zeta's speakers suddenly ceased. Moments later, the sound of a male coughing piped out into her pink and violet bedroom. A few seconds elapsed. Bermuda then continuing blithely.

"Sorry folks. I forgot, with all the excitement of being live on air, that *Tau* - your usual pirate - is standing nearby waiting to greet you. Say hello, Tau," Bermuda instructed. "Speak clearly into the microphone lad. The audience need to be sure that you're not off skylarking somewhere profitable. He is here, listeners, I assure you," Bermuda continued, "supervising me, as he should be. He's just shy and needs a little persuasion."

Unexpectedly the sound of a loud slap resonated from the speakers into Zeta's room.

Surprised she heard Dominic's lilting tenor voice whispering softly from out of her recorder, "Hoist the sails my hearties, for now we sail the winds of time. Leave swords in scabbards - let spirits shine. A bountiful planet will soon be thine!" He paused and asked appealingly, "Did you miss me?" Afterwards adding confidentially, "I'll get rid of this Herculean interloper, Bermuda, as soon as I can, listeners. Then we can resume our usual dignified broadcast."

"I agree. This certainly isn't the usual programme format," thought Zeta. Reaching for an aerosol can of hairspray, she sprayed a fine veil of tiny sparkling white gems over her hair. Then she continued listening.

"Ahem," said Bermuda. "Our show tonight will start with the news. So here am I, jumping into the deep end. Here I go!"

Following the sound of a loud splash, followed by a faint scream, Bermuda began to read the first News Report.

"Thomas Hanepoot, a Knight of the Psychic Forces was this night thrown into prison for a period of not less than twenty days. The police arrested Hanepoot outside of the Science Museum in London for the crime of creating a visual and auditory illusion.

An eyewitness to the illusion said, *'It was an absolutely spectacular illusion. One of the best I have ever seen. At the time, I really believed it to be true. At first, I heard the sound of multiple explosions. Looking up into the sky, I then saw one hundred TT Space Fighters - exploding! I recorded the catastrophe on film - but because it was an illusion, the film was blank, of course. A pity.'*

TT Vox Populi and five of his Intelligence Officers were exiting from an award ceremony within the Museum when the illusion was in progress," Bermuda continued. "TT had just received a plaque for his contributions to science. One of the members of the Award Committee, who let it slip that TT had the highest IQ in his class, thought the illusion was an outrage." Bermuda paused. "Dear, dear, what can we do?" he said softly. "We can only move on - to the next report." Pausing again, he cleared his throat. Then he continued reading.

"Second News Report. The dependable father of a teenage boy has been dubbed 'Parent of the Year' for saving his son from the clutches of an extremist group."

'I had my son detained by the police on suspicion of stealing from me,' the father admitted proudly. *'Once he was back home, I locked him in his room for two weeks. I wanted to give him the chance to pursue a greater commission in life. Now my boy has had time to reflect he admits to the error of his ways. He has realized what a favour I did him.'*

"Thanks, Dad. I wish my dad did that kind of thing for me," said Bermuda sweetly. Knowing that he had neither mother, nor father of his own.

"The third report if you will?" interrupted the cool and steady voice of Dominic.

Silence followed. Zeta's room became quiet. The sound of offended coughing trickled through the speakers into her room. Then she heard Bermuda's voice as he continued to huffily read the news.

"A recent health survey has uncovered that members of our older population carry an enzyme in their bodies making them immune to all existing pathogens. Voluntary blood donors in the age set of 110 to 160 are most welcome at any hospital."

Adding his own personal commentary, Bermuda exclaimed cheerfully, "Excellent! I knew our oldies were first rate! But there's more, listeners! The survey also revealed that citizens over the age of 100 make good judgement calls 90% of the time. Way to go, Pop!"

A brief silence followed. Zeta recognized Dominic's voice, faint in the background. Bermuda, with slighted tone, recommenced the bulletin.

"Our final account for the night is a report about cars," said Bermuda curtly. "Cars, for those of you uncultured enough not to know, were ancient vehicles that had four wheels, rolled over the ground and were powered by, you won't believe this one, listeners - aeroplane engines!"

"Bermuda?" chastised the stern voice of Dominic.

"Do you want me to read this News Report or not, Tau?" Bermuda asked gratingly.

Silence poured from the speakers into Zeta's bedroom.

"Historical interest was fuelled by the discovery of one of these machines in a grand sunny conservatory," Bermuda continued calmly, moments later. "Gardeners found the car hidden under a massive tree fern display whilst digging amongst the plants and flowers. Seizing this antique vehicle, the controlling authorities joyfully put the car - a model Ferrari - under lock and key.

'Look in your own household. Try to find some valuable item,' the president of Earth's principal historical group advised his members. *"Take this conservatory, for example. No one would have ever expected to find a Ferrari in here! So, go on an exciting voyage of discovery! You might find something grand!"'*

Silence followed. Now, with the News Broadcast over, Bermuda unexpectedly begin to sing, slowly and beautifully:

"You captured my heart, and stole it away. It's a great, grand sunny day.

You captured my heart, and took it away. I'm in control of this grand sunny day.

Before I had you, my life was so grey, but now I have you, it's a wonderful day.

You captured my heart, and stole it away. It's a great... great... grand... sunny day!"

Strangely entranced, Zeta automatically picked five chestnut combs out of her holdall. Habitually she put up her light-brown hair. While she did so, she hummed the tune of the song. With a dreamy expression on her face, she listened to the rest of show.

"Proceeding to our live Chat Show," said Bermuda cheerfully. "We have Lieutenant Spears from the Aristau Guards on line one. Lieutenant Spears?"

"Hello," said a whining nasal voice. "I'm ringing to air my grievances about the-"

"Oh dear, the line has gone dead," said Bermuda flatly. "Next call?"

Zeta briefly heard the sound of fingers drumming on a table.

"We have Gerald Hastings on line two," continued the smooth voice of Bermuda. "Gerald?"

"I called to discuss the unfair allocation of living quarters onboard the TT Space Transports," said Gerald in a hoarse crackly voice.

"There is nothing unfair about the allocations," responded Bermuda quickly. "Every man, woman and child is allocated the same amount of living space on the Transports regardless of age, occupation or financial status."

"Exactly my point!" said Gerald. "I should be awarded more space because -"

Zeta heard a distinct clunk.

"The line has gone dead again," said Bermuda quietly. "Such a shame. We won't get to hear why Gerald deserves more than *every other human being on this planet!* Next call?" He briefly paused. "We have Celeste on line three. Celeste? How can I help?"

The voice of a hesitant teenage girl piped through the speakers into Zeta's bedroom.

"I've been listening to your show for some time, and I've noticed that the usual pirate never includes poetry readings in his agenda. Do you?"

"Have you some poetry in mind for us?" asked Bermuda, in a most friendly fashion.

"Yes, I do," she replied excitedly. "The poetry is my own composition and is titled: *Home.*"

"Well, let's have it then," he prompted her warmly.

Celeste began to read her poem in a serious thoughtful voice:

"The breeze touches my face - caresses my hair.

Sweet aromas fill an atmosphere, once dearth and rare.

Silken flowers brush my hand. Oak leaves flutter everywhere.

I run free within our fertile fields, faster and faster - without a care.

Birds sing atop high green boughs. Livestock graze on the grassy plain.

I smell mum's homemade bread while I amble home. Then I laugh and I sing in the summer rain."

"Thank you Celeste," said Bermuda quietly. Then he added cheerfully, "If you happen to be passing T.G's grand Ball tomorrow night in London, please feel free to call in for a chat. We can discuss poetry. Goodbye, petal."

"Bye," said Celeste sweetly. The line disengaged.

"Moving on?" prompted the hoarse voice of Dominic, piping out loudly from the speakers in Zeta's room.

"Yes, of course I shall," responded Bermuda. "The next item on our schedule tonight is our Sports Roundup - beginning with the results of the five Staff-Fighting Tournaments at Aristau Stadium."

Zeta heard the sound of keys tapping on a keyboard and then Bermuda's voice, as he continued eagerly, "The results of the tournaments held this afternoon are - Aristau Vs London:

Juniors: 80 to 40. Aristau wins.

Seniors: 400 to 387. Aristau wins.

Veterans: 500 to 492. Aristau wins.

Psychic Forces: 200 to 180. Aristau disqualified. London wins."

Zeta was surprised to hear the sounds of chairs shuffling, followed by the noise of a table scraping along a floor. She then heard further jostling noises and a low groan.

"Sorry folks for the unplanned interval," Bermuda explained, his voice now back on air. "I wasn't aware until now that the Aristau Knights had lost their particular tournament. Understandably, I am upset. Tau is fine though. He'll get up from the floor in a moment. However, because of the shock defeat, I think I'll postpone the Sports Roundup, *and* the congratulatory announcements. We'll finish up the show listening to a large collection of my granddad's *and my* favourite music."

"Bermuda!" came the hoarse distinct growl of Dominic from somewhere distant.

"I'm the guest host!" Bermuda's voice retorted indignantly, through the speakers, into Zeta's room. "It's my prerogative to dictate the show and your place to allow me some leeway!"

Music began to play. Pumped through the Inbuilt Speaker System it quietly filled Zeta's room with the sound of violins, coupled with the voice of an opera singer.

"This show deviated a lot from Dominic's usual programme," Zeta thought. "Strange News Report." Then she laughed. "I think I'll give granddad's tunes a miss, though. Music off," she commanded.

Suddenly, breaking the silence of the otherwise now quiet room, she heard Cynthia's voice - transmitted through her robotic doll.

"Sebastian and I are waiting at the marina for you, Zeta. It's very busy here. Hundreds of partygoers are filling the platform. I've never seen so many Shuttles moored in the Bay. Just to make it easier for you to spot us amongst the crowd - I'm wearing a pink gown with a beaded bodice. Sebastian is wearing his black coat tails and black trousers. Hurry on. I'm keen to get to the Ball."

"OK. I'll be right along," replied Zeta.

She slipped on her white dancing slippers. Ready now and grabbing her large white bag, she hurried out of her room.

"I'm going now - Dad, Isabelle, Willow!" she yelled out into the apartment. "Bye!"

Running into the hallway outside, she slammed the apartment door behind her. Then she headed briskly for the marina.

Minutes later, seated alongside Cynthia and Sebastian - in an airborne Aristau Shuttle - she was heading towards London. The night was warm. Travelling at a high altitude in a cloudy atmosphere, the wind whooshed against the Shuttle's cone-shaped fuselage. The engines purred faint and constant. Painting a fading trail behind that vessel, a warm white airstream marbled the inky sky. Moonlight shone over the arid chocolate landscape over which they travelled. Beneath their speeding ship, the hills and dales - clear of flora - rolled gently inland. Free from fauna, the terrain stretched away - bare and unsullied.

With the exception of the coloured instrument lights on the Shuttle's dashboard, the twelve-seater cabin was dark. Lightly padded, the black seats were comfortable. Apart from this small luxury, however, the interior was stark and minimal.

"How long before we arrive at London, Sebastian?" Zeta asked.

"We're almost there," he replied. Sitting at the pilot's controls, he smiled amiably. "I'll reduce altitude so you can see the lights of London as we approach. Then I'll hover over the venue for the Ball - for a bird's eye view of Tesla's mansion."

Shortly after, Zeta gazed through the viewing window out over London. Stretching away for many kilometres, thousands of Globe Homes, incandescent on shimmering columns, dotted the landscape. Flying in streams over the locality, a multitude of Shuttles filled the sky with eager partygoers. While at ground level, a labyrinth of luminous Tubular Walkways - crowded with vivacious revellers - connected every venue, shop, municipal building and home.

Out of her seat and standing next to Cynthia, she stared out excitedly. In front of their vessel, presently hovering forty metres above ground level, she saw the most splendid dwelling.

"Is this Tesla's Globe Home?" she asked, not taking her eyes from the window. "Anybody?"

"It's Tesla's home," replied Cynthia.

Ablaze with light from dozens of sparkling chandeliers, the internal four-storey white mansion before them was already alive with hundreds of guests. The ladies wore colourful gowns. The gentlemen wore black coat tails. All of course wore their Roaming-Rings proudly.

Relaxing in the first floor Reception room, many of those guests chatted, languished on sofas or sampled the Lumpo and the sweetened water on the long buffet table. In the ballroom, others waltzed to vibrant music, played by an in-house band.

Subtly sparkling like ice - the marble floors underfoot, the ornate high ceilings and the internal walls of the mansion were white. Upholstered in crushed burnt orange velvet, the furniture was elegant. Draped in that same sumptuous fabric the windows were high, wide and clear. Six metres in front of the Reception room elevator, the glistening white banister of a grand staircase spiralled up to the busy ballroom above. At the top of the stairs, two large shimmering doors hung open - like enormous sheets of opaque ice.

"Quick. Land now, Sebastian," said Cynthia, keen to go inside and join the revelry.

"Zeta might like the chance to see Tesla's rooftop garden," said Sebastian thoughtfully. "I'll hover over it for a moment. Then I'll land."

When Sebastian flew their Shuttle up and over the top of Tesla's Globe Home towards their landing area, Zeta admired the beautifully landscaped rooftop garden. Amass with scented potted plants it was a tranquil haven in an otherwise arid world. Central to the rooftop, a dark-green tubular chute extended from the garden to the top of the Globe Home. Ringing the garden, a brook - fed by a fountain and overhung by ferns - tinkled. Winding through the garden, red glossy pebbles covered a narrow path.

"I like the fountain," said Cynthia. "Shame about the chute."

"What's it for?"

"I've lived in Aristau all my life, Zeta. Not in a Globe Home. I have to admit - I don't know," replied Cynthia.

"It's an escape chute, Zeta," interrupted Sebastian. "Mandatory in a Globe Home this size. It leads to a pressurised service hatch at the top. Now, sit back in your seats please, ladies. We are going to land."

Ten minutes later, after landing and travelling through a busy Tubular Walkway, they stopped at the base of the column supporting Tesla's Globe Home - before a curious elevator door.

Incorporated into that door, Zeta saw a flat robot face - with pleasant, but non-human features.

The robot face, animated due to their arrival, smiled, as best as a flat robot face could smile. Then it spoke.

"All visitors are required to roam into the Gosh residence and greet Miss Tesla Gosh before they are allowed admittance. Thank you for your co-operation."

Zeta was perturbed after hearing the entrance requirements. "I'll have to go back home, Cynthia," she said, tightly clutching her white carry bag.

"Why, what's wrong?"

"I won't be able to roam into Tesla's Globe Home."

"Why not?" interrupted Sebastian.

"Because I don't know Tesla, Sebastian. We've never met."

Suddenly the amethysts in Sebastian's Roaming-Ring began to glow and he stared forward silently - his eyes blank.

"He's asleep, Zeta," Cynthia whispered. "Roaming."

Two minutes later, Sebastian blinked and smiled. Simultaneously the elevator doors opened.

"Tesla bent the rules," he explained, ushering them inside.

After ascending in the elevator and stepping out into the Reception room, all three were soon climbing the white spiral staircase to the ballroom.

"Hi," said a familiar voice, suddenly coming from close behind Zeta.

Turning she saw Eddie, standing on the step below. Dressed in coat tails, he was also heading towards the ballroom. With him, Brooklyn, wearing a lemon chiffon gown, smiled.

"When did you get here?" asked Eddie.

"Just now," replied Zeta, continuing her ascent.

"Bermuda, Keating, Felicity and Parsons are in the ballroom," Eddie said casually. "We've been here for a while."

When Zeta did not reply, he added coolly, "His Lordship isn't here."

Reaching the landing, the group of five walked through the large doors at the front of the ballroom. There they halted. Spinning beautifully under sparkling chandeliers, waltzing couples gracefully stepped out in time to splendid music. Gliding like flamboyant birds, the couples swirled, rose up and down in step and filled the floor with glorious colour. Vivacious, the music - performed on a low curved bandstand on the left of the ballroom - prompted all to the floor.

Therefore, apart from several Roamers, *and* Zeta's group, everyone was waltzing.

Noting their entrance and glancing towards them, a fine young lady, dressed in a splendid navy blue gown, suddenly stopped in her dance. Stepping away from her partner, Miles, she bowed. From the centre of the dance floor, she then threaded her way through the couples, towards them.

"Good evening!" she said, on reaching their party.

"Good evening, Tesla," replied Sebastian.

Cynthia and Zeta looked at Tesla, and nodded in greeting.

"I'm glad you could all join our festive group tonight," Tesla said cheerfully, flicking back her long brown hair, beaded through with tiny sapphires. She surveyed the ballroom, smiling at all her guests. Then she continued. "Next week, the TT Transport Fleet will be flying towards five new planets and the Earth will be empty of our kind. So this Ball marks a very special occasion."

"Indeed," responded Sebastian. "Thank you for your invitation, Tesla. Your hospitality is most appreciated."

"I see you have brought *The Zeta* with you tonight," remarked Tesla coolly. "I also note that we have the privilege of the company of Eddie - our very own 'Stone Age' man."

Turning to face Eddie, she addressed him, in a patronizing, but friendly manner. "You have a captivating personality, Eddie. Truly captivating," she complemented him smoothly. "But tell me, my precious? I need to know! How did your ancestors manage to fight off those beastly dinosaurs? The hardship they endured must have been intolerable. They were undoubtedly very brave men to be born in such taxing times!"

"Yes, they were extremely brave chaps," replied Eddie proudly. "I can share this with you, Tesla, since you are so interested. My grandfather once killed a Tyrannosaurus Rex, with his bare hands!"

"Gracious!" exclaimed Tesla, looking at Eddie admiringly. "You truly are born from fine, strong stock."

Eddie grinned and glanced impassively at Sebastian.

"I read in a history book that people used to believe that the world was flat," Tesla continued, questioning Eddie eagerly. "You don't believe that, do you Eddie? That the world is flat?"

Eddie's reaction surprised her. Appalled, he stared at her crazily. "What are you implying?" he asked incensed. "Are you trying to tell me that the world isn't flat? That the world isn't held up by two giant turtles?"

Although he was winding her up - for a lark - his face was solemn. Tesla paused and not knowing how to reply, quickly turned towards to a more innocuous traveller from the past - Zeta Doherty.

"Zeta, my dear?" she asked coolly. "I believe you come from a time when women used to wash in pots?"

"Not quite. We have advanced to plumbing."

"I believe you are a friend of Tau's. Is that true?"

"Yes," replied Zeta quietly.

"Do you think he likes you, dear?" probed Tesla coldly.

"Yes."

Tesla took an affected deep breath and sighed deeply. "I don't mean to be harsh, my pet," she said scathingly, "but I've heard that Tau only drags you around with him because you make him look good – being *The Zeta* as you are. He can't possibly like you. Why, you are prehistoric! A living fossil! I'm sorry to be the one to break the news. But someone had to tell you."

Zeta glanced across the ballroom and frowned.

"You're a bit of a baby, Zeta," Tesla continued coldly, "not to realize how famous you are." Shaking her head in disbelief, she then asked boorishly, "Why isn't your mother around to look after you, Zeta? You obviously need her."

Zeta's eyes misted. "Excuse me?" she said. Turning away, she moved quickly out of the ballroom.

Brooklyn, disappointed at her best friend's callousness, looked across the ballroom, slightly shamefaced. Cynthia frowned. Eddie remained impassive. Sebastian, however, of a more passionate nature, could only glare at Tesla.

"What?" Tesla asked, staring back at him with a feigned expression of bemused innocence.

Meanwhile Zeta, hurrying out onto the landing, bumped straight into Dominic.

"How goes you?" he asked in his lilting tenor voice.

"Oh Dominic. You're still in your Knight's Raiment," Zeta said quickly. "I thought you'd be wearing your black coat tails like the other young men at the Ball. Never mind. I see you have mirrored. Are you outside of Tesla's home right now, waiting at the elevator doors? Will you come inside soon?"

"I'm in the *Heritage*, Zeta," Dominic answered coolly, staring at her as he spoke. "And I've noticed," he continued sternly, "that you are not correctly dressed. Weren't you supposed to wear your hair down for security reasons? I believe I expressly asked you to do so. We discussed this remember. So it is fair that I ask you now - to go fix your hair!"

Zeta was offended. Taking off her Roaming-Ring she tossed it into her white bag. Then she waved him away.

Still standing on the busy landing, Dominic considered her thoughtfully. "Zeta? If I'm gone for a few days, don't worry," he said quietly. Then his mirror image vanished.

"Is he coming to the Ball or not?" Zeta wondered.

After entering the empty Ladies powder room on the left side of the landing, she took the combs out of her hair. Her brown locks fell in soft waves over her shoulders and down her back. The sprayed white gems sparkled and fine wisps of hair now softly framed her face. Slipping her hair combs into her pocket, she retrieved her Roaming-Ring from her white carry bag. Placing the beautiful platinum band back on her head, she practised a smile in the mirror. She exited the powder room, crossed the landing and strode into the vibrant ballroom.

Felicity, wearing a gauzy blue gown and standing alone on the opposite side of the ballroom - near an inconspicuous elevator - spotted her immediately. Smiling cheerfully, she beckoned Zeta to join her. Zeta waited for the dance to finish. Then she walked across the ballroom.

"Hi, Felicity!" she said warmly.

"What's in your carry bag?"

"Gifts for your brother, Sebastian, Bermuda, and Dominic."

"Oh!" said Felicity, much surprised. "Well, three of the four are standing just a few metres to our right - beside that group of girls. Now is as good a time as any to give them their gifts."

Parsons, Sebastian and Bermuda, all with excellent hearing, pretended not to have overheard this conversation. Standing casually together, talking to Eddie - whilst scouring the room with their eyes - they smiled as Felicity and Zeta approached.

Removing three gifts from her bag, Zeta carefully read one of the gift-tags and stepped towards Parsons.

"Joseph," she said, handing him his present. "My father's companion, Isabelle, has given me this gift to pass onto you. She is extremely grateful that you aided my father when he was detained. This gift expresses her gratitude."

Joseph accepted the gift and tore open the wrapper. "Thank you, Zeta," he said smiling. "And thank Isabelle."

Zeta stepped towards Sebastian. "For you, John Sebastian," she said sweetly. After checking the gift-tag, she handed the tall youth his gift.

Sebastian smiled. "I've only received two gifts in my whole life," he said truthfully. "The first one was from you and this is the second."

Zeta now moved to stand in front of Bermuda. She handed him the third gift - this time without checking the tag.

"Isabelle appreciates how much engineering work was involved when you helped my father with the *Estrella*. So she would like you to accept this token of her appreciation."

Eddie, standing beside Bermuda, abruptly interrupted. "His Lordship has arrived, Zeta - in his mirror form. He has materialized at the front of the ballroom, opposite to us, near the entrance."

Turning around quickly, Zeta saw Dominic. Now dressed in his black coat tails, trousers and brogues, a frilled white shirt and a white bow tie, he was talking to Tesla.

"I'm here for another one of your fabulous parties, Tesla," he said charmingly, having just startled her by his sudden appearance.

"Thank you, Tau, for honouring us with your presence," she responded graciously. "I always love to see you."

"How much did your gown set you back?"

"I wouldn't be so crass to look at the price-tag, Tau," she responded, flattered and smiling.

"Let me in like a good girl?" he asked. Then he promptly vanished.

Entering the lively ballroom, a few minutes later, his mortal self was greeted by Zeta.

"Hi!" she said pleasantly. "I'm glad you're here, Dominic. I was worried you might not come."

"I'd fight off a band of mercenaries to be here tonight," he said gallantly.

Reaching into her carry bag and retrieving the first of three remaining gifts, Zeta handed him a disc shaped parcel. "I hope you like this," she said kindly.

Dominic took the present and tore open the wrapping. Unexpectedly he glared at her coldly. In his hand, he held a heart shaped, gilt edged bone china plate. Painted in large gold lettering on its ivory coloured face was the name *Francis Bermuda*. Underneath the lettering, a fine landscape depicted a rural setting.

Zeta, wondering at her friend's strange reaction, quickly glanced at the gift.

"Oh, Dominic! Please. I've made a mistake. You've got the wrong..."

Too late, he was already striding across the dance floor towards the four youths standing opposite. Approaching them, Dominic marched up to the strongest.

"I believe this is yours!" he said, thrusting the heart shaped plate towards Bermuda.

As Bermuda took the plate from his hand, Dominic glanced over towards Sebastian and Parsons. They too held heart shaped plates on which their names were beautifully painted. Stepping towards Sebastian, Dominic took the plate from his friend's hand. Turning it over, he read the writing on the back: *'To John, with much appreciation, Isabelle.'* Handing it back, he glanced at Parsons. "From Isabelle?" he asked.

When Parsons nodded, Dominic stepped back towards Bermuda.

"A little bit of a mix up," explained Bermuda, handing Dominic an unwrapped gift from Zeta. "The little one forgot to read the label."

Dominic immediately read, then tore off the gift-tag. This he crushed in his hand and tossed onto the floor. Not in a gift-receiving mood, he slid the package quickly into his right jacket pocket. After which he grimaced.

"You're hurt," Bermuda said quietly. Then he barked, "Parsons! Come here!"

Now, as Parsons inconspicuously ran a small medical scanner over Dominic's chest and arms, Bermuda asked, in a voice so quiet that only the other three Knights could hear, "What happened?"

"A forced transfer to a TT Space Transport Ship happened," revealed Dominic bravely, also in a barely audible voice. "I had to put up a reasonable fight."

"Reasonable!" reprimanded Parsons, glancing furtively around the room as he spoke. "You took quite a beating - judging by these injuries." Pushing up the white ruffled cuffs on Dominic's shirt, he saw the 'hammer' worn on his friend's bruised right hand. Slyly he extracted a needle from a tiny First Aid Kit in his jacket pocket. Then he injected Dominic with a mild painkiller.

"Well, Parsons?" growled Dominic. "Just the facts."

"You're fine," responded Parsons. "Black and blue, but fine."

"Who did this to you?" questioned Bermuda.

"Hired associates, I believe," replied Dominic. "I've never seen them before."

"Tau?" advised Sebastian, observing Zeta - forlorn on the opposite side of the ballroom. "*The Zeta.*"

"Yes. I best retrieve my dancing partner," Dominic said calmly. Then he strode back across the dance floor.

"Stow your bag somewhere, Zeta," he asked, after returning to her side. "So we can dance."

"I have two more gifts to give you, Dominic," she said. Reaching into her bag, she withdrew the gifts, then tossed the bag aside.

"Who are they from?"

"One is from me and one is from Isabelle."

"Give me the gift from Isabelle first."

Accepting the gift, he tore open the packaging - to discover a wooden model of a schooner in a small glass bottle. On the base of the model was an engraved message on a small gold plaque, which read: *'To Dominic, good luck, from Isabelle.'*

Dominic put the bottle into the left pocket of his jacket. Zeta then handed him the last rectangular parcel.

What happened next, happened rather quickly and - from Zeta's viewpoint - was quite unexpected. Dominic tore off the packaging and was silent. He held the gift - a Psychic Knight doll that looked exactly like him - in one of his hands. Gazing across the dance floor, he deliberately waited to see a clear gap between the dancing couples.

When gap presented itself, Zeta was appalled to see the fair lad suddenly dropkick his gift across the glistening floor. The robotic doll flew into the air, bounced off the floor, then slid a distance of twenty metres to stop in front of Bermuda. The young magician promptly bent down and picked it up.

Very much aware of Dominic's indomitable presence, Tesla's guests glanced seriously at the lad. Matthew Keating - dancing with a pretty girl - nodded in greeting. Tesla, an admirer of Tau, secretly smiled.

"Dominic? That was a good present," said Zeta. "I was trying to be nice."

Meanwhile, Bermuda - on the opposite side of the room - was inspecting the robotic doll. A sturdy electronic toy, it had suffered no damage whatsoever due to its rude introduction to life.

For a good ten minutes, Bermuda entertained himself by recording amusing short anecdotes and witty insults on the doll's voice recorder - including a beautiful rendition of his own composition: '*You captured my heart.*' Satisfied with his recordings, he set the robotic Psychic Knight doll loose on the busy dance floor. Marching forward, the speaking doll, rather than tripping the dancers up, became a most entertaining and amusing addition to the Ball.

As a by-product of the shenanigans of the robotic doll, a girl wearing a plum gown - called Celeste - introduced herself to Bermuda. Now dancing with her, he waltzed under the numerous sparkling chandeliers.

Zeta was still standing demurely next to Dominic. All of his friends were dancing and Professor Doherty's daughter was seriously regretting her gift-giving blunder. When the band began to play the 'Blue Danube' by Johann Strauss, Junior, Dominic smiled.

"Shall we dance, Zeta? The Viennese Waltz is one of my best."

"If you like."

Together they stepped out onto the dance floor. Sparkling around them, the walls glistened. The chandeliers shone brightly. Whilst the burnt-orange drapes, framing the windows, and treated with a special substance - seemed to smoulder like coals. This was a spinning dance, and Dominic and Zeta waltzed gracefully. Listening to the three quarter time tempo, Zeta's feet slid soundlessly across the shiny floor. Her gown swirled out in a fluid ring and the white feathers on her hem softly fluttered.

Suddenly, half way through the rendition, the room about them began to change. The walls disappeared. Underfoot, rather than a white floor, they discovered billowing violet clouds. Overhead, replacing the chandeliers, an orange sky stretched far away to a distant horizon.

"What's happening?" Zeta asked Dominic.

Dominic, glancing around him, spotted Sebastian and Cynthia. Sebastian's activated Roaming-Ring cast a soft violet hue over the taller lad's face.

"Sebastian is entertaining us all by creating an illusion, Zeta."

As Zeta dreamily gazed at her enchanting surroundings, Dominic suddenly moved his face close to hers. Softly he kissed her on the cheek.

"Thank you for the gifts, Zeta," he said sincerely.

On the opposite side of the ballroom, the conversation was not so convivial.

"Dancing on clouds is so lovely, isn't it Miles?" remarked Tesla, deliberately stepping on her partner's feet. "I can not thank Sebastian enough for making my Ball so memorable - with his... charming illusion."

Stopping in the centre of the floor, she bowed to Miles, left him, and approached Sebastian. Suddenly however, she abruptly halted. Blocked by six Roamers who had unexpectedly appeared, she smiled nervously. Signalling her band to desist, she blushed and bowed.

"We are so honoured that you could join us this evening, TT Vox Populi. Captains," she said in a deferential tone of voice. "I'll let you all in, shall I?"

Dressed in a black frockcoat with a band of cassis red from the elbow to the wrist, grey trousers and a black bowtie, TT smiled at the flustered girl. Behind him, his entourage of five Intelligence Officers - all of stern expression - glanced around the room searchingly.

"Please do, young lady," TT replied, looking curiously at the illusion of clouds and a sunburnt sky.

His spectral image and those of his men instantly disappeared. Simultaneously the illusion waned and the room returned to normal.

Tesla's face flushed. Privileged by TT's unexpected visit, she signalled the band to recommence playing. Then she ran across to Dominic and Zeta. Sombrely, Keating swiftly approached.

"I'm sorry, Tau. TT is our Senior Statesman, so I have to let him in," Tesla apologized. Then she hastened away towards the bandstand, her blue gown swishing.

Now standing by Dominic's side, Keating reached for Zeta's hand.

"Zeta?" he asked urgently. "TT will arrive in person, any moment. He mustn't find you here. We must go."

Zeta glanced nervously at her fair dance partner.

"Go with him," Dominic said quickly. "As fast as you can."

While Keating rushed for the open elevator with Zeta - intending to flee via the rooftop escape chute - Dominic dashed for the door.

Reaching the landing, he abruptly halted. His escape route was blocked. TT and his men were already inside the mansion. Frowning,

Dominic watched them as - followed by a herd of excited guests - they purposefully climbed the stairs.

With obviously no way to sneak through the impenetrable crowd on the stairs, Dominic, with a cool, determined look on his face, returned to the ballroom. There he stood - a few metres to the right side of the entrance - behind a group of taller males. Assisted by an illusion created by Sebastian, he became temporarily unrecognisable.

Watching furtively as TT and his military entourage strode boldly into the ballroom, Dominic closely observed the Intelligence Officers. Three of them were Captains - all over seven foot tall. One of those Captains was Kroll. The other two men were of higher rank. One was a Colonel. The other was the senior physician of the TT Transport Fleet - a Major Goodman.

Hemmed in when the guests from the Reception room surged into the ballroom, Dominic searched out his friends in the crowd. Spotting Bermuda, he covertly signalled.

While two of the Captains took up position as guards on either side of the double ballroom doors, Kroll coldly marched towards the elevator. The doors opened. He stepped inside. Then the doors closed. Dominic, observing, glanced at his timeband. Then he watched TT and the remaining two Officers as they headed for the bandstand.

The musicians immediately ceased to play. The waltzing couples stopped dancing. Everyone stared at the Stage and everyone was quiet. Tesla, already in front of the Stage microphone, introduced TT.

"My dear guests," she said, glancing respectfully at TT. "We have been honoured by a visit from TT Vox Populi. Please put your hands together to bid him welcome!"

TT jumped onto the Stage and approached the microphone stand. Tesla's guests applauded. Once the applause had subsided, TT took the microphone.

"Hello, one and all!" he said cheerfully. "I'm glad to be here! As you are all aware, this coming week you will all be boarding the fine vessels of the TT Space Transport Fleet. All of you, without a doubt, are looking forward to our exciting journey to a bountiful new home!"

Many of the guests nodded and TT beamed.

Cheekily, a winsome voice unexpectedly interrupted the otherwise quiet ambience of the packed honoured ballroom. Hidden behind a group of guests, the Psychic Knight doll, still activated - was singing.

To the surprise of all, TT - his face serene under the radiant glow from the beautiful chandeliers - stopped speaking. Instead of requesting that the doll be found and shut down, he listened dreamily to the mesmeric voice of the electronic toy.

"You captured my heart, and stole it away," the model Knight sang. *"It's a great, grand sunny day.*

You captured my heart, and took it away. I'm in control of this grand sunny day."

Half way through the song, Bermuda, moving stealthily amongst the spellbound guests, found the doll. Turning it off and hiding it under his jacket, he sang the rest of the song himself, to its completion.

"Before I had you, my life was so grey, but now I have you, it's a wonderful day.

You captured my heart, and stole it away, it's a great... great... grand.... sunny day."

With Parsons, Eddie, *and* Sebastian - who covered them all with an illusion - Bermuda then dashed along the front of the ballroom, past the Captains guarding the door, and down the stairs.

TT sighed. "That's a grand little song," he remarked, seconds later, when all remaining in the ballroom came out of their blind reverie. Focusing on the guests before him, TT continued smartly, "Back to the business at hand! Tonight, dear citizens, I have joined you to wish one of your party - my great grandson, Terence Dominic Tau - a happy sixteen birthday! Tau has been assigned the prestigious position of First Officer on my Flagship - Transport 0001. I have arrived here this evening to escort him to his post."

After this announcement, many of the guests heartily clapped their hands together. Others called out excitedly - creating quite a commotion. Moving towards the bandstand, the crowd at the right side of the entrance thinned. Dominic - no longer hidden by an illusion - sidled for the doorway.

"Where is the birthday boy?" TT called above the hubbub.

Under the resplendent chandeliers, the guests hushed.

"TT Vox Populi! I am Miles Sturgeon!" shouted a lad, standing next to the ballroom doors. "I am pleased to inform you that your fabulous great grandson is waiting for you - just outside of this magnificent ballroom - on the landing!"

Chapter fifteen

"Get inside and don't open your mouth!" growled Kroll.

Impassively studying the tall burly man beside him, Dominic stepped into an austere white cabin. He glanced through the large facing window at the planet they were orbiting. Then he sat down on a small metal chair to the left of that window.

"TT Vox Populi will interview you in approximately thirty minutes," Kroll disclosed hoarsely, also glancing through the window at the remarkable vista. "After which you will be attended by Major Goodman."

Placing Dominic's confiscated Roaming-Ring on the metal table to the right of the window, Kroll stared at the lad, still in evening dress. Then he scowled.

"You certainly are the demure gentleman without your Roaming-Ring and Fighting-Staff, Tau," he remarked coldly. "Quite a contrast to your bold persona on the battlefield yesterday."

Disengaging the silver handcuff on Dominic's right wrist - but leaving the left side still fastened - Kroll handcuffed the lad to a pipe that ran underneath the window.

"They gave you a left *corner-cabin* on the highest deck - at the front of the ship," Kroll growled jealously. "Where they've placed you - you get to see everything. Stars. Planets. The Fighters outside. A bird's eye view of any planet we happen to orbit. The rest of the Fleet, if the Flagship desires. I hope you die - soon."

Dominic glared at the man - unreservedly.

Unblinking Kroll stared back. Then he turned to leave.

"Oh," Kroll said smugly, glancing back. "A generated field is blocking all Roamers from entering or exiting this ship, Tau. So don't cry when weeks go by and you haven't received that longed for helpful visit from your extraordinary buddies in the Psychic Forces." Reaching the cabin door and opening it, Kroll added threateningly, with a pleased grin. "I just hope your friends haven't a rescue plan in the making. Because we have orders to shoot down any unauthorized Spacecraft. No exceptions!"

Kroll left the cabin.

Alone, Dominic's previous cool expression changed. Now of thoughtful visage, he remembered Tesla's Ball - and his arrest. He recalled his flight into Space in a TT Space Fighter and the welcome sight of a small purple signal flare from Keating's faraway Shuttle. He called to mind the spectacle of the orbiting Fleet of Transports, stretching out over many kilometres through the black void. Then he considered how he calculated his chances of escape, when the Space Fighter docked in the landing-bay of this - Transport 0001 - the Flagship of TT's Fleet.

Glancing out of his cabin window into the eerie vacuum, he gazed at the Earth below; then farther out at the far-off twinkling stars. Resigned to his fate, he methodically studied the cabin around him.

Inset into the wall, next to his chair, a basic bunk provided the only comfort. Opposite, beside the table, a wall of empty shelving stretched away to the door. Matt and minimal, the door was metal alloy, as were the floors and ceiling. The lighting was bright but simple and the temperature was cool but tolerable. Everything was white and everything was clean.

Dominic looked at the wall above the table opposite - inset with a Safe, a built in state of the art Computer System, an Audiovisual System, Star charts, and a round-faced clock with hands. Reading that clock, his thoughts were sober.

"Seventy minutes to go until a new tomorrow," he considered, noting a square cavity, also above the desk.

Inside that cavity sat a purple, thirty-centimetre wide, Cabin Robot. A spider like creature when animated, but otherwise a ball with two black oval eyes, the Cabin Robot - programmed to clean, chat, and provide a wealth of social information - was a standard complement to all Transport quarters. This particular substitute servant however - being the *secret package* that Bermuda had previously delivered - had several additional capabilities.

Whistling a few short notes, Dominic subversively activated the robot. Opening its eyes, it's legs extended. Subject to instructions, it remained stationary.

"Cabin Robot?" commanded Dominic. "Voice signature activation - Dominic Tau. Secret program TDT5300.6. Initialise."

"Program initialised, Tau," responded the Cabin Robot in a high-pitched mechanical voice.

"Close your eyes. Standby for further instructions," Dominic said quietly.

Finished with the robot - for the time being - the lad settled back on the hard chair. Wistfully, he glanced at the clock. He studied the numeral twelve at the top of the dial. Then he stared out through the window into the dark mysterious Cosmos.

Because the ship was mostly empty, the atmosphere was quiet, but interesting, due to the stellar view. For some moments, Dominic gazed out of his window at the awesome heavens. Then he closed his eyes. The black airless void shrouded the Transport Flagship. Sparkling, the stars glinted in the darkness. A short time passed.

Startled by the sound of his cabin door suddenly banging open, twenty minutes later, Dominic jumped to stand to attention. His handcuff chain clanked against the pipe and yanked his arm down. Moving closer to the window to slacken the chain, he stood tall. Coolly he looked into the green eyes of TT Vox Populi.

After standing in front of the lad and regarding Dominic thoughtfully for a time, TT stepped back. Casually he sat on the table. Minutes later, Kroll also stepped inside. He closed the cabin door behind him. Of smug of expression - with his back to the door - he stood guard.

Dominic, glancing at both TT and Kroll, noted that neither wore their Roaming-Rings. As these devices were integral to their culture, he pondered this strange fact, whilst simultaneously regarding his great grandfather with a mandatory measure of respect.

"Two years have passed since I last saw you in the flesh, Tau," TT said coldly, looking at Dominic reproachfully. Gingerly picking up Dominic's Roaming-Ring from the table, TT turned it over in his right hand. He studied it thoughtfully. "You have grown," he continued. "You're much taller now - my height in fact. Moreover, you have a definite masculine presence. You are no longer a child." Pausing, he glared at Dominic with narrowed eyes and a down turned mouth. "I have had the pleasure of speaking to you recently, however, in your spiritual mirror form. Have I not?"

Reticent, Dominic stared back at his great grandfather with a blank, polite expression.

Suddenly the Roaming-Ring, a projectile in TT's hand, was viciously hurtled at the doorframe. TT observed the diadem crash

against the wall above Kroll's head. Then he watched it clatter onto
the floor.

Although the atmosphere inside the cabin was now tense, no
reaction was forthcoming from TT's small audience. Remaining
impassive, they both stood to attention. Kroll kept his eyes forward.
Dominic glanced at his Roaming-Ring, then stared shrewdly at TT's
bare head.

Moving away from the table and holding his hands behind his
back, TT walked the length of room - from the long rectangular
window at the front of the cabin, to the central door at the rear. He
pursed his lips. His eyes narrowed. He frowned.

"Tau!" he said evenly, turning around. "We met in Professor Hugh
Doherty's apartment in London. There I offered you a job working
for me at the TT Research Facility. Why did you want a job at the
Facility? Were you spying on me?"

When Dominic refrained from reply, TT stared out of the cabin
window at the faraway stars.

"What do I get for not spending enough time with the family,
Tau?" he asked gratingly. "I can't even recognise my own bloodline!
Welterweight menace that you are." After pausing, TT's voice was
harsh. "We'll continue with this interrogation for as long as it takes to
get some answers, Tau. All night if you like. And all the next day.
And the next. *You* have two weeks of incarceration coming to you."
Stepping towards the lad, TT smiled wryly. "Remember Professor
Doherty - so many years ago. Shall I let you in on a few secrets, Tau?
Professor Doherty was not kidnapped, regardless of what the media
of that time reported. I detained the Professor in safe custody. Did
you know that, Tau? Do you disapprove of me?"

Dominic only stared back.

"Are you the interfering wretch who was responsible for the
Professor's liberation?" TT growled. "Tell me where he is?" He
paused. "No comment. OK. What about Zeta Doherty? You *do* know
where she is."

Expecting silence, TT resumed his position seated on the table.
Now with a calculating tone of voice, he studied the lad's face for the
slightest reaction.

"Zeta is a beautiful girl, Tau. Don't you think?" he asked
smoothly. "She reminds me of my deceased granddaughter, Deneisha
- your own dear, departed mother. The apes of Zeta's time can barely
appreciate what a rare gem the child is, so it *is* better that she lives in

our era." Sitting on the tabletop, TT leant forward. "I know Zeta is here," he said quietly. Then he looked at Dominic pityingly. "Such a crime the lovely youngster won't live as long as you will, Tau. Have you thought of that? Her life expectancy is one hundred and thirty years at most, is it not? 'Tis a shame you will have to spend one hundred and thirty years of your own lifetime without her inspiring friendship. No doubt you will mourn her loss until the day you die, as you will mourn all your friends who pass away before you."

After uttering these harsh words, TT stared at Dominic questioningly, but the lad remained impassive.

"Nothing to say, Tau?" said TT, resting his right hand on the smooth tabletop. "No matter," he revealed smugly. "I already know Zeta Doherty's whereabouts. I had a series of local tracking devices grafted into her Roaming-Ring, as a matter of course. We've been tracking her since the day she arrived."

Dominic's expression remained deadpan. TT drummed his hand on the table.

"Professor Doherty has his own crude version of a Chronoguiser, hasn't he, Tau?" TT continued. "No doubt he has travelled through time with his daughter to bring his technology onto my doorstep. I will find his time-machine and destroy it. Do not doubt me."

Dominic pursed his dry lips, but remained silent.

"Well, this is fun, isn't it?" said TT sarcastically. "Don't I just love talking to a brick wall?" Then again, he smiled wryly. "Come now, boy. You are my great grandson, my heir. You can confide in me. You are popular and I know you have many followers. But you must obey me. You have no option but to be part of the colonization plan, whether you like it or not."

With his free hand, Dominic rubbed his face tiredly and looked at TT.

"I am not a monster, young man!" exclaimed TT impatiently. "I only act for the greater good!"

To these worthy words, the fair youth responded by looking out of his cabin window into the black void of Space. Briefly, he watched a TT Space Fighter fly by, one hundred metres out. Then he gazed at the faraway stars.

"Don't turn away from me, Tau!"

Standing up, TT stepped towards Dominic and shook him roughly. When the lad involuntarily grimaced in pain, TT's hidden anger surfaced.

"Several of my hired associates had the misfortune of attempting to escort you to this Flagship, Tau," he growled. "They obviously failed - after some injury to yourself. Why did you resist that escort? Why was your attendance at the Ball so vital? Are the disheartening reports I have been receiving - that you are the leader of a vile resistance group - correct? The stakes are high in this game you are playing, Tau. We are talking about lives. Answer me!"

Dominic's expression hardened. Unconsciously he clenched his fists and his eyes glowered.

Suddenly TT's external mannerisms changed. Now totally aloof and officious, he turned towards the door. "Kroll! Search the lad!" he ordered gruffly. "Confiscate any weapons and empty his pockets!"

Kroll moved briskly away from his position guarding the heavy airtight door. Striding confidently towards Dominic, he roughly frisked the lad. On finding one weapon, he began to yank that device - a series of interconnecting rings - off the fair youth's hand. TT looked on curiously. Dominic stared coldly at the door.

Sparking violently, the device began to crackle. Detached from Dominic's hand, it activated, discharging a nasty electrical shock into Kroll's clenched hand. The large man yelled. Tossing the weapon onto the tabletop, he glared hatefully.

"That particular 'hammer' is equipped with an antitheft mechanism, Kroll," TT disclosed, after the fact. "It will shock anyone who touches it, except for Tau. It was a gift from me for his thirteenth birthday. I doubt very much if my great grandson appreciates my kind generosity."

Dominic suppressed a smile, and TT - watching him carefully - noted that the lad was a lot calmer now and much more docile.

"Tau doesn't relish a fight with me," he deduced gladly.

Kroll, even rougher now, rifled through the pockets of Dominic's evening coat. From the right pocket he took a disk-shaped wrapped gift, which he shook, listened to and squeezed. From the left pocket he extracted a small glass bottle containing a model schooner, plus a paper copy of Dominic's Commission orders. After putting all of these items on the tabletop, he looked to TT for further instructions.

"Get out, Kroll," said TT, already scrutinizing the items on the tabletop. "You have your orders."

As Kroll left the cabin, TT picked up the small glass bottle. Genuinely admiring the model schooner, he turned the item over quickly in his hand. Reading aloud the engraved message on the base of that ornament, his tone was pleasant:

"To Dominic, good luck, from Isabelle."

"Did you show Isabelle your orders, Tau?" asked TT, glancing at Dominic. "I assume you did. She is obviously pleased that you have been invited to take up the post as First Officer on this Transport Flagship. Hence, the apt birthday gift. Was she your dance partner at the Ball tonight?"

Dominic remained silent.

"You refuse to speak," continued TT. "But I am unperturbed, young man. Rather, I am pleased that you carry with you such a positive symbol of our forthcoming journey. My Flagship and the rest of this Contingent all carry the same inspiring emblem."

Finished admiring the schooner and picking up the disk-shaped package sitting tantalizingly on the tabletop, TT carefully tore off the pretty wrapping. Then he held the small gift - a box of fruit jelly sweets - out for Dominic to see.

"Where did you get these sweets?" he asked. Pausing, he placed the sweets back on the tabletop. "You don't have to reply, lad. I know you used a Matter Transfer Device to obtain this food. You have been using one of these illegal devices for sometime. How else did you put a bowl of Lumpo in Professor Doherty's Knightsbridge apartment? I had a sample of that Lumpo analysed to ascertain this fact. The food wasn't one hundred percent chemically perfect, Tau. This being the reason why Matter Transfer Devices are outlawed. They are unreliable." TT paused again. "We *will* find the Matter Transfer Device and confiscate it," he warned solemnly. "Now who is the gift for, Tau? Are the sweets for Isabelle?"

Even though Dominic remained reticent, TT - now of relaxed expression - spoke confidently to his great grandson.

"You will confide in me soon enough," he boasted. "We are much alike, Tau. As soon as you are distant from the influence of your subversive friends, you will begin to see the wisdom and foresight of my endeavours. You will be my ally."

Dominic regarded his great grandfather, not resentfully, but understandingly and a little sadly.

"You haven't spoken a word since you were detained, Tau," TT continued. "I have asked you well over a dozen questions so far, without one reply. However, you have been gracious enough to let me speak without interruption. And you have not argued. After a couple of weeks of sound company, away from the influence of dangerous reckless lads, you will be more agreeable to conversation. We shall become friends."

Suddenly a fleeting look of emotion passed across TT's face and he reached into his left frockcoat pocket. From there, he extracted a folded cassis-red cummerbund in his family colour, which he held out for Dominic to see.

"This is yours, Tau," he announced solemnly. "If you want it."

Turning towards the Safe, fitted into the wall behind him, he placed the item of clothing - a dress symbol of responsibility and honour - ceremoniously inside.

Closing the Safe, he faced Dominic, continuing to speak in a pleasant manner. "What did you think of the Chronoguisers, Tau? You were obviously interested enough to look at the detailed plans in Professor Doherty's home office. And don't say that you didn't!"

Tolerant of Dominic's silence, TT meditatively glanced out of the cabin window. Noting that the stars seemed unusually numerous and bright, he quickly looked back at his great grandson.

"No doubt you have seen the Dandy Lion in the landing-bay of this Flagship," TT further recounted. "A remarkable ship is it not! Once we are on better terms you can borrow her. I know that right now you probably resent the power I wield over you. But I *am* a man of dreams and principles. Don't think I haven't regrets, Tau. I have not embraced *the future*, as my father, Wiggy, hoped I would. Perhaps I should have. But my people neither remember the past nor anticipate the future. They are not ready to see what awaits them - beyond our present."

Dominic, having been the one to use the Chronoguisers to his best advantage, stared at TT.

"You put forward only one point of view and one solution to a difficult problem, great grandfather," Dominic thought sadly to himself. "I wish you had have been open to see other opinions besides your own. If so, you would have given me a choice of action. Then we would never have ever been at odds."

Dominic restlessly pulled against his left handcuff and TT, watching the lad's every reaction, knew that he had struck a chord with the defiant young man.

"Do you know what the initials TT stand for?" TT questioned, continuing to speak to his great grandson, his voice softer and friendlier.

Dominic, although silent, shook his head slightly in answer.

"My name is *Time Travel* Vox Populi," TT disclosed. "Wiggy founded the TT Research Facility in Farnborough. He thought that I would be the one to embrace time travel technology in its entirety. By that, I mean utilizing both the Roaming-Ring *and the Chronoguiser*. But, as I have already explained, my people are not the ones to welcome that sort of responsibility. The Chronoguiser could not be allowed to remain in production, Tau. I have a population to guide and to nurture. And yes, I *can see* the scornful reaction cloaked on your face. I have a population to control." TT's voice rose, commensurate with Dominic's disapproval of him. "Don't look so indignant, boy!" he exclaimed. "We'd all still be living in caves if no-one had the backbone to take command!"

TT stepped up close to Dominic and stared into the lad's restless eyes. "Look carefully at my face, Tau," he directed sternly, his voice level. "See the deep lines. Those lines represent wisdom. I have paid for that wisdom."

Taking a step back, he held his hands up in front of Dominic. "Look at my hands, lad. See how the skin is thick and hard. These hands are measures of my toil. Remember the sight of my hands and know how hard I have laboured for my citizens."

The Statesman lowered his hands and looked at the soft young face of his great grandson. "Do not underestimate me, young man," he warned. "There is still much in me to be revered. I have much to offer my citizens."

"Yes TT, you have much to offer your citizens," thought Dominic compassionately, staring back thoughtfully at his great grandfather. "But you have failed to offer a group of dangerous young rebels what they desire, and for that error they would have brought you great grief. Neither could you offer one thousand of your citizens the chance to remain in their homes, and for that deficit, they would have brought sad discontent to your brave new colonies. I am not your enemy and I have not betrayed you, Sir. I have merely seen the dangers of which you are ill aware, and have made remedy where it was due."

"Your interview is ended," stated TT, judging no hatred for him in Dominic's eyes. "But let me conclude Tau, by saying this," he continued, in a fatherly tone. "There is inherent wisdom in colonizing new planets. I would like you to appreciate that fact. I can visit you everyday in these, your quarters, and we can discuss all the issues - if you like." After pausing, he added thoughtfully. "I know you worked hard to obtain your Doctorate of Physics. Would you be interested in learning something quite different? I could be your tutor in the arena of politics."

Dominic, though pensive, managed to repress a smile, having anticipated these very words many days earlier, during his zeppelin ride with Zeta.

"Perhaps you would even enjoy becoming reacquainted with all your relatives on the Vox Populi side of the family," suggested TT. "Conforming is not such a bad option, young man."

Suddenly, as TT expected, the cabin door opened. Major Goodman - the group's principle Medical Officer - stepped inside. Walking briskly towards the Statesman, he shook TT's hand.

Inside the cabin, the atmosphere was immediately quiet and reserved as TT, adopting a detached demeanour, greeted the doctor cordially.

"Thank you for attending my great grandson, Goodman," said TT in a pleasant voice.

Goodman, a benign man, glanced quickly at Dominic. Then he placed his black medical bag down on the tabletop.

"Please check Tau for injuries, Goodman," TT ordered politely. "After which I suggest he be given a sedative - to be administered daily - for a week."

While Major Goodman opened his bag, TT addressed Dominic coolly. "The sedation will keep you quiet and out of harms way until your injuries heal and you're feeling more amiable, Tau. Plus," he added, "the probability of your escape will be reduced to a tolerable level of zero."

"Sit down please and remove your coat, Tau," asked Goodman, now stepping towards the lad.

Quickly checking the young man over for injuries, Goodman noted the extensive bruising to Dominic's ribs, slightly angular bruising to his back and the slight swelling of his right hand.

"Speak now, Tau, if you object to the sedation?" Goodman asked. "I can refuse the order and file a report in complaint if you decline the treatment."

Dominic remained silent.

"Are the handcuff's really necessary, TT?" asked Goodman. "You're not going to leave him sitting in the chair all night?"

When TT remained unresponsive, Goodman frowned.

Checking that the time was 11.57pm precisely, Goodman grudgingly rolled the right sleeve of Dominic's ruffled shirt to the elbow. Inserting a needle into the crook of the lad's arm, he injected a tranquillising serum.

"The drug is fast acting, Tau," he warned. "You will feel slightly nauseous when you wake up."

Turning to face TT, the doctor's expression was icy, "I'm going to file a complaint, TT," he said sternly. "This treatment is well out of order."

Closing his medical bag, he quickly left the cabin. TT regarded his great grandson soberly. He studied Dominic's passive face. Then he followed, locking the door behind him.

Dominic briefly closed his eyes. He thoughtfully listened to the sound of their footsteps as the two men strode away. Then he glanced at the clock, noting that the hands on the clock were *both* pointing towards the numeral twelve.

Suddenly prompted into action by the advent of midnight, his whole demeanour abruptly changed. Aggressive, his eyes were bright and determined. Eagerly he stared out into Space at the unusual amount of twinkling stars. Seeking the faintest outline of something hidden in the blackness, his eyes penetrated the dark void. Spotting a spherical outline, his expression was taut.

"My invisible Spaceship is waiting outside. If I've programmed what's going to happen next incorrectly," he thought steadily, "the *Heritage* will kill me."

Nervous energy radiated out from his every pore, pervaded his room and activated his Roaming-Ring, lying on the floor.

"Cabin Robot!" Dominic directed urgently, looking to the spider-like mechinoid. "Search for the locking code and deactivate my handcuffs!"

Two seconds later, the handcuff on his left wrist clicked open and he sprang to his feet. Throwing on his coat, he stepped over to the table. He glanced at the 'hammer', which - once free of his hand - had triggered the automatic pilot on his ship. That automatic pilot - homing in on a signal transmitted from a chip hidden in his forearm - had brought the *Heritage* outside his cabin.

Putting all those items belonging to him in his pockets, Dominic moved towards the door. Picking up his activated Roaming-Ring, he placed it on his head. Frighteningly, he then staggered - already feeling the rapid effects of the administered sedative. His head began to swim. The white cabin about him revolved before his eyes. Reacting to the sudden drowsiness, he leant against the heavy locked door.

Very aware of the silence, the bright light overhead and the pure filtered oxygen he was breathing, he inhaled deeply. Concentrating with maximum effort, he pushed away the creeping stupor that threatened his escape. Stomping his feet, he let the adrenaline surging through his veins, take hold.

"Events will happen very quickly now," he told himself soberly. " I must fight against the sedative. I must stay alert."

With his eyes wide open and the quartz crystals in his Roaming-Ring burning bright, he communicated a telepathic message to his nearby Spaceship.

"*Heritage* Computer - run remote pilot program 7887!" he thought aggressively. "*Heritage* Computer - run remote pilot program 7887!"

Glancing out of his cabin window into the darkness of Space he watched for a response to his command. His cabin remained bright and quiet. He remained a prisoner. Angry with himself, he resolved to try harder.

"*Heritage* Computer, run remote pilot program 7887!" his mind screamed his telepathic message. "*Heritage*-"

Suddenly, the force of an outside impact hurtled him against his cabin door. Outside, the *Heritage,* acting on program 7887, was smashing away at the corner of the Habitation Block! Coming down through his ceiling, his ship was driving into his cabin. Nothing, but nothing, was going to impede its progress.

Instantly plunged into terrifying darkness, his cabin thundered around him. Metal crunched against metal. The room shook violently. Splinters and debris flew forward as the ceiling came crashing down over his head and the walls around him folded in. The front wall of his cabin was quickly obliterated. Under his feet, the floor trembled, as it was shorn away - like butter.

Precursor to a swift death, the hissing sound of air escaping from his cabin beat hard on his ears. Sucking him out into the void, a sudden rush of wind turbulence grabbed at his body. Heaved about by the reducing air pressure, his clothes and hair, caught by the suction, blew forward. With harsh vicelike hands, the suction tugged him and pulled him, trying to drag him out into Space. The lad - fearing for his life - instinctively held fast to his cabin door.

Warning him that there was no way out, he heard a loud click. The Safety System within the Habitation Block sealed his cabin door shut. Screaming throughout the entire vessel, he heard the Transport's alarm sirens, alerting the crew.

With all his willpower, Dominic struggled against his body's impending collapse. Thin all around him, the air was barely breathable. Thumping in his ears, his heart pounded. His lungs struggled for oxygen. His face paled.

Three seconds after his *Heritage* breached the Flagship he could still hear crushed metal being sheered away before him, but looking ahead, he could see nothing but blackness.

Sensing the nearby *Heritage* was moving forward towards him, he reached out one of his hands. There he felt an invisible curved wall of metal edging closer and closer.

"The *Heritage* is going to squash me like a bug," he speculated. Then he thought, with a certain amount of cheerful resolve. "And the door behind me - my future as a colonist - is locked."

Life threatening, the *Heritage* moved closer. Pinned against the door and barely able to breathe, the lad's solemn face, illuminated by his Roaming-Ring, was still determined.

"I don't have any regrets," he thought stoically.

Just as Dominic feared the end, the *Heritage* stopped its advance. All became quiet. The suction dragging at his body abruptly ceased. The hissing stopped. The sound of metal tearing against metal halted and the cabin around him ceased to implode. All was eerily still.

Screaming out in his mind, surrounded by blackness and thinning air, Dominic's psyche once again contacted his ship - now stationary - halted only centimetres away.

"*Heritage*, open hatch! *Heritage*, open hatch!" his thoughts roared.

In rapid response to his panicked telepathic message, a large vertical shaft of light, half a metre high, suddenly beamed out through the darkness onto the shredded floor of his cabin. With the light came a gust of fresh oxygen that filled the lad's lungs, and gave him strength. Carefully sliding down the door and crouching in his now cramped confines, Dominic gratefully espied an open hatch.

"Not dead!" he thought elatedly. "I can hardly move for lack of oxygen, but I'm not dead! Yesterday I programmed the thrust required for the *Heritage* to smash through this Flagship correctly. Today I live!"

Still struggling for breath, but calmer, he hastily glanced up at the area in front of him, now illuminated by a shaft of light beaming out from underneath his ship.

Uncannily he could see no part of the *Heritage* except for the open hatch and the shaft of light beaming forth. He only saw a faint reflection of what was left of the room behind him. Above his head, the ceiling was demolished. So too, the side partitions and the floor were crushed and crumpled. Sharp shards of metal hung down dangerously. Electrical wires - loosed - sparked red and yellow, threatening fire. Whilst burst water pipes - spilling liquid over the remaining floor space - were flooding the crushed remains of his cabin with icy water. The wall behind him was intact however, and the door behind him was still sealed shut.

"This is great," Dominic thought wryly. "I only have a choice of electrocution, drowning or suffocation now. Being crushed or killed in the vacuum - are no longer options."

With the water pooling around his knees, Dominic was surprised to see his Cabin Robot looking up at him.

"You're a fast little spider," Dominic determined to himself. "But you'll be a drowned one soon, if I don't make a move on."

Stretching out one of his arms, Dominic quickly felt the smooth silvery underbelly of the invisible *Heritage,* smooth against his fingertips.

"The cloaking device of the *Heritage* is a fine mirror," he thought wonderingly. Then he exclaimed to himself elatedly, "By jingoes! How good is this ship! Who says Chronoguisers can't pass through walls!"

Collecting his thoughts and wasting no further time, Dominic quickly crawled underneath his ship, on the flooding deck, towards the shaft of light. Fast filling what remained of his cabin, the cold water bubbled and splashed against the underbelly of the *Heritage*. Consequently, on reaching the glowing hatch, and climbing through, the lad was soaked to the skin.

A welcome haven, the *Heritage*, a ship invisible from the outside but visible and brightly illuminated inside, contained some air. Rushing through his ship's cabin, past the walls lined with scientific equipment, Dominic fell into his silver pilot's chair. Glancing about his familiar ship, he immediately activated the manual pilot, threw off his wet coat and strapped himself in, ready for lift off.

Unexpectedly however, appearing inside his ship with him, he spotted his Cabin Robot. Fully animated it approached him. Looking like a huge innocuous spider, it blinked silently at its young Master.

"Cabin Robot, since you are here, you can remove the homing device from my forearm," Dominic commanded. "Quick as you can!"

Pushing back his wet shirtsleeve, Dominic thrust out his left arm. He observed the robot remove a slither of metal from under his skin, in a mere fraction of a second. Taking the homing device from the robot and crushing it in his hand, the lad spoke quickly.

"Secret Program TDT5600.6. As soon as you are able, Cabin Robot, proceed to the landing-bay of this Flagship via Space. Then take up your assignment in your new quarters. Go!"

Seeming almost forlorn, the robot scuttled away. Returning to Dominic's wrecked cabin, it clung fast to the door, where it stayed, half submerged in the icy water.

Now as Dominic closed the hatch, his Chronoguiser filled with oxygen. Shaking from the shock of the last two minutes, he took a few well-earned breaths.

"Here we go now," he said to himself out aloud. "You got in, my *Heritage*. Now you have to get me out - without being fired on by the Fighter pilots outside. They are sharp enough to hazard a guess that an invisible ship is in the vicinity. If they fire blindly out into Space when I make my exit, I'm done for."

Setting his ship's power at minimum thrust, he moved the *Heritage* slowly away from the Transport in which it was tightly wedged. Groaning in complaint as the metal ripped and the decking was further torn away, the larger ship splintered and cracked.

Looking out through his viewing window into black void, Dominic spotted a squadron of Fighters moving cautiously toward the Flagship. Suddenly pressed back in his seat - as the *Heritage* broke free of the wreckage - his invisible ship surged forward, notably on a collision course with the Squadron Leader's Spacecraft.

Quickly shrouded by the cold blackness of Space, the stars twinkled around the lad's fast moving vessel. He could see the face of the unsuspecting Squadron leader - sitting in the Fighter's cockpit - getting closer and closer. While the Earth, over which the Flagship orbited, dominated this charged scene.

"Even if the entire squadron sense I'm here, they are not going to shoot at their own Squadron leader," Dominic gambled.

As he had anticipated, the Fighter pilots did fire a sudden volley of shot out into the blackness where they determined an escaping ship might fly. Dominic, however, was not were they expected him to be. Nowhere near the firing site, the *Heritage* was ten metres away from the Squadron leader. Turning ninety degrees left at the last minute, Dominic avoided collision. Then he looped back towards the Flagship. There he hovered the *Heritage* directly over his wrecked cabin, watching as the Fighters continued to fire in the opposite direction.

Behind the Transport Flagship, he could see the rest of the TT's Fleet. Those nine hundred and ninety nine Transport vessels moved forward serenely. A spectacular site - orbiting their home planet Earth - they filled the cold darkness with endeavour and hope.

TT's Flagship however, was a different matter.

Crippled, floating in the black heavens, its streamlined structure was badly damaged. The left corner of the Habitation Block was torn away and the attached box-wing was shredded at the joint. The entire ship - including the wings - was no longer illuminated. Even the Control Room - not far from the site of destruction - was plunged into darkness. Thus, unlike the rest of the Fleet, travelling behind and flying brightly through the void, the Flagship - a sad testimony to TT's massive accomplishment - was hardly visible.

Solemnly surveying the damage to the Flagship, Dominic cautiously watched the Fighter squadron fly in a close circle around that distressed vessel.

"A fine mess I've made of great granddad's Flagship," he thought to himself soberly. "No doubt I've lost my status as his *favourite* person."

Now that the Fighter pilots had stopped firing blindly into Space, Dominic readied to move away from the Transport Fleet. Spotting his Cabin robot, floating over the top of the Flagship, he watched it as it propelled itself down the rear side. Then he saw it fly quickly into the landing-bay.

"I hope TT likes his new Cabin Robot," Dominic thought shrewdly. "I spent a long time programming that little beastie."

Recalling TT's interview, he thought about Zeta, her whereabouts, and the sly tracking devices that TT had admitted to concealing in her Roaming-Ring.

Thoughtfully, only two minutes after his initial perilous exit from the Flagship, Dominic set his heading on his onboard computer.

"Time to collect my passenger," he decided coolly.

Drowsy now that the adrenaline rush had left him - but still lucid - he was pressed back in his seat as the *Heritage* surged away from the Flagship. Quickly heading for his next destination - the moon - he thought about Zeta once again.

"She's a nice girl and I like her. Just as well."

Emptying his coat pockets of their contents and opening the confectionary box, he put one of the sweets into his mouth. Up ahead, he saw the moon.

Meanwhile, screaming with the piercing sound of emergency sirens, the damaged Flagship was in complete and embarrassing darkness.

"I've been conned, Colonel," TT said vehemently.

Standing in the dark Flight Control Room on the highest deck of Transport 0001, he glanced at the man standing by his side. He stared out of the large square window at the stars outside, specks of light in an otherwise black environment. He observed the Earth revolving huge beneath his damaged vessel. Frowning, he then watched as a squadron of TT Space Fighters flew by, searching for a body.

Holding Snookums - his pet Koala in his arms - TT stepped away from the window. Turning into the room, he gravely scrutinized his busy surrounds. Edging the Flight Control Room, a continuous black bench, fronted by padded black chairs, cosseted the human and robotic occupants. Soberly he peered through the darkness at his ship's skeleton crew, seated at intervals around that bench. Critically he then watched those ten solemn humans, plus four robots, as they ably coped with the current catastrophe.

Glancing at the surrounding blue walls - lined with apparatus - he determined that all the Flight Instrumentation, Communications and Defence Equipment were still operational. Noting the soft blue laminate floor underfoot, the pale blue ceiling, and the array of dysfunctional overhead lights, he frowned. Finally, after surveying the empty chairs and the black desks in the centre of the area - particularly the empty First Officer's station - he scowled.

Disgruntled and walking across to the left side of the room, TT retrieved his Roaming-Ring from a locked wall compartment. After placing it on his head, he slumped down heavily into a vacant chair.

"Get them to turn off those irritating sirens, will you, Colonel?" he shouted across the room. "And see if you can do something about the lights. It's not good to have my Flagship suffering a blackout."

When the Flight Control Room was quiet and illuminated and the Colonel had rejoined him, TT asked soberly.

"How bad is the damage?"

"Not too bad," replied the Colonel. "The ship's Space robots are already outside initiating repairs. We can't tell what caused the damage, as yet. Possibly an explosion."

TT glanced across the large Control Room out into Space. Once again spotting the squadron, he frowned.

"Did the squadron find a body?"

"No," replied the Colonel.

"I don't expect they will," TT said stonily. Pausing, he glanced at the crew, busy with their duties. Then he continued quietly, "You heard the news over our ship's radio. Am I a fool?"

"No," replied the Colonel, shaking his head. "Tau is your flesh and blood. I would not have expected any less of him."

"I've lost one thousand of my people, Colonel," TT said in a hushed angry voice. "They just vanished off the Earth - on the strike of midnight - as if they never existed. Some were in Aristau. Some were on Satellite25. The rest were in London."

"Tau's interest in the Dandy Lion was not without purpose, TT," said the Colonel coolly. "I assume he has manufactured three large makeshift Chronoguisers. That is the only explanation for this mass disappearance. Obviously these machines must be found and destroyed."

"His splinter group left him behind," said TT.

"At his say so, most probably," responded the Colonel.

Suddenly, recalling the Pirate Radio Station Broadcast, which he had recorded and greatly enjoyed, TT sang slowly in his pleasant baritone voice:

"You captured my heart, and took it away. I'm in control of this grand sunny day.

Before I had you, my life was so grey, but now I have you, it's a wonderful day.

You captured my heart, and stole it away, it's a great... grand sunny day."

Then he threw back his head and laughed bitterly.

"Tonight, Tau acted the lamb, placing himself willing in my hands, as a diversion. I should have been suspicious, Colonel. None of his friends tried to free him. He offered no resistance when he was arrested at the Ball. He just stalled for time - distracting me - while his followers escaped!"

"You have to make a decision on what to do about our missing citizens," prompted the Colonel. "Are you going to let them leave, or are you going to search for them and force them to return? You have your own time-machine."

"Give me a few moments, Colonel," replied TT. After pausing and deliberating thoughtfully, he replied. "I am roaming outside this Flagship now - for ten minutes or so. I must check something for myself. The answer to one important question is necessary before I can make a decision."

"You're going roaming into Outer Space?"

"Yes."

"That's going to frighten the wits out of the Squadron pilots. Space Roamers are an anomaly."

"Good," said TT darkly. "They might wake up and guard my Fleet properly. If I discover any evidence that we've actually been rammed by a Space vessel, I'll take the cost of repairs out of their pay."

Holding Snookums comfortably on his lap and closing his eyes, the three amethysts in TT's Roaming-Ring began to glow. An instant later, he was asleep.

Outside of TT's Flagship, Outer Space was dark, cold and forbidding. Apart from the Control Room, the rest of his ship was still without generated light. Only the twinkling stars, the far off Sun and light reflected off the Earth kept his fine vessel visible in the eerie darkness. Thus the star of the Fleet, his Flagship - now marred with an ugly cavity - moved forward unremarkably in its constant orbit.

Searching for answers, it was before this cavity - once Dominic's cabin - that the transparent image of TT Vox Populi suddenly appeared.

Looking quite dignified, dressed in his black frockcoat with a band of cassis-red from the elbow to the wrist, grey trousers and his black bowtie, his ghost glanced away to his far left. He waved reassuringly to a worried female ensign he saw staring out at him through his Control Room window. Then he admired the symbol of a schooner in the core of a planet, painted beautifully, he thought, underneath that window.

After reading his Contingent's motto, *'Exploration champions freedom'*, he floated regally into the ugly dark cavity.

Turning about once he reached the rear wall of the demolished cabin, TT stopped. Floating with his back to the sealed door, he inspected the damage to the gutted, ragged accommodation. The front cabin wall was obviously gone, as was most of the adjacent cabin. The top left corner of the Habitation Block and the adjoining box-wing had also suffered major damage. Investigating the wreckage in more detail, TT searched for something. Noting that the innards of the two cabins were gone, and presuming the missing wreckage was drifting out in Space, he floated across the sheered-away deck to check his theory.

Stopping in the area where the cabin window had previously been, his ghostly image peered out into the eerie black vacuum. Spotting what he sought, drifting away from his Flagship, his spectre began to vanish. An instant later, TT's roaming spirit reappeared hundreds of metres in front of his orbiting ship.

Floating in the inky heavens, his psyche looked very wonderful indeed. Glowing in the darkness, his black frockcoat sparkled. His grey trousers shimmered and the cassis-red bands on his sleeves radiated warm rosy light out into the blackness.

Around him, the stars never twinkled so brightly. The Earth spun large and bright beneath him. While faraway, the Sun shone golden, radiating starlight onto TT's round thoughtful face. He glanced back at his Flagship.

Flying out from his Flagship's landing-bay and heading towards Dominic's wrecked cabin, TT curiously watched what looked like a bunch of enormous headless beetles. Over three metres high, these mechinoids each had ten arms and six legs. As a group they all carried hull plating and tools. Critically watching these Space robots, TT made a mental note to take up the issue of aesthetics with the Robotic Industry Board - at their next meeting.

"Those particular mechinoids are hideous," he thought fairly. "They should be kept under lock and key - except in emergencies. It's reasonable to say that they would give even the most stout hearted of my citizens - the collywobbles."

Distracted from watching the robots by the panoramic view of the Transport Fleet, flying behind his Flagship, TT stared proudly. Each wide, silver Transport vessel gleamed in the darkness. Light shone out from the many portholes in the square Habitation Blocks.

Outlining each set of rectangular box-wings, bright white lights sent cheerful rays out into the void. Whilst the large green safety lights on the wing tips blinked comfortingly.

Finished enjoying the spectacle of his Transport Fleet orbiting the Earth, TT remembered the reason why he had made this journey. Floating forward, he moved towards something small and black that was speeding away from the Flagship, into the darkness.

"Aha!" he said gladly, on reaching that object.

Grabbing Dominic's Safe with transparent arms, he briefly travelled along with it.

"The Safe is still in one piece," TT thought soberly. "Now I'm going to find out where I really stand with my great grandson. Whether he is friend or foe."

Of anxious expression, TT quickly grasped the latch on the Safe. Pulling open the small heavy door, he carefully peered inside.

"The Safe is empty," he thought to himself happily. "Tau has taken his cummerbund." His eyes brightened. "I'm glad he has accepted my family - even if we don't agree."

Pleased and settled, he spun his spectral image. Seconds later, his roaming image disappeared. Simultaneously he awoke in his Flagship's Flight Control Room. Extremely bright compared to the darkness outside, the Control Room was warm, but confined. The blue and black décor was positive. Happily, most of the crew - now that vital repairs were underway - were cheerful.

The Colonel, still seated next to him, anxiously waited for TT to speak. As did the quiet crew, who intended to eavesdrop. All except for the female ensign, however. She had watched TT all the while he had been roaming. Still standing at the window - most impressed by his ability to roam in Space - she regarded TT with a high degree of reverence.

"I have made my decision, Colonel," TT said, on the instant of awakening. "This decision is my own - made without external influence. I want you to find Tau and bring him to me for interrogation. Once captured, he will tell us where the thousand escapees are hiding. It is impossible to bring any vessel close enough to this Flagship to aid him. Therefore, Tau is injured, sedated and alone. Probably he is still onboard. I'm guessing the gutted cabin is a ruse. It shouldn't be too difficult to find him."

"A small Chronoguiser - travelling fast enough - could have slipped through our Surveillance System undetected, TT," said the

Colonel. "It could be responsible for the damage to this ship. Perhaps our Security has already been compromised, many times over. You should take account of this possibility."

TT waved him away dismissively.

"There isn't a pilot born who can fly a Chronoguiser fast enough to invalidate my Surveillance System, Colonel. The lad's alone. No one is helping him. Follow your orders. Find him."

Acknowledging his instructions with a nod of his head, the Colonel temporarily left TT, to attend to his duties.

During the Colonel's absence, TT fished a handful of eucalyptus leaves from his frockcoat pocket. Feeding them to Snookums, secure in his arms, he patted the cuddly grey marsupial. The Koala, clinging onto TT - as if the man was a tree - munched contentedly on the fragrant leaves.

As TT watched his pet, he reflected on this midnight's trauma. He glanced out into Space. Then he hummed Bermuda's song. After which he sat back in his chair and smiled.

Several minutes later, when the Colonel returned, TT began solidly discussing Affairs of State.

Chapter sixteen

"Go free, my little ones," the large man said quietly.

Swirling around his feet the dusty earth spun in low eddies. Overhead the early morning sky was blue, clear and cloudless. Covering the lowlands of this hilly desert region about him, a vast body of water - London Reservoir - stretched away for many kilometres.

Adjusting the breathing apparatus covering his face, the man swept back his dark hair. Looking towards the cold rippling water lapping at the Reservoir's stony banks, his face was thoughtful.

Moments before he had held Jack in one hand and Jill in the other. He had looked at each of their pointed faces. Then he had lowered them carefully into the cool water. Now he watched them gently swimming away.

Turning away from the Reservoir, he stepped across the soft earth. Leaving deep footprints in the sand he headed for his Space Fighter, landed nearby. On reaching his vessel, he glancing admiringly at that triangular, streamlined black battleship. Then he jumped up onto the wing. Stooping under the large curved windscreen, he eased himself into the cockpit. When the windscreen snapped shut, he started the engines.

Finished reminiscing about the secret release of his squadron mascots - two baby Nefarids named Jack and Jill - earlier that day, Kroll speculated on their high chances of survival. Then he grinned.

Flying away from the Transport Fleet through the black vacuum of Space, darkness fell like a shroud over his darting Spaceship. Little noticing the twinkling light from the faraway stars he settled into his generous brown pilot's chair - mounted forward of an adjacent chair on either side. He adjusted his Roaming-Ring. He checked his timeband. It was 11.50pm. Turning his hand over, he then darkly scrutinized the superficial burn, inflicted only ten minutes before - by Dominic's 'hammer'.

"I will enthusiastically enjoy watching that fledgling statesman - Tau - suffer his captivity," he thought vengefully.

Reaching that same hand towards his mahogany coloured dashboard - fitted with a Communication, Navigation, Artillery, and of course, an Audio System, he flicked two switches. Filling his cockpit with music, he coldly set his heading - for the moon.

Racing through the Cosmos with easy grace, Earth's massive bulk quickly reduced in size behind his sleek Space Fighter, whilst up ahead, the stars blinked invitingly.

His being a fast ship, the silver circle of the moon loomed quickly into view. A fanciful glowing place from afar, it shone a bright face into the cold black void. Reducing speed and altitude as soon he reached that planet, Kroll flew over the rocky grey terrain. Critical of the arid bleak landscape, he considered the moon thoughtfully.

"Ominous dark shadows fill the deep ragged craters on this small grey planet," he mused. "Cold and desolate, this gigantic rock has no gravity, atmosphere or water. A lifeless place that looks beautiful from afar - the moon is deceptive. Once man is close, the surface is inhospitable, pocketed and marred. Bright on one side, yet dark on the other, I find the moon prohibitive. Yet, at the same time it is wonderful. For it freely offers the most glorious vista of my world - the Earth."

The time had gone midnight and Kroll - being a perceptive man - was suddenly agitated by a nagging suspicion about his abject assignment. Unexpectedly displeased by the small planet over which he flew, Kroll's temper darkened.

"Stinking bad luck to be born when I was," he reasoned, finding excuse for his sudden black mood. "The poisoning of my planet - seventeen years ago - has left me embittered. Almost overnight, Earth turned into a desert. At the time, I was only eight years old. Some childhood I've enjoyed - thanks to conservative planning. Our leaders guessed Earth was going to be barren one day. The best contingency plan they could come up with was the colonization of distant worlds. Not good enough - by my estimation. I'll be thirty by the time we get to the colonies. I haven't been given the opportunities I deserve due to bureaucratic bumbling. What a waste of my years!"

Done grumbling to himself, Kroll reduced altitude. Scrutinizing the moon's terrain with hard-hearted precision, he glanced at his dashboard instruments. A few moments later, he visually detected two distinct structures on the rugged dry surface.

Nearest to his low flying battleship, he observed the first structure - a modern compact Moon Station, built for the dual purpose of Defence and Astrological research. Following protocol, Kroll signalled the Moon Station in passing. Then he looked to the second structure - an intriguing abandoned Dome, forty kilometres further forward.

After checking his ship's Console and homing in on the local tracking devices planted in Zeta's Roaming-Ring, it was towards this large solar-powered Dome that he directed his ship.

"Once I've completed my assignment and have returned my captives to TT's London Globe Home," Kroll thought confidently, "I'll help myself to a well deserved glass of TT's fine sherry."

Putting thoughts of his success temporarily to the back of his mind, Kroll stealthily approached, then flew over the top of the ancient Moon Dome. From the cockpit of his Fighter, he observed the illuminated webbed framework and the yellowing semi-opaque fabric that covered the Dome.

"This Dome is over a thousand years old," he marvelled.

Utilizing his ship's cameras to zoom in on the large area inside of the Dome, he observed a yellow, 'L' shaped building complex fronted by a red-fenced quadrangle. The buildings were aged and decrepit. On the longest side of the 'L', which stretched from the right front of the Dome to the rear, he observed a ticket booth, an open plan spacious restaurant and an entertainment area. The cracked walls of the ticket booth were a dismal flaking pink. The décor of the restaurant was fading lilac, teamed with rusted brown metal. The open entertainment area - full of dusty lilac sofas - was littered with smashed toys and broken games. On the shorter side of the 'L', extending along the rear of the Dome from right to left, he saw an office building.

"Zeta is hiding in that building," thought Kroll, after glancing at the tracking device, worn on his belt. "I can taste the sherry now."

Smiling confidently, he looked at the quadrangle, covered with tired olive-grey synthetic turf. Raising his eyebrows in quiet astonishment, he studied the interesting and simply hair-raising range of amusement rides he saw - undamaged - within that large enclosed space.

Finished perusing the Dome from on high, Kroll set down his ship in an old Spacedock - built for Spacebuses - at the front of the Dome. Disembarking with the aid of his magnetic boots and his full gold flight suit, he hurried through the airless dock towards a pedestrian airlock.

On reaching that airlock, he keyed a standard combination of numbers into the outside keypad and the outer airlock door slid open. Once through - that door slammed behind him. He keyed in a further sequence of numbers into the keypad mounted on the side of the interior door. That also slid open. Moving forward, he stepped into the uninhabited, but air-filled Dome.

"I had expected it to be bright in here, since the webbed Dome framework is illuminated," he thought. "But it is as dark as any typical night on Earth."

Quickly running across broken blue paving, he stopped at the ticket booth several metres ahead. Carefully hiding his helmet and gloves under the counter inside of the booth, he looked around clinically.

"In its heyday, this place was a popular tourist attraction," he surmised. "Now it's neglected and dusty. The overall atmosphere is bleak and forlorn."

After warily glancing around him, he ran a distance behind the 'L' shaped building complex. Stopping in front of a single black exit door at the rear of the office building, he activated his life-form scanner. Surprised at the reading, he checked it again.

"Yes, my scanner definitely says there is only one entity inside," he thought to himself, his body relaxing and his heart beat slowing. "Weighing in at fifty kilograms the entity is located in the rear room, to my right." He paused and considered. "So, Miss Doherty has been left here alone. This is an appallingly neglectful way to treat *The Zeta*. Fortunately for me, it means I don't even have her father to deal with." Kroll smiled. "My mission couldn't have been easier!"

Quietly Kroll turned the handle of the unlocked rear door.

"It's so dark in here," he thought soberly, stepping inside the chilly building. "I can hardly see my hands in front of me."

Standing in a green corridor that led to the Reception area at the front of the building, he briefly watched stray rays of fine white light flow through the grubby front windows, then filter through the thick dusty air, down the gloomy corridor towards him.

Peering through the darkness, he observed three red doors on either side of that corridor, each leading into a square and windowless dark room. Each door was open, except for the door on the first room to his right. That room being the place where he believed Zeta to be hiding.

"It couldn't be any more gloomy or dusty in here, than it already is," he thought warily. Cautiously stepping back, his foot went through the cracked floor, down into the moon dust below.

"Lovely. I hope the roof doesn't cave in on me as well as the floor disintegrating."

Extracting his foot, he stepped forward. On cue, a stream of dust fell gently from the ceiling onto his head.

Under the cover of imposed darkness, Kroll furtively approached the mysterious closed room. Creeping forward slowly, stepping carefully on the uneven untrustworthy floor, he stopped outside the closed red door. There he listened for the sound of movement inside. Smoothing the dark hair on his head above his Roaming-Ring with his hands, and brushing his thin black moustache with his thick-skinned fingertips, he smiled meanly.

"TT said that the little girl, Zeta, is beautiful," he considered slyly. "But more importantly I know *she is rich*! I will act nice, make a good impression. She will admire me. Once I have gained her trust, I will line my pockets with the fruits of her labours. After which, I will spend many enjoyable hours squandering her wealth." Kroll's expression briefly changed to reflect his nastier side. "Zeta's father, Professor Doherty, was easy to oppress when I held him captive," he remembered. "Therefore, I am guaranteed to keep his tender little offshoot under control."

Having decided how he was going to conduct himself in the presence of the little girl, Kroll eagerly gripped the silver door handle of the dark closed room. Speaking softly through that door - in his most non-threatening tone of voice - he called out quietly.

"Hello, Miss Doherty." he said. "Don't be frightened, young lady. I'm here as a friend. TT Vox Populi sent me. I am Captain Kroll. TT has asked me to escort you to his home in London, where you will stay with him until the Fleet leaves. Then you will travel with our citizens to five new Earths. It will be a truly wonderful journey." Kroll paused. His right hand slowly turned the silver door handle.

"I'm going to open the door now, Miss Doherty," he cautioned. "Please don't be alarmed. I won't hurt you. I promise."

After this short comforting speech, Kroll, smiling pleasantly, pushed open the red door. Expecting the room to be dimly illuminated, he was surprised to step forward into utter blackness.

Suddenly he gasped. Widening in shock, his brown eyes filled with fear. Draining from his ruddy young cheeks, the healthy pink colour left his face. Affronting his ears, he heard a horrible death snarl. Filling his nostrils, he smelt the putrid scent of inhuman breathing. Coming at him out of the darkness, he saw a huge terrible set of menacing jaws. Looped around the lower jaw of the beast lunging at him, he could faintly see a corroded Roaming-Ring. Compelled to stare at that small diadem, he was rooted to the spot.

"No time!" he thought hopelessly, losing his chance to jump away.

Towering over him in the pitch-black room, a monstrous hairy biped lashed out at him with a large clawed paw. Hurtled out into the dingy corridor, the man's body smacked against the wall with a thud. No longer the predator - Kroll was the prey. His knees buckled underneath him. He slid heavily to the floor. Dust from the dingy cracked cream floor flew up around him where he fell. Blinded by that dust and disoriented by the sudden attack, he gasped in panic.

"For the life of me, I can't even see what's attacking me!" he muttered.

Concealed by the darkness, the black creature descended upon him. Pinning him down, it tore at his suit with serrated teeth. It scratched at his chest with pointed claws. Growling, the man pushed the jaws of the beast back from him. Heaving both himself and the creature up from the floor, he hurtled the monster into the office from whence it came.

Hastily he looked about for anything he could use as a weapon - a club or a shield.

"No luck," he thought, dashing along the dim green corridor, towards the front of the building.

Already bounding out from the office, the monster gave chase. Growling horribly, the beast jumped at his back, tried to knock him down and slashed at his flight suit. Reaching the Reception area and the wooden front exit door, Kroll found that way blocked. Throwing himself at the door, he knocked it down.

Outside the building, glancing behind him, he could now *see* the monster - a bear-sized beast with an enormous head - snapping at his heels. Close behind him and running on all fours, the predominately black creature blended easily into the darkness. Jumping over a low faded red fence, it chased him out onto the olive green quadrangle, snarling and gnashing its teeth.

Loath to listen to the frightening thump, thump of the beast's paws on the hardened turf underfoot, coupled with its rasping heaving breathing, Kroll ran as fast as he could. Weaving his way between the once exhilarating amusement rides, he headed across the quadrangle. He leapt over the low faded red fence surrounding that quadrangle. Then he dashed towards the ticket booth. Reaching the booth, he grabbed his helmet and his gloves.

Hounding him, the creature took this opportunity to throw itself violently at the big man's chest. Kroll staggered back against the booth. Baring its razor-like teeth before his eyes, it drooled disgustingly onto his ashen face. Again, he threw the monster back from him. Clutching his gold coloured helmet and gloves he sped towards the pedestrian airlock. Thumping the red button on the airlock keypad with his fist, Kroll pushed inside as the door slid open. Pounding the keypad again, he watched that same door close.

Quickly looking back, he was aghast to see the creature hurtling itself against the reinforced glass. Trying to break through and attack him, it struck at the door with all the weight of its big hairy body. Then it pressed its horrible open jaws against the thick clear glass. Disgusted, Kroll observed its slimy thick drool sliding down that transparent surface.

"I can see you clearly now, you disgusting wretch!" Kroll called loudly, while donning his helmet and gloves. "Count yourself lucky that I didn't kill you!"

Checking his flight suit for vital damage, he keyed in the numbers required to open the exterior airlock door. Running with difficulty in his magnetic boots, he headed out into the Spacedock towards his Space Fighter - without looking back.

Breathless when he reached his Fighter, Kroll jumped up onto the wing. He threw himself under his forward opening, top hinged windscreen, and into his cockpit. Within the safe confines of his familiar battleship, his windscreen access closed and his gun close, Kroll took time to catch his breath.

"No wonder I felt agitated when I neared this planet," he thought angrily. "My gut instincts are always right. Finding the little girl was never going to be easy - not after we kidnapped her father... and he escaped to tell the tale. TT underestimated the Doherty family. Zeta's friends or father must have spotted the tracking devices right from the start." He glanced at his grubby scratched flight suit. Then his brooding eyes narrowed. "Zeta and her friends all going to pay - for messing with me."

Looking back towards the Dome, he was surprised to discover the place now quiet. The creature that had attacked him was neither prowling along the perimeter, as he had expected, nor was it smashing itself against the pedestrian airlock. The Dome seemed empty of all life. The monster was nowhere to be seen.

Visually searching for the beast and scrutinizing the glass fronted Spacedock, Kroll did not notice anything unusual. Silent and sleepy, the abandoned Leisure Park was deserted. The tired buildings were vacant. The cracked blue paving, untrodden by crowds for so many years, showed no footprints - other than Kroll's and those of the monster that had given him chase. Even the amusement rides in the quadrangle remained stiff and still.

"Perhaps the beast has returned to the office building?" Kroll speculated.

Wanting to be sure of its whereabouts, Kroll retrieved the life-form scanner attached to his belt. Activating that device, he ran a thorough scan for the monster - attempting to pinpoint its exact location.

"What the dickens!" he exclaimed. Then his voice rumbled in a low growl. "Great!" he thought warily. "My equipment tells me there are now two entities, besides myself, in the local vicinity. Stationary, they weigh in at fifty and seventy kilograms. Located in the Spacedock - forty metres away from my ship - they are stopped outside the... Spacebus airlock."

Peering out from the curved windscreen of his Space Fighter, he attempted visual confirmation of these facts, but saw nothing. Staring at the Spacebus airlock, he checked his scanner again.

"Of all the rotten luck!" he grumbled out aloud.

With his heart beginning to race, he grabbed his gun.

"I've got a couple of invisible monsters in this Spacedock," he thought anxiously. "Monsters that are smart enough to get out of an airlock. Added to that, the vicious creatures don't even need air. Part of me wants to stay inside my battleship and fly away. The other part of me wants the satisfaction of capturing the brutes."

He deliberated. "I'll rise to the challenge!" he concluded.

Determined, the Intelligence Officer decided to leave the safety of his vessel. Pushing a button on the Flight Console in front of him, his windscreen access quickly popped open. Jumping out of his battleship onto the wing, he leapt gingerly down to the ground.

Working against the grip of his magnetic boots, he dashed towards the Spacebus airlock. Taut with fear he held his primed gun in his large wide hand. With his finger poised over the trigger of his gun, Kroll was ready to shoot at anything.

Fearful for his safety and believing there were two monsters in the Spacedock with him, keen to tear him to shreds, Kroll noticed every single detail of the area around him. Every ridge on the orange metal floor was noted and magnified. Every particle of dust around him and beneath his feet was assessed and judged for movement. The struts supporting the dock's frame, the blue colour of the flat old roof, the thin layer of moon-dust covering the tracks that his landing battleship had made. Every single aspect about this location was indelibly stamped into his brain.

Reaching the raised Spacebus airlock in what seemed to be an eon, Kroll searchingly looked through the glass access gate. Spotting something, he pressed a keypad mounted on a panel at the side of that airlock. The gate, positioned two metres above ground level, quickly slid open. Kroll, pulling his magnetic boots free from the dock's metal floor, easily climbed through the opening.

Immediately disgusted, he looked down at what was lying at his feet. Picking up the corroded diadem that he had seen in the beast's mouth his expression was cold.

"I'll take Zeta's Roaming-Ring back to TT," he decided.

On activating his life-form scanner, however, his thoughts differed. "The reading now indicates that I am the only entity in the local radius. Strange? Where did those two monsters go?" He shook his head. "I can only presume they left the Spacedock and are lurking outside, somewhere on the surface of the moon." Looking at his battleship, he mumbled hoarsely, "I'll discover the whereabouts of the beasts."

Jumping hastily back out of the Spacebus airlock he ran for his ship, still clutching the corroded Roaming-Ring. Once safely inside his vessel, with his hinged windscreen slammed securely shut, he extended the range of his scanner.

"I will pinpoint the location of the two elusive entities," he thought purposefully.

Detecting twenty life forms on the surface of the moon - each weighing in at between seventy and ninety kilograms - he groaned impatiently.

"Those twenty are all the Staff of the Moon Station. I knew *they* were there. I'll try again."

He extended the scanner's range. Finding the two entities, his dark hair bristled underneath his helmet. His brown eyes glowered with rage.

"The entities are hundreds of thousands of kilometres away - in the vacuum of Space," he exclaimed angrily. "Two monsters my eye! The Master has collected his vicious pet!" Thereafter Kroll exploded into a tirade of cursing, whilst simultaneously taxiing his Space Fighter out of the large old Spacedock.

As his ship shot like an angry black dart out into Space, Kroll's thoughts were dark. "This whole episode was a nasty trap. Two grisly beasts can fly a Spaceship as well as open an airlock. Sure!" Pausing in thought, his eyes were hateful. "I do so despise those Psychic Knights! I bet a member of their elite extraordinary group is flying that escaping Spaceship right now. He must be an Illusionist," he deduced incorrectly. "How else did I fail to see his Shuttle landed beside my own ship? How else can he control that hairy monster that he has taken with him?"

Staring meanly out into Space, and following the entities, by using both his natural instincts and the life-form scanner, Kroll continued to bellyache.

"That cunning Psychic Knight was right under my nose when I ran out of the Dome. He must have coupled his invisible Shuttle to the Spacebus airlock when I was running for my own ship," he thought, bitterly fuming. "Now he thinks he's getting away. He won't escape. I am going to catch up to that clever piece of work. Then I'm going to fire on him until his ship explodes into a million spectacular pieces." Kroll smiled. "With the stealth capability of my Space Fighter, he won't even realize I'm chasing him."

Dominic, however, did know that he was being followed. Slumped half asleep in the pilot's seat of his Chronoguiser *Heritage*, flying through Space towards Nefaria, he had just heard the warning sound on his ship's Console.

Alarmed, he stared blearily at his radar. Previously registered with all of the Space Fighter frequencies, his radar now told him that one of those Fighters was within range, and fast approaching.

Fighting against the sedation, he forced himself awake. Glancing through his viewing window, he was thoughtful.

"Splattered onto an endless black fabric, the distant stars look like blurred flecks of white lint," he noted. "A minute seems like a second. What I hold gently in my hand I actually crush. When I should feel fear, I feel confident."

Looking towards the many gauges on his ship, he then considered carefully. "The administered drug I was given has altered my perception of time, space and distance. My instruments tell me I am travelling at an extremely high velocity. But looking outside my viewing window, my eyes tell me my ship is moving quite slowly. I need automatic evasive manoeuvres. My automatic pilot must prove its worth now."

Leaning forward towards his ship's onboard computer, he programmed the automatic pilot of the *Heritage* to the task of evading the pursuing battleship.

"Firstly, the *Heritage* will travel forward in an erratic zigzag pattern," he thought coolly. "She will perfectly match the speed of Kroll's Space Fighter. In addition, she will send out a false electronic reading telling Kroll's Computer that she is a high speed Shuttle. I can't have one of TT's men knowing that I have my own personal Chronoguiser."

Minutes later, Dominic programmed the final routine.

"At 1.10am, when the *Heritage* reaches the rings of Nefaria she will time jump three hundred years into the future. Then she will set down outside my favourite subterranean cavern."

Now that the programming of these critical evasive measures was complete, Dominic slumped back into his pilot's seat. As he looked seriously at his onboard computer, his face was thoughtful. Softly glowing with fine blue light emitted from the gravity drive, the cabin around him was conducive to sleep. Shaking his head in an effort to stay alert, the quartz crystals in his Roaming-Ring caught these blue rays of light and reflected them back over his solemn face.

"It is important that Kroll arrives at Nefaria just before sunup," Dominic considered. "So that when my invisible *Heritage* disappears off his instruments, he will assume I have landed on Nefaria and will not follow. Therefore," he thought, leaning towards his onboard computer and typing slowly onto the keypad, "I will loop back behind him if he's travelling too fast, or speed up to prompt him forward if he's going too slow."

Finished typing the necessary data into his onboard computer, Dominic soberly gazed out of his viewing window into Outer Space.

Then he pondered as to his chances of escape from Kroll's TT Space Fighter.

"If Kroll gets close enough he will fire on me," Dominic thought pensively. "Even though his eyes will never see the *Heritage*, and his ship's instruments will falsely tell him she is a Shuttle, his life-form scanner will accurately pinpoint my location. I can't fly fast enough in the state I'm in to avoid that little piece of tracking technology." He glanced at his gravity drive. "I can only hazard a guess as to what effect an attack will have on my gravity drive. The extra power of an explosion might push the *Heritage* further through time. Or it might light her up like a beacon - just before she explodes."

Suddenly the sound of a low ominous growl startled the lad. Reacting to the sound, he swivelled his pilot's chair around to face both the stern of his ship, and the source of the noise.

Dozing at the back of the *Heritage* - on a mat on the floor - was the ferocious beast that had attacked Kroll. Its black fore and hindquarters were curled up underneath its round heavy body. The wet fur on its flanks spiked upwards. Its large head lay resting on its paws.

While Dominic watched its belly rise and fall in sleep, the monster growled again. Blinking its black eyes open unexpectedly, it pricked its small round ears forward to listen.

"Go back to sleep, Angle," suggested Dominic in a soft slow voice. "*You've been a good boy.* I saw you chasing Captain Kroll through the Moon Leisure Park. You're very brave to chase such a big tough man. And you're obedient too. As soon as you heard your whistle, you dropped that rusty old Roaming-ring and jumped straight through the Spacebus airlock into my invisible ship. Weren't you glad to see me, eh? Bermuda will be well pleased when he hears what an exemplary job you've done tonight, Angle. He'll be very proud of his big brave guard dog."

The monstrous dog, reminiscent of a Panda, but with much larger jaws and much longer claws, gazed at Dominic trustingly. Knowing the youth since it was a pup, it stretched and yawned.

Dominic returned his chair to its original position.

"My automatic pilot is going to play a cat and mouse game with Kroll for the next forty-five minutes, Angle," he said. "Kroll will be livid by the end of it. If he can shoot us, he will. It is his nature." Dominic's voice became softer, hardly audible. "I can't stay awake anymore, Angle," he whispered. "Nefaria is almost twelve thousand million kilometres away, and I can't stay awake! This is the second time tonight that I gamble with my life. But I can be pleased that over a thousand people are away safe, three hundred years into the future. Whatever happens, even if I don't make it to the future to join them, I have won."

Travelling into the depths of the Universe, through the Milky Way Galaxy, the *Heritage* raced onward, surrounded by billions of faintly glowing mysterious stars. The Earth's hot Sun was left far behind. Cold blackness shrouded the small humming Chronoguiser. The Space vacuum pressed in around the vessel and while Dominic slept, time moved forward.

Slumped unconscious in the pilot's seat, the lad was a miniscule mortal compared to the galaxy around him. Within the infinite speckled black canvas of the Cosmos, however, the dimensions of the young man's heart far surpassed his diminutive physical size. Whilst the lifetime of his chaste spirit knew no certain bounds.

Following in menacing pursuit, the TT Space Fighter, piloted by Kroll, was flying its fastest. Slicing through the darkness, twisting and turning in an attempt to gain on its elusive target, the engines of the Fighter - running at maximum - were softly humming.

Catching thousands of particles of stray starlight, the splendid glossy bodywork of the Fighter glistened like the silky feathers of a great black bird. Streaking through the Cosmos - almost invisible in the vacuum - the swift menacing vessel pushed forward, plunging into the darkness. Left behind in the blink of an eyelid, nearby planets were indiscriminately passed by. Glimpsed for but a moment - the stars twinkled softly.

Many minutes had elapsed since Kroll had begun the pursuit of what he mistakenly believed to be a fast Space Shuttle. Now, softly illuminated by the instruments on his busy dashboard, he leant slightly forward in his seat. His helmet was off. Relaxed, one of his hands rested on his manual flight controls. The other fell comfortably onto his knee. Glinting as it caught the stray rays of cabin light, his platinum Roaming-Ring sparkled. Underneath that Ring his face was calm. Gazing wistfully out into Space, Kroll's voice - speaking to his Squadron leader via his Fighter's Communications System - was clear.

"Yes, Sir," he responded to a command just set to him. "I will intercept and disable the escaping vessel. Yes, Sir. Yes." Resentfully he flicked a switch to end the communication.

Confident of his ship's ability to catch his quarry when he had left the moon, thirty minutes before, the brawny Officer had been alert and eager. Increasing the velocity of his TT Space Fighter, he had activated his Weapon System in readiness to fire. Alert in the dim cockpit of his ship, he had focused his mind and his body on the chase. He had fixed his eyes on the fleeting stars in the distance and on the blackness into which he travelled. Only occasionally had he glanced at his Flight Console to check vital instrument readings. Only occasionally had he checked the passing time.

Thirty minutes later however, with Earth's Solar System far behind him, Kroll's attitude had changed. Finished speaking to his Squadron leader, he was sitting indifferently in his pilot's seat. Since multitasking was his favourite pastime, that's what he was doing.

Simultaneously weaving his way through an asteroid field, he was polishing his gold coloured helmet, he was listening to energetic music - interspersed by updates transmitted on his Squadron channel - and he was admiring the shining planets as his ship quickly passed them by.

Full of the musical strains of a delightful array of orchestral instruments, his cockpit was a most pleasant place to be, and the overall expression in the man's deep-set brown eyes was calm and confident. Still flying his threatening black battleship forward through Space, he happily had only one eye focused on what was in front of him, and only one half of his concentration devoted to piloting his fast moving Spaceship.

What had brought about this drastic change of outlook was recent intriguing information. Information that came from his three sources: his onboard computer, his surveillance equipment, and his Squadron Leader.

During the initial stages of his pursuit of Dominic, Kroll thought to activate his life-form scanner every two minutes, as a way to plot the position of the vessel he was chasing.

"My quarry is flying in an extremely erratic, zigzag pattern," he discovered, after imputing these co-ordinates into his onboard computer. "Plus it is matching my speed."

Pepped up by this enlightening information, he determined what type of craft he was tracking. Utilizing his surveillance equipment, he established that he was indeed following, as he had first thought, a high speed Shuttle.

"I'm following a Shuttle on automatic pilot," Kroll mistakenly concluded from this methodical analysis.

Finally, the announcements on his squadron channel concerning Dominic's escape, confirmed his suspicion that he was indeed pursuing one of the elite members of the Psychic Forces. That Knight most probably being the rebel, Tau.

Captain Kroll, now being of certain mind of the guaranteed capture of his quarry, was confident - even enthusiastic.

"Since the Psychic Knight inside of that fugitive vessel is probably Tau, I can be confident that he will be fast asleep for the next eleven hours," Kroll thought smugly. "My ship is faster than any Shuttle, and with the aid of my onboard computer, I can easily out manoeuvre a vessel on autopilot. I have already gained on the fugitive ship and I should catch up with it shortly. Without doubt, Tau knows the whereabouts of Miss Zeta Doherty and her father. Soon I will be able to deliver those two absconders to TT Vox Populi, plus his great grandson. Surely I will be well credited for that achievement."

Routinely now, Kroll checked his life-form scanner for the position of the two entities.

"Not true!" he exclaimed out aloud. "The two entities have gone. Disappeared!" Shaking his scanner roughly, he tapped it against his dashboard. "Bit of rubbish equipment," he complained crossly. Checking the scanner again, he extended the range, but had no luck.

"Since I still can't find them, I'll shorten the range," he thought impatiently. "Tau may have stopped his vessel." With the tips of his large fingers, he tapped on the keypad of his life-form scanner. Then he read the results.

"He's behind me. Balderdash! He can't have backtracked," Kroll deduced incorrectly. "His Shuttle's not fast enough to achieve that feat. Impossible. I must have caught up with him and passed him - four minutes ago!"

Angry with himself, Kroll switched off the lively music filling his cockpit. Putting his helmet back on his head, he turned his ship about. Heading on a course back to Earth, his ship slid forward at phenomenal speed.

Like strings of gossamer webbing - spun by a mysterious spider hiding within the great black void - the light from the faraway stars on either side of his ship streamed together in fine white threads.

Shielding his eyes from the bright glare emitting from the stars before him, Kroll dropped the black visor of his helmet down. Keeping his eyes fixed on his instruments and on his course, he readied two low explosive missiles set under his ship to fire.

Four minutes later, he was at the spot where he believed the Shuttle had stopped. Peering out from his curved windscreen, he saw only blackness and distant flecks of light from surrounding stars.

"The Shuttle must have drifted," he guessed incorrectly. Checking his life-form scanner again, he couldn't help but shout, "Atrocious piece of electronic garbage!" Throwing the scanner down onto his cockpit floor, he thought dubiously, "Now the scanner says that Tau's ship is nine hundred and sixty kilometres ahead of me! I'm better off using my wits to track the lad, rather than this piece of electronic refuse!"

Kroll turned his ship about, back to his original course. His eyes narrowed. Thinking hard about Tau, his background and his abilities, Kroll reasoned aloud. "Dominic Tau copes extremely well with monsters."

Astutely he then set a direct course at full speed - for Nefaria.

As Kroll's threatening black battleship rushed through Space, the clock on his ship's Console counted the seconds, and then the minutes before he reached Nefaria. One minute passed. Two. Three. Four. Five. Six, then seven. Before eight minutes time had elapsed, Kroll had the pleasure of viewing the beautiful planet Nefaria - ten times larger than the Earth - that he was fast approaching.

"Nefaria is a peacock twin of Saturn," he noted appreciatively. "Surrounded by three glistening azure rings and illuminated by two great crimson moons, this blue and purple marbled planet before me offers an inviting haven to any naïve Space traveller. Unsurpassed in superficial beauty, the planet is huge. The colours of the terrain are amazing - vibrant and warm."

Now that he was close to the exotic planet, Kroll slowed his vessel. Coldly he studied the pale blue rings of Nefaria, composed of millions of ice fragments, the size of icebergs.

"Those rings will do nicely as a hiding place," he said to himself.

Amongst those huge floating blocks of ice, he hid his Space Fighter. Glancing at the clock on his Flight Console, he read the time to be 1.08am. Eagerly waiting for his quarry to arrive, he primed his weapons. Then he stretched his shoulders, as, for the first time during this mission, he felt the aches and pains ensuing from his previous high-speed chase.

Picking up the discarded life-form scanner from the floor of his vessel, Kroll activated that device. Nervous that he may have guessed the fugitive's destination incorrectly, he scanned the vicinity for the two entities.

"Yes!" he exclaimed proudly. "There they are! Only three hundred kilometres out from Nefaria's rings and fast approaching!"

Armed with his victim's location he set his target seeking missiles to launch. Right on 1.10am, he fired. Curious, he crept his Space Fighter forward to the outer edge of the pale blue ring. Lifting his helmet visor, he ceremoniously watched the results of his attack.

"Confounded!" he shouted, staring disbelievingly out of his windscreen.

Where he hoped to see a disabled Shuttle, he now saw something completely different. Hurtling towards Nefaria, one hundred kilometres out from the icy rings, he saw a large golden and blue fireball. Amazingly, the fireball - a great fiery mass - rushed forward at an unbelievable speed. Suddenly, just as the fireball reached the massive ice fragments composing the rings, it mysteriously and astonishingly vanished.

"Oh no!" Kroll shouted. "Did I just destroy a Spaceship or what?"

He activated his life-form scanner, read the results and groaned. Sitting back, he leant his helmeted head against the headrest.

"I only launched two low explosive missiles," he reasoned. "But?" He shook his head in disbelief. "The two entities have gone!"

After several moments of contemplation, he hit on an idea.

"The fireball was heading towards the atmosphere of Nefaria," he thought to himself calmly. "I didn't actually see it explode. The fireball was probably just a surface fire, and the Shuttle is sure to be intact." Pausing, he deliberated. "Since Nefaria has an atmosphere that has plenty of oxygen, and gravity commensurate with that of the Earth, the pilot could have landed and be sitting down there on the surface, laughing at me, thinking he's escaped. Wrongly, he presumes I'm too much of a coward to fly down to Nefaria at sunup to look for him."

The time was 1.12 am. Captain Kroll turned his black battleship about and headed through the three ringlets of floating ice towards Nefaria. Emerging quickly out from those rings a minute later, his battleship descended rapidly into the striking colourful moonlit world of that prohibitive planet.

At a moderated speed, comparable to the velocity of an ancient jet plane, his ship streaked like a black arrow across Nefaria's violet night sky. Whistling about his wingtips as he cut through the oxygen rich atmosphere, the wind shrieked a howling warning.

Activating his night vision and heat seeking equipment, Kroll reduced altitude. Flying over the thousands of large black craters that pocketed this entire planet, he scanned the salty green crater pools searching for Dominic. Gouged into the sides of those black craters, inside a multitude of warm dry caves, thousands of Nefarids were awakening. Since human brain waves were painful to the cephalopods, they had already sensed the presence of Kroll. Holding helmeted heads upright, they gnashed their teeth angrily.

The orange Sun of Nefaria was beginning to rise on the horizon. Kroll, failing to sight a Spaceship in the craters below, soared his black battleship over the purple canyons. Shooting forward over the spectacular rocky terrain, his Space Fighter gleamed, glinted and glistened spectacularly in the light of the rising Sun. Heedless of the danger posed by thousands of active Nefarids, Kroll sped forward through the lightening sky.

Most of the canyons below the Fighter were over two kilometres deep and finding no sign of Dominic's ship from above, Kroll swooped his ship down, sending the sleek black bird darting inside one of the rocky fissures. Manoeuvring his vessel between the rugged walls of the purple canyon, he observed, through his ship's daytime monitors, the blue canyon floor far below.

"Nefaria is a right pretty place - if you like rugged," he thought soberly. "A forest of tall thin trees covered in blossom sweeps along the canyon floor like a silvery orange river. Large leafy purple ferns grow profusely at the base of those trees. Whilst trying to hide underneath the ferns, feeding on fallen seeds, rabbit-like creatures hop about happily."

Watching with amusement, he saw those furry fragile creatures nervously scurry underground into their protective deep burrows, as daylight suddenly broke.

"Obviously blue rabbits are a Nefarid delicacy," he laughed.

The temperature of the planet quickly rose. From a comfortable fifteen degrees Celsius, it was soon twenty, then thirty degrees. The canyons began to bake. Rising to a blistering fifty degrees Celsius, the atmosphere hung hazy and the air thinned.

Kroll had still not discovered the whereabouts of the ship he hoped to find. Searching in daylight should have been easier for him, but the strong Intelligence Officer felt unusually tired and unexpectedly drowsy. Closing his black visor against the vicious glare of the searing Nefarian Sun, he pushed his way further into the canyon. Although his cockpit was cool, he felt feverish.

Suddenly Kroll saw not one, but many of this planets' dominant species. Perturbed by their numbers, he instinctively punched at a red button hidden underneath his busy Flight Console. Instantly illuminating, that button - an emergency timer - began to blink, every two seconds.

"Just to be on the safe side, I've set the timer for my escape capsule," he reasoned. "I hardly expect to be benumbed by these pathetic Nefarids. It's just standard procedure."

Looking out from his windscreen, Kroll was now reluctant witness to the sight of a multitude of slimy-grey, three-metre long cephalopods, rushing out from their caves or from the crater pools, onto the purple cliffs. Uneasily he watched them.

"Either side of my ship, they are crawling and slithering - by the thousand - down the purple canyon walls," he noted. "I can barely see the rock face." Vexed and sickened by the sight of so many heinous monsters, Kroll's mouth was dry. "I had no idea what they were like en masse," he thought warily. "I'll find the Shuttle quick smart and get out of here."

Clinging onto the canyon walls, he observed that most of the revolting Nefarids had stopped to bask languidly in the hot Nefarian Sun. But some, he saw, stretched out their thick tentacles and dropped, parachute fashion - like giant macabre grey starfish - onto the blue canyon floor below. There they sat gruesomely devouring a tardy fluffy blue creature or two.

Nervously now, Kroll continued his search for Dominic's crashed vessel. Occasionally, on route, a ghastly Nefarid would glide into his flight path and collide with his ship. During these times, Kroll had to stomach the horrible sight of the white puckered face of the monster, then the gore, as after impact, the Nefarid was hurtled away in a nasty mishmash.

"Fine mess they are making of my ship," he grumbled.

After searching for Dominic's ship for some time and finding nothing, Kroll was feeling ill. Surrounded on both sides by Nefarids, stress was beginning to tell on his nerves and overheated, he took off his helmet. With the back of his hand, he wiped the sweat from his brow.

"I'll have to call it a day," he decided. "There's something wrong. My mind feels sluggish."

Suddenly Kroll saw the glint of metal far below him on the blue canyon floor and he sat back in his chair, relieved and pleased. Guessing he had just seen Dominic's disabled Spacecraft, he immediately reduced speed and altitude. Then he brought his Space Fighter around in a tight circle, intending to take a closer look.

Just as he did so, he heard a loud thud on the hull of his Spaceship. This was followed by an intense high-pitched predatory scream. Smacking straight into his windscreen and sticking there - obstructing his view - a large gliding Nefarid was now fiendishly smiling at him. Inside its open red mouth, a set of long jagged teeth gnashed grimly. Running out of its nose, a black tarry substance oozed over its chin.

Wincing as a series of sharp pains - transmitted from the monster - shot through his temples like burning hot needles, Kroll's mind began to numb. Staring blankly at the revolting face before him, he let his arms drop from his manual flight controls. His hands fell like dead weights by his sides. Automatically, the power cut out from his vessel. Unwittingly Kroll then let his fine black battleship fall gently downwards.

All seemed tranquil. Large purple leafy ferns brushed against the sides of the black battleship. A faint breeze rushing along the canyon floor rustled those ferns. The hot Nefarian Sun beat down on the silver trees lining that canyon. In the raw heat, the seeds on the trees baked.

Some twenty minutes had passed since Kroll's Space Fighter had fallen onto the sandy blue canyon floor. Sitting a prisoner in the dark cockpit of his TT Space Fighter, the large man was breathing lightly and quickly. With the exception of one small red glow, still blinking underneath his Flight Console housing, all of his instruments were dead. Inside his closed cabin, the temperature was well over fifty degrees Celsius.

"I bet the fiends all over my ship," Kroll mumbled unhappily to himself. "What horrible pestilence have I unleashed onto the Earth? I'm a despicable cad."

Spread out over his undamaged Space Fighter, ten Nefarids, bathing in the hot sun, offered up a chilling and repulsive picture. Their tentacles overlapped each other. Their long ghastly helmeted heads were upright. Exaggerating their elongated pointy chins, their mouths were open.

Suddenly suffering another predatory scream from the Nefarid stuck on his windscreen, Kroll felt the painful experience of burning hot needles searing through his brain. Several seconds later, he groaned.

"I've no idea how long I've been sitting here and my cockpit is getting hotter by the minute," he thought anxiously. "I'm trapped inside. Getting out isn't an option. Added to that, the benumbing experience is killing. My IQ is dropping away. I'm totally inert." Then he added ruefully. "Ten more minutes of this and I'll be a dead cad."

Fortunately, for Kroll, only another five minutes elapsed before the red light underneath his Flight Console - the emergency timer suddenly stopped blinking. Two green lights illuminated. The pilot eject program - activated when Kroll had punched the red button underneath his Flight Console - now initiated.

Humming quietly, the sound of the escape apparatus broke the previous silence of the dark hot cockpit. Abruptly Kroll's seat began to move. Mounted on tracks it slid through a newly opened access panel towards the stern of his vessel. Using a pneumatic system of elevation, the seat containing the large inert man rose up into the escape capsule at the rear of his ship.

"Thank technology," he thought gratefully.

Kroll's face was pale. His mouth was parched and the dark hair covering his head was soppen with sweat. He was safely inside the capsule however, and that small ship was initiating lift off.

Outside, clinging onto the escape capsule's hull, two large Nefarids had sensed his proximity. Aware that sustenance was near, they bent their grisly heads forward. Peering into the small triangular window of the escape vessel, they regarded him curiously.

Looking out dazedly, Kroll saw their evil hungry faces and winced at their ugliness.

"Torturing devils - I bet you two are getting ready to split my head open with your fiendish shrieks," he guessed.

An instant later, the pair screamed horribly. Pain pierced Kroll's brow and he lost consciousness.

Seconds later, the Control System of his small escape vessel thumped into life. Instigating a countdown procedure, the automatic pilot, in front of Kroll - in the tapering nose of his escape capsule - activated. The Nefarids outside heard several clicking and sliding noises as the capsule sealed, inclined, and rose slowly from the hull of its Mother ship. Comfortingly, the sound of rushing air filled the capsule and cool fresh oxygen flooded the cabin.

Following, the sound of an explosion reverberated through the deep quiet canyon. Golden flames burst out from the rear of the escape capsule. The engine roared into life. Now as the small vessel lifted off from the back of the battleship, a patch of purple ferns behind the Fighter burnt clear away.

Shooting out from the rocky purple canyon - with Kroll safely onboard - the escape vessel rose quickly, higher and higher, through the troposphere. Tenaciously, clinging on top of that small ship, two gruesome hitchhikers were peering through the window at the unconscious Kroll. Reacting to the dropping temperature outside, however, the two Nefarids quickly began to lose their deadly hold.

Up into the stratosphere the small escape capsule rose, then into the ionosphere, but the temperature had now increased and the two slimy Nefarids had regained their grip. Meanly and hungrily, they continued to peer fixedly through the capsule's small window.

Finally, when the escape capsule broached the final layer of atmosphere - the exosphere - the Nefarids totally lost their hold. Falling away from the hull of the capsule, they floated away, screaming with hatred.

Reaching Space, the capsule began to transmit an automatic distress message. Weaving its way easily amongst the ice fragments of Nefaria's pretty rings, it headed towards Kroll's home planet - Earth.

Captain Kroll was fortunate. Revived by the cool fresh cabin air and the decreased cabin temperature, he was beginning to waken. No longer in the painful grip of the Nefarids benumbing power, his mind was functioning normally. Therefore, apart from suffering a splitting headache, he was unaffected by his terrible ordeal.

Bleary eyed, but fully conscious, Kroll stared glumly at the escape capsule around him. Then he rubbed his face with his hands. Sitting up and frowning, he glanced at the instrument panel in front of him. With a strange sheepish expression, he leant forward and switched off his distress beacon. Resting his dishevelled head back against his chair, he was greatly peeved.

"Damn, I've lost my ship!" he thought to himself angrily. "This is *really* great! What sort of cock and bull story am I going to invent to explain how I mislaid a TT Space Fighter? That battleship was worth more than one man can earn in a hundred lifetimes. I just let her fall into the canyon. She's probably a write-off, smashed and crumpled against some canyon wall. Blast!"

Leaning his chin on his right hand, he further deliberated. "I can't tell a soul what really happened tonight. I'm certainly not fool enough to admit to anyone that I shot down TT's great grandson. I'm never going to let on that I flew down to Nefaria to search for him. In fact, I'm not going to own up that I was anywhere near Nefaria!"

Exhausted, he closed his eyes to rest. "I'll reactivate my distress beacon in a few hours," he decided. "Then someone in my squadron can come and tow me back to Earth. That should give me enough time to concoct a suitable excuse as to why I failed in my mission to collect Miss Doherty. *And* managed to lose a beautiful Space Fighter in the bargain."

The large man's thoughts were now quiet. His chest rose and fell. His fingers spread out. His hands rested on his knees. Scratched on the outside, his gold flight suit was soaked on the inside. His helmet was missing and the dark hair on his head was in strange disarray. He opened his brown eyes, looked up through the small triangular window of his escape capsule at the twinkling stars outside. Then he closed his eyes again.

"The official report will say what I want it to say," he mumbled tiredly. "I'm not going to be Captain of a cargo ship - ferrying wares between the five colonized planets."

Once again, he opened his eyes, but this time he reclined his chair and gazed at the twinkling stars outside for a very long time. In this vast black realm of brilliant stars, shining colourful planets, grey asteroids and blazing comets, his tiny escape capsule headed slowly back to Earth.

Suddenly he frowned. "Too bad I won't get to see the blue-eyed great grandson suffer his two week incarceration," he grumbled to himself quietly. "That would have been much more entertaining than killing him off - as I most probably have done."

He brooded for a while. Then he rummaged in an inside pocket of his flight suit. Retrieving a paper-thin chip, he thought sulkily, "I think I deserve some music after what I've been through tonight."

Sitting up, he placed that chip onto a tiny drawer on the dashboard in front of him. Then he pushed in the drawer. Instantly the small cabin of his vessel was alive with an orchestra of wonderful music. Kroll reclined back in his chair. While his tiny vessel coursed its way through the Milky Way Galaxy, he gazed at the black fabric of the Universe, twinkling with bright starlight, and he began to listen.

Chapter seventeen

"Shush, you two," said Celeste. "As a Library Assistant I have to advise you to speak quietly or leave this library."

Glinting through the long rectangular windows of the ultra modern library, built within a huge translucent Globe, the sun shone over many parallel bookcases packed full with volumes. Filling the library with warm light the sun played over the shining wooden floor. Flickering and dancing, it splashed bright patterns over the glossy white walls.

"But Celeste. Our Globe library is empty except for us," said Felicity.

Celeste's stern glance did not waver.

"No matter," said Eddie, standing beside Felicity. "We wouldn't want to step beyond bureaucratic boundaries, would we, Celeste. Heaven forbid. By the way, Celeste," he added, "your blue library uniform is quite appealing. Even if it is exactly the same frock that Felicity is wearing, except in a different colour."

While Celeste, seated behind the Librarian's desk at the front of the library glared at him, Eddie grabbed Felicity by the arm and dragged her through an aisle of books, past the screened off elevator area, then through another aisle. Stopping at the rear of the library in front of a large window, he immediately stared out at the Dome webbing covering their city.

Dwarfing towering oak trees, rivalling adjacent green Downs and reaching tentatively towards a blue cloudless sky, the colossal saucer-shaped London Dome rested compellingly within the heart of a lush Oak forest. Sharp and dazzling, summer sunbeams glistened off its translucent latticed structure. The imperceptible hum of an electrified barrier coursed through the square tubular webbing, forming the ground to ceiling roof of the massive Dome. Whilst a cool breeze, slightly impeded, blew through the apertures of that webbing, bringing to the occupants of the city the fragrance of the forest, mingled with another peculiar scent.

While Eddie stared through the window transfixed, Felicity adjusted her embroidered blouse and the sash on her white dome skirt. Preferring to face into the library, she avoided looking out of the Dome at the strange chaos outside.

"You cant deny that killing a whole bunch of evil aliens isn't exciting, Felicity," Eddie remarked.

Directing her gaze towards a gaggle of Nefarids - one hundred metres away - writhing horribly on the Dome's webbing, his face was earnest.

"In fact," he continued enthusiastically, whilst listening to the faint noise of gunfire outside their Dome, "our entrance to a future Earth couldn't have been better. Greeted by millions of infesting Nefarids has to be the best welcome home to a verdant green Earth that anyone could ever wish for. Isn't it fun? We get to see Nefarids throwing themselves against our electrified Dome webbing, twenty-four seven. And, if you're privileged enough to go flying in a Shuttle outside the Dome, as I am, you even get to see the slimy aliens rushing around ablaze or exploding spectacularly - after they've been shot, of course. Plus, don't let me forget, you get to admire the splendid Oak forest encircling our Dome." Eddie laughed. "We have nice fresh air to breathe - even if it does smell of smoked cephalopod - lots of plants and trees to admire, and we have the added bonus of monster hunting. Life couldn't be better!"

"You're horrible, Eddie. Even though the Nefarids are a pestilence to us, they are still living creatures. You have no sympathy."

"Sympathy for what?"

"For me, for starters. You know my head hurts and you're being a bully. Now let me go!"

"No, I won't."

Felicity purposefully avoided looking behind her at the electrocuted Nefarids stuck on the webbing. Instead, she looked across the high Globe Library towards the centre of their city - five kilometres away.

Nestled comfortably amongst spreading mature trees, the city boasted thousands of new Globe Homes. Underneath those homes, charming landscaped gardens with smooth green lawns, shrubs and flowers, gave the city a garden ambience. A normal part of everyday life in the new city, a variety of robots rolled through the paved tree-lined streets, attending to their duties. Whilst overhead at the top of the gigantic Dome webbing, a large central portal used for incoming and exiting aircraft and Spaceships, gave the city a futuristic appearance.

Finished admiring the city, Felicity glanced back at Eddie standing beside her. Indignantly pulling her arm free from the grasp of the adamant lad, she stated crossly.

"I'm Zeta's friend, Eddie. Everyone is feeling bad with thousands of Nefarids gathered outside our city. I want to talk to her and you're stopping me!"

"Give it up. Leave Zeta be," he advised in determined voice. "She's hiding out in this library for a reason."

"For what reason?" asked Felicity.

Trying to discourage his company, Felicity paced up and down between the aisles of books. Looking for Zeta, she stopped at the front of every white aisle, peering searchingly along its length.

Eddie stubbornly followed.

"Zeta obviously wants to be alone," he said.

"Well, you didn't cheer her up with all your gossip about two strangers you left behind, called Green and Faith. Did you? I'm sure she was keen to know they have a chat show together. Moreover, you could have been more tactful when you revealed that her Auntie Marjorie married a scientist colleague. Marjorie is her aunt, Eddie, not yours."

"Don't get too niggled because my brother and I enjoy roaming to see friends, family and acquaintances in past times. I do all right," said Eddie. "I tell it like it is." Pausing, he continued in a stern reproachful voice. "Tau has been missing for over two weeks. Why don't you girls get over it? Everyone else has."

"That's a lie, Eddie," retorted Felicity. "Everyone is shocked. Our beautiful new city is under siege by aliens. We've all got splitting headaches due to that never ending Nefarid shrieking - coming from outside. Moreover, we've lost our leader. Just because people aren't being vocal about the fact that Tau is missing, doesn't mean they are not suffering. Tau is more than just popular. He is…"

"Ahem," said the cool voice of Bermuda, interrupting.

Suddenly appearing phantom-like in front of Eddie, Bermuda's transparent image floated one metre above the polished library floor. Wearing a fine-linked gold chainmail vest over a brown ochre shirt, together with loose brown cotton trousers and sturdy brown boots, he stared at Eddie with hazel eyes narrowed. Only Bermuda's curly brown hair softened a face much hardened over the last two weeks.

"I remind you of your duty, Eddie," said Bermuda gruffly. "The roster has you and your brother down to start work in five minutes. Collect your silver chainmail vest and your Radar and Battle Grid Tablet from the armoury. Then report to Matthew Keating."

"Sure," Eddie replied. "Where are you roaming from, by the way?"

"I'm in the library elevator, coming up. I'll pass you on your way out."

When Bermuda's spectre disappeared, Eddie turned to leave the library. "Come along with me, Felicity," he said. "You are in good company. As from today I wear the uniform of the London Dome City Guards - until this crisis is over."

"Why should I spend any extra time with you?"

"Look. I know you can't think straight with the Nefarids benumbing your brain and all. Don't give me that face that it's not true. Zeta has probably already snuck off by now. In addition, you're safer with me than wandering around the city alone. Plus, Celeste is giving us the evil eye for disturbing the delightful ambiance of this fine quiet library."

"You can see her from here?"

"She's just roamed behind us. Let's go."

Glancing behind them, Eddie and Felicity nodded goodbye to Celeste's roaming spectre. Then they threaded their way back through the aisles of books towards the lift area. Moving behind the elevator's opaque partitions they disappeared out of sight.

Zeta, hiding behind one of the high shelving units at the front of the library, quite close to Celeste's station, watched them leave. Selecting a novel from the shelf before her and walking towards the Librarian's desk, she suddenly heard the sound of footsteps.

"Hello Bermuda," she said, turning to face the muscular youth standing behind her. "I'm glad to have this opportunity to speak to you."

Bermuda glanced at her fleetingly but did not respond.

"Aren't I speaking loud enough or are you just rude?" she asked.

"If you want an escort to go out of the city, you can forget it, Zeta," he responded curtly. "We're too busy. Once the Nefarid problem is solved you will be able to wander about freely."

"That's not what I was going to say," said Zeta. "I know you are trying to find Dominic. I...."

Suddenly Bermuda looked very tired. "Please, I'm very busy," he said tersely, glancing at Celeste seated at her desk - a few metres in front of Zeta. "I've just come back from attending our Town Meeting at the Civic Centre. Everyone over sixteen who was well enough and who wasn't outside of the Dome burning Nefarids, attended. Aristotle gave a speech. The news so far is not promising."

"What is the news?" Zeta asked.

"I recorded Aristotle's Address," replied Bermuda, pulling a small device out from his shirt pocket. "You can listen to the bits of news that are of interest to you. Now if you like."

Holding up a recorder the size of his thumb, he pressed a switch on the side of that apparatus. Zeta and Celeste then heard Aristotle's voice, clear and brisk throughout the library.

"Dear citizens of London, I am pleased to announce that Professor Doherty, the inventor of the Chronoguiser, and Sir Kepplar Holmes, an eminent scientist of high repute, have both decided to honour us by becoming part of our community," said Aristotle's optimistic recorded voice. "They are seated on the Stage with me to your left. Kepplar has also recently brought his mother and father from the past to join him. Professor and Mrs Holmes are both seated in the front row with us today. On behalf of all of us, I would like to extend to them a hearty welcome. Please, put your hands together for Professor Doherty, Kepplar Holmes and their friends and family!"

The three in the library all heard the sound of an audience clapping.

"We are all glad you're here, Zeta," said Bermuda, fast forwarding through the recording. "I'm rude to everyone right now. Sorry."

Stopping at a point of interest to Zeta and Celeste, he continued to play the recording. The three in the library heard Governor Aristotle's voice again, but this time his tone was sober.

"I would like to address the issue of the Nefarid scourge," he said sternly. "I will finish with the missing persons bulletin. As you are all aware, we encountered an alien pestilence on our arrival. Consequently, apart from our Knights and Guards, everyone has had to remain within the safety of our Dome City for the last two weeks. Naturally, we have postponed the release of the livestock and wildlife from the orbiting satellites."

"That means no eggs, milk or honey," interrupted Bermuda, pressing pause for an instant.

"We have instigated precautionary measures to safeguard our community," continued Aristotle. "Those precautionary measures are a relaxation of the previous fortnight's restrictions but must be strictly adhered to for your own safety. You may leave the city now, but only with an armed escort. You will organize this escort with either Francis Bermuda or Matthew Keating. If you wish to venture out of our Dome City for any reason, you must obtain a gate-pass or flight-pass from Inspector Maniscallo. All permits must be signed by the Inspector and counter-signed by either Keating or Bermuda."

"I expect you've been pestered to counter-sign, by half of the town already, Francis," interrupted Celeste sympathetically.

Bermuda fast-forwarded the recording again. Smiling at Celeste, he nodded. All three in the library continued to listen.

"On the subject of how to get rid of the alien pestilence," continued Aristotle. "We have a team of scientists, headed by Kepplar Holmes, formulating a plan to deal with the Nefarids. They are working on a device that they intend to install into the Communications Satellite orbiting our planet. The device they are constructing will transmit a signal, harmless to us and our flora and fauna, which should be unpleasant to the Nefarids. We will be able to use this device to generate a protective shield around our city. We are uncertain as to the completion date, so please be patient and adhere to the safety restrictions. Rest assured we will endure no food shortages for we have a large complement of robots which can be safely sent out - temporarily unsupervised - to harvest any desired produce."

Fast-forwarding the recording for the final time, Bermuda gravely listened to the end of Aristotle's speech.

"The last item on my agenda this afternoon is the missing persons bulletin," said the serious voice of their Governor. "Unfortunately, we have not received any further information as to the whereabouts of my great grandson, Dominic Tau, since I spoke to you last week. Our emissary, Francis Bermuda, scouting to the past, has information that Tau did not leave for the colonies with TT's Fleet. Bermuda has discovered that during the night of Tau's disappearance, an Intelligence Officer named Captain Kroll pursued a vessel through Space at high speed. We believe that vessel may have been Tau's ship, the *Heritage*. Kroll's TT Space Fighter was subsequently lost during that pursuit. That is all the information we have been able to uncover, Ladies and Gentlemen. I am sorry." Pausing, Aristotle concluded. "I would like to wrap up this meeting by adding that Francis Bermuda is continuing his search for Tau. We do however have to face the prospect that the founder of this fine city, my own flesh and blood, and dedicated guardian of you all, may be lost to us."

Switching off the recording, Bermuda addressed Zeta. "You've had your News Bulletin. See you."

Stepping past Zeta, he moved towards Celeste.

"No. Stop," said Zeta. Moving in front of him, she blocked his progress. "You've tried to roam to see Dominic and couldn't find him. Is that correct?"

"Haven't you got somewhere to go, Zeta?" Bermuda asked dismissively. "Where's Felicity? School starts at the London Dome Ladies Academy next week. Shouldn't you be at home prepping up on the syllabus?"

"Please, answer my question," Zeta entreated.

"You are insulting me, Zeta," he responded coldly. "Naturally I have tried to roam to find my friend. I failed. Alright."

"Have you considered teaming up with someone else?" Zeta suggested earnestly. "Teaming up works very well. When I wanted to roam to see my dad and I couldn't manage it alone, I teamed up with... someone else... another girl."

"Guys don't team up," responded Bermuda.

"What about me? Would you team up with me?" Zeta suggested. "We could try to find Dominic together. I might be able to help."

Met with a sudden reproachful stare from Bermuda, she added meekly, "Dominic could be hurt or stranded somewhere. I don't like to think he's suffering out there alone."

"Go on, Francis," interrupted Celeste, who all the while had been listening. "Let's give teaming up a try. There are three chairs back here behind my desk. We can put Zeta in the middle between us. Come on. You know roaming is all about feelings. Why should Tau be lost when he has people here who care?"

"Alright then," Bermuda conceded. "On one condition. You two are not to go blabbing to the whole of London about this. Agreed?"

Celeste smiled.

"Yes, we agree," replied Zeta softly.

Soon the three were seated in a row, three metres behind the Librarian's desk with their backs to the large library front window. Celeste held Zeta's right hand. Bermuda placed his larger hand over the top of both Celeste and Zeta's. All of their Roaming-Rings were beginning to glow.

"Wait a moment!" exclaimed Zeta. "I'm not ready! I have to call someone else to help!"

"Someone else!" Bermuda growled. "This is humiliating."

Celeste laughed. "No. She's sweet, Francis. Go on."

"OK, Zeta. Get your fourth person. If you wish," he conceded.

"Temerity, Temerity!" Zeta called out into the quiet library. "Please, I need you! Please come and help! I need to find Dominic!"

Surprised and astonished, both Bermuda and Celeste could only stare at what they now suddenly saw - floating before them.

"Oh my, you are a clever little thing, Zeta," said Celeste, breaking the silence of the tranquil library. "I've read about Salubes in books. This one is your friend. Does he mind that we're staring? Because I can't help it."

Never having had the opportunity of seeing a Salube before, both Bermuda and Celeste took time to study the alien creature. Marvelling at Temerity's silver gauzy cape-like wings, they watched him hovering gracefully before Zeta. They observed his human face, his white hair and his delicate alluring features. They wondered at his cream arms and limbs, his toddler size and the demure white shift that he wore. Then they looked amiably into the large thoughtful green eyes of Temerity.

"He's telepathic," said Celeste. "He's going to help us find Tau."

After Celeste spoke, Temerity landed gently on Zeta's lap. His wings dropped around his shoulders and holding up both of his little arms, he wrapped them around Zeta's neck.

"I am ready to roam now, Celeste, Bermuda," Zeta said quietly.

Both of the older teenagers glanced at Temerity. Silent, they nodded to Zeta.

Given the go ahead, Zeta reached her free hand up to her forehead. She activated her Roaming-Ring. Then she closed her eyes. Bathed in a soft glow as the nine amethyst crystals in her platinum band shone pink and violet, her face was thoughtful. Simultaneously the quartz crystals in Celeste's Roaming-Ring began to glow and the three amber stones in Bermuda's diadem sparked.

"Tau can never say I'm not a good friend," thought Bermuda. "This is embarrassing."

Suddenly, just as he commenced to roam, he was stunned for a second time, by the sight of a thin silvery ring of light emitting from Zeta's Roaming-Ring. Floating one metre above her head, the Ring glistened and sparkled, even in the bright sunlit library.

"Zeta's trying to link to Tau's psyche using a Guardian Ring," he considered thoughtfully.

Glancing down at the innocent face of the little Salube sitting on Zeta's lap, he closed his eyes. Concentrating on a mental image of his friend Tau, he fell asleep.

Zeta too, was thinking of Dominic. She thought of how he had liberated her father from the kidnappers and how he had promised to help her find her absent mum. She remembered the happy fun times they had spent together and then finally she thought of the anguish she had felt when Aristotle had suggested that Dominic was dead. With all these thoughts revolving around her mind, she fell into a determined emotive sleep.

Opening her eyes a split second later she was immediately puzzled. Finding she was no longer in the library, but in a strange alien dreamlike world, she guessed her roaming had failed.

"I've fallen asleep and I'm experiencing a vision," she thought pensively. "Through dreaming eyes, I can see the beautiful subterranean cavern on Nefaria. Grey rock walls glisten softly around me. Hazy blue sand, speckled with hundreds of tiny orange gems, lies tossed and uneven underfoot. Beyond that sand, in front of me, a low wall of blurry white boulders edges a blue half-moon pool. Before the pool, I can see a charming misty waterfall. Cascading in an enchanting silvery streams over the face of that waterfall, the water tumbles softly and slowly. Strangely," she thought. "I can't hear a sound. I should be hearing the tinkling and splashing of the water. But, just like in a dream, I can only see tunnelled images. All is quiet."

Quickly glancing to her left and right, Zeta was surprised to suddenly see the faint spectral images of Celeste and Bermuda. Standing on the blue sand, they were staring at the waterfall.

"Oh," thought Zeta optimistically. "Perhaps I have roamed after all, since they are here. Hello," she said quietly.

Unable to hear any sounds she was not surprised when she did not hear them reply. Unexpectedly however, the quiet was abruptly shattered. Calling to her, Zeta heard a familiar warm voice.

"Zeta!" the voice warned. "I'm about to give you a little fright."

Startled, Zeta suddenly saw - standing a metre before her - a vision of Dominic. Barefoot, he wore black trousers, rolled up to the knees, and a white frilled evening shirt. Tousled over his Roaming-Ring, his sandy hair fell onto his temples. Sparkling, his deep blue eyes were vibrant.

Running up to Dominic, a large animal - something like a cross between a wolf and a Panda bear - stopped. At the same time, Zeta saw the hazy images of both Celeste and Bermuda weirdly evaporate.

"No you don't," she heard the stern voice of Dominic say. Seeming to be speaking to her from very faraway, his voice was faint. "I'm not letting you disappear on me, Zeta. Not when you're so close."

Jumping in fright, Zeta suddenly gasped. Catching her and wrenching her from her dream-like state, she felt two strong hands on her shoulders. Pressed against her face, clear as day, she saw the dusty frills of Dominic's shirt.

No longer did everything about her seem like the disjointed fragments of a hopeful dream. She heard the sound of water as it cascaded over the falls. She smelt the fragrance of the sand and the sweet cavern air. Clearly now she saw the orange gem speckled sand underneath her feet.

Glancing to her left, she also noted the real, monstrous Panda-dog beside Dominic. Instinctively she tried to move away.

"He won't hurt you. He's trained," said Dominic cheerfully, keeping his hold on her.

Innocently the large black eyes of the animal stared up at Zeta.

"My roaming was successful," she now thought elatedly. "I've found Dominic! Hey!" she then exclaimed, finding her voice. "You can't catch hold of me, Dominic!"

"And why not?" his lilting tenor voice laughed in reply.

Pushing her back from him, but still holding her firmly by her shoulders, Dominic quickly studied the teenage girl before him. After which he exclaimed joyously, "Am I glad to see you!"

"Dominic, I'm a spiritual reflection. It's impossible for a mortal to hold a roaming entity."

Zeta's comment only served to make Dominic laugh even louder.

"You have to face the obvious, Miss." Letting go of her shoulders, he held one of her arms. "Look at your hair."

Pulling a lock of her hair forward, Zeta glanced quickly at the long strand. Then she looked at her pale arms and hands.

"Hey, my hair has changed colour to blonde! I'm not transparent! I'm solid! I'm guessing my face and eyes are pale as well. Dominic?"

"Yes," he answered solemnly. "It seems you've been keeping an important secret from me, Zeta," he continued, in a mock censuring tone. "You disappoint me. I thought we were good friends."

Zeta was embarrassed. "Secrets? No. I didn't know I could mirror, honestly. When I activated my Roaming-Ring, Temerity had his arms around my neck. Celeste and Bermuda were holding my right hand. That's probably why I was able to mirror. They helped me."

Dominic smiled. "Well just as well they did, Zeta, for I was growing a little impatient waiting for someone to find me. Now, you must help me. The first thing you need to know is *where I am*. Nefaria of course, you recognize this grotto. Tell Bermuda the time in Nefaria is the date on your calendar today, plus twelve thousand years. Ask him to come alone in the *Warrior* to assist me. I need a replacement gravity drive for the *Heritage*, an Assembly robot and a Matter Transfer Device. Plus food of course! For Angle as well as for myself. I've been living exclusively off the seeds that those blue creatures eat." He pulled a face and laughed.

"Dominic? Who's Angle?" asked Zeta, looking around the cavern for a third person.

"He's right in front of you, Miss. Angle is that big hairy brute of a guard dog standing beside me. He belongs to Bermuda."

With his free hand, Dominic scratched the beast affectionately behind the ears.

"How did you manage to end up marooned on Nefaria, twelve thousand years in the future?"

"At the precise moment the *Heritage* switched over to her time travel function and proceeded to time jump - to join you all - a TT Space Fighter fired on me," Dominic replied. "The explosion damaged my computer and my gravity drive. I ended up here. The *Heritage* is in the canyon, in front of the cavern entrance. She's a little singed, but otherwise undamaged. Working during the nights, when it's cool, I manage a few repairs." Dominic laughed. "Two months more of this vacation and I would have patched together a gravity drive of sufficient merit to get me back home."

Pausing, he smiled at Zeta warmly. "Enough about me. Tell me, Zeta. Did my followers all get away safely to their new home, three hundred years into the future? Are they happy? Did they like the Dome City I had built for them?"

Zeta, rather than answer, looked decidedly uncomfortable.

"What is it?" Dominic asked, puzzled by her expression.

Zeta took a deep breath. "The Earth is infested with millions of cannibal Nefarids, Dominic!" she exclaimed quickly. "They have surrounded us. They fry themselves on our electrified Dome constantly. The smell outside the Globe dwellings is horrible. Everyone has a headache."

Dominic's face relaxed. "Any other problems?" he asked calmly.

"No, apart from the plague of Nefarids, everything seems to be rather perfect. The Earth is lush and green. There is plenty of food for everyone. The air is sweet. London Dome City is absolutely beautiful." Then she added quickly, "Don't tell me you're not disappointed or worried?" She glanced at his face. "You're not even concerned!"

"OK. It mustn't be very nice living under siege, but I can't see why I should get bothered, Zeta. Nefarids are not a problem. Come. Sit down on the boulders in front of the pool with me. When you wake up you need to speak to a few people on my behalf. Once you relay the information I am about to tell you, the Nefarid crisis will soon cease."

Pulling her by her right arm, Dominic walked towards the blue pool. Plonking himself down on a shiny white boulder with Zeta sitting close beside him, he dangled his bare feet into the clear warm water. The charming waterfall before him splashed over the rocks and bubbled into the pool. Tinkling, that cascading liquid filled the glistening cavern with a soft musical score, a soothing sound that was broken only by the gentle snoring of Angle - asleep on the sand behind him.

"Did you know that the life span of a Nefarid is only six months, Zeta," Dominic began. "Whereas mine, and yours, is two hundred and sixty years."

"I won't live two hundred and sixty years!"

"Yes, you will, Zeta," he calmly insisted. "That is the life span of anyone who has the gift of mirroring. Mirroring is extremely beneficial for the physical being."

Zeta saw the pleased, sincere expression on Dominic's face and although shocked at this new revelation, decided to believe him.

"Well, Zeta, back to the vital topic of Nefarids," he continued pleasantly. "Nefarids lay eggs that hatch after a period of exactly fourteen days and the creatures reach maturity two months later. In an ocean environment, predatory fish would quickly eat most of the eggs, or tiny tasty young. The Nefarid population would be contained. Eventually they would become extinct, being rather moreish as they are. When the Nefarids breed on land or in lakes, however, there is nothing to prey on their young. They flourish, quickly proliferating to plague proportions."

"So if we can drive the Nefarids permanently into the sea we can get rid of them?" interrupted Zeta.

"My point exactly," replied Dominic steadily. "To eliminate the problem of the Nefarids, the creatures must all be driven into the oceans and kept there. Once in the sea, the fish will eat the Nefarid eggs and young, and the sharks will eat the adult Nefarids."

"You're smiling," remarked Zeta, glancing quickly at his face. "You have a plan. Tell me."

"Every sunrise and sunset since I've been stranded on Nefaria, I've gone out into the canyon and tested a gun I constructed. I call it a Cerebral Wave Gun. It is an altered version of a Hate Scanner that Kepplar Holmes invented. The gun amplifies human thought waves and transmits them. With me so far?"

"Yes, I understand."

"Well, I tested the gun out on the Nefarids, and you know what? It caused a stampede! The Nefarids scuttled away. They headed for the crater lakes at quite a pace. Then they disappeared underwater for the next twelve hours. The next time I tested the Cerebral Wave Gun I extended the range, and the power. Then I left the gun activated for twenty-four hours. The Nefarids didn't come out of the crater lakes until twelve hours after the gun was deactivated."

"So you think we can use the Cerebral Wave Gun to force the Nefarids into deep water, and keep them there?"

"I'm certain of it!" replied Dominic. "What I would like you to do, Zeta, is to speak to Aristotle, Kepplar Holmes and your father and pass on the information I have told you. Ask Kepplar to visit the Communications Satellite that is orbiting the Earth and wait there. Once Bermuda arrives here, I will use the Matter Transfer Device he brings, to send Kepplar a Cerebral Wave Gun. Using the Satellite Broadcasting System, Kepplar can transmit the gun's signal across the entire Earth. The Nefarids will be affected by the thought waves. They will stampede for the oceans. The deep water will provide their only relief from the Cerebral Wave Gun Broadcast. The city will be saved."

"What can we do if the monsters decide to hide in our rivers or lakes?"

"Most of our rivers and lakes are too shallow," replied Dominic reassuringly. "And those that are deep are usually too cold to encourage them to breed. Our Marine robots will be useful to track down any stragglers. As well, it is a good idea to tag the Nefarids. That way we will always know where they are, and how much they are breeding."

"Dominic? Whose thought waves are recorded on the Cerebral Wave Gun?"

In reply, the lad only grinned happily. Then he stared into the clear waters of the pool. When he turned to look back at Zeta, the expression in his eyes was both grateful and kind.

"Go on, wake up now Miss," he instructed her cheerfully. "Sorry you were worried about me, because I know you were."

Dominic let go of her arm.

"Bye," said Zeta. "I look forward to seeing you again... soon."

"Hey, I have a new psychic ability," he added at the last minute. "Something the Salubes taught me."

"What is it?"

Dominic grinned. "Wait and see. Adieu, Miss Zeta."

"You're going to leave me guessing?"

"Yes. Goodbye."

Zeta closed her eyes. She remembered her father's face and all of the faces of the people belonging in her world. Quickly fading from the beautiful glistening cavern, her mirror image vanished.

Once she was gone, Dominic immediately threw off his Roaming-Ring, tossing it onto the clean blue sand. Jumping up, he enthusiastically threw himself into the refreshing blue pool. Angle woke, growled happily and followed.

Swimming about exuberantly and splashing the monstrous black Panda-dog, Dominic shouted happily. Stopping for a moment, he treaded water. Then at the top of his voice he yelled out earnestly, "TT was wrong about Zeta! She will live as long as I will! She will live!"

Four hours later...

The Cerebral Wave Gun Broadcast had commenced. The atmosphere was taut, hectic and brutal. Fleeing from the Satellite Wave Gun transmission - on every land, on the blue, green planet of Earth - thousands of Nefarids stampeded for the sea.

Monstrous, the large helmeted heads of the stampeding aliens swayed from side to side as they dashed across the tree-covered Earth. On all ten thick tentacles, they sombrely lolloped along at a hectic pace. Drool spilled from their red gaping mouths. Oozing out from each pencil thin nose, a black tarry substance dripped over each pointed chin. Out of each of their lungs came a horrible screeching sound. The look in their eyes - reflective of their dedicated panic - was glazed.

Over most of the Earth, the stampedes were unsupervised. The Nefarids ran randomly through the trees - seeking the ocean.

One region, however, differed. For in this area, droving a stream of aliens - between London and Portsmouth - twenty cone-shaped black Shuttles soared through the clear blue sky. Their engines hummed out over a frantic location while their guns boomed out over the surrounding locale. Working both sides of an alien stream by laying down intermittent fire on the Nefarid flanks, these Spaceships contained the torrent of monsters, keeping the cephalopods moving quickly forward towards the coast.

"This stampede is spectacular!" shouted Eddie excitedly.

Seated before the Weapons System in Keating's lead Shuttle, he briefly paused to reflect on his assignment. Then he listened to the sound of the wind as it whooshed noisily around his vessel.

"In fact," he added earnestly. "I don't think I've ever had so much fun!"

After his enthusiastic outburst, he glanced at his brother seated to his left. Then he briefly gazed out of the viewing window at the terrain below. Underneath Keating's Shuttle, an undulating landscape of low hills and shallow valleys, bedecked in various hues of comforting green, stretched towards the sea. Pushing between the trees in that verdant landscape, he saw thousands of Nefarids. Destroying all the low-lying vegetation and trampling each other in their panicked flight, they filled the surrounding area with clouds of dust, hideous screams and a sickening odour.

"Just make sure you keep the Nefarids heading for the coast, Eddie - while you're enjoying yourself!" growled Keating, seated in his pilot's chair, beside the exuberant lad. "And give your happy shouting a rest, will you? I can hear an ant crawling on the ground and you're yelling in my ear."

Garrulous in his Keating's Shuttle, Eddie - gunman for the day - was too excited to listen. Using his Radar and Battle Grid Tablet, he fired on any aliens foolishly straying from the mainstream. While Ret, also dressed in black and silver, quietly filmed the stampede with their ship's external cameras.

"I give this Cerebral Wave Gun Broadcast ten marks out of ten," Eddie commented. "It is doing a dandy job of encouraging the Nefarids to race for the sea. But I'm concerned, Keating. Bermuda took the *Warrior* to help Tau over four hours ago and the two have not returned. I would have expected his Lordship to relish the chance to participate in this droving experience."

"We're managing fine, Eddie. Tau didn't use a Matter Transfer Device to send the gun to Kepplar because he wanted to join us."

Eddie frowned.

"Don't question Tau's motives," Keating continued. "His IQ is double yours. Just keep working your Tablet."

"Oh, I wondered why you wore a gold vest instead of a silver one, Keating. It's because you're so clever."

"I'm not saying you're stupid, Eddie," said Keating, suddenly increasing speed.

Breaking sharply away to his right and swooping down in a steep dive, Keating took their Shuttle close to the herd below. Chasing a gaggle of Nefarid strays, their vessel wove between clusters of Oaks. Eddie readied his Tablet to fire. Ret, seated next to Eddie, eagerly filmed the chase.

"There are at least one hundred Nefarids, trying to escape!" said Eddie quickly, in an excited raised voice. "I'll pick off the front-runners. The others will then rejoin the herd!"

Around their vessel, a checkerboard of green and golden English meadows warmed under the gaze of a benign sun. Mingled with these meadows, apple orchards flourished. Leaves rustled on the boughs of the small laden trees and the ripening red produce sent forth a heady bouquet into the surrounding rural locale. Into this picturesque scene, the gaggle of Nefarids ran.

Flying low to the ground, their Shuttle darted through the orchard - after the aliens. The creatures scattered. Within firing range, Eddie - with his hand working his Tablet - lined up the front-runners.

"Try not to singe too much of our flora when you burn these suckers," said Keating coldly.

"Get them quick, Eddie," urged Ret. "Every time we reduce altitude my head feels like a mallet hit me."

Without further prompting, Eddie instinctively fired. A jet of searing flames shot out from the guns on their Shuttle. Directed at the leading Nefarids, the golden stream of flames stretched forth like a striking snake, lashing out at the aliens. As quickly as it had emerged, the whip of flames vanished. Ten of the front-runners were instantly incinerated. Singed, the grass around their remains was black. Nearby wildflowers wilted. The remaining strays changed direction. Running for cover under a forest of nearby trees, they tried to escape.

"Eddie! Get the ones up front, quick as you can!" directed Keating, following in swift pursuit.

An instant later, five Nefarids, running amongst the tall Oaks dramatically exploded - without damaging the trees. Covering the ground, their slimy remains seeped into the soft fertile loam. With their leaders gone, the rest of the dissident pack turned back to the herd. Subsequently Keating increased altitude.

"Are you getting all this on film, Ret?" asked Eddie.

When Ret nodded, not taking his eyes from his task, Eddie continued eagerly. "This will be my favourite movie when you've finished, bro. I always fancied myself as a Star. Parsons is in Sebastian's Shuttle filming as well. I hope he gets all the impressive firing I'm doing - on camera."

"You're a conceited monkey," remarked Keating. "No wonder you ran your guts out during the Satellite Cup."

"Why, thank you," replied Eddie, grinning broadly. "You believe in giving praise where it's due."

"We are going to fly close to a water source soon, Eddie. We already have small robots out scouring the banks of the lakes and rivers destroying Nefarid eggs," Keating said quickly. "Don't hit any mechinoids. They are expensive."

Suddenly   Keating   was   speaking   into   their   Shuttle's Communications System. "Drive the herd South West!" he instructed the other nineteen Shuttle pilots. "There's a lake six kilometres up ahead that we have to skirt around!"

Attempting to push the Nefarid herd in a different direction meant that Keating was constantly reducing altitude and darting towards the horrible stream of Nefarids. Simultaneously Eddie was firing jets of searing flames into the pack of aliens, whilst occasionally exploding others.

"Noisy, stinking, messy beggars they are," Eddie remarked, noting how the innards of several of the creatures splashed horribly over the course bark of a cluster of large trees. "Did you know that they have red blood and they're all jellylike inside?"

"How could we not notice," said Keating. "After all your enthusiastic eliminations. Have you considered, Eddie," he continued, "that the aliens may be quiet in their own domain. We may disturb them as much as they disturb us. Before you become too attached to those guns, I would like to remind you that we are not here to exterminate these aliens. Nature will do that for us. Nefarids are more valuable to us as fish food than fly food."

"Yes, settle down, bro," added Ret. "We have two more hours of driving this alien herd forward, before we reach the coast. That gives you oodles of time for target practice."

"Thrills galore and it will be over soon," said Eddie, pulling a disgruntled face.

Ret laughed and Keating smiled.

The remaining hours herding the aliens did indeed pass very quickly, especially so for Eddie, in his role as gunman.

Reaching Portsmouth and the coast, Keating's Shuttle cruised in tandem with Sebastian's - above a Strand packed with Nefarids. Behind them, stretched out across the lush countryside, the other eighteen Shuttles were finishing up driving the dribbling rear of the herd to the beach. Continuing to push forward through the picturesque rolling farmland the remaining Nefarids were hunched over, parched, and their previous hasty gaits had slowed.

Proof of the alien's passage to the ocean, a dusty narrow road now swept from London Dome City to Portsmouth. On that road lay the remains of many aliens, trampled and crushed during the stampede. The road was grim. The small plants growing there, only four hours previously, had perished. Beside the long road, the charred or exploded remnants of diverging aliens dried in the afternoon sun.

In front of Keating's Shuttle however, the picture was more promising. Flat and wide, the pebbled beach below his cruising vessel reached out into a deep Harbour. Sheltering that Harbour, low green hills covered in trees cooled the atmosphere of a heated afternoon. At the mouth of that calm Harbour, the crests of the ocean waves spilled inward. The sea was cool and the incoming breeze was fresh.

Additions to this natural pleasant scene, crowds of jostling Nefarids, kicking up the sand, crushed together on the pebbled shore. Congested by the same species - trying to wade forward to deeper water - the shallows were dirty and foul smelling. Being filled as they were, with thousands of angry grey cephalopods.

"Look at all those grisly monsters, throwing themselves off the hilltops over yonder," said Eddie, watching the Nefarids from their

Shuttle's viewing window. "I wouldn't want any one of those beasties gliding down on me."

"The Nefarids dashing across the crowded beach below are more interesting," remarked Ret. "They actually stop to eat the weaker Nefarids, before they hurtle themselves into the sea. They are churning up the shallows horribly. The water is really frothy and red. Plus, they continue to trample each other mercilessly to death. Nasty species."

"I expect they'll be relieved to be free from the effects of the Cerebral Wave Gun Broadcast," said Keating. "I can see their white, puckered faces relax as soon as they hit the water. No doubt, they will dive down into the salty depths to congregate and rest."

"I'm hungry," said Ret.

"Don't think we've finished yet," said Keating, looking out over the blue Harbour before him. "We'll be seeing the Nefarids away until nightfall. You'll be waiting a while for a good supper. There's bread and water in the back of the ship, though. Compliments of the ladies."

"What's that about nightfall?" asked Eddie.

"Once this herd of Nefarids has been driven into the sea, we will group together and fly in a squadron to the next location," Keating said calmly. "I'm waiting to hear from Samuel and Winston who are piloting the two Shuttles at the rear of the herd. Once they signal me that the last few stragglers have spilled into the sea, the job here is finished. Then we move on."

"Do you want me to stop filming?" asked Ret.

"No," replied Keating. "Your filming is much appreciated, Ret. We will especially enjoy the next reel of footage you have for us."

"Why's that?"

Keating grinned. "You know how I mentioned fish food. Well, while we are waiting we are going to give our local sea-life a taste for Nefarid."

"No you don't!" said Ret quickly. "He's going to plunge our Shuttle into the sea, Eddie. There are thousands of monsters in there. They'll be all over us in an instant!"

"Is that right, Keating?" asked Eddie.

"It sure is," Keating replied. "Activate your Grid Tablet, Eddie!"

Not dissuaded by their reservations, Keating surged their vessel forward. While Sebastian's Shuttle waited on the coastline, he flew their ship over the beach. Plunging with a splash into the Harbour, he took their Shuttle down to the depths.

"Thrilling or terrifying, take your pick," remarked Ret. Staring out of their viewing window, he filmed at an ocean teeming with Nefarids.

"I'd say exciting," said Eddie, with his hand poised over his Grid Tablet, ready to fire.

A very different world from the realm above, the sea, churned up by the influx of Nefarids, pressed murky against their viewing window. Limited to only a few metres in front of them, their range of vision was poor. Water bubbled around their cone-like vessel as they descended. Sinking deeper and deeper, the sea swallowed them up.

Quiet, except for the sound of the engines gently purring, their cabin suddenly felt confined.

"Rejuvenated by the three centuries without fishing, the sea is alive with many familiar indigenous fish, as well as Nefarids," remarked Keating, peering through the murky water below them.

"Let me rephrase," said Eddie sarcastically. "Teeming with Nefarids, the salty water is practically opaque, cold, oppressive and forbidding. The indigenous fish are all fleeing for their lives to avoid the suckers of the hungry aliens. The atmosphere inside the Shuttle is rigid. And Ret, still filming, will break his camera if he holds it any tighter. Plus, my head is starting to pound painfully."

"It's the suspense of waiting to be attacked that's causing your headache," said Ret. Then he added quietly, "I'm only young. I don't want to die."

"Have you two anything positive to say?" asked Keating.

"Out of the thousands that are in the Harbour, most of the aliens are lying on the seabed resting. That's good," said Eddie. "Comparatively few are swimming through the water - reducing the probability of an attack on us." Eddie paused, then he suddenly seemed eager and excited. "I'm guessing, Keating, that you are not going to be sympathetic about the extermination of these alien ghouls while we are underwater. Have we plenty of ammunition?"

"More than enough," replied Keating, reducing their Shuttle's rate of descent. Heading towards a particularly large group of Nefarids lying in layers on the sandy seabed, he directed the brothers sternly. "Make sure you film this, Ret. I'm close enough to the seabed, Eddie. Fire at will!"

"Sensational," Eddie whispered to himself. Moving his hand quickly over the Tablet, he caused a tremor through a group of lounging Nefarids, as hundreds of small exploding projectiles rained down on them.

Instantly, the sea outside the submerged Shuttle's viewing window turned bright red. Bits of slain Nefarid floated with the current. Small hungry fish quickly fed on the tasty jelly-like remains. Equally hungry seabirds hovering above the surface were squawking with delight. All of the surviving Nefarids, previously lying on the seabed, swam frantically away.

"Wait for it!" said Keating.

"Wait for nothing," said Ret, keen to be away, airborne and safe. "Let's go, Keating. We've agitated the aliens beyond measure. They will attack us."

"Look, bro!" exclaimed Eddie, peering through their viewing window and grinning. "You have to keep filming. Scavengers with large fins and razor sharp teeth have just arrived. They are not big. But there are hundreds of them. I doubt very much that they even have brains to benumb."

Cruising through the scene of carnage, a multitude of sleek grey sharks had suddenly appeared. Armed with razor sharp serrated teeth, large jaws and even larger appetites, the sharks - excited by the bloody water - were in a feeding frenzy.

"Look at how they are tearing the Nefarids to shreds!" remarked Eddie. "They swim around their victims in a tight pack and all attack at once. Once they get a grip with those jaws of theirs, they shake their victims until they are ragged. You find them fascinating, Keating?"

"Yes," replied Keating, whilst watching hundreds of torn off Nefarid tentacles float through the sea.

"The Nefarids have met their match with our sharks," said Ret. "Problem solved, eh. Let's go. Now."

"Yes. That's our job done here," said Keating, noting the distinctive fin, the manoeuvrability and the high speed of one particularly large white attacking shark that was presently savaging a rather large Nefarid. "We move onto another coastline and repeat the exercise."

"Sounds good to me," said Ret.

Watching the white shark suddenly turn toward them, Keating moved away from the scene of carnage. Starting their ascent to the surface, their Shuttle moved through an ocean that gradually changed from pink to blue as their vessel quickly rose.

"We'll be clear of the Nefarids any minute now," said Ret.

"I enjoyed that," said Eddie. "Hunting is..."

Suddenly, abruptly terminating his discourse, he was jolted forward in his seat. The Shuttle rocked violently. Only minutes from breaching the surface of the sea, their vessel came to an abrupt stop. Simultaneously something crashed onto their Spaceship. Attacked by a group of Nefarids that fouled their engines and stopped their ascent, their Shuttle hung submerged beneath the waves, powerless and vulnerable. Clinging tenaciously onto their vessel, one of the fiends peered hungrily through their viewing window and seemed to grin.

"I will get rid of them," said Keating.

Just as he spoke, all of the attacking aliens began to scream. After hearing the horrible nerve racking shrieks - even through the medium of water - the occupants of the Shuttle all felt a searing pain stab at their temples.

Instantly benumbed by the close range screaming, Ret dropped his camera apparatus onto the floor. Eddie, in a stupor, let his Radar and Battle Grid Tablet slide off his lap. Keating frowned. Then he punched a button on his Flight Console.

Charged instantly with electricity, the outer plating of their Shuttle's hull was immediately aglow. The Nefarids screamed again, finding they were now clinging to what seemed to them to be a glowing black monster. Promptly letting go of the Shuttle, the singed Nefarids swam hastily away.

Now on automatic pilot with its engines clear, the Shuttle continued its ascent through the ocean. Rising quickly, the vessel broke the surface of the sea. Flying high in the air, it hovered over the Harbour.

"We're fine, Sebastian," said Keating, already recovered and speaking to the other nearby Shuttle through his Communication System. "Samuel and Winston have given the all clear. Good. Our next heading is the coast of America. Follow me in two ticks." Ending the communication, he glanced at the Bourne brothers, now also recovered.

"We predicted we would be attacked, Ret," Keating explained. "The hulls of all of our Shuttles can be instantly electrified - a necessary modification introduced just before this mission. However," he added. "That wasn't a pleasant experience. We won't hang around after our next underwater excursion shooting Nefarids."

"What's that I heard you say about shooting Nefarids *and* America?" said Eddie.

Keating grinned. "What about you, Ret? Any objections to more of the same."

"I'm good," said Ret.

Smiling, Keating turned his Shuttle towards the ocean. Now, with the rest of his droving team behind him, he headed his vessel at high velocity towards the coast of a distant land.

"Let's go to the coast of California first," suggested Eddie.

High over the waters of the Harbour they flew. Their engines hummed. The wind whistled softly around their Spaceship. Excited, noisy, feeding seagulls, flying in flocks below them, hovered over the gentle waves. Underneath those waves, darkened by the forms of thousands of swimming Nefarids, the Harbour water was shadowy. Quickly flying out through the mouth of the Harbour, the sea glistened underneath their high soaring vessel. Waves rolled green. Stretching away a distance before them, the ocean kissed the horizon.

Chapter eighteen

Ruffling his dark blonde hair, a wisp of wind caught the wing of the Space Fighter on which he stood, whooshed around that vessel, then whistled away. Squinting his large deep blue eyes against the glare of the bright sunshine he admired the beach flora, the trumpet shaped pink blooms on the sheer cliff-face, the flowering cushions of sea grass and the small white flowers blossoming on the wavy sea kale. Freshwater Bay was tranquil and the heat of the sultry afternoon brought a calm ambience to a previously chaotic setting.

Glancing towards Parsons and a group of five females - standing together before a chequered rug, twenty metres away - he jumped down from the Fighter's wing. Striding confidently across the sand, he stopped when he reached them. He nodded to Parsons. Bowing courteously, he addressed the females.

"Good afternoon, ladies. Is anyone hurt?"

Pausing, he studied their silent faces.

"What about you, Miss?" he asked, glancing at Zeta. "Tough day?"

"I'm OK," Zeta said thoughtfully.

"We're fine," the others finally replied.

"Why do you want to see us, Tau?" asked Tesla.

"I would like to check your gate-pass. It has been barely a fortnight since the Nefarid stampede. I hardly think you were authorized to fly to the coast."

"Oh, my gate-pass!" said Tesla, quickly stepping forward. "I left it in my shop. Sorry. You don't really need to check it, do you, Tau?"

Taking Dominic by the arm and with a definitely sheepish expression, she walked with him over the sand towards the water's edge. While they faced the Bay and Dominic's underwater childhood home, Tesla ventured quietly in an embarrassed tone of voice. "About my gate-pass, Tau, I..." Then her voice trailed off. She dropped his arm, her face flushed and she stepped slightly away.

Dominic looked at her questioningly. "I was not allowed to leave the Dome without an armed guard. I was foolish. I put my companions in danger. Is that what you were about to say?" he chastised sternly.

"So, you know everything. Please, don't blame the other girls. It was all my doing."

Dominic listened to the waves tumbling onto the shoreline. Letting the sea wash over the toes of his boots, he looked out over the beautiful Bay.

"Will I be punished, Tau?"

"We will drop the subject of the gate-pass, Tesla, and not speak of it again."

Tesla's manner relaxed. Her face brightened. Instantly she reverted to her normal haughty self.

"Do you like my clothes, Tau?" she asked cheekily.

Dominic glanced behind him towards Zeta. Smiling at her, his blue eyes twinkled warmly. Turning back to Tesla, he took time to observe the black vest top and the short pink skirt that Tesla wore.

"Those ancient clothes now exposing your sensitive skin to the vicious rays of the sun, my dear, only pale in significance to your own fashionable creations," he replied.

Tesla beamed, then looked contrite. "I've caused you some trouble today. I'm sorry. I also need to apologise for the behaviour of Miles Sturgeon on the night of my Ball."

"He went to the colonies with TT," said Dominic. "Do you miss him?"

"Yes, I do."

"I will ask TT to relax visiting restrictions so that the colonists can roam to our city and we can roam to the Transport Ships. Then you and Miles can visit each other."

"You'd do that?"

"Yes. I will also extend an invitation to any colonists whose future family tree will not be affected by the change in time, to join us on Earth."

"Will Miles be extended an invitation?" asked Tesla hopefully. "Have you checked his future family tree?

"Miles will be invited."

"Oh! How simply marvellous!" exclaimed Tesla, moving back to join the others.

"No. I want you to return to London. Now," Dominic said sternly. "Take Brooklyn with you."

Obeying his instructions and several minutes later, Tesla stood before the aircraft controls of her Globe shop. Standing beside her was Brooklyn. At Brooklyn's feet sat the Clode, Pinky.

"What?" asked Tesla, noting Brooklyn's sudden reproachful stare.

"Why did you wear Zeta's clothes?" asked Brooklyn.

"I thought I should," Tesla replied sheepishly. "Call it premonition if you like."

"Well, I've had a smashing day, Tesla!" congratulated Brooklyn. "But make sure to tell me if you have any more premonitions. Being your best friend I need to be kept in the know."

Tesla released the clamps holding her shop secure to the beachfront Globe column. Once the floating shop was level with the cliff top, she activated the globe propeller and *Tesla's House of Gown* flew towards London.

"I am roaming now," she advised Brooklyn. "I'm going to spread the word that Tau is coming home. Once they hear, everyone will want to celebrate."

When Brooklyn nodded agreement, Tesla smiled. Stepping away from the window and the aircraft controls, she activated her Roaming-Ring. She closed her eyes and roamed.

Earlier that day…

Three hours earlier, bathed in the warmth of the mid-morning sun, two stocky men blissfully filled their lungs with fresh scented air. Squinting their eyes against the bright daylight, beaming down on them from a blue cloudless sky, their keen eyes swept their general location.

Wearing the garb of the Dome City Security Group of a grey open neck short-sleeved shirt and grey trousers, both these men were cool and relaxed of demeanour on this pleasant hot day. Crowned with their slim Roaming-Rings they took it in turns to meander casually back and forth across the red paved road that stretched from inside the closed gates of their London Dome City towards their City Plaza.

While one man marched, the other smaller man - seated in the Gatekeeper's Sentry Box, inside and to the right of the Dome Gates - leisurely gazed out over the black tarmac road outside of their Dome. With little to do - unless called upon to open the gates when a laden robotic market trolley approached and sought access - he drank in the vista of the encircling Oak forest, a mere twenty metres away.

"Hey, come here!" shouted the larger man.

"What?" the smaller chap responded. Leaving his Sentry Box, he strolled towards his colleague.

"When will the Satellite's be emptied? The birds have been freed but I'm keen for the farmyard animals to be released. I want to taste coffee again - made from full cream milk."

"Probably when Tau returns."

"He's not back yet?"

"No."

"The sooner we see his face, the better then," came the measured response. The larger man paused. Glancing away from his colleague, he stared a distance along the red paved road issuing from the Town Centre. "Look over yonder at the bunch of teenage girls coming towards us," he said. "Two of them I recognize. One is the Gosh girl. The other runs *Brooklyn's Bakery* in Town. I've heard she gives complementary samples as part of her advertising campaign. Correct me if I'm mistaken, but I can already smell the aroma of freshly baked goods."

"You're not mistaken," replied the smaller man. "Bon appetit."

Curiously, the gatekeepers watched as the approaching four girls, dressed in dome-shaped gowns of light patterned fabrics, crossed the bridge over the River Thames. Three of the young ladies carried baskets and both men could now positively smell the aroma of freshly baked scones.

Unusually, trailing the girls, the men also took note of an empty silver market trolley that bounced along the red paved road towards the gates. They saw its Robotic Driver Head swivelling from side to side as the automated machine drove slowly forward. When the girls reached the gates and stopped, the trolley, travelling two metres behind, also abruptly halted.

"Good morning!" Tesla said cheerfully. "I am Miss Gosh."

Exuding her most charming manner, she smiled beguilingly. As she stepped forward in greeting, the gatekeepers could see gingerbread, scones and raspberry tartlets arranged tantalizing within the basket she carried.

Handing the largest man the collection of baked goods, Tesla continued generously, "These few samples are from my friend, Brooklyn. If you like the fare, please pay a visit to *Brooklyn's Bakery* in our City Plaza. I guarantee you will enjoy all the Bakery has to offer!"

Eager to taste the food, the men quickly walked across to their Sentry Box. Putting the basket on the counter, they immediately began sampling the scrumptious contents.

Leaving Brooklyn, Felicity and Zeta standing by the gates, Tesla - after retrieving her gate-pass from her skirt pocket - quickly followed. While the largest man was munching into one of the delicious scones, Tesla handed him her crumpled Pass.

Casually, the man glanced at the two signatures. One signature belonged to Inspector Maniscallo. The other was Matthew Keatings.

"So, you want to go out into the forest, Miss Gosh?" he asked - between mouthfuls of scone.

"Yes," she replied. "I want to go to my shop. I have valuable stock that I wish to collect. My shop is located one half a kilometre south of our Dome - near my parents mansion."

"I know where the Gosh Mansion is," he said. "Where is your armed escort?"

Tesla patted her hair, worn up and held in place by pale pink and white slides. "There they are!" she suddenly exclaimed, pointing up at a black Shuttle hovering high above the Dome outside.

"You've no ground escort," the smaller man said, shoving two raspberry tartlets into his mouth.

"We'll be in clear sight in the middle of the road for most of our short journey," said Tesla. "Once we turn right at the 'T' junction up ahead, it is only a very short way to my dress shop. We'll stop at the shop and spend an hour or two there, then we'll come back."

"The escort are going to watch you from the Shuttle?" the largest man asked.

"Yes, I expect so."

"Very well," he said, handing her back her gate-pass. Finishing off his last piece of gingerbread, he waved Tesla away.

"Come on! We have the go ahead!" Tesla called, walking towards the trolley. Gathering up her pale pink gown, she seated herself on the trolley tray. When the others approached, she took the second basket - a hamper that Brooklyn carried - and placed it on the tray. Then she held Zeta's pet basket containing the Clodes, To-do and Pinky, while Zeta climbed aboard. "Don't tear your dress climbing up, Zeta," Tesla warned, admiring the pink frock, edged with lace, which Zeta wore. "That particular gown has to be one of my finest designs."

Several moments after receiving the go ahead from the gatekeepers, the four girls, seated in a row, were ready to leave. Tesla

took a commanding position at the front of the trolley, closest to the
Robotic Driver Head. Next to her was Brooklyn. Felicity and Zeta,
holding the puppies, sat towards the rear.

"Proceed, market trolley 017," Tesla commanded.

Passing out from the safety of the Dome the girls travelled into the
shadowy forest. All around them, small red-breasted robins, grey of
body, competed in song with beautiful bronze, high perching
chaffinches. Tiny willow warblers and Tree sparrows fluttered from
tree branch to branch, whilst larger violet wood pigeons cooed
contentedly within lush thickets.

After glancing at this delightful feathery orchestra - performing in
their Earthy woodland home - all the girls looked up to admire the
heavenly mantle overhead. Flowing calmly, like a pale blue river with
occasional rippling white clouds, the moving sky was serene.

"I haven't spent the last seventeen years living in a Globe Home
and walking within airtight Tubular Walkways, as the others have,"
thought Zeta. "But, even I can't help but appreciate the freedom of
being able to travel on an open vehicle under such a clear blue sky."

Once the initial novelty of being outside the Dome was over,
however, both Zeta and Felicity realized that the Shuttle they had
believed to be their escort, was no longer in sight.

"Tesla, why can't I see the Shuttle? Who is the pilot and why isn't
he keeping an eye on us?" asked Felicity, the first of the girls to voice
her concerns. "We should stop the trolley immediately, turn around
and go back to the Dome."

"We're not going to stop, Felicity," replied Tesla. "As you can see,
we are already well on our way."

"But the Shuttle?" questioned Felicity.

"You can't see the Shuttle because I presume the pilot is scouting
the area. And I'm sorry, but I don't know who the pilot is."

Appalled by Tesla's answer, Felicity stared into the deep forest.
Suddenly she tensed. Having just spotted a glint of bronze between
the distant trees, she conscientiously peered forward.

"There's a Psychic Knight staring at Zeta," she wondered. "From
this far away, I can't see his face clearly. Unusually, on this hot day,
he's wearing bronze Knight's Raiment."

She turned to tell Zeta, but the Knight was gone. Nervously she
smoothed her indigo and white striped skirt and retied the neck-bow
on her pretty, white blouse. Cupping her hands together in her lap,
she spoke again.

"Tesla, we should stop!" she reiterated, while Zeta and Brooklyn listened soberly. "For our own safety. There may be unknown dangers in the forest. I thought I just saw a man hiding in the trees."

"What sort of man?"

"A Psychic Knight."

"Nonsense!" retorted Tesla, unconcerned. "All of our Knights are far to busy to waste their time spying on us from the forest. As for the possibility of Nefarids stalking us, I overheard Governor Aristotle say that there are no large alien beasties still existing in England. Our men, assisted by robots, are still collecting Nefarid eggs of course. Nefarid hatchlings are only the size of mice. They bite, but they can't paralyse our minds, so they can't eat us."

"Great, the prospect of being bitten by hundreds of mice-sized walking squids makes me feel so much better than the possibility of being murdered by a strange man," said Felicity, still pondering on her brief glimpse of the Psychic Knight.

"We only accompanied you out here to keep you safe, Tesla," said Zeta, now speaking up. "You should listen to Felicity."

"Do you think I would have ventured into the forest if I thought I was going to get hurt," retorted Tesla. "You and Felicity insisted on coming with me. You can always get off the trolley now and walk back to the Dome, if you like. I'll stop now and let you off. Yes?" Glancing at their worried faces, she frowned. "That's a no, then. The two of you are so conservative. Honestly."

Bumping along the shadowy road, the slow turning wheels of their market trolley rolled noisily over the tarmac. The girls sat comfortably, their legs dangling over the side. No one said anything for a while. Rather, they admired the cool green forest. Noting the wildflowers growing in the clearings, they appreciatively listened to the songs of the birds.

"Even though I'm not keen to be in this forest, I am glad to be on Earth," said Brooklyn, breaking the silence.

"Beats spending five years cooped up in a Transport Ship," agreed Felicity. "How horrid!"

"Did you all know that that the five colonies can be reached in a TT Space Fighter in less than three hours," Tesla divulged, in her most knowledgeable tone of voice. "A Chronoguiser is so fast that it can reach the colonies in one hundred and forty five seconds. That's two and a half minutes!"

Interested in this discussion about how far away in travelling time the colonies actually were, Zeta listened attentively. "I remember what a thirty second ride in a Chronoguiser felt like," she thought prudently. "I fainted."

"Oh, how cruel!" exclaimed Felicity. "TT is making everyone spend five years travelling with him in his Transport Fleet when they could get to the colonies in three hours."

"I don't believe you are right about the speed of the TT Space Fighters or the Chronoguisers, Tesla," Brooklyn interjected. Looking unexpectedly troubled, she stared thoughtfully out at a large bed of red poppies growing alongside the road. "TT wouldn't have behaved so horribly," she then continued. "Five years of life wasted travelling against a possible three hours is downright unethical. TT wouldn't have made people spend so long travelling in Outer Space when they didn't have to."

Tesla was irritated. "I didn't say they didn't have to. I just said there was a faster way. Look, I've already done the calculations to explain why the decision was made to travel in the TT Space Transports, rather than in the Space Fighters. It wasn't feasible to transport one million people to the colonies in the hundred Space Fighters available. A Fighter can only take two passengers at a time. With a round trip taking approximately six hours, each Fighter would require thirty thousand flight hours to complete the job. That's nearly three and a half years flying time per ship!"

When Brooklyn was not impressed with Tesla's calculations, she added snappily, "You should have bought your gown from me, Brooklyn. Orange and peach are not your colours, my dear. Neither is math your subject!" Then she glowered at the row of girls with her, seated on the moving trolley.

"How do you know these things, Tesla?" asked Felicity, unperturbed by Tesla's stare.

"Tau told me."

"Sure he did," said Felicity.

Tesla's alert blue eyes flashed angrily and her face flushed. Pretending to ignore Felicity's remark, she watched their trolley pass under a low hanging bough. Then she spoke again, directing her conversation to Zeta.

"Zeta?" Tesla asked coldly. "Your father is a Professor of Mathematics and Physics. You then are obviously skilled at your math. *Do you* disagree with my calculations? Or do you consider this discussion too banal to waste your precious thoughts on?" Pausing for a second, she continued bitingly. "Obviously Tau doesn't discuss physics when he converses with *you*. Is that why you are so quiet? Are you jealous that he speaks to me? Or are you sulking because it has been two weeks since you contacted him on Nefaria and he still hasn't shown his face."

Zeta petted To-do and Pinky seated in the basket on her lap. Not wanting to be drawn into an argument, she remained silent, giving Tesla opportunity to continue acidly.

"Tau is avoiding you Zeta. He had to hide all the way out there in Nefaria, twelve thousand years in the future to get away from you. And you still managed to find him!"

When Brooklyn tittered and Zeta blushed, Tesla turned away from them all and stared out over the road ahead. Turning back a little while later, she began to converse with Brooklyn on lighter subjects.

When the trolley reached the 'T' junction, it turned right into a lane. Travelling past the Gosh Mansion, it stopped at *Tesla's House of Gown* - a pink, two-storey shop, built inside a Globe, atop a thin white column.

Looking up at the Display window on the first level of the shop, Zeta and Felicity observed three dressed animated mannequins, going through a sequence of poses. Above that display, two smaller upper floor windows provided a glimpse of the shop's aircraft control area.

Jumping down from the trolley, the four girls strolled towards the shop's elevator entrance, along an orange cobbled path - set between borders of blue forget-me-nots. Tesla took the lead. Walking ahead of the others and carrying the hamper, she was puzzled to detect several circular nests of strange looking white oval stones, positioned haphazardly on either side of the column supporting her shop.

"I'm doubtful whether they are stones," she considered, touching the shop elevator and deactivating the lock. "I'll hurry everyone inside - just in case the stones are eggs containing baby monsters!"

Sealed for over three hundred years, the elevator door slid open.

"As you can see, the lower floor is exclusively devoted to the presentation of beautiful gowns," Tesla boasted, standing in the centre of her shop, moments later. "Displayed on racks in the front section are Day and Evening Wear. Ball Gowns and Leisure Wear are in the rear section. The winding silver staircase in the front corner to your right accesses my workroom and is out of bounds. Please feel free to browse."

Leaving he companions to admire the gowns, Tesla placed the hamper on her shop counter, near the stairs. After removing a small package of Zeta's borrowed clothes from the bottom of that basket, she slyly hid the clothes in one of the counter drawers. Mentioning that she wished to check her workroom, she ran up the winding silver stairs.

Tesla's private sanctum on the second floor was a most interesting level, for her Globe, as well as being a shop, was also an airship. Silver aircraft controls - comprised of an array of dials, lights, buttons and gauges - were mounted on a moulded bench underneath the shop front windows. Devoted to dress design and manufacture, the rest of the floor space was minimal. Packed into floor to ceiling shelves - wound on long spools - many rolls of coloured fabric gave the area an industrious aura. A large silver cutting table took centre place in the room. Before the table was one chair.

"Time to check out those weird white stones outside my shop," Tesla thought decisively.

Moving towards the table, she sat down on the chair. Activating her Roaming-Ring with a trigger word, she closed her eyes and slept.

Simultaneously Tesla's spectral image appeared gliding outside her shop. Transparent, her roaming self melted into the fragrant air around her. Forget-me nots tickled the soles of her floating feet. Rushing along the cobbled path to her shop, a faint breeze blew through her ghostly form. Filtering through the surrounding forest, the sun shone soft light beams onto her inquisitive face.

"Curiously, I feel ill at ease," she thought warily. "After dismissing Felicity's sighting of a stranger, I now think she may have been wise to be worried." Glancing around searchingly Tesla peered out at the lane before her, then into the forest behind her. "Is anyone there?" she called. She waited. "No reply," she thought. "Everything looks normal. My senses must be deceiving me."

Tesla, however, was right to be concerned.

Concealed in the depths of the forest was a dangerous stranger. With narrowed eyes, and activated Roaming-Ring, he stood staring at Tesla. Seriously observing the teenage girl, he watched her as she picked up a stick fallen from a nearby tree. His eyes followed her while she moved towards a circular nest of oval stones, heaped against her shop column. Using her stick, he saw her roll over one of those stones.

"Oh!" she exclaimed in surprise. Moving back suddenly, she dropped the stick. "The egg I touched is breaking open. Did I just call it an egg? Oh dear!"

Tesla floated a little higher. Watching the egg crack apart, her racing heartbeats counted the seconds until the creature hatched. Breaking out from the stone-like egg, a Nefarid with a small helmeted head and ten slimy wiggly legs opened its mouth and hissed. Without hesitation, it sprang a metre into the air. It snapped its teeth. It leapt about madly on its ten upright tentacles. Jumping at Tesla repeatedly, it tried to bite her transparent feet. Failing, it let forth a high-pitched shriek.

Prudently, in response to this sudden belligerent attack, Tesla's spectral image rose higher in the air. Frightened, but fascinated, she inspected the other nearby nests of Nefarid eggs.

"The hundreds of eggs surrounding my shop are all beginning to hatch," she concluded. "Am I to soon to reign over a praising army of minions?" Pausing for a moment, Tesla seriously considered the situation. "There may be more nests further out in the forest? If there are more and those eggs are also hatching, I certainly can't take Brooklyn and the other two girls back home the way we came." Deciding to survey the area, her ghostly image floated into the forest backing her shop.

Seeing Tesla's spectral image gliding towards him, the Knight ran for thicker cover. Concealed in the undergrowth, he crouched down. Although his large brown eyes remained open, he slept. Appearing in Tesla's upstairs workroom, a split second later, his transparent bronze chainmail glowed warm around his translucent form. Stopping before the bench housing the Globe's aircraft controls, he glanced at Tesla sleeping. Squatting down to avoid detection from outside, he swiftly opened the Navigation System panel. After quickly tampering with that system, his ghostly image vanished.

A short time later, Tesla's floating spectre returned from the depths of the forest. She stopped before the elevator doors. Glancing at the trolley waiting a short distance away, her face was glum.

"The eggs in the forest are also hatching. Every time a Nefarid hatches, it runs straight for me, snaps its jaws hungrily and tries to jump up to where my ghostly feet dangle. I've seen enough!" she decided. Her spectral image vanished from outside her Globe shop. Simultaneously she awoke, pale and shaking.

Panicked, she ran towards the aircraft controls. Pulling down a lever, she released the column clamps holding her buoyant Globe stationary. When the Globe floated above the treetops, she pressed the ignition switch to start the engine. Gratefully she listened to the sound of the rear propeller whirring.

"We'll be back in London Dome City in five minutes," she reassured herself. However, after glancing through the windows, she groaned. Instead of heading forward, she watched while her shop turned 180 degrees about.

Hurriedly Tesla tried to reset her course for the Dome, but the helm of her floating Globe did not respond. "After being out of operation for over three hundred years, I expect my Navigation System has malfunctioned," she surmised incorrectly. Glancing through the windows, she watched her shop float through the sky. "What am I going to tell the girls? Rather than head for our Dome, my airborne shop is now heading for the coast. I bet those two gatekeepers are snoozing in the sun after feasting. They probably haven't noticed our departure. So no help there."

As she had guessed, the dozing gatekeepers had indeed failed to see her mobile Globe shop rise from the trees like a high-soaring bubble. *Tesla's house of Gown* had floated away without either of them being any the wiser.

"Tesla!" shouted Felicity, running up the winding staircase. "What are you doing? You didn't say anything about taking us on a journey!" Behind her stood Zeta and Brooklyn.

"Excuse me! This is my private sanctum. My workroom," said Tesla. "And you ladies have not been invited. However," she continued, "I will let you in on my surprise now. Being that it is such a grand day, I thought we should all make the most of it, and take a sightseeing excursion to the coast."

Clearing the stairs, the three surrounded Tesla. From the windows, they could see that they were sailing over green forests, intermittent Heathland and blue rivers.

Zeta sternly confronted Tesla. "We can't go to the coast, Tesla!" she warned. "The coastal waters are plagued by Nefarids."

"I am flying this Globe shop to the beach front of Freshwater Bay, Zeta," Tesla responded haughtily. "A huge underwater net still surrounds Aristau and encloses the whole Bay. I heard that Marine robots cleared the Bay free of alien monsters a couple of days ago."

"I can't believe that you were given permission to fly to such a dangerous area," said Zeta. "Bermuda wouldn't authorize anyone to leave the Dome at all. I would expect that Matthew Keating has adopted the same attitude."

"Go back downstairs, Zeta!" Tesla demanded. "Bring Felicity with you. I'll not tolerate this invasion into my private workroom any longer. You'll find chairs near the Display window. You might like to sit and look out at the scenery while we are airborne. We are going to the Bay and that's final."

"You've made up your mind," Zeta said.

"Yes. I have."

Suspecting that they were heading into danger, Zeta followed Felicity downstairs. Brooklyn lingered.

"Tesla, I know you didn't plan a trip to the coast," she said quietly. "We were meant to lunch in the shop."

"No way was I going to travel back to our Dome City sitting on the trolley," Tesla said vehemently. "Not after what I just saw. I decided to fly back to the Dome. Thwarting me, my Navigation System has jammed."

"What did you see?"

"Nefarids hatching."

"OK," said Brooklyn, taking a deep breath. "I appreciate that you decided it was best if we flew back to Town in this shop, rather than ride on the trolley. But, you'll have to tell the other two that the steering is wonky."

"We're not flying willy-nilly over the place, Brooklyn. We're heading for Freshwater Bay," said Tesla. "I did check the destination co-ordinates. We'll reach the Bay in forty minutes. Once there, I'll shut down the Globe engine. We'll stop and I'll fix the steering problem myself. I am endowed with a little computer savvy."

"Tesla, why don't you ask the pilot who is supposed to be supervising us to come and help? It is the least he can do," suggested Brooklyn. "Tesla?"

Tesla remained silent.

"Tesla, you didn't get permission to leave the Dome, did you? I was with you when Inspector Maniscallo signed your gate-pass. Matthew didn't sign though, did he?"

"No. I copied his signature. I signed the gate-pass myself."

"Oh, Tesla! Why?"

"Matthew Keating is impolite. Since Tau has been away, all the Knights have lost their manners. When I last saw Bermuda - a fortnight ago - he said I was a useless decoration. I replied by saying, *'Isn't this a pleasant day, Francis. Please excuse me. I must hurry home, sprinkle some glitter on myself and hang myself up on a tree!'* Once Bermuda went to help Tau, Keating took his place in the league of callow youths. How can I be expected to approach a person who is rude and disrespectful?"

"I can't disagree," acknowledged Brooklyn. "I was standing in the City Plaza yesterday, outside my own Bakery, when Keating told me to go and spin my dress somewhere else."

Tesla regarded her friend fondly. "Come on, we'll join those two downstairs. There's no piloting required from me until we reach the coast. We're sure to spot an empty beach-column. Then all I have to do is to activate our magnetic anchor and we'll land. Everything will be fine. But mum's the word!"

When they returned to the shop floor, Tesla stopped at the Display window and stared out. There she stayed, little realizing that a Chronoguiser was furtively flying above her airship. Hidden by the clouds it stalked her floating Globe. Blue light beams radiated out from its core and diffused into the surrounding blue sky. Occasional rays of sunlight caught against its silvery hull and the ship glistened.

Skimming over the dark green treetops, soaring over grassy plateaus and dotting shade over a rainbow of wildflowers, the Globe shop flew onwards. Thirty minutes later, the stalking ship vanished.

Flying at a much higher altitude over a short stretch of salt water - between the Southern Coast of Britain and the Isle of Wight, Tesla's shop was now quite close to Freshwater Bay. Underneath her moderate spherical aircraft, the sea rolled steadily in smooth rounded waves.

Still looking out from the first floor Display window, Tesla could already see the shoreline of the picturesque Isle.

"I hope I can land my Globe shop as I promised," she thought, keeping up a brave face in front of Felicity and Zeta. "Else we may fly out over an ocean teeming with horrible Nefarids. Then I'll have to call Matthew Keating for help. He will be cross."

Chapter nineteen

"I have yet to ingratiate myself with TT Vox Populi," thought Captain Kroll, seated in his pilot's chair in the small beige Chronoguiser cabin. "My career hangs on the successful capture of *The Zeta*." Looking out from the viewing window of the invisible hovering Dandy Lion, he cast a shrewd eye over the calm blue water of Freshwater Bay. "Today just might be the day I end up in TT's good books," he thought optimistically. Then he flew that Spaceship into the mouth of the Bay. Glancing inland at the chalky cliffs in the distance, he checked his radar. Noting an approaching vessel hidden beyond those cliffs, he spoke to the four Knights seated behind him. "Screw up this mission and I'll make your lives a misery! Got it?"

"We've got it," answered the oldest Knight, a man of twenty-four years, dressed - like those beside him - in bronze raiment.

Moments later the seagulls nesting in the Bay's cliff face took fright. Flapping their white wings as a loud thud resonated across the theatre of their quiet home, they squawked in unison. Flying from their nests they circled above the aberrant noisemaker, a transparent Globe, enclosing a pink house. Thus, they marked the auspicious occasion of the successful landing of *Tesla's House of Gown* atop a beige beach-column at the base of their cliff.

Looking out from her upstairs windows, Tesla admired the beach onto which she had just landed. A sheltered curved sanctuary of soft toffee sand stretched out before her in a half-moon shape, edged where it met the waves with a shiny layer of smooth cream pebbles. Sparkling, the inviting seawater was warm. Blue and cloudless, the sky was bright. Dazzling and golden, the sun shone hot overhead.

Tesla listened as the elevator doors on the floor below, opened and closed. After watching her three companions step out onto the beach, she opened the navigation access panel on the bench before her. Squatting down she began to tinker with those controls.

Outside, the three on the beach walked across the soft dry sand, stopping where they found the air cooler, three metres from the sea.

Zeta let the pets run free on the beach. Felicity spread out a purple and orange chequered rug over the soft toffee sand. Brooklyn placed their hamper in the centre of that rug. Sitting down, they formed a circle.

Shallow blue waves lapped rhythmically against the shore, repeating a soothing mantra of ebb and fall, to which the young girls listened. With a natural ageless beat, these low banks of salty tidal fluid washed forward and broke with a familiar crash onto the porous sandy surface at the water's edge. Once fallen, they were sucked back instantly with a uniform whoosh, into the vast body of saltwater from which they came.

Lulled by the oceans natural melody, bathed by the hot sun and dissuaded from thoughts of Nefarids in the sea by the sight of a flock of gulls floating peacefully in the shallows, the girls relaxed. Zeta let down her hair and took off her shoes and stockings.

Suddenly, interrupting their quiet respite, however, the three anxiously sighted a Chronoguiser. Swiftly landing a distance away - on the otherwise deserted beach front of Freshwater Bay - the hatch of that vessel opened and the boarding steps descended.

"Tesla's got us into trouble," said Felicity. "I knew we weren't supposed to be here. A Chronoguiser visit isn't for socialising. We are going to get a telling off."

"The only Chronoguiser we have of those dimensions is the *Heritage*," said Brooklyn. "Tau's vessel."

"No. This is something different," Zeta warned. "The Dandy Lion is that size too."

The girls stood up. Surprised, they observed a lady step out from the Chronoguiser. On her head, she wore a bonnet tied under the chin with a satin ribbon. Dressed in a cream cotton jacket and a closely pleated ankle-length, dome-shaped cream skirt, she was pretty and petite.

After the boarding steps retracted and the Chronoguiser shot up into the sky, the lady walked towards them. Blowing the pleats of the lady's skirt, the sea breeze whooshed around her. Overhead the sun, shining brightly, brought a warm glow to her already rosy complexion. Five metres away from the three girls, the lady could not help but stare at Zeta. He dreamy grey eyes smiled warmly. Stopping, she held out her arms.

Staggered by the sight of the lady, Zeta was initially rooted to the spot. A second later she dashed forward. Her bare feet dug into the soft beach sand. Fine dry grains of sand kicked up behind her heels.

"Mum!" she shouted, surprised beyond measure. "It's you. It's really you!" Reaching the lady, she abruptly halted.

"There have been two great moments in my life, Zeta," said the lady. "The first was seeing your face when you were born. The second is seeing your face now."

"Mum, how did you get here? I mean - who brought you? Was it Dominic?"

"I'll explain everything shortly, but for now, let me meet your friends." Putting her arm affectionately around her daughter's shoulders, the lady walked towards Brooklyn and Felicity. Zeta was positively beaming.

"Well, who are *you*?" called Tesla, with both interest and anxiety in her voice. Finished adjusting her Navigation System, Tesla had just left her Globe shop. Now wearing Zeta's black vest and pink pleated skirt - for a lark - she hurriedly approached, running across the sand.

"This is Kaira, my mum," responded Zeta.

"No dearest. That's not who I meant," Tesla called back. "The lady is obviously your mother. I do however suggest that you *all* look behind you, and move back from the water. We have a sudden problem!"

Heeding her advice, the four females looked behind them. Startled at the sight of four unfamiliar Roamers, they backed away from the shore. As they did so, Tesla strode boldly towards the waters edge.

"How do you do?" she said, addressing those four ghostly Roamers - all Knights - presently floating eerily above the breaking waves.

With a considerable degree of trepidation, she peered at their transparent booted feet - dangling millimetres above the water. Peeping through one of their bronze clad translucent bodies she watched a seagull flutter down to the sea and float casually, bobbing up and down on the gentle waves.

Remaining reticent, the phantom Knights formed a tight circle around Tesla. Surrounded, she turned away. Blocked by the oldest Knight, she halted.

"Did you enjoy the illusion I gave you of hatchling Nefarids, Zeta?" the oldest Knight asked. "I have been watching you for some time. I am the one responsible for programming your Globe aircraft to bring you here. Freshwater Bay is a nice location - is it not?"

"You have no right to deceive me with an illusion," Tesla said angrily. "Who are you?"

"I am an emissary sent by TT Vox Populi," he announced in a deep confident voice. "TT would like a chat with you, Zeta."

Tesla suddenly rushed forward, making a move to force her way through the enclosing circle of spectral Knights. Too late, the oldest Knight's ghostly form menacingly barred her progress.

"Don't even think about trying to get past me, Zeta!" he warned, pushing his transparent face close to hers. "I might not be able to physically hold you, Miss Doherty, but I can still knock you down with my psychic energy."

Stepping back, Tesla glanced past the Knight at the worried faces of the real Zeta and Zeta's mother, Kaira.

"Remove your Roaming-Ring, Zeta, and throw it down!" the oldest Knight growled. "We don't want you calling for help!"

After Tesla grudgingly complied, throwing her Roaming-Ring onto the sand, he stared at the other females. "You too!" he ordered gruffly. "Throw your Roaming-Rings down. Don't you dare try to run away! And don't speak!"

As three of the four spoken to, threw their diadems onto the sand, Tesla suddenly called out, "To-do! Pinky! Come here, my darlings!"

Bounding over the sand towards their owners, Zeta and Brooklyn, the little dogs stopped. Looking towards Tesla with their gentle brown eyes, they happily changed direction. Tesla caught the two puppies. To-do yapped noisily and wriggled in her arms. Pinky tried to climb up onto her shoulder.

"Hush now, dears," she said to the pets in a soft soothing tone. "Be still."

Several awkward moments later, a Spaceship - the Dandy Lion - appeared glistening on the horizon, far out in the Bay. Glowing silver and radiating three thousand azure light beams, it raced across the calm aquamarine seawater towards the middle of the beach.

Reaching the small group of Knights and females within seconds, the silver Sphere hovered above them - bathing everyone in a sea of blue light beams. Mingled with the sound of the rolling sea - the cry of the gulls hovering near the cliffs, the whistling of the breeze and the faint rustling of the beach flora - everyone could hear the gentle musical hum emanating from that aesthetic craft. Subsequently the silver Sphere moved away to stop twenty metres away to their right, near the water's edge.

Zeta, staring at the hull of the buoyant vessel, immediately recognized the large embossed lettering on the side, as did her mother. Fearing that TT was inside the Dandy Lion and would recognize them, Zeta's usual rosy complexion paled. Her head felt light, her knees felt weak and she fell onto the sand.

"Hey, stand up!" barked the oldest Knight, staring in her direction. "What do you think you are playing at?"

Kaira quickly pulled Zeta to her feet.

"You've got no manners, Sir! Apologize!" Kaira said crossly. "Can't you see you're being horrible?"

The oldest Knight frowned. "I'm sorry, young lady," he said, addressing the real Zeta. "Remain standing so I can easily see you." Then he glanced at the Dandy Lion, noting that the hatch had opened.

Captain Kroll, wearing his gold flight suit and carrying a lethal gun - plus a Fighting-Staff - jumped out. With his square jaw jutting forward, he strode across the sand towards the Knights. Squinting against the glare of the sun, his mean brown eyes critically scrutinized his surrounds. Reaching the chequered rug, he abruptly halted. Ignoring the females, Kroll scooped up the Roaming-Rings previously dropped onto the sand.

"I can see five of the fairer gender, yet there are only four Rings," he complained.

"The lady wasn't wearing one," the oldest Knight responded.

"I see," said Kroll, scowling at Kaira. "You're not hiding yours are you?"

"Don't you dare try and find out," she retorted.

After glaring at Kaira, he threw the four platinum crowns into the shallows. Kroll then marched up to Tesla.

"She's Zeta alright!" he thought to himself soberly. "She matches the description that TT Vox Populi gave me – light brown hair worn up with sections at the top, plus pink and black bathing clothes. Zeta's supposed to have grey eyes though? This girl's eyes are blue. No matter, blue, grey, there's hardly a difference!"

Stepping behind Tesla, Kroll hooked his right arm under her chin. While a flock of white winged seagulls circled overhead and cried shrilly, Kroll threatened the girl.

"Don't give me any trouble!" he growled. Then he whispered vehemently, "If you're waiting for help from your friend, Tau, you can forget it, Zeta! No one will ever see him again. He was strawberry blancmange for the Nefarids - weeks ago!"

"I'm looking forward to the day when life dishes out your comeuppance," thought Tesla, equally vehement.

Feeling his arm against her throat and his voice hissing in her ear, she stiffened nervously. Inadvertently she dropped the puppies onto the sand. The escaped pets immediately ran towards Zeta and Brooklyn, but Felicity - quick to react - intercepted them. Safe in their pet basket the puppies quickly settled, to peep out inquisitively at the Knights and Kroll.

"You're totally out of order, Kroll," reprimanded the oldest Knight. "There's no need to be so rough with *The Zeta*."

"Don't judge me! Wake up and remain inside the Dandy Lion. I will deal with everything from now on," Kroll growled.

"No way!"

Kroll reacted to this disobedience by tightening his grip on Tesla. "Ladies are such fragile creatures. Don't you agree, Sir Knight?"

Glancing at Tesla and frowning, the oldest Knight signalled to his colleagues. He nodded to Kroll. His spectral image and those of the other three Psychic Knights with him then vanished. Simultaneously, their sleeping bodies wakened onboard the Dandy Lion. Grumbling, they waited for Kroll.

When the transparent images of the four Psychic Knights disappeared, Kroll removed his arm from around Tesla's neck. Gripping her firmly by her right shoulder, he marched her roughly towards the Dandy Lion.

Kaira quickly and with a determined expression, glanced at Zeta, then at Felicity and Brooklyn. With a united purpose, the four unexpectedly dashed towards Kroll. Brooklyn hurtled herself at the large man, trying with all her might, she attempted to pull his hand away from Tesla's shoulder. Kaira, Felicity and Zeta, on the other side, pulled his Fighting-Staff from him.

"Let her go!" Felicity screamed.

"You're a horrible bully," said Kaira.

"You've made a mistake!" shouted Zeta. "I'm Ze -"

Briefly letting go of Tesla, Kroll grabbed at his Staff and pushed the females away. "Any more interference and you will all join Zeta as my prisoners!" he growled.

Kroll again seized Tesla. Consequently, the look on her face was desperate. The others paused - at a loss what to do.

Suddenly, taking all on the beach by surprise, a thundering blast reverberated throughout their locale. Simultaneously a spectacular pyramid of water dramatically exploded out from the centre of the Bay. Suspended in midair for an instant, the fluid structure shimmered. Out from the apex of that pyramid, a split second later, a sleek black Space Fighter burst forth. Water fell, roaring, in great watery slabs off the sides of that Spaceship. Tiny droplets of seawater sprayed out, creating a transient mist. Collapsing, the pyramid fell back into the sea in a churning white froth.

Rising up high in the air, the Fighter turned towards the beach. Laying down fire that spread inflammable fluid from the shore to the cliff face, the pilot created a high wall of flames. Thus, he cut off Kroll's access to the nearby Dandy Lion.

Beautifully glistening under the Sun's golden rays, the Space Fighter then flew forward, sounding like a whisper. Seconds later, it hovered over the shallow shore water. Unexpectedly, the Fighter's curved windscreen snapped opened. Thrown out, golden and etched, a jewelled Fighting-Staff spiralled downwards. Concealing the pilot, the windscreen closed.

Witness to the intriguing sight of a beautiful black-tipped Fighting Staff spinning down to the sea, Zeta - along with the others on the beach - took note of its distance from the water.

"Fifteen metres... twelve metres... ten metres... eight metres... five metres," Zeta counted to herself.

Before she had time to count further, she suddenly gasped. Her eyes shone. Materializing from thin air - easily catching his Fighting-Staff in midair - she saw the welcome sight of Dominic. Dressed in a fine linked gold chainmail vest worn over a brown ochre shirt, together with brown trousers and boots, he flew his mirror image over the beach. Floating gently down to the ground, he stood confidently before Kroll and the captive Tesla.

"What brings you here, Knight?" Kroll growled. Whilst hiding his astonishment at seeing a lad who he had previously believed dead, he glared meanly. "Levitating your solid spiritual manifestation is a new gift, is it not?"

Dominic looked past Kroll and smiled at Zeta. "I'm here for the Dandy Lion, Kroll."

"My Space Fighter isn't enough for you?"

"It's not your Space Fighter anymore, Kroll," said Dominic, glancing at the hovering Fighter wherein he slept. "Finding it next to my parent's wrecked ship makes it mine under the rules of salvage."

"Why do you want the Dandy Lion?"

"Using a small familiar ship gave me a higher chance of convincing a lady to travel with me."

"*Gave* you? What lady?"

Dominic winked at Kaira. "Your thirty second question time is up, Kroll," he continued. "Hand over the Chronoguiser."

Kroll tightened his grip on Tesla's shoulder. "Get out of my way or I'll hurt *The Zeta*!"

"She's not *The Zeta*. The person you are holding in such an unpleasant manner is *the* Miss Tesla Gosh."

Instantly annoyed, Kroll released Tesla and threw her away from him. Together with the other females, she ran back along the beach and stopped a safe distance away.

"The last thing you are ever going to do is fight me!" Kroll threatened. Glaring at Dominic, he pulled his gun from its holster.

"Negotiation is a preferable option. Not interested?"

Without hesitation, Kroll fired his gun at the lad. A stream of small metal projectiles loudly shot forward. Astoundingly, Dominic's mirror image moved at an incredible speed. Easily dodging the bullets, he listened as the projectiles hit the side of the Dandy Lion.

"Your wall of fire is dying, Tau," said Kroll, watching his four men - armed with Fighting-Staffs - jump out from the Dandy Lion. "Two of my men have the gift of telekinesis. The other two are Illusionists. We'll see how easily your flying mirror self can dart my bullets when your mind is confused and you have a pair of bigger Knights floating in the air, hemming you in."

Dominic glanced at the wall of fire between the Dandy Lion and his opponent. Now only two metres high, the fire was indeed dying.

"Look, another Chronoguiser has appeared at the top of the cliffs behind us!" said Kaira, from where she stood with the four girls. "Reinforcements!"

Observing the *Warrior* land on the beach behind them, moments later, the females watched as Keating, Bermuda, Sebastian and Parsons leapt out from that vessel. All armed with Fighting-Staffs and all wearing the same raiment as Dominic, they ran straight for Kroll's troops. Not hindered by small obstacles, they somersaulted over the wall of fire.

Now the thwacking sound of eight Fighting-Staffs - wielded in combat - resonated across the beach, as Dominic's allies fought Kroll's troops.

"You will prove your Staff-Fighting skill, Kroll, or you will lose the Dandy Lion!" challenged Dominic.

After that statement, he flew at Kroll and knocked the gun from Kroll's hand. When Kroll raised his Staff to fight, Dominic struck at the man with his own Fighting-Staff - swiftly and in mirror flight.

Henceforth everything happened rather quickly and *rather strangely*. For this was no ordinary Staff-fighting battle, with nine of the combatants actively using their psychic powers to their best advantage.

Kroll's two Illusionists - seeing their leader beset by Dominic - initially tried to gain the advantage by using their psychic powers to create consecutive imagined realms. In a bid to confuse Dominic and his team, they took it in turns to create these illusions. In the first realm created, Dominic and his allies saw a mirage of a foggy red cliff top. In addition, they saw their enemies transform in appearance - to clones of themselves.

After battling their clones on the cliff top for a mere two minutes, Dominic and his team saw the next illusion. The secondary realm was a gloomy, misty swamp and their opponents now looked like skeletons, brandishing Staffs.

Imagining he was standing in muddy water, surrounded by three skeletons, Dominic was in reality, battling very hard. Keating and Parsons - unable to help him, and suspended upside down in midair - were suffering the enemy's telekinesis power. Bermuda and Sebastian, he saw, each battled against a belligerent skeleton.

"Give up, Tau," growled the imagined skeleton, Kroll, smashing at Dominic with his Staff.

Frowning, Dominic wielded his own Fighting-Staff fiercely in return. Lunging at him, he saw three bony skeleton faces. He heard the sound of their Staffs slicing through the air. Several times the Staffs hit against his back and grated against his chainmail vest. Seeing the blows rain down on him, he felt the pain of the attack.

Agitated, he shouted at his troops, "I could do with a little help!"

Keating listened to Dominic's voice. Breaking out from under the enemy's psychic power, the crystals in his Roaming-Ring began to glow. Using his own gift of telekinesis, he quickly released Parsons and himself from their suspended midair state.

Urged on by the sound of Dominic's voice, Sebastian's will also prevailed. Rather than his own team, it was Kroll and his accomplices who now experienced a disturbing illusion.

The beach around them seemed as normal. Coming at them, however, Kroll and his men saw fearsome mechinoids, born from their own worst fears. Concurrently they heard Bermuda's voice, seeming to whisper around him like a creeping wind. "You are lost. You have lost!"

Dominic saw Kroll unnerved. Currently standing near the shallows, Dominic's eyes narrowed. Charging at Kroll, he hurled his enemy into the sea. They hit the salty liquid with a loud splash. Grappling with Kroll, he pushed his assailant's head under the water.

"You're drowning me!" Kroll protested, coughing and spluttering.

The illusion waned.

Looking at Dominic's determined face, Kroll conceded. "The Dandy Lion is yours, Tau," he said. "I give up. Do you hear me, Knights?" he shouted. "Tau has won!"

The illusion ended.

The female spectators - also prey to the hypnosis, now observed all on the beach in their true form. Watching, they saw Dominic drag Kroll from the sea. They noted how the two enemy Knights empowered with telekinesis were hanging suspended and powerless in midair. One of the enemy Illusionists was asleep on the sand. Finally, they saw the oldest Knight wandering lost along the shoreline.

Dominic signalled to his troops to relax their psychic powers over Kroll's Knights. Then he addressed Kroll commandingly.

"Get up, Kroll," he growled. "I will only speak to you once. After that, you will be interviewed by Bermuda. I am sending you back to TT after a spell in our gaol."

"You can't send me back. Not after having lost two of TT's ships!"

"It is not your place to dictate to me what I can and cannot do," responded Dominic in a moderate tone of voice.

"But I'll be working until the day I die to pay for those lost ships," complained Kroll. "You are punishing me for following orders."

"Don't stand in front of me acting the innocent!" Dominic growled. "You have persistently operated outside the scope of your instructions, Kroll. You have committed a host of crimes ranging from assault on a Professor to the attempted murder of myself. In addition, you are entirely responsible for infesting a whole planet with Nefarids. And don't you dare tell me that you were ordered to beat up Professor Doherty, leave me to perish on Nefaria, or release your squadron mascots into the water supply, or I swear I will feed you to the Nefarids in the adjacent cove!"

Kroll remained silent. Avoiding Dominic's reproachful stare he glanced sulkily at his troop of Knights, now all standing together quietly, guarded by Sebastian and Keating.

"My interview with you is over, Kroll," Dominic said with finality. "Stand there and don't move."

Kroll sheepishly obeyed. Dominic, determining that the Officer was unlikely to cause further trouble, stepped towards Bermuda.

"Take the *Warrior* and return to London Dome City, Bermuda," Dominic instructed his friend coolly. "Bring this lot with you," he added, glancing first at Kroll and then at the enemy Knights. "Keep Kroll handcuffed and under guard at all times. Throw him into a goal cell as soon as you land at London Dome City. Give the Knights a good feed."

"I could also do with some fresh food," said Kroll carefully.

Bermuda laughed and stared at Kroll sternly. "What would you like - pasta with cheese, broccoli, walnuts and a smidgeon of peppers, accompanied by a fine red wine? If you behave yourself you may be rewarded." Bermuda then turned to face the group of females, still watching from a distance. He bowed in parting. "Ladies," he said.

Keating also spoke to them. "My compliments," he said politely, much to Tesla's embarrassment. Swiftly the girls saw four Roaming-Rings rise from the shallows, fly across the beach and land on the chequered rug before them. Kaira, also watching, smiled.

Marching the vanquished men before them - carrying the enemy's five Fighting-Staffs, as well as their own - Dominic's team moved towards the *Warrior*.

"Not you, Parsons!" said Dominic, calling the youngest of the Knights back to him. "You stay here." Glancing across at the group of females, Dominic again called out, "Wait until I land my Space Fighter, ladies. I wish to speak to you all."

Handing his Fighting-Staff to Parsons for safekeeping, the mirror image of the fair lad promptly faded away. Simultaneously his mortal self awoke in the cockpit of the Space Fighter, still hovering quietly over the sea.

Moments later, when the *Warrior* had gone and the Space Fighter had taken its place, Dominic jumped down from the wing and strode confidently towards the six remaining on the beach.

After questioning Tesla concerning her gate-pass, he sent her off home in her Globe aircraft with Brooklyn. Smiling charmingly, he joined those remaining.

"You've all been introduced, I take it?"

"Yes," replied Felicity. After which she asked quickly, "You won the Dandy Lion in battle, Tau. Then you flew it back in time to before you won it and dropped Zeta's mum off on the beach. Is that right?"

"Yes," replied Dominic, grinning. "I've yet to get my timing perfect. Perhaps it would have been better if Kaira had arrived *after* the fight."

"Tau. You're returning to London, now?" asked Parsons.

"Yes," replied Dominic. "Kaira, would you like to fly home in the Space Fighter?"

"The journey through time in the Sphere was quite turbulent, Dominic. The black Spaceship parked nearby looks promising. Is it a smooth ride? Can it fly slowly?"

"As slow as you like. It's a very safe vessel."

Watching Zeta put on her shoes, he took his Fighting-Staff from Parsons.

"Tau, can I squeeze into the Fighter as well?" asked Felicity.

"No problem," he replied casually.

A few moments later, Felicity, Zeta and Kaira carefully jumped down into the cockpit of the Space Fighter. Zeta placed the pet basket with To-do inside, at her feet. Outside, Dominic stood on the wing of the Fighter. Nearby, Parsons was waiting for further instructions.

"Parsons, collect Hanepoot from Aristau," Dominic called. "Go back in time three hundred years. Find the exact position of the TT Transport Fleet in Outer Space. Return with the co-ordinates."

"Fine," replied Parsons. Running across the sand, he disappeared into the beige cabin of the Dandy Lion.

Concurrently, Dominic took his place in the pilot's chair of the much larger Fighter. While those seated in the Space Fighter watched, thousands of beautiful pronged azure light beams radiated from the core of the Dandy lion. At an amazing velocity that special craft shot forward like a fast moving beam of blue light. A split second later, the remarkable vessel plunged into the sea with a splash to disappear fathoms below the gentle rolling waves.

Gazing at the Dandy Lion until it was out of sight, Kaira sighed. "That machine threw me into the past and I was lost. Finding me, it hurtled me into the future. I am sorry I have been away for five years, Zeta."

Dominic activated the controls of the Space Fighter and the engine of that beautiful stealth vessel purred quietly. Lifting slowly off the sand, the landing wheels retracted.

"Mum?" asked Zeta quietly. "Do you know about Isabelle?"

"Yes. When Dominic found me, he told me," she replied. "Your father roamed to see me shortly afterwards. We are friends."

Continuing to rise on an inclined plane, the black Spaceship gained altitude until it was high over the chalky white cliff tops surrounding Freshwater Bay. Levelling off, the Space Fighter - soaring through the clear blue sky - headed inland towards the South of England, London and home. Echoing its flight on the surface below, a dart shaped shadow danced a rippling routine underneath the sleek aerodynamic vessel. Dominic activated the Music System and the cockpit filled with a pleasing orchestra of sound.

"We'll catch up to and pass Tesla's floating Globe shop soon," Dominic advised, glancing behind him at his passengers, seated to his left and his right.

"We can wave at Tesla and Brooklyn from our cockpit window!" said Felicity excitedly, grinning at Zeta.

"Only month away and I had forgotten what softies you two are," remarked Dominic. "You *cannot* wave from this ship."

"Excuse me," said Felicity.

"Hey Dominic?" said Zeta.

"Yes, Miss?" he asked, glancing around.

"Thanks for everything."

"You're welcome, Zeta."

Several minutes later, the Space Fighter in which they travelled caught up to Tesla's Globe shop. Maintaining the same altitude, the Fighter briefly acted as grand company to the more moderate aircraft.

"Oh, my goodness!" laughed Kaira. "We're flying next to a little pink house built within a floating bubble! The house is called *Tesla's House of Gown* and inside are the two girls from the beach, waving at us from the upstairs windows!"

"You didn't notice the Globe aircraft when it flew away from the Bay?" asked Dominic.

"I did, but I didn't like to stare. Now I can't help it."

Leaving the Globe aircraft behind, Dominic raced the Fighter through the clear blue sky. Sitting before the controls of the sleek Spaceship and soaring high above a world he loved, he looked forward wistfully through the curved windscreen. Deeply appreciating everything his planet Earth offered, he marvelled at the lakes and the rivers over which they passed, at the green forests, the grassy meadows and at the crop filled valleys.

A short time later, London Dome City loomed into view. An imposingly latticed structure on the landscape, the Dome towered splendidly over the surrounding Oak forest.

Kaira was gazing out over the left wing tip of the stealth Space Fighter when Dominic, proud of his city, reached his left arm back towards her and touched her jacket sleeve.

"We're home, Kaira," he said kindly, prompting her to look ahead.

She glanced at the fair lad diagonally seated to her right. Looking forward, she suddenly stared transfixed at the mammoth translucent Dome, looming large before their fast moving vessel.

"Is that London?" she asked, her face bright with interest.

"Yes. That structure you can see before us is the Dome shielding the city. In a moment, we'll fly inside the Dome and you'll enjoy a bird's eye view of the Globe Homes. The city is original. Many new ideas have been incorporated into the entire project. Be ready to see lots of harmless robots, both inside and outside of the homes."

Zeta watched the delighted expression on Kaira's face.

"So much has happened in the last few weeks," Zeta said thoughtfully. "My head is spinning. But in a good way."

Flying in through the large central portal at the top of the gigantic webbed Dome, the Fighter descended to the city. Underneath the vessel, hundreds of Globe Homes, mounted on their pastel columns, sparkled in the sunshine. Everyone in the city had come out of the buildings and all were looking upwards, watching the Space Fighter land.

Zeta could see her father, Kepplar and Aristotle, grouped together. Isabelle and Ret were waving to them. Eddie was standing alone, looking up and beaming. The returned Knights were smiling.

Suddenly, the air rocked with a series of explosions - the sky around them ablaze with lights from exploding fireworks.

"London is celebrating your return, Tau," said Felicity.

Around London, the British Isles stretched out, a flourishing forested garden of oak and fir trees, of deep lakes and rugged picturesque mountain ranges, of wide rivers and winding canals.

Beyond Britain, from the Artic tundra and its adjacent coniferous forests, to the warmer wooded southern regions, and finally to the jungles, prairies, and savannas in the middle latitudes, the Earth turned. Breathing, sighing - changing with the seasons - the fertile planet moved forward, once again cradling humanity in her magnanimous embrace.

Epilogue

Voyaging through the Cosmos at high velocity, the inspiring Fleet of one thousand TT Space Transports - safeguarded by a squadron of Space Fighters - appeared at a distance to be a simple conglomeration of gently moving cognate objects, floating like plankton in the depths of an infinite, fluidless, inky sea. Slivers of starlight, born in aeons past, stretched needle-like fingers into that inky sea. Sheer white mists floated mystically in the vacuous ocean of Space. Stars - as if caught on a time-lapse camera - twinkled golden, lilac, blue and pink.

Shortly to receive an unexpected visit from a Space traveller, the Commander of that Fleet calmly walked through a brightly lit cream corridor towards his cabin. Wearing a grey frockcoat banded with cassis red from elbow to wrist, grey trousers, a white shirt and a rose coloured tie, he stopped when he reached his quarters. After stating his name loudly and clearly, 'TT Vox Populi', the curved metal door before him opened.

Entering his illuminated domicile on the right front corner of his Flagship - Space Transport 0001 - TT glanced through his two cabin windows out into the Cosmos. Noting that the hour on his timeband was 2am, he took one step forward. Again, he spoke loudly in the manner of instruction, "Routine cabin check," he stated solidly. "Close my cabin door in ninety seconds."

Ever vigilant, he withdrew a security scanner from his frockcoat pocket. As a precautionary measure, he pointed that scanner towards a mahogany desk in front of the left window, then into the centre of his room where four burgundy armchairs encircled a marble coffee table. Next, he scanned his extensive floor to ceiling mahogany library - stretched across the entire right side wall of his cabin. Lastly, he checked the left side of his room where an opaque partition subtly screened his compact bathroom and tidy cream divan.

TT took two further steps forward. His programmed cabin door clicked quietly closed behind him. Recorded music filled his room with the sweet clear sound of tinkling piano keys. Looking towards a dwarf eucalyptus tree - in the metre gap between the windows - he spoke to his pet. "Hello, Snookums," he said kindly.

Resting in the branches of that tree, Snookums turned his head towards TT and blinked.

"You'll soon have a fresh sprig of eucalyptus leaves, gathered from our onboard garden," he reassured his Koala. With his grey shoes clicking on the cream tiled floor, TT walked briskly forward towards his mahogany desk.

"Cabin Robot, fold down my bed linen," he instructed Dominic's secret spy robot, sitting idle on the desktop. "Lay out clean clothes for tomorrow. Circulate a memo to all my citizens that they are each to be given a small portion of produce from our onboard vegetable garden during their next meal."

TT watched the spider-like legs of the small spherical robot extend. Always amused at its movements, he observed it float off the desktop, drop down to the floor and scurry away to perform its duties. With the robot away, he looked at several gold-framed family photographs arranged neatly on his desktop. Staring at one particular picture, his face softened. The man to the left of the photo was himself. Next to him, a young woman - his granddaughter - stood close beside her handsome husband. The fourth face in the photograph belonged to their three-year old son, Terence Dominic Tau, held securely in his mother's arms.

"We're waiting on news from the Dandy Lion, aren't we, Snookums?" TT said, turning towards his pet. "It has been a week since I heard from any of her crew," he continued in thought. "That can only be a good sign. Their absence implies that collecting Miss Doherty wasn't such an easy undertaking. It most positively suggests that Tau is still putting up a fight, whilst simultaneously convincing my younger citizens to join him. I'm second-guessing the lad here, but if I don't know my kin, who do I know."

TT patted the Koala's head, brushed its grey fur with a nearby wide-toothed comb, and deftly inspected the long claws of the gentle marsupial.

"I really should have been more receptive to Tau on the night of his sixteenth birthday," TT further mused. "Being the statesman for so long, I'm in the habit of people listening to me. I'm not practised at listening to them. Tau's voice should be familiar to me, but its not. That is an issue I will address in future."

Taking the promised leaves out of his frockcoat pocket, TT fed the fragrant food to Snookums. Glancing through his windows into Outer Space, he spoke his thoughts aloud to his pet in a gentle, rhythmic and heartfelt tone.

"I am a man who does not accept darkness, Snookums. When a room I am in starts to dim, I notice immediately. I press on the light.

At nightfall, when I was on Earth, I always took time to look outside, raise my eyes up to the heavens and gaze at the multitude of stars - tiny specks of light in the darkness. I never believed that there was so much darkness and so little light. I knew that the stars were actually big and beautiful, and that in reality there was so much light that I would have to shield my eyes or be blinded.

Daybreak on Earth was always something special to me, something marvellous. Always, even as a young lad, I would throw back the curtains in my bedroom at the first glimmer of light. My heart cheered that the darkness had gone and was replaced with a bright colourful world full of people I loved. Together with the sun, my heart rose."

TT's large eyes sparkled as he said these words, and although his face was that of a man of one hundred and twenty, his spirit at that moment in time, was ageless.

Moving away from his desk, Snookums and the dwarf eucalyptus tree, TT strode past the second of his cabin windows, towards his well-stocked library. Selecting a fine volume from one of the higher shelves, he opened that book and slowly turned the cream leaves. Deep in thought, he read many transcripts in the book. With the volume open in his hands, and still absorbed in reading, he stepped towards the nearest burgundy armchair. With his back to the windows, he sat down.

Several minutes passed. TT lifted his eyes from the volume. Startled, his gaze fell on the coffee table before him. Surprised at what he saw, he sat back in his armchair. Closing the heavy volume in his hands with a loud snap, he laughed.

"Oh my! This is definitely the best illusion I have been subjected to so far, Snookums!" he exclaimed with good humour.

Sitting on the coffee table was a sizeable bamboo hamper, tied with a wide lilac bow. Arranged tantalizingly within that hamper was a generous selection of golden honey, raspberry jam, orange marmalade, cheese, fruit scones, mince pies and red apples.

"This hamper definitely wasn't here when I entered this room," TT thought. "Everything inside looks delicious."

Leaning forward in his capacious armchair, TT placed his book down on the table. Curiously picking up one of the mince pies and turning it over in his right hand, he thoughtfully observed the pale golden colour, the round shape, the indents around the edges, and the neat little star shaped cut made in the centre of the pastry.

"The aroma wafting from this food is so fragrant," he considered, holding the mince pie closer to his nose and breathing in the tempting bouquet. "The scent is heady and quite wonderful. This phantasm is quite a work of genius." Inquisitively he bit into the pie. "I can taste fresh butter, wheat and raisins!"

Reaching again into the basket to sample a spoonful of honey, TT was surprised when his hand brushed against a small, framed portrait. Withdrawing the frame, he settled back in his chair. Thoughtfully he then studied the portrait's subject - himself.

Keen to know the artist, TT peered at the signature in the right hand corner. Surprised, he read the words: 'Zeta Doherty'.

"I am not seeing an illusion. This art is real," he thought, warily scrutinizing the room around him.

Hurriedly reaching into one of his trouser pockets for a white device - the size and shape of a small comb - TT activated a screen on the wall opposite. Quickly he viewed a security recording taken of his activities in his room, from the time he entered to the current time.

Amazed, he observed himself feeding Snookums a handful of leaves while his cabin door silently opened behind him. He watched incredulous as a generous bamboo gift hamper floated inside his room and the door closed. He saw the hamper - suspended in midair - move onto his coffee table. Moments later, he watched himself, oblivious of the hamper, move towards his library and select a book from one of the higher shelves.

Having seen enough to form a conclusion, TT terminated the recording.

"I know you are in here!" he called out loudly. "I have seen you entering this room as an invisible Roamer. Show yourself!" When TT received no answer, he continued speaking to the invisible intruder, but this time in a calmer, quieter voice. "We have a field generated around each ship to stop unauthorized roaming. Would you be so good as to explain to me how you managed to get through that field, Roamer? You might follow that up with a brief communication as to why I didn't hear my cabin door open or the hamper being placed on my coffee table. Finally, you could kindly enlighten me as to why my intruder alarm didn't sound."

"There was no need for your alarm to sound in this instance," replied a pleasant tenor voice from somewhere inside TT's room. "For your benefit, your Security System is not programmed to keep me out, whether I am roaming or mortal. Neither will the generated field around your ship dissuade my visits. I am very much aware that you didn't hear me come into your cabin, having overheard your sweet soliloquy I apologize for any offence caused by my stealthy intrusion."

"What do you want?"

"The painting in your hand is a nice likeness of you, don't you think?" said the pleasant voice, ignoring TT's question. "Miss Doherty did a good job of capturing your finer side."

"Why are you here? Explain yourself immediately or I will call for assistance and have you removed!"

"I am here to negotiate. There is no need to call for assistance. It is better if this visit remains private."

"Of all the audacity!" exclaimed TT. "State your business! I give you five minutes!"

"Do you like the hamper?" asked the voice. "I thought you would appreciate some fresh food. All those tasty items are a token of my goodwill."

"Where is my Chronoguiser - the Dandy Lion? If you know Miss Doherty you also know what happened to my ship and her crew."

"The Dandy Lion has been confiscated. Until I am sure I can trust you she will remain my ship," replied the voice. "As for her crew, Kroll is bundled up nicely on the landing deck with four Knights for company. If you send someone down after our meeting, I suspect those prisoners will be relieved to be untied from their bonds. Don't worry if their behaviour is slightly different, and they can't remember where they've been."

"Who are you?"

"You have a fine library, TT Vox Populi, including excellent works on socio-economics and law. You have many years of successful experience as a politician," the voice continued casually.

"What does my library or my expertise have to do with you?" TT growled.

"You mentioned you would like to be my political tutor," said the voice. "I would be pleased to take you up on that offer, if it still stands?"

"Dominic?" asked TT expectantly.

Suddenly the mirror image of Dominic materialized in the capacious burgundy armchair across from TT. Seated casually, he wore tailored taupe trousers and matching shoes, a long-sleeved cream shirt and his cassis-red cummerbund. Encircling his blonde hair, his platinum diadem gleamed. His pale blue eyes were smiling and his expression was most sincere.

"We have much to discuss, TT," said the fair youth amiably. "And many agreements to make."

TT's face lit up with charm and vitality. Reaching across the coffee table, he extended his hand in friendship. Dominic, accepting TT's goodwill, stretched out his own arm and they shook hands.

Eagerly leaning forward with his hands clasped together, TT spoke enthusiastically. His fine baritone voice filled his cabin with warm optimism. "Where would you like to begin?" he asked.